Praise for *Fleet of the Forgotten*

Author Dan Thornton created a wonderful story of resilience, courage, and leadership. The story is packed with action, suspense, mystery, and twists that had me in awe. ... While the concept of an alien invasion isn't exactly new, it is handled so perfectly that it makes reading this story eventful. The author effectively builds a sense of urgency and high stakes ... This is a great start to a series that I know will be fantastic!

- Rabia Tanveer

—

Fleet of the Forgotten isn't just a sci-fi space adventure; it is also a bit of a thriller ... Dan Thornton's story of Fleet Academy hits all the right notes in this high-stakes adventure. There's friendship, romance, intrigue, class struggles, artificial intelligence, and all while in the midst of an alien invasion. ... this action-packed story held my attention from beginning to end.

- Natasha Jackson

—

Paying great attention to detail, Thornton brings the scenes to life with vivid depictions. The sentimental edge and the dramatic touch accompanying the storyline, alongside the juxtaposition of the cast's complex traits, allowed me to connect with the latter. Through the cast, Thornton explores the themes of social class disparity, corruption, technological advancement, family, friendship, jealousy, power, and more. The story mirrors the real world in many ways. The rich and powerful often seem eager to abuse their power if it helps them enhance their status or maintain access to their privileges. ... If you are looking for a novel flavored with military, space opera, adventure, and suspense, you will find Dan Thornton's *Fleet of the Forgotten* an enthralling read.

- Keith Mbuya

EXILES WAR: BOOK 1

FLEET OF THE FORGOTTEN

DAN THORNTON

EXILESWAR.COM

I've always said that the only things in this world that I care about are pizza and—like—two people.

This book is dedicated to my wife and daughter.

(Sorry, pizza.)

PROLOGUE

Outer Asteroid Belt

The clang and clatter of objects striking the hull of the commercial mining vessel *Bison* woke its surly captain with a start.

He slapped the red button near the head of his slowly rotating bunk bringing it to a stop and easing the centrifugal forces acting on his body. As weightlessness returned and he regained his bearings he growled into the com panel.

"Jackson, what the fuck are you doing, mate? I told you to keep an eye on the scopes!"

The crackling speaker made the reply almost unrecognizable until Captain Foster, using his free hand, slapped the grill several times.

"...Cap, nothing on the scopes at all."

"I'm on the way up, slow us down for god sakes, we don't need another hole in the hull."

He flipped the com switch to standby, making a mental note to tell one of the mechanics to fix the damned thing.

He gently pushed off the grab handle and got one toe on the side of his bunk, pushing his body toward the hatch in a practiced ballet of zero-g maneuvering.

"Swear to God, that idiot," he muttered. Jackson was a solid hand with the remote tractors they used to ferry ore from the asteroids they mined to

1

the cargo containers, but behind the controls of the hauler, he was impatient and hotheaded.

Gliding up the small, cramped passage, he used his outstretched hands, tapping the sides of the bulkhead. The contact slowed his glide bringing him to a stop at the bridge hatch. The *Bison* was a large ship, but it was mostly cargo and utility spaces, affording very little room or comfort to the crew.

Beeping alerts grew louder along with a steady stream of curses as he approached.

When he passed onto the bridge Jackson was clearly struggling.

"Cap, I can't bring the piece of shit thrusters online. I'm getting a 209 error. What the fuck is a 209 error?"

They were in the thick of a particularly dense part of the asteroid belt. Normally, they would burn from one large rock to another, sometimes a million kilometers apart, but here a strike not so long ago left several large, and hundreds of smaller chunks of rock orbiting nearby—along with a lot of small rock and dust.

It was a rare find and if harvested correctly, one that could cut the length of their cruise down from twelve months to ten—sending everyone home early with full pockets. That was if Jackson didn't get them killed before then.

"I swear if you mangled that array, it's coming out of your share. Do you know how much they charge to fix one of those?"

Jackson slapped the release on his harness and pushed over to the co-pilots chair while Foster locked himself into the newly vacant seat.

Foster studied the diagnostic display. "The combustion chambers fouled. Whoever ran that thing last time ran it rich." He looked over, knowing it was Jackson.

"I ran it normal! Ten-minute burn, totally by the book."

"I did it by the book…" Foster mocked him. "You have to lower the mix by hand on the forward thrusters, you know it runs rich asshole."

"I hate this tub," Jackson said, crossing his arms.

Captain Foster overrode the thruster safety lockout with a practiced hand and fired the forward thruster array. He let it burn hotter than normal allowing all the carbon deposits to dislodge from the chamber. When the temperature warning lights started to squawk, he did a silent ten count before shutting the array down.

"Right on the money," he said slapping Jackson on the arm.

Jackson wasn't looking at him, his face slack.

"Cap..." he said, his voice colored with concern. He pointed out the window of the command deck.

Foster looked in the direction Jackson pointed, not seeing anything but a large, slowly rotating asteroid.

"What the hell are you getting at?" he said before a shadow engulfed a smaller asteroid just to the starboard side of the larger rock.

"Not a shadow," he thought slowly moving forward in his seat until the harness went tight against his shoulders. Whatever it was, it was gigantic, larger than some of the largest chunks of the asteroid they were heading toward. Many times larger than the *Bison*, which was no small brig.

He couldn't quite make out the shape of the thing, the little sunlight this far out cast harsh shadows across everything making the dark object confusing... but it was slowing down.

A feeling of unease settled over Foster. Too many years of dealing with dangerous jobs on the frontier had amped up his sense of self-preservation, and unknowns immediately raised his hackles.

"Log that and... send a message to the company, I want them to know where we are... just in case." He looked at Jackson, who was staring out the window slack-jawed. "Now!"

As Jackson snapped to his duties, he cinched his acceleration harness tightly across his shoulders and chest. The musty smell of old nylon and years of grease and grime was comforting. He pondered for a second, watching the huge shadowy object intently, his brain trying to make sense of what the thing was.

"Trying the satellite network." Jackson tapped the button on the communications screen, each time it spun a small pixelated logo that looked like the head of a buffalo before returning to the word "Send." "Shit no luck, it won't connect…" He slammed his fist down on the armrest. "I lost the nav beacons and the satellite ping! Got nothing at all now." He tossed his hands in the air.

Captain Foster touched his own communication controls, picking up the auxiliary headset that was tethered to his chair by a frayed bit of elastic. The wired headset was old tech, but great when they were around the massive metal asteroids that played havoc with their wireless systems. He held one of the cups to his ear and closed his eyes, listening to what should have been the ever-present background static that filled the system. There was only the slightest crackle.

"I don't like it," he said flipping a switch on his console and pressing a well-worn button several times, each press causing a horn to echo through the living spaces of the small vessel.

He bent over the console raising his voice. "Listen up, everyone, drop whatever you're doing and strap in, we're turning the ship around."

He grabbed the maneuvering console and pulled it toward him. Fingers flew over the keys in a practiced dance. Foster decided to forgo the usual safety checks and had fuel flowing to the maneuvering pods in record time.

"Hang on." His voice echoed through the cabins of the blunt nosed hauler.

A low roar reverberated through the structure as the thrusters fired. Bits of unseen debris clattered around the inside of the cabin as the nose of the *Bison* slewed to port slowly away from the shadowy menace. "Point eight… point nine… that's one G, Cap," Jackson said, holding his arms across his chest trying to keep the straps from digging into his skin. "Cap?"

A veritable orchestra of squeaks and rattles came from every panel, bolt, and support strut surrounding them.

Captain Foster grimaced as they passed one and a half G, pushing the limits of the old tub. She wasn't a very nimble ship pulling a half a million tons of ore behind them, but whatever that thing was had stopped and he didn't want to goad it… or them… into a chase.

"Nice and easy." He dropped the output of the thrusters as the nose of the *Bison* was pointed 90 degrees away from the thing.

He slowly pushed the main engines up to 10 percent thrust dragging the chain of modular containers along with them, gaining speed and hopefully safety.

Jackson craned his neck trying to see through the starboard side of the bridge windows.

"Well? What's it doing?" Foster said after a few tense moments.

"Nothing that I can tell… it's just sitting there."

The screeching sound of the master caution alarm caused both men to jump in their harnesses. Between the bridge chairs a flat panel where a row of red indicators sprang to life. The right most lights were blinking in time with the screeching caution alarm.

"Did we shake one of the containers loose?" Captain Foster pushed away the maneuver panel and pulled the general computer display closer silencing the alarm.

Jackson, whose specialty also dealt with the cargo, was already on it. "Maybe," he said, tapping a button. The last four containers are showing red, but containers ten and eleven are both yellow."

A shudder ran through the ship along with the renewed screech of the caution alarm as several more lights came to life on the panel between them.

"Shit, Cap, I think we just lost all the aft containers. Eight through sixteen are red." Concern lined his face.

Foster turned to his panel and started typing in commands bringing up the topside docking camera. He ordered it to swivel around and point straight aft, and the picture made his heart sink. Behind them was half a years' worth of ore slowly spreading out in a long tail. Tattered tangles of metal interspersed amongst the partially processed rock were all that was left of the tough modular containers. They looked like chewed-up tissue paper.

His heart leapt into his throat as he noticed that the mysterious shadow had moved in behind them, slowly, like some sea creature of legend. A flicker of light, more like a row of sparkling dust leapt from near the shadowy object making a bee line toward the *Bison*, it registered in Foster's mind that it was the ore. Solid chunks of asteroid iron flaring to life as if subjected to an arc furnace before it reached the remaining containers behind the hauler.

Both Foster and Jackson looked on in abject horror as they flared red hot and started to melt.

"It's shooting at us!" Jackson cried flinching away from the screen instinctively.

Captain Foster's hands started to shake as his fingers caught up to his brain. He slapped the emergency cargo release. A series of explosive bolts cut the cargo away from the haul craft making it leap forward, and pushing both men awkwardly back into their seats. Without thinking, he commanded the engines to full power.

While underpowered for hauling a half million tons of ore, when unleashed, the haulers engines were enough to turn the crew to paste if allowed to run full out. Thankfully for Foster and crew, the computer systems responded instantly, cutting the acceleration to a manageable five G.

"Jesus Christ..." Jackson managed to grunt out.

Foster barely heard him; his eyes locked on the rear facing camera display as another line of twinkling light caught up to the hauler.

"Maybe it won't be that bad," he thought right before the *Bison* disintegrated in a flash of light and heat.

CHAPTER 1

O n Earth, amidst the manicured lawns of the Interplanetary Security
Alliance Fleet Academy, Ryan Anders tightened his grip behind his
back, the stiff fabric of his uniform pressing against his knuckles. His
gaze swept past the white-walled classroom buildings and pristine sidewalks
toward the horizon. Beyond the Academy's sterile perfection, just barely
visible in the haze of morning light past the outer security fence, he could
make out a squat grey apartment block surrounded by a squalid slum. Like so
many others, it was a standard government design: cold, dark, utilitarian to
a fault. It was too distant to see clearly, yet clear enough to stir a memory. A
different block. A different life.

The whine of turbofan engines grabbed his attention. Overhead, a grey
short-haul shuttle banked sharply, circling the campus once before angling
toward the northern landing field. Ryan tracked its movement until it
disappeared, then exhaled, forcing his focus back to the present.

Around him, his classmates gathered in tight clusters, their voices a low
murmur of anxious speculation. The entire class had been ordered to muster
at dawn in the green space outside the chow hall, an unusual and unwelcome
surprise. The Academy—where the North American Federation trained
its next generation of fleet officers—was built on discipline, routine, and
hierarchy. Mysterious impromptu gatherings on the Green had everyone's
hackles up.

Three years of relentless study brought Ryan and his class to the edge
of graduation. In a few short weeks, they'd receive their first assignments

and their official ranks before shipping out to the fleet. It was a moment he should have looked forward to, but instead, he felt only relief. The campus was becoming overcrowded. Each new class swelled in size, their numbers doubling, then tripling. The war drums were beating somewhere, even if no one dared say it aloud.

His gaze swept across the assembled cadets. They were the sons and daughters of politicians, corporate moguls, and high-ranking officers. Legacies. Their uniforms were custom-tailored, their brass buttons polished to a mirror shine—probably by some overworked household staffer who was little more than an indentured servant. They clustered in their usual groups.

The corporate kids, or "corpos," stood in one corner, their conversation a mix of smug one-upmanship about weekend getaways, private shuttles, and luxury vacations. Across from them were the politicals, or "pollys"—children of the ruling elite. Unlike the corpos, they not only had richly tailored uniforms but were also bedecked with commendation ribbons and chevrons on their sleeves for "volunteer service." Technically, any cadet could earn them, but in practice, only those with a powerful political sponsor ever did.

Then there was Ryan's group—the Citizen Officer Corps. The lottery winners. The afterthoughts. Years ago, the program had been a public relations stunt to prove that the system wasn't completely rigged against the working class. Back then, each Academy class had a dozen citizen cadets. Now, there were only three. The rumors whispered through the Academy halls lately hinted that next year, there would be none.

Ryan shifted his stance, his fingers flexing behind his back. He could feel eyes on him. The corpos and pollys didn't even try to hide their disdain. It didn't matter that he'd worked harder than any of them just to be here. The moment he stepped onto this campus, the system had already decided his worth.

The rich kids liked to joke that even the fleet needed someone to unclog toilets—which wasn't entirely untrue. Regulations dictated that all leadership positions aboard spacefaring military vessels had to be filled by Academy graduates. Less glamorous departments—maintenance, supply, waste management—still needed officers, and the lottery program conveniently filled those gaps—for now, as automated and AI controlled systems were rapidly taking over.

Ryan had always considered himself lucky. Not only had he managed to secure a scholarship to university, but against all odds, he had won one of the coveted spots at the Academy. It was a miracle, really, considering his past.

"What's the matter, Anders? You look like you smelled something."

The voice was unmistakable. A slim cadet stepped out from a cluster of his taller peers, a smirk tugging at his sharply defined features. Cadet Slaunder—heir to Mazim, one of the largest multinational defense contractors in the system. His father had only recently slipped out from under a corruption probe, and Slaunder carried himself with the arrogance of someone who knew money could buy anything, including the law. He was also conventionally handsome, with a chiseled jaw and sharp blue eyes that turned heads. His perfectly tailored uniform and expensive, custom-made shoes—just a little too thick in the sole—hinted at a quiet insecurity he'd never admit. From the first week at the Academy, he'd latched on to Ryan, relentless in his harassment.

Nose in the air, his eyes swept over Ryan with the practiced disdain of the privileged.

"He's probably just smelling his future career," one of his toadies croaked. "Good luck unplugging those toilets grub!" another added.

They brayed like donkeys, and heat flared in Ryan's chest.

He took a breath, about to fire back, when a gentle hand landed on his shoulder, short-circuiting the anger surging through him.

"Don't give them the satisfaction, Ryan."

The soft but firm voice belonged to Anna Rodriguez—one of the only people in this place he considered a true friend. Another lottery placement. Another outsider.

Slaunder, emboldened by Ryan's lack of response, made another snide quip to his friends, but Ryan barely heard it. Anna's fingers tightened on his arm, guiding him away.

She tilted her head, studying his face, and a stray curl of dark hair slipped from beneath her garrison cap. At barely five foot three and 110 pounds, she was dwarfed by Ryan's six-foot frame, but he'd seen her take down men twice her weight in hand-to-hand combat class without breaking a sweat. Six older brothers had trained her well.

"Don't tell me he's actually getting under your skin?" she asked.

Ryan shrugged, trying to play it off, but the weight in his chest had nothing to do with Slaunder.

He was relieved that graduation was a few weeks away and wanted to focus on what came next—but instead, his thoughts kept circling back to his past. He tried to keep his mind in the present, in the here and now, but it wasn't working. Stray thoughts, glimpses of his painful past, would come unbidden like flashes of lightning in the dark. The struggles of his poor family, his father's disapproval, his mother's death. They left him exposed, and a familiar, suffocating darkness swept over him in those moments, urging him to lash out.

On top of everything else, Ryan never understood his place in the world. He always felt like he was destined for something more, something bigger than scratching out a living in the slums where he grew up.

Behind Anna, another cadet walked up, offering a small wave. It was David Kim, the last of the lottery cadets in their class and the closest thing Ryan had ever had to a best friend.

"Not like you guys to be running late," Ryan said, forcing a change of subject.

"We don't have servants to tidy up our bunks like some people," David replied dryly, his Korean accent barely noticeable. He adjusted his cap, brushing his thick black hair back into place, but his nervous glance toward the corpo kids didn't go unnoticed. Their laughter quieted, but their sideways glances and whispered conversations meant trouble wasn't far behind.

Ryan clasped both David's and Anna's shoulders, pulling them farther away from Slaunder's group. "Whaddya say, pal? Any heads-up on this meeting?"

David's slight stature and quiet demeanor made him a target for the Slaunders of the world, but it also allowed him to go unnoticed around the staffers. "Nothing at all, Ryan. The barracks chief seemed to be as surprised as we were."

"Maybe you two are finally getting recognized?" Ryan said.

Anna and David were both top of the class in different areas, and, had they not been born to working class parents, would probably be class leaders and able to take their pick of the very best fleet assignments.

Ryan was another story. Hard sciences and mathematics had always been a struggle, but thankfully, his command and combat scores gave him an overall passing grade. This wouldn't have been the case if not for the mediocrity of most corporate and political candidates dragging down the average.

As David and Anna joked about the possibility of receiving some kind of recognition, Ryan couldn't help but think that whatever was happening wasn't going to be good... at least for them. The world wasn't a fair place. The strong preyed on the weak, and the weak preyed on each other. In fact, they found each other during their first week at the Academy precisely because of that.

He'd been minding his own business, getting the lay of the land, when Anna had come sprinting into the hallway, wild-eyed. She blurted out that someone named David was in trouble—backed into a dark corner by five corporate cadets who were laughing as they detailed exactly what they planned to do to "his kind."

Ryan had no intention of getting involved. He'd learned the hard way that stepping in usually ended badly for people like him. Before he could say as much, Slaunder flew out the door—clearly trying to stop Anna—and ran straight into Ryan. The impact sent the shorter cadet bouncing off Ryan's chest and sprawling to the floor. His limbs flailed gracelessly, and the look of stunned outrage on his face was so ridiculous that Ryan burst into laughter.

A mistake.

Slaunder scrambled to his feet, humiliated, before slicking his hair back and running inside; in that instant, Ryan saw the birth of a lifelong grudge.

Moments later, Slaunder was back with four large, albeit cow-eyed, corpo cadets, dragging David behind them. Ryan had two choices—fight and risk expulsion back to a life of poverty, or submit and spend the next three years under Slaunder's thumb.

He'd never been good at making those kinds of choices. So, he winked at David and sucker-punched the nearest corpo in the jaw.

To David's credit, he hadn't hesitated. Within seconds, they were both swinging, fists connecting in a flurry of adrenaline-fueled defiance. It hadn't been pretty—by the time it was over, they were both bruised and bloodied—but Anna had escaped and found an officer just in time to keep them from getting their asses kicked too badly.

Of course, nothing happened to the corpos. The Academy turned a blind eye to their indiscretions. Only Ryan and David were handed demerits for "unbecoming conduct." He was sure he was bound for a shuttle back to the slums, but the officer who broke up the fight was called away, and for whatever reason, they hadn't been expelled.

Anna helped them limp to Medical, and by the time they got to their barracks, they had all become fast friends.

"Here they come again," David muttered now.

Before Slaunder and his gang made it more than a few steps, an unfamiliar officer emerged from a nearby building, the slam of the metal door echoing behind him. His purposeful stride and crisp uniform, conspicuously adorned with a bright blue aiguillette, marked him as Academy command staff. This froze everyone in place.

Elizabeth Miller, their class leader and one of the most politically connected cadets at the Academy, snapped to attention. "Cadets, form up!"

The students fell into their usual formation—political cadets in front, corporate-sponsored recruits behind them, and Ryan, David, and Anna relegated to the rear.

"At ease," the officer ordered, his voice raspy but sharp. The cadets relaxed into a more neutral stance—hands clasped behind their backs, legs shoulder width apart, eyes forward.

Ryan studied the man. He was older, with visibly white, closely cropped hair beneath his command cap. He carried himself with authority, but not the haughty air of a polly or the loose dismissiveness of a corpo. A long scar ran down the left side of his neck, disappearing beneath his gold collar insignia. Below that, a thick stack of ribbons adorned his breast. One stood out above the others—a dark red Unit Combat Commendation with three bronze stars. That meant this man had earned it in real battle. Four times. Whoever this officer was, he'd seen more action than most would in a lifetime.

"Good afternoon, cadets," the officer said, his voice steady, measured. "I'm Commander Young, ISA Fleet liaison." He glanced at the tablet in his hand, swiping once before continuing.

"No doubt you're wondering why I've called you to muster before class. I'll get to that. But first—credit where it's due. I've reviewed your latest fitness reports, and I'll admit, I'm impressed... though also a bit troubled."

His gaze swept the formation, pausing briefly on Ryan before moving on. "It seems there's been a fair amount of friction and some insubordination in your ranks." He let the words settle before adding, "...but these things have a way of working themselves out."

Ryan's stomach dropped. Had Slaunder followed through on his threat? Had he finally found a way to get them expelled just weeks before graduation? A glance at Slaunder seemingly confirmed his worst fears—the bastard threw a quick look over his shoulder, smirking. A spark of rage ignited in Ryan's chest before he could force himself to stamp it down.

Young continued. "Now, I know you're all looking forward to your upcoming graduation ceremony. Unfortunately, some of you won't be attending." His tone was serious.

Ryan's jaw clenched. His face burned as his worst fears seemed to come true. Was he about to follow in his mother's footsteps and blow the opportunity of a lifetime? His fists curled, an overwhelming urge rising—to break Slaunder's smug face before anyone could stop him.

A subtle touch on his arm. Anna. Her hand barely brushed against his, but it was enough. Without looking at him, she gave a small shake of her head.

Ryan exhaled slowly, releasing the breath he hadn't realized he was holding.

"The following cadets will step forward," Young said, motioning to his right. "Cadet David Kim. Cadet Ryan Anders. Cadet Anna Rodriguez…"

Ryan barely heard the rest. His mind reeled. David and Anna? They were model cadets. Was this his fault?

Moving like prisoners to the gallows, the three stepped forward. Ryan caught sight of Slaunder, his shoulders bouncing with barely contained laughter until Commander Young continued.

"Cadet Percival Slaunder. Cadet Maxime Dubois. Cadet Elizabeth Miller."

Ryan blinked, the names catching him off guard. Elizabeth? He flicked a glance at her, but her face remained a practiced mask of control. Slaunder, however, looked downright frightened at first before quickly hiding his feelings behind a facade of arrogance.

"The rest of you, fall out and return to your regular class schedule. Dismissed!"

A stunned silence followed as the other cadets hesitated, then began dispersing. Slaunder's posse exchanged furtive whispers and glances before they scurried off.

Commander Young waited until the last of the cadets walked out of earshot. Then, in a measured tone, he turned to them. "At ease. I'll get straight to it—you six will not be attending the graduation ceremony."

Confused glances shot between the cadets before Elizabeth Miller snapped to attention. "Sir?"

"Stand at ease, Miller. Let me explain."

Young continued, "You've been selected for immediate fleet assignment. Due to extenuating circumstances, command has chosen to accelerate your graduation. You'll be on the next shuttle to the Forge, where you'll receive your final duty stations."

Miller stood at attention again, voice firm. "Sir, with all due respect, I must point out that Cadets Abbas and Chen are eminently qualified for fleet assignment. Cadet Petrov as well—"

Young raised a hand, cutting her off. "I made several of these recommendations myself, based on your academic and simulator scores. I don't agree with every selection, but I know how to follow orders." He arched a brow, his tone making it clear the discussion was over.

Miller hesitated, then squared her shoulders. "Understood, sir."

Young nodded and consulted his tablet. "When I call your name, step forward... Cadet Kim."

David stepped forward, standing at attention.

"Cadet Kim, you have been recognized as your class's top navigator. For your performance, you are awarded a meritorious commendation and hereby given the rank of Ensign in the ISA Combined Fleet. Congratulations."

Young handed him a small, polished wooden box containing his new collar insignia and shook his hand. David stepped back and they exchanged salutes before he returned to formation, his face shining with pride.

"Cadet Rodriguez."

Anna stepped forward, eyes locked straight ahead.

"You have been recognized as your class's top tactical specialist." Young glanced at his tablet again, then smirked. "Impressive scores, Cadet. You would have given Captain Armstrong a run for his money back when we went through the Academy together."

Anna's spine somehow straightened even more. A small, triumphant smile flickered at the edges of her lips before she forced it down.

"For your performance, you are awarded a meritorious commendation and the rank of Ensign in the ISA Combined Fleet. Congratulations."

She accepted her insignia with a crisp salute, face neutral, but the glint in her eyes betrayed her excitement.

One by one, Young called the other cadets forward, awarding each the rank of Ensign. Finally, only Ryan and Elizabeth Miller remained.

"Cadets Miller and Anders, step forward."

They moved simultaneously, though Miller edged slightly ahead, positioning herself directly in front of Young. She wore a smug, expectant expression.

Young withdrew two additional boxes from his pocket and studied them both for a moment.

"Cadets Miller and Anders, you have both demonstrated exceptional performance in command simulations, survival training, and hand-to-hand combat." He let the weight of his words settle before continuing. "Each graduating class produces one Lieutenant Junior Grade. However, this time command has made an exception."

A beat of silence.

"Both of you will graduate with the rank of Lieutenant Junior Grade."

Ryan blinked, barely processing the words. Beside him, Miller stiffened. Her smirk morphed into a barely concealed frown.

Young handed them their insignia and gave a firm nod before snapping off a salute.

"Congratulations, Lieutenants."

When they fell back into formation, Ryan felt like he was going to faint. The world seemed too bright, his vision swimming as he struggled. He forced himself to take a slow, deep breath, willing his pulse to steady.

Not being summarily expelled was unexpected, the promotion was shocking—but more than anything, it left him confused. He'd ranked second in the command simulator, true, but Elizabeth dominated the written exam with her encyclopedic knowledge of ISA Fleet regulations. Now he was headed to the fleet as a Lieutenant JG? Was he delusional or was the other very large shoe about to drop?

"Now," Commander Young continued, his voice cutting through Ryan's racing thoughts, "fall out and return to your rooms to collect your things. A jumper will be standing by on the airfield to transport you to the spaceport at 0900 hours. Dismissed!"

The six cadets snapped to attention before pivoting sharply on their heels as a unit, heading toward the barracks and then naturally separating into their social groups with the pollys leading the way.

Slaunder glanced over his shoulder at Ryan, making eye contact. A hard scowl drew down the sides of his mouth.

"Relax... Percival," Ryan said. "I won't make you salute me every time I see you." Ryan gave him the biggest gloating smile, which caused Slaunder to stomp off toward the chow hall without a word, fists in tight balls at his side.

"He looks really mad," David said, absently flipping the lid of the small wooden box open and closed.

"Screw that guy. In an hour we'll be on the way to the spaceport and he won't matter," Ryan said with bravado he didn't feel. He probably shouldn't antagonize someone like Slaunder, but it felt good.

"Oh my god, Ryan," Anna said, throwing a playful punch at his arm. "I mean—Lieutenant Junior Grade Anders." She gave him a mock salute before turning to David. "Ensign."

David relaxed a bit and returned the gesture. "Ensign."

Ryan let out a half laugh, shaking his head. "I thought for sure I was getting booted… or arrested."

"Me too," David admitted, his shoulders tightening up again. "When he called my name, all I could see was my parents' disappointment flashing before my eyes. I almost ran away."

Ryan and Anna both did a double take, exchanging glances. David rarely talked about his family, and when he did, it was never with anything close to sincerity. He assumed his parents were very strict from the few jokes David had made about his childhood.

As they made their way back to the main hall to gather their things, a quiet unease settled over Ryan. The promotion, the sudden orders, the way Commander Young had phrased things—it all felt off.

He couldn't shake the feeling that trouble was on the way.

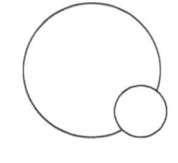

CHAPTER 2

Three hours later, the newest members of the Interplanetary Security Alliance (ISA) Combined Fleet sat strapped into their seats, their old cadet insignia replaced with official ranks. As was customary, they traveled in their dress uniforms, everything they owned stuffed into a large black rucksack. The military shuttle hummed around them as it was slowly raised into launch position, the whine of hydraulic motors echoing through the cabin. A dozen or so other passengers—some in uniform, others in civilian clothing—were seated, scattered around the cabin, waiting in silence.

"Have either of you ever been to space?" David asked, gripping the sides of his chair so tightly his knuckles turned white.

Anna shook her head, glancing across the aisle where two of their classmates, Elizabeth Miller and her friend Maxime, were seated a couple rows ahead. They were giggling and chatting like middle schoolers on a field trip, oblivious to the fact that they were about to leave the planet.

"Looks like some of us have," she muttered to herself, her eyes scanning the rest of the passengers before landing on Slaunder's rigid back at the front of the cabin.

Ryan remained silent, staring straight ahead. The hissing of cryogenic propellant loading faded, replaced by the groan of supercooled metal contracting. Then the cabin went quiet as the pilot's voice crackled over the intercom.

"We've been cleared for takeoff. Stand by."

Ryan barely registered the words, lost in a memory he rarely allowed himself to revisit.

His tenth birthday. His mother had surprised him, taking a rare break from her job as a security officer at the Federal Employment Center. She'd arrived home with a hastily wrapped box and a huge smile. Inside was a model of the *NAF Columbia*, the battleship depicted in his favorite reality show, which would soon be christened as the first true battleship in the North American Federation fleet. Young Ryan always dreamed of joining the fleet and captaining a ship just like it and spoke of nothing else but protecting the planet from real or imagined perils to the chagrin of his parents.

He wondered what changed; his mother had always discouraged the idea of him having anything to do with the military. She never spoke about her own time at the Academy—only that she'd dropped out before he was born. Whenever he brought it up, there was only sadness in her eyes.

That day, though, had been different. They played and laughed. His mother was beaming, beautiful and happy.

That night was just as perfect. She dimmed his bedside lamp the way he liked it—to a soft blue hue, almost as if he were floating below the sea, and the shadows swam by like fish as she sat stroking his hair.

"Follow your dreams, Ry," she'd said. Her voice was heavy with melancholy. "Join the fleet, go to space… get out of this place."

As she stroked his head, he drifted off to sleep, lulled by her hum. The melody was familiar. *Twinkle, Twinkle, Little Star.*

That was the last memory he had of her. The last time he saw her smile. The last time she gave him a wink and a thumbs-up, just like the captain in that show he loved. Hours later, she was gone.

Blinking back his emotions rapidly, Ryan glanced up at the cabin ceiling and, as subtly as he could, gave his mom a thumbs-up, his hand trembling.

A moment later, the roar of the shuttle's engines reverberated through the cabin. The force pressed them deep into their thickly padded seats as the ship shot skyward.

Ten long minutes passed. The outside light dimmed, replaced by the harsh white glow of the cabin lights. The engines, which had been slowly ramping down, cut out entirely, and they found themselves totally weightless.

Through the small windows, a much larger craft loomed into view, casting a deep shadow over their shuttle. A metallic clank reverberated through the cabin, followed by a slight jolt.

"Capture complete," the pilot announced.

A strange prickling sensation crept up Ryan's legs. He strained against his seat belt, trying to figure out what was touching him, before realizing it wasn't something external—it was the larger craft's pseudo gravity field engaging. The sensation became strongest on his fingertips and lips, a peculiar, tingling pressure. He read about it before, but experiencing it firsthand was different. Judging by the looks on his friends' faces, it was their first time too.

When the field stabilized, his hands dropped naturally to the armrests, as if gravity had finally remembered to pull them down.

"Weird," Anna muttered, rubbing the back of her neck. She lifted her hand up and down experimentally, feeling the slight shifts in the field. Catching sight of Ryan's slightly pained look, she leaned in. "You OK?"

He blinked, clearing his throat. "Strange feeling, huh? How long until we reach the Forge?"

David, seated closest to the window, croaked, drawing their attention. He looked a little green and was still gripping his armrests, staring straight ahead. "The... Forge is at the L1 Lagrange point, about... a million kilometers..." His voice trailed off, his breathing growing shallow. "...past the Moon..."

He froze.

Anna narrowed her eyes. "David. Breathe."

He didn't respond.

She reached into the seatback pocket in front of her. "Alright, maybe just take this." She handed him a zero-g sickness bag.

David's eyes widened in horror a split second before he grabbed it and promptly threw up his breakfast.

Ryan and Anna exchanged cringing looks as the sounds of David's misery stretched on far too long.

Across the aisle, their other classmates had taken notice. Elizabeth was staring at them with barely concealed disdain, while her friend whispered something, giggling. Others in the cabin ignored the sound but mostly had gone quiet.

Ryan sat back and sighed. It was going to be a long trip.

Sometime later, a click and mechanical whir vibrated through the craft as external shutters slid down over the windows, locking into place. Another, even stranger, sensation washed over them as the large carrier vessel engaged its slip drive, accelerating the assortment of docked craft to nearly 700 kilometers per second.

Ten minutes later, the feeling subsided, and the shutters retracted. "Incredible," Anna whispered breathlessly, drawing Ryan's attention outside.

The large carrier craft had already passed the Moon's orbital plane, the cratered surface still visible in the distance as they decelerated. Another announcement from the cockpit was followed by a metallic clunk as the shuttle was released from the hauler.

The pilots expertly changed orientation and fired the main thrusters. Momentum caused the craft to slide sideways as it adjusted course, positioning the windows closest to Ryan and his friends directly toward the Forge. Ryan grabbed David's arm, causing him to open his weary eyes and take in the view.

It was the largest structure humanity had ever built. Officially called the Earth-Moon Assembly Platform, it was a titanic construct, its form vaguely resembling a colossal, mechanical mushroom. The upper dome-shaped section, composed almost entirely of solar collectors and reflectors, faced the sun, generating power for the massive foundries below while also providing shade to the lower station against the constant solar bombardment.

Beneath the reflectors, the station's core was a vast, layered structure. An immense scaffold ringed the midsection, allowing for the simultaneous construction of several capital ships and smaller vessels. Below that, a central tower—resembling an inverted skyscraper—extended downward like a dagger, always oriented toward Earth.

Over the past two decades, the Forge had evolved from a simple orbital foundry into a sprawling construction hub. Initially tasked with producing hulls for the ISA Fleet, it had since expanded to accommodate corporations supplying the manpower and materials to complete those vessels. Now, it launched fully outfitted warships into service.

In its current form, the station was a self-contained city packed into a massive structure. It housed living quarters, lounges, shopping areas, green spaces, and even hotels for visiting family members. Most recently, the Interplanetary Security Alliance headquarters had relocated from Geneva, Switzerland, following the addition of twenty-five new decks to the station's lower levels. Altogether, the station was home to 12,000 permanent civilian and military personnel, all living and working together.

Ryan's sharp eyes picked out the shape of one seemingly complete vessel partially obscured by the scaffold. Its stern faced them, revealing a row of four engine nozzles.

"Which ship is that?" he asked, admiring the craft as their shuttle descended toward the station.

A man in civilian clothing seated in front of him turned, glancing between the seats. "That's the *Cosmic Explorer*," he said with a proud smile. "Newest ship in the ISA Fleet. I worked on her, you know." His tone invited further questions.

Ryan nodded but remained focused on the ship. Its silhouette didn't match any ISA vessel he recognized. It looked almost civilian, except for the squared-off stern, reminiscent of a destroyer or cruiser.

The man opened his mouth to say more but a commotion from the other side of the shuttle drew their attention.

The slow turn revealed an equally impressive sight: the battleship *Buenos Aires*. Hanging in the distance, it filled the shuttle's windows with its imposing bulk. Boxy and angular, the ship wasn't built for speed or beauty, its form was pure function, a fortress of dull steel-gray armor plates wrapped around an equally dense superstructure. At the rear, six massive fusion engines sat buried within a broad, heavily armored aft section. Bristling with weapons and sensor arrays, the vessel carried a single vivid green stripe across its bow. Ryan couldn't make out the emblem from this distance, but the stripe was a dead giveaway: this was the pride of the South American Union. A huge smile bloomed on his face before he caught himself.

Buenos Aires was the third ship of the Columbia class, its structure nearly identical to the original, a design that deliberately echoed the massive, steel-plated warships of centuries past. Huge turrets were mounted in strategic banks across its surface, their enormous barrels visible even from this distance. But those were only the secondary batteries. The real firepower lay along the ship's centerline: four 120-centimeter main guns housed deep within the armored core, capable of punching through the thickest of warship armor. These were battleships in the truest sense, slow-moving behemoths clad in thick plating, designed to absorb punishment and return it a hundredfold with a devastating mix of guided missiles and direct-fire cannons.

As the shuttle moved into the station's shadow, another sight caught their attention—the immense docking section of the Forge. Ships and shuttles of various makes, sizes, and designs criss-crossed everywhere like bees buzzing around a hive. Several larger ships hung outside, tethered to the station by long docking arms, while smaller craft like their own fifty-person shuttle entered designated bays.

The shuttle touched down in one such bay, and a large door thudded shut behind them, allowing the space to pressurize. Once sealed, the inner doors opened, and the shuttle's landing gear locked into a mechanism in the deck that smoothly guided it into the vast hangar. The passengers stood, grabbing their bags as the shuttle finally stopped, then the port-side door swung open automatically.

Once they disembarked from the shuttle, Ryan, David, and Anna stood in awe at the sheer scale of the hangar. A dozen shuttles ranging from small personnel movers like their own, to big cargo craft occupied the bay. Several gangways on the upper levels extended toward larger vessels, allowing direct boarding for the really big passenger liners and transports.

Above them, orange-white lights cast a diffuse glow, so high that the atmosphere blurred them at the edges. The sharp scent of machine oil, lubricants, and fuel hung thick in the air, carried by unseen currents.

A buzzer sounded as the mechanism attached to their shuttle rotated it back toward the airlock. Taking that as their cue, the three hurriedly followed the large yellow arrows painted on the floor toward the passenger terminal.

"Did you see which way Elizabeth and the others went?" David asked, shifting the weight of his large duffel over one shoulder.

Ryan and Anna shook their heads.

"Gotta be this way," Ryan said, scanning the terminal ahead. "Look for an ISA desk."

They wove through the growing crowd, passing clusters of people who seemed to naturally sort themselves by profession. Ryan took note of the emblems stitched onto their various uniforms—many bore the symbol of a hammer striking a star, framed by an outline of the station itself. Probably the Forge's official insignia.

Workers in blue coveralls with red stripes carried tool bags and test equipment, one even hauling a power pack and welder over his shoulder—maintenance crew, no doubt. Others, clad in soot-stained khaki jumpsuits, bore a bucket emblem, likely tied to the massive industrial forges that gave the station its name.

Mixed among them were civilians, some likely workers returning from the Moon or Earth, others looking just as lost as Ryan and his friends. But what struck Ryan most was the absence of uniformed ISA personnel.

"There." Anna pointed ahead.

A small manned kiosk stood near a row of snack vendors, a backlit triangular ISA emblem glowing above it.

As they approached, a somewhat rumpled petty officer looked up from his tablet. "How can I help you... sirs, ma'am?"

Anna stepped forward. "Hi, we were told to check in and get our final orders."

"Huh, you're the fifth group today." The petty officer tapped at his tablet and began rattling off instructions with the weariness of someone who had repeated them a dozen times. "Report to the quartermaster on Deck 17 first. Once you get your PDDs, your orders and room assignments will be uploaded automatically. You can—"

"What's a PDD?" Ryan cut in.

The petty officer exhaled sharply, clearly annoyed at the interruption. "Your Personal Data Device." He held up his wrist, showing a wide black band. "Everyone gets one when they join their first command. Makes communication and getting around a snap."

"Oh, of course." David nodded, looking a little less green. "I've read all about those."

Ryan smirked, briefly wondering where David had stashed his sick bag.

The petty officer had already returned to his tablet, barely acknowledging them.

"Uhh… that's it?" Ryan prompted.

The man perked up slightly as if remembering something. "Oh, right. If you three need food or entertainment, the Level One promenade has just about anything—shopping, too." Lowering his voice, he added, "If you need anything else… go to the Nebula and tell 'em Charlie sent you." He winked at Anna.

"Thanks Charlie." Ryan said, steering the others away.

Once out of earshot, David frowned. "What do you think he meant? Like drugs?"

"Drugs, sex, whatever." Ryan shrugged. "You hang around enough seedy spots, you get to know how these things work. Our guy Charlie's probably got a deal with the Nebula—sends people their way, gets a little commission in return. Believe it or not, it's probably a decent place."

"Ewwwww." Anna wrinkled her nose.

"No, not like that. Maybe overpriced drinks for the tourists, but get in good with the owner, and it's the kind of place where you can get decent food, cheap drinks, and information. I'm telling you, bartenders can be your best friends if you ever need to know what's really going on."

The others looked skeptical, but Ryan made a mental note to check the place out when he had the chance.

After a bit of searching, they arrived at a massive elevator bank. Several other new ISA recruits were already waiting.

"He said Deck 17, right?" Anna pressed the already-lit call button.

CHAPTER 3

After hours of administrative runaround, and even more hours of checking into the ISA housing division, the exhausted trio met back on the main deck, having changed into more comfortable civilian clothing. After a short walk, they found a pod of chairs off to one side that had been placed there by one of the many corporate partners of the Forge. Above, a video screen played an endless loop of advertisements and snippets of news.

"How was your room?" Anna said, slumping down into the comfy chair.

The other two followed suit. "Actually decent, I can't believe they assigned us singles," Ryan said.

"You got a single room?" Anna pouted. "I'm stuck with two other ensigns... of course *you* get a single."

"You're lucky," David said. "I've got three roommates."

Ryan shrugged, leaning back in the chair, head rolling until he was staring straight up at the ceiling high above. For a few seconds he let himself just sit there, taking it in. Then he flicked his wrist and tapped his PDD. The screen popped awake with its usual flood of menus and links. He started scrolling, eyes skimming across page after page.

The Forge was set up like a small city. The main deck they were on now was like the main street of a small town. The cavernous space was at least four stories high and was a place where people gathered around commercial shops and services. Lining either side were stores, restaurants, bars, and all manner of entertainment.

When they first entered the space on their way to the housing division, none of them could believe the sheer scope of it, especially given that it was located on a space station so far from Earth. Anna was the first to notice that it actually had living plants and trees growing here and there. The ceiling was even made from high-definition panels that mimicked the day-night cycle of the station with various clouds flying high above.

At this time of day, the virtual sun had set with orangey red hues, giving the whole thing the feel of a small planetside town if you didn't look too closely.

"So, where did they say to report again?" Ryan said, struggling to navigate other menus on his PDD.

Anna tapped hers clumsily before finally answering. "It just says report to the Temporary Training Division on Deck 6 at 0700 tomorrow."

"Yes," David agreed. He swiped his PDD a couple more times before an icon lit on Ryan's PDD.

"You got the hang of that pretty quick," he said, opening the message. "Looks like all us newbies are in the same division."

"When do you think we'll get our orders?" Anna said, still struggling.

"We find out tomorrow."

"I didn't see that anywhere," she said, giving up and letting her arm fall back to her side.

"Ryan?" a hesitant voice called out nearby.

The three friends looked over as one, spotting the young man in civilian clothing. Ryan, never good with names, took a second before pushing himself out of his chair and holding out his hand. "Marcus? Hey, man, good to see you."

To say that Ryan didn't know many people would be an understatement. His time at the Academy taught him to stay far away from anyone not named David or Anna. The one exception was Marcus Batista. He was a bottom tier polly from the class before theirs and had graduated weeks before. Even amongst the elites, he was sort of an outcast. From a middling family with no real political power, and he was a strange duck to boot.

They first crossed paths during a joint SERE training exercise. The upper-year cadets played the opposing force, tasked with tracking and capturing

Ryan's class in the wilderness near the Academy. Not long into the exercise, most of Ryan's classmates were quietly granted the option to call a timeout, a privilege reserved for those with the right names and connections. Only Ryan, Anna, and David were left in the game. That made them the foxes… and the hounds were all too eager to chase them down.

It was Marcus who found them and let them go for reasons Ryan still didn't understand.

"Hey, Marcus!" Anna said, holding out her hand as David did the same.

"Your class already graduated?" Marcus asked pointedly, as he shook their hands. He was about as tall as David, with about the same build. Ryan assumed he was in his early twenties like the rest of them, but he had a bearing that made him seem older.

Ryan was the only one who didn't seem to mind talking to Marcus. Both David and Anna had heard strange stories about him, rumors whispered by other cadets and even echoed by a few instructors. They said he was unlucky, often close by when something went wrong. A few even claimed he caused the accidents somehow. But Marcus had done Ryan a solid, and that counted for something.

"Nah, man, we graduated early. You're looking at Lieutenant Junior Grade Ryan Anders." Ryan smiled broadly, eliciting an eye roll from Anna. "We got bumped up with some others. No idea why, we haven't received our orders yet. Where did you get assigned?"

Marcus didn't seem fazed by the news of Ryan's promotion. "Oh, that's good. I'm a… I requested assignment to the *Rio de Janeiro*. I'm on third watch coms."

"Requested?" Ryan asked. "You can request a ship? I thought that was assigned by fleet."

Marcus shook his head. "No, anyone can request. Let me send you the link." He quickly swiped his PDD a few times and a chime sounded in Ryan's embedded earpiece, signifying the message.

The screen behind them flicked back to a news broadcast that Ryan did his best to ignore, but Marcus seemed immediately enthralled. Ryan turned, seeing the same report he had heard in passing. Two very attractive anchors were talking about a cargo craft that had been found after disappearing a week before. The authorities were pinning it on a reactor accident.

"Ryan, I… well, I need to tell you something," Marcus said, his voice a little shaky. He glanced around as if looking for an escape route. "I don't know why, exactly, but when I saw you, I just had this feeling. Just… be careful, okay?"

Ryan tilted his head, watching Marcus flounder. His reputation for being strange certainly wasn't misplaced, but he didn't care. Still, something in his voice felt different, earnest, even anxious.

"Hey, I never got to say thanks for what you did in SERE," Ryan offered, trying to lighten the mood. "You really saved our asses out there. We probably would've failed if not for you, right guys?"

Marcus gave a tight, uncertain smile. "Yeah. No problem." He hesitated, then added, "Sorry to bother you," before turning and disappearing into the crowd without another word.

"That guy is… weird," Anna said, plopping back down into her chair. David nodded vigorously beside her.

"We all are." Ryan shrugged. "Hey, look at this thing, he wasn't kidding."

Swiping his PDD, he sent the link Marcus had given him to the others.

"ISAPERF 203.5 Request for Posting or Reassignment." He read the title before scrolling down to several pages of instructions.

"I don't get it." Anna looked dubiously at the form, which to her surprise looked legitimate and had very few caveats. "I thought all assignments were handed out by fleet… and if it was this easy, why isn't everyone doing it?"

"Says here that you can request postings on heritage, family legacy, corporate citizenship, religious grounds, just about anything."

"Ryan, we don't have any of those things," David said.

"Ah, but we don't have to," he said triumphantly. "There is no requirement that we submit supporting documentation. We can just request it. It's all automated by the system."

He could see both of their expressions soften a bit. Ryan didn't tell them Marcus was actually a legitimate heritage, as his family was from Brazil, but the way he figured, there was no way he was going to get an assignment on the *Columbia* going the standard route.

"Hey, it says here that we can submit them as a group. What do you guys say? Keep the band together?"

"Sure..." David said, waffling.

"You two would be lost without me." Anna shook her head while starting to tap out her application.

"OK, send them to me when you get finished."

Several minutes later, a couple notifications popped up and Ryan tapped the two applications, adding them to his submission. When he had the three bundled, he tapped "send" and got confirmation that they had been received. "OK, it's asking which ship or ships we would like to be considered for."

Neither of his friends had given much thought to ship assignments, assuming they would be put wherever the ISA needed them. Anna slumped back in her chair and blew a lock of hair from her face, tapping her fingers together.

"Umm," she said.

"How about... the *Columbia*?" Ryan said, pretending to just throw it out there.

David's head tilted to the side as if he were weighing the pros and cons of being on the fleet flagship. He also knew it was Ryan's favorite even if he wouldn't admit it openly. Anna gave a little nod before agreeing. Ryan took David's noncommittal response as a yes.

"OK, *Columbia*," he said, tapping the screen. "Maybe we should pick some backups?" After nobody raised objections, he scrolled and chose the *Seoul* and the *Buenos Aires*. He was gambling that submitting three applications amongst the thousands of crew on each of the battleships wouldn't raise any eyebrows.

"Done!" Ryan said, tapping the send button, then closing the tab.

Ryan let out a long breath, the knot in his stomach loosening. A posting on the *Columbia*—his mom would've... He stopped himself, jaw tightening. No use going there. Shoving the thought aside, he pulled up the mapping feature on his PDD and searched for "Nebula," the bar the petty officer had told them about when they'd first arrived. It wasn't far, just a few minutes from where they sat. "Now, it's time to celebrate."

David yawned, stretching his arms above his head. "I don't know, we have an early morning. We should probably get some rest."

"What? Come on, we're on the Forge! The biggest space station in existence. Let's at least get something to eat. The guy said that our PDDs have full access to our accounts. I'm itching to spend some of that sweet ISA cash, so… first rounds on me?" He smiled, waiting.

"OK, how about first round AND dinner," Ryan proposed a few seconds later.

Both of his friends perked up.

He hadn't even checked his account for almost a year. When he had seen his first paycheck, he was floored by how much a cadet made. Growing up in the refugee camps skewed his concept of money, so he wasn't quite sure how to react to the windfall other than to ignore it. Both of his friends, however, sent almost the entire balance of their checks home as soon as they received them. He bet that they were supporting a dozen people between them—parents, siblings, extended family, maybe more.

Not long after arriving at the Academy, Ryan had tried sending money to his father, but the messages went unanswered. He told himself he'd look again on leave, but the camps weren't really home, and people there drifted constantly, chasing scraps of work. The closest he came was a week in a Seattle airport hotel, drinking and ordering room service, hoping his father might surface. He never did. Truth was, Ryan doubted he'd ever see the old man again, and wasn't sure he wanted to. His father had never shown him much affection, even before his mother died. Afterward, he just… unraveled, vanishing for longer stretches until one day he didn't come back at all.

After hearing no other talk of calling it a night, Ryan popped to his feet and held out his hands. As both of his friends grabbed them grudgingly, he pulled them up out of their chairs. "I know the perfect place to start," he said with a big smile on his face.

The three walked like a group of tourists, doing everything but snapping pictures while making their way down the wide faux street of the Forge's main promenade. It was fairly crowded and only seemed to increase as the neon lights and shopping storefronts gave way to the "outdoor" dining areas of restaurant row. Owners of the various businesses had added small touches like lampposts, painted signs, benches, and even some fake animatronic birds. Ryan imagined that this was what one of those fancy theme parks must be like with a thin veneer of pretty eye candy slapped over the machinery that made the place run.

As they continued their journey, the restaurants gave way to nightclubs and bars. There were even some darkened side "alleyways" complete with shifty-looking characters and bouncers. Neither of his friends could figure out if it was more decoration or if these places really were as seedy as they looked.

*

Nearby, a small gathering of people chatted in lowered voices just to the side of a gaudy corporate nightclub; the low, muffled thud of the music they were blasting within could be heard half a block away. One figure took notice of the three walking by, his eyes locked on Ryan, following him and his friends till they moved out of view. Teeth clenched, Slaunder pivoted on his heel and walked away toward the main promenade, several of the others in the group calling after him.

*

"Down here," Ryan said, studying the map on his PDD as he led them into one of the narrow, dimly lit alleyways. They passed what was unmistakably a brothel—holograms of men and women in barely-there outfits flickered in the air, beckoning passersby inside for a "drink."

David drifted toward it like a moth to flame, but Anna caught his arm before he could veer off course and steered him firmly down the alley.

They passed several other establishments of unknown type before coming to the end of the alley where they saw a small wood paneled facade with a purple and pink glowing sign: Nebula.

"This place?" Anna said, crossing her arms, slowing slightly before picking up the pace to catch up to Ryan and David.

Ryan could feel his excitement growing like it did every time he went into a dive like this. He swung the door open, expecting to be greeted by a dozen hard-nosed characters who would all stop speaking and give him dirty looks. Instead, besides the bartender, the place was empty. David and Anna were hot on his heels and nearly collided with him as he stopped inside.

Ryan took a quick scan of the bar and wasn't disappointed. The place was dimly lit, forcing his eyes to adjust for a second. The air smelled of stale beer, sweat, and what he guessed was machine oil. Like every dive bar from here to Washington state, the layout was familiar: well-worn booths lined two walls, their padded burgundy coverings scarred with gray-white slashes from years of abuse. Heavy tables clustered in small islands, leaving just enough room for foot traffic to reach the bar that dominated one side of the room. Near the back, a row of unmarked doors suggested bathrooms or maybe storage.

Behind the bar stood an older man with graying hair and a beard to match. His thick arms and barrel chest were inked with faded tattoos that blurred in the low lighting. A questionably clean, threadbare towel hung over his left shoulder. He hadn't moved since they walked in, eyes fixed lazily on a newscast reporting a missing ship.

After a few moments, he spoke. "What can I get you three?" The low, gravelly voice startled Anna, who'd been moving in slowly, half convinced he was asleep on his feet.

Ryan made his way over, noticing a vague yet familiar stickiness to the floor.

"I'll take a beer—whatever you got."

"What about them?" the bartender said, still not turning from his news program.

"Make it three." Ryan sat on one of the stools bolted to the floor and put his feet up on the railing near the base of the bar. Anna and David joined him on either side while the bartender finally moved from his spot, turning in their direction.

Ryan scanned the room, noting that if the place had ever been popular, that day was long past. Like the bar, some of the furniture was painted, textured metal made to look like wood, but other pieces were just bare metal. Some pieces were haphazardly painted, and everything was scratched or dented.

"Credits or chits?" the bartender grunted.

"Uh, credits?" Ryan held out his arm as the bartender waved a dirty white puck over his PDD, then turned to fill three questionably clean mugs and thumped them onto the bar.

"Oh, uh… Charlie sent us," Ryan said as he grabbed his drink.

The bartender crossed his arms. "You don't say. Well, if you see him again, tell him I still have that…" He stopped, lips tightening, then waved it off. "Never mind. That doesn't concern you."

He studied Ryan for a moment, his expression shifting. "Academy," he said flatly. "Guess you three are here for the simulator."

Ryan had no idea what the man meant, but the mention of a simulator caught his interest.

"Don't know why I let him talk me into buying that shit." The gruff man paused for a moment, considering something. "Maybe I let you use it and you bring your Academy buddies here." He pointed toward a nondescript door in the back wall of the room. "No freebies for them, but you can use it as long as you're drinkin'." He turned and went back to wiping glasses and watching his news program.

Intrigued, Ryan stood. "Sounds like a deal. What was your name again?"

"Robert," the bartender said, not turning.

"Nice to meet you, Robert. I'm Ryan, this is Anna and David."

He let out a grumble, picking up another glass.

Ryan shrugged, then gestured towards the mystery door. They grabbed their beers and all walked back, not quite sure what to expect. The door opened surprisingly smoothly on well-oiled hinges. Inside, a small hallway led to another door. As they opened it, lights started to snap on, revealing a clean, well-appointed simulator room. About fifteen feet wide and ten feet deep, there were four mechanized chairs built into the floor at the rear.

Hanging on each chair were a set of clear wraparound AR glasses that looked like they'd never been used.

A chime in Ryan's ear indicated "Nebula Simulator" attempting to pair with his PDD. He accepted and saw a menu pop up on his display.

"Ryan, look at the second page. Bridge simulator!" David said, having paired his own PDD.

Ryan grabbed the nearest set of glasses and put them on. The clear lens immediately showed the same menu as well as outlines around his hands. He took a long draw of surprisingly good, cool beer, then tapped the bridge simulator option.

"I guess we're supposed to sit?" Anna said, taking a sip and sitting in one of the seats, which had a built-in cupholder. Her glasses were a bit oversized for her small face but adjusted easily. As she sat, the chair immediately started to shift position to Ryan's left, eliciting a small squeak from the petite woman.

"I selected 'tactical,'" she said, now scanning the room with a look of wonder on her face.

David jumped into the next chair, putting on the glasses, and started furiously swiping the air as his chair moved forward.

Ryan sat, selecting "captain" from the menu. As his chair slid smoothly forward, the world around him changed. Now instead of a nondescript beige and grey room, there was a high-resolution rendering of the bridge of a destroyer. To his left and a little forward of his position, Anna sat, looking slightly out of place in her civilian clothing. To Ryan's right, David's chair moved into the Navigator's position. They all looked at each other, then back to their stations.

"Oh look!" she said, tapping the console in front of her. "I can feel the glass on this screen. The buttons feel real," she said with awe.

They had used simulators at the Academy, but they must have been several generations behind the one at the Nebula. Ryan shook his head as he tapped his controls randomly. "This is going to be fun, but I think we're going to need more beer... a lot more beer," he said, draining the rest of his frosty mug in one long gulp.

*

At a small two-seat table in the heart of Restaurant Row, Elizabeth Miller absently swirled her drink, scrolling idly through the news on a sleek new tablet. Her fleet-issued PDD was adequate for navigation and messaging, but its design was awful, its holographic display too small for comfort—and worse, it was ugly.

Her classmate Maxime ran into some sort of housing issue, leaving Elizabeth with a few hours to spare. This place, she supposed, was the best she could do under the circumstances. Personally, she had eschewed the standard-issue accommodations for new arrivals and checked into a so-called well-appointed hotel that barely met her minimum standards.

A soft chime cut through the ambient hum of the faux street. Elizabeth glanced at her tablet, took a sip of her drink, and tapped the notification.

The message was from Lieutenant Jameson, a minor contact in Forge personnel, the sort of overeager social climber Elizabeth would never befriend under normal circumstances. Still, she'd proven useful.

Setting her drink down she scanned the message. There it was: the preliminary crew roster for the *Cosmic Explorer*.

She had hoped for a position on First Watch, but her mother's chief of staff had already warned her that the maiden voyage's principal bridge crew had been handpicked by the ISA's inner circle. Second Watch, however, was well within reach. A posting at the weapons control station for the shakedown would be more than respectable. With the right maneuvering, it could lead to a secondary command role within the year. Two, perhaps three tours, and she could be running the ship herself.

She filtered the list for bridge assignments and began scrolling. Her finger traced down the column, past one name after another until she reached the end.

Frowning, she scrolled back up, slower this time. Still no entry with her name.

She scrolled again. And this time, her breath caught.

Miller, Elizabeth, Bridge, Communications Specialist, Third Watch

She sat bolt upright, her drink forgotten.

"What on Earth…"

It had to be a mistake. She scrolled back to Second Watch, hunting for some sign of a clerical error. But what she saw next stopped her cold.

Anders, Ryan, Bridge, Weapons Specialist, Second Watch

Her pulse spiked. That post was hers. The notion that anyone else could take it was absurd, but a lottery pick? Impossible. The insult stung like a slap. No one rose that far without someone powerful dragging them upward.

For a moment, she simply stared at the screen, her expression unreadable. Then she reached for her drink with deliberate calm, the kind of stillness that settles in just before a storm breaks.

"If it isn't our illustrious class leader," a familiar voice called from nearby. "I'm glad I ran into you."

Elizabeth blinked once, slowly, her gaze fixed on the tablet. "Ensign Slaunder."

Corporate candidates like him were mannerless to the point of offense, and she had no patience left. Her mother had exposed her to their type early, through fundraisers, galas, and diplomatic functions. She had watched them closely: always circling, eyes sharp behind counterfeit smiles, treating every introduction like a transaction. Unlike the political class, who cloaked ambition in subtlety and restraint, these boardroom brats were obvious, transactional to the bone.

Slaunder, as if on cue, took Elizabeth's greeting as an invitation and slid into the empty seat across from her.

"I'm surprised to see you here." He looked around, picking at the rolled napkin in front of him. A practiced smile played on his lips. "My father says the best place to eat on this dump is Stellaré. I can get you a private table there if you want."

"No thanks," Elizabeth said coldly. "What do you want, Slaunder." She put her tablet down on the table, careful to close the message, and picked up her drink.

He blinked, thrown off for just a second, then recovered with a tight smile. One hand casually swept back his carefully styled hair, the gesture more habit than necessity. "Right to business. I like that." He motioned to the server, who brought Elizabeth a drink earlier. "I'm working on a little project, and I need some… assistance from someone with ISA connections."

Elizabeth took a sip. "Why on Earth would I help someone like you?"

"Staying at the Spire?" He switched quickly; his predatory grin was back. "I know that place is nice enough."

The young server appeared at the table. "What can I get you, sir?"

Slaunder looked at her like a piece of meat, his smile and wandering eyes made Elizabeth want to retch. "I'll take a glass of *Rubio7* on the rocks, darling." he said, adding a wink that earned a giggle and hair toss from the girl as she turned away.

Without missing a beat he turned back to Elizabeth, all smooth entitlement.

"I can get you a private apartment. Fully furnished with its own concierge." He tapped at his PDD. A glossy sales brochure blinked to life on her tablet without her asking.

Elizabeth didn't even glance at it. "Not interested."

"The job's simple," he said, pressing on as if she hadn't spoken. "You get the apartment for as long as you need. And I want Anders. Gone, out of the ISA for good. Arrested, if you can swing it. But gone."

There was a new sharpness to his voice, tight and focused. When he said the name, his expression twisted into something darker, almost feral.

Elizabeth's eyes flicked to his for the first time since he sat down.

Now he had her attention, and he knew it. His smile changed—not wider, but sharper, hungrier.

She paused as the waitress returned with Slaunder's drink, her thoughts spinning. She didn't trust him, not even slightly, but she didn't have to. What mattered was that Ryan Anders had somehow bullied his way into her spot and was now standing firmly in her way.

"What's your name, cutie," Slaunder said, interrupting her train of thought, grabbing the waitress by the wrist.

"I can make that happen," Elizabeth said, her voice sharp and deliberate.

Slaunder's hand dropped away as the waitress retreated. His gaze snapping back to Elizabeth, still hungry, still watching.

"I'll message you when it's done..." she picked up her tablet and began scrolling.

"No," he said quickly. "I want to be the one who does it." He licked his lips. "I want to send the dumb idiot back to his nothing life."

Elizabeth looked up, her eyes icy over the top of the screen. He flinched, just slightly.

"This isn't how it works," she said coolly. "I'll set things in motion. When the time comes, he's out. You can tell him whatever story makes you feel powerful."

She returned to her tablet as if the conversation bored her, then added, almost as an afterthought, "Oh, and the rest of my things are with a porter at the dock,"

With a flick of her finger, she sent a message to his PDD. "See to it they're delivered to my new apartment."

She met his eyes one last time. "Goodbye."

Slaunder stood, his mouth opening and closing as if still assembling a reply. Then, without a word, he threw back his drink, slammed the glass onto a nearby table, and stalked off.

"Pathetic," she muttered.

Elizabeth lifted a hand to signal the waitress. With Anders finally out of her path, her appetite had returned.

*

The next morning, Elizabeth lounged on a fairly comfortable hand-crafted chaise flipping through some files on her tablet. The apartment Slaunder procured was indeed much more nicely appointed than the supposedly luxury hotel room. The bed was even better, offering her the first proper night's sleep she'd had since her last visit to the family estate in Kensington.

She skimmed another file, her thoughts circling back to Ryan Anders. How someone like him—a nobody, from nowhere—had managed to secure a coveted position aboard Earth's newest and most advanced vessel was beyond comprehension. Even Lieutenant Jameson in personnel had come up empty when she asked.

Elizabeth let the thought drop. She would find out sooner or later, but first she needed to figure out how to remove the tick from her position. She could use her family connections, but that sort of brute force approach wasn't her style. It was best to use the system and let others handle the dirty work as her parents had so skillfully done in the past. She had watched her mother, a seasoned member of Parliament, unseat a political rival with nothing more than a few carefully whispered suggestions to the press. That was how power worked: subtle and clean... mostly.

Elizabeth opened the files of Anders friends first. Her mother had also taught her that friendships were easily leveraged to get what you wanted. Perhaps they had problematic pasts that she could use to force him to resign his commission.

She assumed they were all chosen randomly, probably based on some formula a long-dead populist politician had dreamed up. Surprisingly, both David Kim and Anna Rodriguez were near the top of the class. Their scores weren't as high as her own, of course, but uncomfortably close. If not for the extracurricular credit granted to her by the Academy, she might actually be below them.

Scandalous.

In their respective specialties of weapons and navigation, she had to admit that there were few who could challenge them. David especially was frighteningly good. His instructors said he could plot complex courses through dense asteroid fields by feel alone, without AI assistance. He was so talented, in fact, that the Academy had quietly monitored him for weeks, suspecting he was cheating. He wasn't.

Anna had shown a knack for weapons employment with an emphasis on large scale tactical coordination. She had several notes recommending her for further tactical training, which of course went unanswered due to her low political and social standing. The best Anna could hope to achieve would be a posting to third shift bridge watch stander, but she was most likely destined to be a supply officer.

Had David been born to a better family, his technical expertise would have guaranteed him a spot as First Navigator or even Chief Engineer but he'd most likely be assigned as a maintenance crew officer.

Swiping to the last record, she crinkled her nose.

"Ryan Anders," she said, her British accent becoming more pronounced with his last name. She used two fingers to enlarge his picture. Just about everything from his fake easygoing manner to the way he laughed reminded her of her brother, Harry, which made her stomach turn.

She swiped away the picture in disgust, scrolling down the record.

Ryan was hotheaded and not particularly well educated. His grades were decent for a public university, but his disciplinary records were filled with notes showing a complete disregard for political or social nuance and a problem with authority.

From his first days at the Academy, he had racked up demerits. Fist fights, talking back to his betters, even having the gall to tell one of the instructors that the system was rigged against the poor.

She shook her head, swiping to the next page. Having been born into a well-to-do family, she had always heard this talking point.

The world, or at least her own beloved country, wasn't rigged or biased, she thought; it was complex. Her mother had lectured her many times that the difference between rich and poor was drive and intelligence. Obviously, it wasn't the fault of the grubs that they were born dumb and unable to navigate the complexities of government or business; that was a factor of family heritage, education, and probably genetics. If they were too lazy to fight to better their place or compete for a better spot in the world, that meant that they would have menial jobs and be poor forever. That wasn't the fault of the system or the people who used it to their advantage, she told herself.

"I've had to fight for everything I have," she thought to herself, anger swelling.

Competition was her whole world. Her mother constantly tested her, made sure she was ready to take the mantle of family leadership, or so she thought. Accepting nothing but the very best from Elizabeth, her mother would demand she perform at a high level even as a child.

Elizabeth let out a small, joyless laugh, remembering the requests she had made as a little girl for things her mother deemed unnecessary. She had begged no less than twenty times to keep a tiny cat she'd rescued near their estate, a fragile helpless thing that her mother claimed was diseased. It vanished shortly afterward. Even as a child, Elizabeth suspected who was responsible but felt powerless to do anything.

By the time she was in secondary school, she had learned that attachments like that were weakness waiting to be exploited. So, she buckled down and became quite adept at managing the fickle family bureaucracy, finding loopholes in the rules to get what she wanted.

Her younger brother was another story. He never seemed interested in anything his mother said, or her father for that matter. He wouldn't participate in the games and eventually just did whatever he wanted. Her parents, more often than not, had to use their family influence to pull him from the fires of his own making.

She could have coasted by on her name like her brother had, but she didn't; she was driven to do better, to be better.

The day her mother called her into a private meeting, she was riding high. The path to the future assured.

Then came the shock of all shocks, something that sent her into a rage unlike any other. Her mother, the woman who had done nothing but prepare her to take control, had selected Harry as her successor.

That same day, she had packed her things and moved to their vacation home in New York. If her mother wanted a war, she would give her one. Elizabeth decided to take a different, more roundabout way to power— through the military, the one place she could make some very powerful friends and where her mother's reach was stunted.

Elizabeth waved away the line of thought getting back to the records.

Like her brother, Anders seemed another dumb brute who had somehow wormed his way into a spot he didn't deserve… or perhaps, like him, he had a powerful benefactor pulling strings on his behalf.

Elizabeth couldn't understand how he'd even been considered for the Academy. By Anna's and David's entrance scores alone, far more qualified candidates must have existed. She flipped through his record again, irritation rising. He'd excelled in the command simulations, showing a natural grasp of information processing and resource management. In high-altitude flight training, a module she personally loathed, he'd scored in the top percentile. She blamed her own mediocre performance on the archaic, bulky pressure suits, but even so… something about his record didn't fit.

She tapped her fingernail on the glass of the tablet before finally backing up and looking closely at his application.

Before nearly tossing the tablet in frustration, she spotted a short note in his admissions paperwork made by some nameless clerk.

> ISA member recommend (r)

She sat back in disbelief. It had to be a mistake—the only people who could recommend students to the Academy were high-ranking government officials, corporate board members, or flag ranked officers. She tapped the "(r)," not recognizing the notation. It brought up the explanation: "redacted."

Elizabeth bared her teeth. So not only was this mystery person someone with real clout, but they also had the ability to redact their name from the official record. A feat that Elizabeth doubted her own family could accomplish.

She swiped to his profile, showing all his recorded family members. To her surprise, she saw that his mother, born "Chloe Davis," had made it to her third year at the ISA Fleet Academy under the same program Ryan had weaseled his way into, before she dropped out for reasons unknown.

After she met Ryan's father, she changed her name.

"Oh, a little drama there." Elizabeth smirked as she noticed the dates. Chloe had already been pregnant before the wedding.

"Probably met him in some cheap tavern," she scoffed.

His mother had gone on to become some sort of security guard before being killed on the job.

Not finding anything there, she turned to his father's profile. Keith Anders was another dead end, showing only that he was some sort of factory worker who had apparently gone missing after the mother's death with his whereabouts marked unknown.

Swiping to older records, she found that his maternal grandparents were both dead and equally unremarkable with nothing noted on his father's side. None of his family records could explain the discrepancy.

She tried to switch perspective. "What would my brother do?" she whispered to herself, imagining her lazy, good-for-nothing sibling squirming out of even the barest of responsibility. "He would probably blame me, and then Mother would give him anything he wanted."

Then it dawned on her.

"Ah." She smiled, looking at Ryan's intake photo. "You must have paid the clerk to slip that note into your file." She flicked his picture with a carefully manicured nail. "Typical of you grubs to try to game the system for what you don't deserve."

She would have to send a note to the personnel office, warn them to watch for irregularities. If he'd done it once, she was certain he'd do it again.

The soft chime of the door announced the arrival of the masseuse she had summoned. Elizabeth set the tablet aside and stretched. "Come in."

CHAPTER 4

T he following morning, Ryan sat at the same set of chairs where he had met his friends the day before. His work uniform was a bit wrinkled, having just pulled it from his bag, but seemed passable. He swiped his PDD, getting familiar with the layout of the interface, its holographic screen displaying his daily plan, which had been downloaded sometime last night. He saw David exiting the elevator and waved him over.

"Hey, Davey, how you feelin?" He smirked, knowing he felt like trash.

"I feel awful, and my roommates were angry with me for waking them."

"You get locked out? Don't tell me you already lost your PDD?" Ryan said.

"No, I got sick again," David said, head low.

"Hey, there she is," Ryan said, ignoring David's shame display, instead waving to Anna, whose hair was pulled back into a damp bun. He admired her walk, noticing her work uniform was a bit tight across the chest.

Having long ago learned to ignore Ryan's wandering eye, she brushed it off. "Come on, you two, let's go grab some breakfast, we need to be on Deck 6 at 0700."

"What's the hurry? I'm sure we can be fashionably late," Ryan said.

"This is the fleet, not some elective. When they say 0700, they mean it," Anna said, walking off.

*

After breakfast, the trio strode through the large doorway to the Deck 6 Temporary Training Division, mouths agape. They hadn't known what to expect, but there were hundreds of people milling about. The room they occupied was large enough to accommodate the crowd, with rows upon rows of chairs. It could have been any hotel conference room with an empty area near the front where a lone podium stood. The only other notable things were the two-meter-tall Training Division logos emblazoned on the walls to either side, which to Ryan looked like swords stabbing a book that was on fire.

"Who are all these people?" Anna said, standing on her tiptoes trying to see farther into the room. "They aren't all ISA Fleet."

Ryan noticed there were a lot of different uniforms, some familiar, some not. To his left about twenty feet away was a large group of boisterous men and women. "Are those guys U.S. Marines?"

Anna and David both looked at the group decked out in grey digital camouflage and caps.

"I believe so," David said, pointing farther back. "That group looks like SSA regulars."

Ryan nodded. The South Sea Alliance, which patterned itself after the old European Union, had distinctive tan uniforms with dark red accents at the shoulders. This group was made up of "regulars," or the equivalent of enlisted personnel in other space borne forces.

A chime interrupted their musings, and people started taking seats. A minute later, at the far side of the room from where Ryan and his friends were standing, a projection shimmered into existence, showing a larger-than-life woman in a splendid ISA Fleet uniform. Her hair pulled back into a tight bun, she held her cap under her right arm. Beside her, the normal-sized podium looked child-sized.

Anna urged them to take several open chairs about midway up the aisle.

"Good morning," the woman began. "My name is Admiral Samantha Hayes, head of the combined ISA Fleet. I'd like to extend a welcome to you all from the men and women of ISA Fleet headquarters." She paused as if waiting for something.

"Recorded," Ryan said to nobody, slumping back into his chair.

"The ISA was formed in the aftermath of the terrorist attacks that decimated..."

A moan sounded from several points in the room as the pre-recorded Admiral Hayes started into a well-known and often recited history lesson. Ryan, too, added a small moan before Anna's elbow found his rib. She shushed him and urged him to pay attention.

"...so devastated and horrified the Earth. Since that time, we have welcomed the best and brightest from every country into our ranks."

"Damned right!" one of the Marines yelled nearby, causing some scattered chuckles.

"Acting as a sword, the ISA brought the perpetrators of the Rogue Five organization to justice. Now we act as a shield, and for the past twenty years, we have protected the Earth and her vital stations and space lanes, helping to expand humanity's reach to the rest of the solar system."

Ryan could have sworn they were going to add music to her little welcome speech.

"With its inclusion as a full member of the Orbital Security Convention, we have now added Mars and her citizens into the fold."

At the mention of Mars, a small roar went up near the front of the room. A rowdy group of crimson and brown clad soldiers shook fists into the air. Elsewhere a smattering of boos sounded.

"For the first time in its history, humanity has been united as one. I salute you, the newest members of the fleet, for your dedication to the Earth and the ideals set forth in the OSC."

The projection shimmered again and disappeared with a few half-hearted claps around the room.

Up front, an older man in a black ISA Fleet uniform stood from his seat. He walked stiltedly to the podium, carrying a tablet. Waiting for a few background conversations to come to an end, he swiped the screen a few times.

"Like the admiral said—welcome to the fleet. I'm Lieutenant Commander Compton with the personnel division here on the Forge. For most of you, this will be the first and last time we talk—so you're welcome." This elicited a few laughs, but he plowed ahead with his well-rehearsed speech.

"Please refer to your PDDs for your final assignments, which I have just sent. If you don't see a muster date for your next command, you'll need to contact the travel office for further instructions. You'll find that number under the fleet services tab."

All around the room, people raised their arms and tapped their devices. A new round of murmuring took hold. Ryan looked as well, seeing a new notification in his message queue.

"Mine just says: Please contact Lieutenant Commander Compton," David said.

"Yeah, mine too." Anna looked toward Ryan, who smiled.

"Probably our preferential posting request." He rubbed his hands together. "We might actually be going to the *Columbia*. At the very least, we'll be together since we all three got the message."

"Settle down." Commander Compton raised his voice over the din. "If your transfer date is more than seven days from now, you will muster here tomorrow morning for temporary duty assignment until the Friday before your transfer to your final command." He paused, looking around the room, satisfied there weren't any questions before continuing. "OK, now the good news. You might have noticed the new ship hanging in assembly yard one. That's the *Cosmic Explorer*, and I just got word that she will be launching in two weeks."

All around the room, hoots and hollers sounded. The low din had become a loud and rowdy cacophony.

"What?" Ryan looked at his friends, who seemed as perplexed as he was.

He turned to a young ensign next to them, getting his attention. "What's the big deal?"

The smiling ensign got closer, practically yelling over the noise. "Launching Day! Whenever they christen a new ship, they throw an all-out party! My brother was on the *Seoul* when she was launched, he said it went on for three days." He held up three fingers to accentuate the point. "Everyone will be here, man. Politicians, actors, CEOs, sports stars. Shit, my brother said he was hungover for a week after."

Ryan smiled at the thought of an authorized three-day bender, not to mention all the girlfriends and wives of the VIPs who would be hanging around, probably bored out of their minds.

The ensign seemed to read his mind. "My brother volunteered to help with the party, and he was giving tours to the VIPs." He smiled like a cat getting ready to eat a plump mouse.

"Thanks, pal," Ryan said, clapping the young man on the shoulder.

"Listen up!" Commander Compton said with a booming voice that short-circuited the early celebration. "We have some Mars personnel here."

Several of the Mars soldiers who had been some of the loudest and most rowdy clanked their forearms together, making a metal-on-metal sound. Ryan craned his head till he could see them more clearly. They were wearing some kind of power-assisted harnesses on top of their fatigues. Thin plates of some type of alloy covered the arms, legs, and chest like tactical body armor.

"Since Mars PDDs haven't been integrated into the Forge network yet, you people will need to report here every morning for your assignments."

After getting the thumbs-up from the Mars contingent, Compton looked over the rest of the gathered service members.

"Now, most of you on temporary duty will be assigned to help set up the Launch Day party, so it isn't all fun and games. We've got a lot to get done, and ships from all over the system are headed here to join in, so rest up, you're going to need it."

The background conversation started to swell again before Compton added a seeming afterthought. "Oh, and one last thing." He paused for dramatic effect. "I hope you all get laid. Dismissed!"

The roar from the young service members was booming. Before long, most of the crowd, and noise, left the room. Scattered pockets of people in groups were still sitting or standing around.

"OK, looks clear, let's go talk to Compton about our assignments," Ryan said and started making his way up front with Anna and David close behind.

"Commander Compton," Ryan said, giving a not-so-perfect salute. "We were told to report to you."

Commander Compton, seated at one of the chairs near the podium, looked up from his tablet. He immediately looked at Ryan's name tag, then at Anna's and David's in turn.

"Anders, Anders…." he said, scrolling on an open document. "Lieutenant Junior Grade Anders. You mind telling me what this bullshit preferential posting request is all about?"

Ryan became still, face hot. Compton paused, scanning the three now petrified young officers. "No? What about you?" he said to David, who started to turn beet red.

"OK, so here's how this will go. Submitting a false posting request can land three people like you in the brig," he said, emphasizing the "like you" part. "It could even get you booted from the ISA if the wrong people find out."

"Sir," Ryan said, finally screwing up enough courage to speak.

"Go ahead, Anders," Compton said, rubbing the top of his left leg absently, which Ryan noticed was artificial.

"Sir, it was my call. I submitted their applications, they didn't know."

"I would have believed that if Ensign Kim here didn't look like he was going to pass out when I first mentioned it." He sighed heavily, looking at the tablet that Ryan could now see had his request – with a big fat review flag plastered on the front of it.

"Fine." He looked at David and Anna, both of whom were now white as ghosts. "You two are dismissed. Report here for temporary duty tomorrow at 0600 sharp."

"Yes, sir!" they said in unison, snapping off salutes before turning on their heels and retreating from the room.

Turning back to Ryan, he crossed his arms. "So, what's so special about the *Columbia*? Why possibly ruin your career before it even got started just to get on that ship?"

Squaring up his shoulders, he debated saying something like "I wanted to serve on the best ship in the fleet" or something patriotic, but something about the commander told him he would see right through that lie.

This wasn't the time nor the person to bullshit.

"Sir, it was my mother's dream to serve on the *Columbia*, talked about it all the time. She made it to the Academy, she…" Ryan swallowed hard. "Well, she gave that up when she got pregnant with me… after she left the Academy… I wanted to." Ryan could feel a lump in his throat, but he plowed forward. "She never made it to the fleet, sir. I wanted to make sure I did." Ryan stopped talking, unsure if his rambling explanation had made any sense, but Commander Compton just looked at him before giving a curt nod.

"Not the answer I expected from you."

Compton pressed his hands into his thighs and lifted himself from his chair, his leg making a soft whir as the servomotors assisted the movement.

"She die serving?" he said in a matter-of-fact tone, his face softening somewhat. Ryan was surprised at his own reaction to the question. Normally he wouldn't even allow himself to think of his mother's death; it was just too painful, too raw after all these years, but with Commander Compton, he felt something he hadn't experienced before—someone who understood.

"No, sir. She left the service and worked as a security guard at the local employment office. She died in the line of duty."

"Employment office… The riots?"

"Yeah, I mean yes, sir. They told me she was the only one who stayed at her post, trying to protect the people working there. They held out for a while, but the local cops never showed, and the mob burned the building."

"Sorry, son, that was a shit deal. I read about the riots; it was a damned shame so many good people died." Compton looked him in the eye. "Sounds like your mother would have made a great officer, but this." He held up the tablet. "This doesn't do you or your family name any favors. You will never make it onto a battleship, much less the flagship of the fleet, if some political officer got wind of a low-born grubber trying to game the system. We have to do it better, cleaner, and by the book. You get me?"

Ryan looked forward, trying to stand even straighter, looking like a new recruit on his first day. "Yes, sir!"

He glanced at the commander. "*We*, sir?"

"You're not the only one who grew up in a slum, Anders, so believe me when I tell you. Do better." He consulted his tablet briefly. "I can see from your file that this isn't the first time you've been in a spot." He pondered for a second, shaking his head. "Report here with your friends tomorrow morning, and don't make me regret this. Dismissed."

Ryan managed a perfect salute, probably the first of his career, which was returned just as precisely by the commander before turning on his heel and marching out of the room.

Compton sighed. Ander's little stunt hadn't gone unnoticed by the personnel division higher ups. He tapped the reassignment button and turned off his tablet.

*

Across the room, Slaunder leaned against a support column, his arms crossed watching the scene play out. "What's happening?" he said.

Elizabeth sat a few chairs away, casually scrolling on her tablet without looking up. "Exactly as I predicted. My contacts in the personnel office spotted an irregular application in his records and flagged it. The commander had no choice but to handle it."

Slaunder looked like he ate a puppy. "What did you add?" He licked his lips, moving closer. "Stealing equipment? Maybe spying?"

Elizabeth frowned; the scent of his overused cologne wafted over her. "Nothing of the sort. I merely nudge the system in the way that benefits... you. I didn't have to do much really, like all low born they try to get ahead without putting in the work." She held her finger under her nose to partially block the strong scent.

Lowering her tablet, she watched the tense exchange with amusement. Compton was clearly berating the group, then dismissed Ryan's friends who scurried out of the room with their tails tucked firmly between their legs. She noticed Slaunder literally rubbing his hands together in anticipation.

Once Compton had the squirming Anders alone, she assumed that, like her brother, he would either skulk away to gather his things and wallow in self-pity or perhaps fly into a rage and even strike the commander. Either way she didn't want to miss the excitement, especially if it ended up with him being carted off to the brig in cuffs.

Instead, something very unexpected happened—they talked. This had Elizabeth's full attention. What could a low born schemer like Anders and the decorated officer have to talk about? From their body language she could tell there was some deeper meaning being shared. Then Ryan actually saluted the commander and marched out like he had been given an important assignment.

"What the hell was that, Miller? I thought you said he was done?" Slaunder stood there, jabbing his finger towards her. "How did you fuck that up!"

Elizabeth stood calmly and smoothed her slacks tucking her tablet under her arm before turning to meet him inches from his face. "Don't you dare speak to me in that tone." She locked eyes with him, watching the realization of who he was speaking to push away the anger he was feeling.

She took a step forward, causing him to retreat a step.

"We… we had a deal," he stammered. "You were supposed to—"

"I know what I was supposed to do, and I'll do it." She bent down and retrieved her purse from the chair, returning to her former calm and detached self. "I'll just have to take another path. I'll let you know."

Slaunder's anger flared again. "No." He flinched as her eyes darted toward him. "No, thank you. I'll take care of it *my way*, but please stay in the apartment as long as you want." He turned and strode away. His stilted walk and balled fists gave away his barely controlled emotions.

"My way?" Elizabeth said to herself, shaking her head. During her research of Anders and his friends, she had widened her net to include Slaunder. She regretted that she hadn't done so before involving herself with the insect. The buried records she uncovered from his university days showed him as spiteful, vindictive, and petty, willing to do whatever he wanted to whoever he wanted. She could see just from the police reports and class records that he was probably responsible for no fewer than five expulsions and a few unexplained "accidents" that left one classmate in a coma.

She composed herself, checking her tablet for one message in particular. As if on cue, the chime sounded and Lieutenant Jameson's short note popped up on screen: *He's Out.*

Elizabeth allowed herself the faintest smile. She slipped the tablet into her bag and turned toward the opposite door.

That's settled, then.

*

Outside the large Training Division conference room, Ryan took a moment to compose himself before looking for Anna and David. His conversation with Commander Compton had shaken him.

"Anders," a venomous voice called to him.

He glanced over, knowing the voice and the tone far too well.

"What can I do for you *Ensign*." He made sure to emphasize the rank, knowing it would stick in his craw.

"You think your so fucking clever, don't you grub?" He spit the reply.

Ryan turned toward the fast-approaching man. Something in his voice told Ryan to be ready for anything. When he was within striking distance, Slaunder's demeanor changed. He went from rage to cold so fast it gave Ryan the chills.

"Oh, was that you that tried to get me in trouble?" He hitched his thumb toward the conference room. "Pretty sloppy work, *Ensign*, you're going to have to do better next time." He smiled.

"Anders," Slaunder said, clearly struggling to put his thoughts to word. "I just want you to know, when you're lying on the floor with your guts in your hands." He moved closer, hissing. "That it was me."

He stepped back, smiling like a serpent, his eyes almost bloodshot. Without another glance, he pushed past Ryan, headed toward the elevator, which was just arriving.

Ryan knew he should just shut his mouth and let things cool down. He'd been threatened so many times growing up in the slums that it was almost a non-event, but Slaunder... the way he said it chaffed.

Thankfully they were alone in the passageway, so disengaging was easier, as he didn't need to feed that part of his ego. That was until he saw his two friends walking around the corner.

He could feel the comment start to form on his lips, and before he could stop himself, he blurted it out.

"I'll keep that in mind, Percival!"

Slaunder's step hesitated for a moment before he bullied his way past Anna and David to stand in the elevator with his back to the door breathing heavily.

After it closed, both his friends turned toward Ryan.

"Should we ask?" Anna was the first to speak.

"Probably not."

He led his two friends toward the elevator, plastering a grin across his face. As they strode forward, he decided that whatever die he just cast would play out regardless, and worrying would be pointless. Work the problem, his mother had often told him growing up, don't worry about the what ifs.

"Well?" Anna said. "What did the Commander have to say?"

"Oh, Commander Compton is cool, I just played dumb." He lied, not wanting to divulge the real conversation he'd had with the man. "I saw a flag on our applications though."

"They didn't get flagged, Ryan," Anna said, hands on her hips. "They probably saw three lottery recruits headed for the *Columbia* and said 'no way.'"

"I saw the flag as clear as day on the commanders tablet." Ryan started walking. "It was Slaunder, he basically just admitted it to me."

Ryan watched as David furiously tapped away on his PDD behind Anna before snapping his fingers and saying, "It wasn't Slaunder."

Anna turned on him, furrowing her brow. "How could you possibly know that?"

David squirmed a bit under her intense gaze. "I was doing some digging. Nothing illegal, I swear. I just noticed earlier that there were some bad holes in their security. Just like the Academy."

Ryan snickered.

"You hacked into the Forge's network?"

David inched backwards before Ryan put his hand on his shoulder, startling him.

"I was curious. Anyway, it was our class leader Elizabeth, not Slaunder," David said.

"Why am I not surprised." Ryan scoffed. "Corpos and polys workin together to screw over the little guy, ain't that always the way."

"That doesn't make any sense, we barely know her. I don't think I've ever spoken to her besides saying 'yes ma'am,'" Anna protested.

"Forget it. Come on, you two, it's almost lunchtime, and it seems to me that we could all use a drink and something to eat... I know a place," Ryan said, calling the elevator as David vigorously nodded in agreement.

"Oh my god, you two," Anna said, looking first to David, then to Ryan before finally acquiescing. "We can grab *one* drink, but I want to go to that new German place."

As they rode the elevator down, Ryan silently chastised himself.

So many times over the last three years, he thought he was sure to get kicked out of the Academy after mouthing off to teachers and students alike. He must have been born under a lucky star to have graduated with only a few demerits and notes in his record. Too many small strokes of luck to be entirely random, he thought. It was almost as if unseen hands had steered him clear of disaster. He shook his head, pushing the notion aside; some things were better left unexplored.

"What are you up to?" Anna said, eyes squinting as if she could see in his head.

The elevator doors opened, revealing the grand promenade.

"What do you know about Slaunder?" He deflected.

"Just the usual. His father runs the defense contractor Mazim. He's supposed to be anointed as king whenever the old man dies of natural... or unnatural causes."

"Anointed?" Ryan said, angling toward a less busy part of the promenade.

"Business is like politics, well and the military for that matter. The titles all pass to the kids." She looked at him closely as he chewed on her words. "Seriously, you don't have to study this stuff to understand it. No wonder you get in trouble so much."

She shook her head before continuing. "Haven't you ever noticed that the names of the ship captains are all so similar? Windsor? Wei? Vargas?" She ticked them off on her fingers.

"Those are all different," Ryan said, goading her.

"No, not similar with each other, with other captains. Sofia Vargas is the captain of the Battleship *Buenos Aires*, right? Well, Manuel Vargas, her son, is captain of the cruiser *Salvador*." She nearly bumped into a customer leaving one of the retail shops who had several large bags.

"Well, that can't be the only way you get to be a captain, how'd Vargas get the spot? The ISA hasn't been around forever," Ryan said, winding his way through the crowd. "I'm thinking once I'm Admiral of the fleet, I'm gonna make some changes."

Anna rolled her eyes. "OK, Admiral. So why were you asking about Slaunder, anyway?"

"No reason," he said urging her on.

"Anyway, his path is set—with his connections and money, he's making Captain in five years. Especially since Mazim is such a big contractor for the ISA. They've got some real pull."

Now Ryan was really worried; in the back of his mind he berated himself for making such a powerful enemy.

As they skirted around an unusually loud and tight knot of people, he noticed the rest of the promenade. "Is it way more crowded down here or is it just me?"

"Yeah, there must be a new ship docked or something," Anna said, following Ryan across the street, still taking occasional glances at the gaggle.

After several more minutes, he turned down a now familiar alleyway.

"No, absolutely not, Ryan. I'm serious," Anna said, stopping so quickly, David ran into her with a half-hearted apology, head still buried in his PDD.

He absentmindedly navigated around her to follow Ryan. She crossed her arms as she watched the two head down the alleyway toward the Nebula. "I thought we were going to that new place first. Fine, wait for me! Does Bob even serve real food?"

CHAPTER 5

The weeks leading up to the induction of the *Cosmic Explorer* into the ISA Fleet had been busy. Anna and David had each been assigned to help lead a mixed crew of ISA enlisted, readying several areas of the station that would host the throngs of people who had already started arriving.

David was helping to prepare the large residential sections, which included temporary quarters for dignitaries and hotshot civilians, CEOs, and stars from screen and field. Anna was assigned to help set up a massive party room known as the Dome. She and her crew were arranging hundreds of tables, moving in countless chairs, and setting up the longest bar anyone had ever seen.

Ryan, however, through chance or more likely Commander Compton's creative punishment, was stuck as a glorified security guard at the main entrance of the *Cosmic Explorer*. Ironically, he didn't even need to check identification as the door, like all others on the Forge, was fully automated.

Ryan stretched his back for the millionth time. At first, standing outside the ship with very little to do was great. He wore his reasonably comfortable blue working uniform and would scroll news posts and watch video's all day long. There was a never-ending stream of workers that would come and go through the main gangway only occasionally stopping to ask him for directions to the nearest bathroom or, more often than not, ask why he was standing there.

Even though he hated the job, he was endlessly curious about the ship.

When he first saw it the day they arrived, he recognized it was different from the others, but as he gleaned little tidbits from talks he had with bored workers or overheard conversations between corporate muckety-mucks, he realized it wasn't just different; it was one-of-a-kind. She was the first and probably the only one of her class. Built not for war but exploration. Best he could tell, the Frontier corporation, who ran most of the haulers and mining ships in the belt, had wrangled a huge contract with the ISA to explore the outer reaches of the solar system.

The elevator chimed and a small group of engineers from Frontier wandered past. Trailing that group was a lone straggler, dressed similarly in blue and green coveralls but wearing grungy and well-worn grey athletic shoes and not the customary black boots. He stopped in front of Ryan's podium blowing his nose and drawing Ryan's eyes up from his PDD which was streaming a "History of" show that had become one of his favorites.

"Bathrooms are down the passageway to the left," Ryan said, pointing back the way the man had come.

"I know you," the man said, stuffing his handkerchief into his front pocket.

"Not ringing any bells, pal," Ryan said, all sense of military decorum stripped away by the seven hours he had been standing there.

"Ah, the shuttle, on the way here. You and your puking friend were behind me."

"Oh yeah," Ryan said, rolling his shoulders and killing the stream on his PDD. "You worked on this boat, right?" He nodded toward the ship.

"Indeed I do," he said with pride. "I designed the power systems."

Holding out his hand, he waited for Ryan to grab it before clasping it in his other. Shaking vigorously, he smiled. "Miles, Miles Carter."

"Lieutenant Junior Grade Anders," Ryan responded, noticing the very moist hands of Mr. Carter.

"If you don't mind me asking, Ryan… what are you doing here? Are the door access mechanisms broken? I can get mechanics to send someone."

"It's a long story, Miles." He covertly wiped his hand on the side of his trouser changing the subject. "So maybe you can answer a question I had?

I heard a couple techs talking about the power conduits. They said that the *Explorer* uses more superconductive cabling than a Columbia class. Is that right?"

Miles smiled broadly. "Indeed! Not many people know that." He lowered his voice. "Not even the other engineers know why, but I do." He looked around before turning back to Ryan, giving him a once-over. "You look like a trustworthy sort."

Ryan thought the man was a bit kooky but played along. Maybe the last hour wouldn't be so boring. "Completely." He answered the unasked question.

Miles leaned in a little too close for Ryan's comfort. "They're searching for something out there on the rim and using some top-secret stuff to do it."

"You don't say," Ryan said, letting the man do his thing.

"Yes. In fact, the superconductive cabling I designed wasn't just run to the engines. It runs to some really interesting equipment on the hull. The power requirements are fantastic!" He almost yelled the last part, making himself flinch and lower his voice.

"What, like a weapon?"

"No, there are separate lines for the weapon systems, all completely isolated from these." Miles frowned. "They run to these huge actuated arms with some kind of pods on them. I had to approve the swiveling components and connections." He paused again, lost in thought.

"So, what do you think they are? The pods, I mean."

Miles seemed to remember they were still speaking and focused back on Ryan. "I think they're scanners. Huge, absolutely gigantic scanners that can penetrate miles into asteroids. You need that kind of thing if you're hunting for secret bases."

Ryan almost rolled his eyes. Miles had gone from interesting dude to conspiratorial nutjob pretty darned quick.

"I can see you're skeptical, but R5 didn't just disappear overnight like they say in their stories. Think about it." He tapped the side of his head with his finger. "How does a shadowy terrorist organization with the resources and intel to drop asteroids onto cities just suddenly disappear."

"They didn't disappear, they were hunted down and killed by the military, well a lot of them... and the leaders."

"That's what they want you to think. They're still out there. They have bases hidden deep in the asteroid belt, just waiting for their time to strike." He looked feverishly at Ryan. "Why do you think so many ships go missing out there?"

"It's deep space, man. All sorts of stuff can happen out there. Bad equipment, shitty maintenance. One wrong move and poof... you're dust."

Miles laughed, palming his face. "Don't be naïve, Lieutenant, and don't listen to what they tell you. Watch what they do!" He started to pace.

"OK, let me ask you this. What happed right after they supposedly 'wiped out' R5?" He used air quotes. "Nothing. No big inquiries, no raids. Just a slew of low-level arrests and investigations that all came to the same conclusion: The Rogue Five were gone. Gone? Ha!"

He waved his hands around franticly before coming to a stop in front of Ryan. "Then what did they do? I'll tell you; the world signed the Orbital Security Convention. Just like that, they signed away their sovereignty? Not likely."

"What does that have to do with a bunch of terrorists?" Ryan said, yawning and checking the time.

"Everything! Awfully convenient that R5 appears out of nowhere, terrorizes the planet then disappears. Don't you see? They let it happen—our own governments were complicit in the attacks. We were so scared we gave up our freedom for safety. We even signed away our militaries to the ISA!"

"Then why are they searching for them now?"

"Because! They want to shut them up once and for all. Do you know what would happen if anyone found out? How many millions died in New York alone?"

Ryan shrugged. "Seems like a stretch if you ask me."

The inner hatch to the ship cycled open cutting their conversation short. A rather pinched looking corporate suit strode up to them. "Miles. You were supposed to sign off on the change orders an hour ago. The inspectors are waiting." He spoke in short clipped tones before pivoting on his heel and walking back onto the ship.

"Things are not what they seem," Miles whispered to Ryan before following the man onboard.

When the hatch cycled closed, Ryan whistled and went back to scrolling the news on his PDD. "Glad it's my last day."

He swiped a few stories away before he saw a new article that caught his interest.

Little Hope for Missing Mining Ship.

Ryan didn't believe the engineer's wild theories, but the missing ships did pique his interest. He skimmed the article to see where it had gone missing.

"Huh. Asteroid Belt." He read to himself, shaking his head.

Thankfully, before the boredom could kill him, his final shift ended. Stretching his sore back, Ryan took the elevator down to the main promenade level. As usual, his shift ended first, so he sat cooling his heels at their second most frequented establishment: *Le chat noir.*

According to Anna, their new favorite restaurant was the best and only French bistro in orbit. He had never sampled French food, but they did serve a pretty good approximation of steak and fries, so he went with it. The place was a bit off the beaten path, being almost as far from the primary walkway as Nebula was, but in a much more reputable area tucked behind a clothing store. The faux brick walls and black wrought iron fence made it almost feel like they were back on Earth. A fortuitous bit of luck had one of the main air supply ducts for the level mounted very near the courtyard, meaning they got a regular breeze blowing through, adding to the effect of being outdoors, never mind the peculiar odor of the sanitized and filtered air.

"Hey, guys." Ryan raised his hand, waving to Anna and David, who looked like they just got done breaking rocks. Their uniforms were disheveled, and Anna's hair was partially pulled free from her normally neat bun. They swung open the low iron gate to the patio where he was sitting.

As they plopped down, the waiter walked up with a serving tray laden with three large pints of beer, a large plate of sliced bread, and a small ramekin of olive oil, which Ryan had ordered a short while ago. When he placed it on the table, his friends jumped on it like sharks in a frenzy.

Between delighted moans, his two friends grunted thanks in his direction.

"So, looks like you two are still pretty busy?" he said, knowing full well that they probably had the busiest jobs on the station.

"Mmmmf," was the only thing David could manage as he shoved an entire slice into his mouth.

The little bistro was so far out of the way that it rarely had more than a few other guests, but for the past few days, they had found it harder and harder to get a table.

"That isn't the half of it, Ryan." Anna wiped her mouth, sitting back, finally putting the napkin in her lap. "Three other battleships are on the way. That's like ten thousand more people!"

"Almost twelve," David said, finishing off his beer.

"Huh, isn't that a little low for three battleships?" Ryan said, motioning for the waiter.

"No, only three of the four duty sections will be on shore leave for the party," David added in his familiar know-it-all way.

"Ah," Ryan said as the waiter walked up. "Can we get another round and three of the usual? Thanks, Pete."

"So, how's guard duty?" Anna asked with a devious smile. She knew he hated it, but after his little special request debacle, things could've been much worse. A reminder now and then kept him humble.

"At least I'll never have to do that again—what a joke," Ryan deflected as he sat back. "Hey, at least I got to catch up on some of my favorite shows. Oh, and I know everything there is to know about interplanetary news. Did you know both the Martian and Earth ambassadors will be here for the party? This is the first time they have been in the same place since Mars signed on to the OSC Treaty."

"I'm impressed—look at you, Mr. Politics," Anna said playfully, patting him on the shoulder.

"Har har. You guys have no idea how bored I was."

Both Anna and David gave him a deadpan look.

"Okay, I may have complained once or twice," he said, raising both hands in mock surrender. "Anyway, the rest of our class should be arriving soon."

"Yeah… I'm so glad. Maybe I can get Petrov to steal my boots again," Anna said in disgust.

The waiter returned with three identical plates, setting one down in front of each of them. The smell of freshly cooked meat wafted up into Ryan's face, the peppercorn sauce slathered on top immediately making his mouth water. On the plate was a metal cup stuffed with thin cut truffle fries, or frites as they were called here, which he immediately grabbed a handful of and stuffed into his mouth.

"Some of our assignments posted," David said, then went back to eating his steak like it was nothing.

Anna bolted upright. "Are you kidding? What? Where!"

Ryan started at the news, but David's reaction said everything he needed to know.

Anna rapidly tapped her PDD, read something, and became silent.

"ISA *Sweetwater VSC*… What the hell is that?" she said finally.

"New patrol ship. The second part is your designation," David answered, still keeping his head down. "We're on the same ship."

"We are? Well, that's good news, right?" Anna looked to each of them, not understanding.

Ryan looked down at his own display, seeing no pending messages.

"I'm still unassigned."

"Yeah," David said.

Anna took a long draw of her beer, then plopped the mug back onto the table. "That's just great. It just figures, you know, whatever we do, however hard we work. We will always be at the bottom. This is such bullshit." She sniffed, taking another drink. "God, I'm exhausted."

David and Ryan looked at each other for a few seconds before David shrugged. Always kind of a pessimist, he had never held out much hope that they would get posted together. Ryan felt the same way if he were being honest, but they were a kind of family now, and it hurt.

Ryan cleared his throat. "Come on, finish up, at least we still have some time. It's not like we can't ever talk again. We keep in touch and request transfers until we're back together, right?"

Anna grabbed some fries and swirled them in the dark sauce on her plate. "Sure," she said half-heartedly, not seeming the least bit comforted.

*

After dinner, they made their way towards the familiar alleyway that held the Nebula. Since landing on the Forge, the bar had become their second home, far away from their duties and roommates. For all her complaints, Anna did actually like the place, and right now, they needed a distraction.

Walking in the dusky light of the artificial sky above, something was nagging at the edges of Ryan's consciousness. He couldn't quite put his finger on it, but something was off.

He slowed his pace as they entered the alley, nearly causing his two friends to bump into him.

"What's up?" Anna said, stopping next to him.

"Look." He pointed with his chin.

Anna saw a smallish well-dressed man standing outside the Nebula who seemed none too pleased. He was gesturing to another larger man wearing a gaudy crimson colored blazer before shoving him toward the door to the bar.

"Slaunder," Ryan said, pulling his two friends to a small alcove situated between the brothel at the top of the alley and the empty storefront next door with grimy windows.

"What's he doing here?" David said, peeking around the corner. "Doesn't seem like his kind of place."

"You see the guy he was with?" Ryan leaned against the wall. "I've seen my share of hired thugs. Bet he's looking for me."

"...or us," Anna added.

The large man exited the bar and said something to Slaunder, who stalked away, thug in tow.

"Come on," Ryan said, not waiting for a reply from either of them. As he approached, he put on a practiced smile and walked in like he didn't have a care in the world.

The midday crowd, even with the influx of new visitors, was normally pretty sparse, but the place was empty…even the drunks were gone. Several tables were knocked over near the bar, and the door to the back room behind it was wide open.

Anna and David somewhat hesitantly entered behind him, looking around, concern on their faces.

"Bob?" Ryan called out.

Some muffled sounds could be heard over the low hum of the air circulators.

A large tattoo-laden man appeared from the back room. "We are closed," he said in a thick Slavic accent.

"Aw, shit, we aren't here to drink or anything, I came to pay my tab from last night. Bob around?" he lied.

The man looked at Ryan, then Anna and David. "Are you Anders?"

"Athos," Ryan said without missing a beat. "Tim Athos. These are my friends Porthos—"

"Then fuck off," the man interrupted, the veins on his thick neck pulsing with each word. The door to the simulator room opened and two other men, each of them nearly as big and tattooed as the first, entered the room taking positions behind them.

Adrenaline dumped into Ryan's system. His breathing quickened and vision narrowed as his body automatically prepared for a fight. He turned and looked at the newcomers, knowing that he might get one or two good hits in, but from the look of them, he would have to be the luckiest man on two planets to walk out with all his bones intact. He glanced back at David, who looked absolutely petrified, taking a hesitant step away from the nearest man. Anna seemed concerned, but from her stance and the look in her eye, Ryan could tell she was ready to brawl if need be.

Ryan held up both hands in surrender. "H-Hey, fellas, we don't want any trouble." He stammered putting some fear into his voice. "We just came in to pay our tab."

"Go away, little girl," the man behind the counter yelled. The other two laughed. "Maybe you come back later with more friends, eh?"

"Uh, yes, sir..." Ryan said, turning and ushering his friends out the door in front of him.

When they gained some distance from the bar, Anna turned. "We have to call station security," she said, raising her arm to activate her PDD before Ryan put his hand over her wrist.

"Don't bother." He shook his head.

"Who were they? I... I think we need to leave. We can't be involved in illegal activity, we could be court-martialed," David said, his rapid cadence making him hard to understand.

Ryan wiped his sweaty palms on his pants, trying to calm himself. "Station security won't help. Something was bothering me when we first walked down here, and I think I know what it was." He hurried to the entrance to the alley and looked down either direction of the main promenade, confirming his suspicions. "Look at all the cameras."

David and Anna both looked up—every 25 meters along the street, the ubiquitous security cameras were powered off, their ever-present green status lights dark.

"Can we call ISA security?" David asked, head whipping around when a passerby tossed a can into a recycler across the street.

"No chance. This isn't military jurisdiction; they'll just refer it to the station," Ryan said, rubbing his chin.

"We have to help Robert," Anna said, her concern was growing by the second. "If he gets hurt, or worse, because of us..." She let the thought hang in the air.

Ryan wasn't about to let that happen, but without an armed response team, the thugs in the bar weren't going anywhere. Nearby, the blinking neon and holograms of the brothel caught his attention. Through the doors he could just make out a section of a bar and several of the patrons within.

"You two relax," Ryan said, the beginning of a plan forming. "If we want to help Bob and stay in one piece, we're going to need information. David, do you have access to the security cameras in there?"

"Why would he?" Anna said before reversing her thought when David started to swipe his PDD. "Of course, why wouldn't you."

"Here," he said as a new message pinged Ryan's PDD. Ryan brought up the message, which had several windows embedded. On each was a miniature view of a camera feed. He brought up one after another before he settled on a group of men standing over the beaten bartender.

Anna gasped.

"He's still breathing. That stupid sombitch probably told them to screw themselves when they asked about me," Ryan said, his plan coming into focus. "Come on."

"Where are we going? I thought you said no security," Anna rushed to catch up to Ryan.

"We might need guns; did you see the size of those guys?" David said, following close behind.

Instead of heading out of the alley, he unexpectedly turned to the right and walked into the brothel instead.

David walked ahead and entered right behind Ryan. "Good idea, we can hide in here."

Anna ran inside, girding herself, expecting to witness unknown forms of debauchery but instead was met by a small bar with some overstuffed couches and low coffee tables spread around. It was… comfortable and, while dimly lit, seemed oddly nice to her.

"What? I thought this was…" she said, trailing off.

Ryan was already leaning over the bar, talking in hushed tones with the bartender, who Anna thought was much too attractive to be working here. After a few moments he set a bottle of liquor down on the bar and nodded over his shoulder to a door on the opposite side of the room.

"Be right back," Ryan said, grabbing the bottle and heading to the door, disappearing within.

"What is he up to?" Anna said, looking to David, who was still watching the feed on his PDD before becoming distracted by a scantily clad man wearing an elaborate headdress walking past them.

"He'd better hurry, I think they're getting ready to do something." David sounded worried, noticing something on the feed.

A muffled shout and bang followed by the crash of glass broke the silence. From behind the door, a chorus of voices were chanting something before it swung open, banging into the wall.

Ryan stumbled out first, rubbing his shoulder, followed by a gaggle of rough-looking men in crimson and brown fatigues.

The leader, a barrel-chested man with salt-and-pepper hair, grabbed Ryan by the arm. "Where?" he demanded, his voice slurred but serious.

"At that dive down the street. Listen, we don't want trouble."

"Well, you got it, mate. Com'on, boys," the man said in an accent Anna couldn't quite place.

Six of the men stomped out of the brothel looking determined and a little pissed.

Anna and David stepped up to Ryan, who was asking the bartender for ice.

"Ryan, what was that all about?" Anna said, touching Ryan's shoulder lightly, eliciting a wince.

"I was doing what that asshole told me to do. I got some more friends..." He placed the towel filled with ice on his shoulder and passed the bartender several pieces of printed paper, which Anna recognized as chits, or the unofficial currency of the Forge's less legal establishments.

"I told them that I overheard a couple of really big guys saying Martians shouldn't be allowed on the station and that we should turn up the gravity a bit so we can watch 'em wriggle on the ground." He smiled wickedly. "That last part almost cost me my arm."

Anna cocked her head and looked at Ryan.

"What?" Ryan said, still nursing his shoulder.

"Nothing," she said, turning and heading out the door. "Come on, we can't miss this."

Ryan looked at David, who wasn't really paying much attention as the same man who had passed by earlier was now leaning on nearby couch speaking to an equally underclothed woman. Ryan followed Anna out into the alley, towing the sputtering David by his arm.

When they reached the Nebula, the door was wide open, and Ryan could clearly hear the first gangster they had spoken with earlier.

Ryan poked his head through the door and saw the older Martian man flanked by his compatriots in a standoff with no fewer than eight of the gangsters surrounding them. He thanked his lucky stars he didn't try to take them on himself. David and Anna were standing on the other side of the door peeking in.

"You Ryan Anders?" the man behind the bar called out.

"Dunno who that be," the bearded Martian said, cracking his neck. "But I hear you been talkin' 'bout my kin and me."

"Fuck off, Martian asshole," the thug snapped.

"That was a mistake." Ryan chuckled, wagging his eyebrows several times at Anna.

The older Martian's arm flashed out, accompanied by the whine of servomotors and grabbed a fistful of the thug's clothing hoisting him from behind the bar with ease. Grunting, he tossed the gangster like a sack of cement across the room where he crashed awkwardly into a booth, bending the tabletop and popping the padded back off the metal frame.

A roar went up from the rest of the Martian soldiers and thugs as they clashed. Ryan smiled as he noticed that the Martians weren't angry; they just looked excited. Like a pumped-up team right before they took the field, they gleefully waded into the group of thugs, fists flying. A few were chanting something—either it wasn't in English or their odd accents were so thick he couldn't make it out.

A chair flew through the air, connecting with the doorframe next to Ryan with such force that it caused all three of them to take cover. David raised his arm, tapping his PDD.

"Robert's alone, but he isn't moving." He spoke with urgency.

Ryan peeked around the corner, then motioned for them to follow. "Stay low."

The three ducked another chair and hugged the wall nearest the door. They had to skirt around the fight and make it to the end of the bar itself where you could raise a hinged section and get behind it.

As they approached, a figure in Martian fatigues jumped up onto the bar in one swift motion. The crown of the man's bald head was tattooed with unfamiliar geometric patterns and he held a bottle of liquor in each hand. He wore an unhinged look that Ryan had only seen once before when he was growing up, and that man was having a full-blown psychotic episode. The bald man let out a scream at the top of his lungs and launched himself into a crowd of fists and legs, bowling over the entire group. He bounced to his feet and smashed both bottles together against the sides of the largest thug's head who happened to be holding another Martian in a chokehold. The gangster crumpled under the assault as the bald man howled with glee.

"Jesus," Anna said, towing David along. "Something is seriously wrong with these guys."

The three ducked under the hinged bar top just as a section of metal table thudded into the wall crashing down onto a row of bottles and glasses, showering them with sharp fragments.

Ryan pushed them both forward into the back room behind the bar and closed the door. The fight was still going strong behind them but muffled quite a bit when the door latched.

Anna rushed past a row of coolers and storage cabinets to the prone figure near the back. Robert the bartender lay on the dirty floor near a drain caked with grunge. The footprints in the dirt and grease surrounding the man told a story of pain.

She knelt beside him. "Find a med kit or something."

Both Ryan and David started opening cabinets and rummaging through drawers around the dimly lit space.

When she pressed her fingers on the side of his neck, Robert thankfully stirred. He struggled to raise his bruised head from the tile floor, his own blood streaking his face.

"Did I get 'em?" he said, speaking through swollen lips.

"Stay down, we'll get a medic."

He grunted pushing himself upright, plainly regretting it, holding his ribs. "With all due respect, miss, I just need a hand up."

Ryan walked over and held out his hand and with Anna's help carefully hoisted him up onto unsteady legs.

"You look like shit, Bob," Ryan said, gaining a harsh look from Anna.

"Here, this is all I could find," David said, holding out a dirty towel, which the man grabbed with bruised fingers and stowed on his left shoulder.

He coughed wetly and walked over to the nearby sink turning on the water and holding himself upright. "Give me a minute, will you?"

Ryan grabbed his friends and walked to the door. The room beyond had become quiet.

He pulled the handle and found himself looking at four Martians sitting at the bar slapping themselves on the back and hooting like they just won the big game.

The three stepped out to survey the damage. Overturned tables and chairs were scattered everywhere. Glass and blood smeared parts of the floor, and one of the hanging lights had lost its shade—its bare bulb casting harsh, angular shadows across the room.

The Martians were dragging the last of the thugs out the door and unceremoniously dumping them onto the street. Near the entrance, the man in the crimson brocade blazer they'd seen earlier speaking to Slaunder stood watching, a deep scowl etched on his face.

Ryan and the others emerged from behind the bar just as the two Martians, who'd ejected the gangsters, slammed the front door shut and walked past them, laughing as they rejoined their friends.

"Crazy bastards," Ryan said, reaching down and lifting one of the metal tables from the floor trying to straighten up.

"Ryan," Anna said, giving him an awkward hug. "You probably saved Robert's life."

Ryan shrugged. "Eight to one is just unfair. I wasn't gonna let them get away with that. Anyway, where else we gonna hang out?"

Robert appeared behind the bar, battered and bloody, eye swollen shut with two of his fingers on his left hand at an odd angle. Ryan thought he would call it a night and go to the medical center, but he reached down slowly and grabbed a mug from a lower shelf and started serving pints to the Martians, who were pounding their fists against each other's chests, their laughter echoing off the walls.

"I have you three to thank for my new friends?" He raised his voice, more gruff than usual.

"These guys said they needed a new hangout, so I told 'em this place was nice and quiet," Ryan said nonchalantly.

Bob the bartender beckoned them over, reached below the bar and grabbed three large mugs. Filling them one by one, he placed them in front of Ryan and his friends. Before Ryan could grab his drink, Robert stuck out his good hand.

"Master Sergeant Robert Harlow. Retired."

Ryan firmly grasped the hand, a smile forming on his face.

"Lieutenant J.G. Ryan Anders. Nice to meet you, Master Sergeant." They locked eyes for a split second before Bob the bartender quickly withdrew his hand and absentmindedly grabbed for the dirty towel that was perched on his shoulder.

"Those are on the house. Next ones you pay for," he said.

"Sounds fair, guess we'll be in the sim," Ryan said, hefting his beer and turning to his friends. "Shall we?"

CHAPTER 6

T he trio finally stumbled out of Nebula at nearly two in the morning. Bob the bartender wasn't true to his word and seemed to forget to ask for payment when he delivered round after round. Ryan wondered to himself what Slaunder would do when he found out. There was probably hell to be paid, but with the Martians seemingly liking the place, maybe it would be okay.

Ryan lost count of the number of simulations they had run or the number of beers they drank. He, David, and Anna were finally starting to gel as a team, now that they had started to trust in each other's strengths.

David unsurprisingly was an amazing navigator; he was always great at the Academy, but working with him in the simulator had cemented his skills in Ryan's mind. Anna had taken to the tactical role like she was born with weapons specs clutched in her hands. She was fast, accurate, and deadly, which, from the outside, was in complete contrast with her kindhearted nature, but to those who knew her well, it fit.

For his part, Ryan was doing okay. He had assumed that the more he practiced, the faster and better he would become, but it really wasn't working out that way. Sure, he was more adept at the command interface than he was at the Academy, but when the computer would get creative with the scenarios, he was often at odds with himself. He would second guess his decisions, costing them precious seconds. More often than not, he would have to rely on Anna's weapons work or David's creative maneuvers to get them out of tight spots, leaving him mentally kicking himself. He wondered if he actually had what it would take to be anything more than a second-rate button pusher.

"Hey!" Anna put her arms around both of them they stumbled down the alley. "What's next, boys?" she smiled, hanging on their shoulders. "Want to hit a club or maybe duke it out with a few more gangsters?" She laughed.

"Ugh, I need to get back and press my uniform," David said, blowing a raspberry a little too vigorously with flecks of spittle flying off his lower lip.

Ryan nodded, for the first time siding with David. "Yeah, we should get back and prepare… don't wanna get too sauced right now, it might interfere with the big party tomorrow. I heard that Rubio will be there." He rolled his R and flashed his hand into the air like a matador. That started another round of laughter. Anna was obsessed with the famous singer.

She became a little more somber. "You guys think we'll ever have a shot at getting on a bridge crew? For real, I mean." Ryan didn't want to say what he really thought. With no patron or political connections, it was a one in a million chance. Looking at David's crestfallen reaction, Ryan knew he was feeling it too.

He put on his best smile, turning towards them both. "Hey, the ISA would be fools if they didn't see our potential. Who's top ten high scores are on that sim?" he said, pointing towards Nebula. "Ours, right?"

"We're the only ones that use the sim," David said which wasn't especially helpful.

"Who cares, I looked it up and we are definitely the best on this station in any sim," Ryan said, lying through his teeth. "Anyway, who is the best damned navigator in the fleet? You are! Hell, besides that, you're the only one I know who has ever hacked one of the most secure networks in the system." He looked at Anna, smiling. "And this lady… this legend right here took down three pirate ships with one shot… one shot! There isn't another person alive or dead who has ever done that."

Ryan looked the two of them in the eyes. "You guys are the best… now who wants to hit Hyperion and do some dancing?" He put his arms around their shoulders and ushered them forward towards the row of nearby nightclubs.

*

Several clubs and hours later, Ryan stumbled back to his room. Opening the door, he was met by an all too familiar and distinct unwashed clothing smell. Luckily, being a lieutenant junior grade came with the perk of a single room, albeit tiny.

He staggered over to the bed and collapsed onto the rumpled mess of sheets, drifting into a fitful and dreamless sleep.

When the incessant warbling of his PDD's alarm dragged him from his slumber an unknown time later, he woke with a pasty sour taste in his mouth and an accompanying thumping headache.

He shook the cobwebs out of his head and painfully walked to the small sink in the back corner of his room. Waving his hand over the sensor by habit, the bright white lights over the sink came to life, causing a stabbing pain in his temple. He washed his face and took a few big gulps of water from the tap before drying his face.

"News," he called out as he brushed his crusty teeth. A display popped to life, projected onto the wall at the foot of his bed. A distinguished older man was speaking with the picture of what looked to be an ore freighter behind him.

…carrying a crew of fifteen, including engineers and miners, and was scheduled to arrive at the Forge two days ago. However, communication with the vessel was lost shortly after it entered the asteroid belt.

Yusen Freightliner, the company which owns the Bison, *has also released a statement expressing concern for the well-being of the crewmembers and stating that they are working closely with the ISA to help with the investigation.*

The disappearance of the Bison *is the latest in a series of incidents involving deep space freighters in the past few months. The ISA has been investigating and has dispatched patrol craft to the area. While not commenting specifically about the disappearance of the* Bison, *a spokesman for the ISA has reported an increase in pirate activity in the region …*

"Off," Ryan called out, shutting down the display and rubbing his temples. He grabbed his dress uniform, which he had hung out when they first heard the news of the upcoming party, and laid it on his bed. "Poor bastards," he mumbled as he put on his pants and shirt, struggling to get his belt adjusted properly. After wetting his fingers, he ran them through his hair and flashed his best smile at the reflection in the mirror. "Okay, now where's my hat?"

A chirp in his ear announced an incoming call. He tapped the receive button on his PDD, seeing his friend's contact card. "Yo, Davey!"

"Hey, Ryan." David sounded like death warmed over. "I'm... not feeling so great." Ryan didn't doubt that he was feeling the effects of the long evening, as his friend was nothing if not a lightweight.

"You'll be fine, David, just pop a couple stims and power through. When we get to the party, you'll forget all about it. I heard those ladies from docking are going to be there."

"I don't like them," he answered back quickly.

"What? You're down there all the time. Come on, you can't fool me."

There was silence before he finally responded, "Did you hear from Anna? Hope she's okay."

Ryan didn't remind him that Anna could hold her liquor far better than he could. She was probably already dressed and waiting for them. "I'll check on her. You sober up and meet me near the Dome."

"Maybe, but—" David sounded skeptical.

"Sounds great, see you there, buddy," Ryan said, quickly cutting the link before David could change his mind.

Anticipation cut through his headache as he imagined tonight's party in the Dome. One of the most spectacular spots within the Forge, the Dome boasted a colossal semicircular window that overlooked the bustling construction docks. It had been fully outfitted as a party space, mostly thanks to Anna and her crew.

"Call Rodriguez," he spoke to his PDD. It rang several seconds.

"Ryan," she answered, a far-off wispy quality to her voice. "I was meaning to call you. I don't think I can make it. Not really feeling like partying, you know?" Ryan rolled his eyes—what was up with these two? It was only the biggest party in the solar system.

"Hey, none of that, Anna. Remember, I'll be getting my posting soon—who knows, I could get assigned to the *Sweetwater* too."

"It's not that... I talked to my dad this morning. My mom's sick and he's really pushing for me to come home."

"Damn. Is it serious?"

"They don't know yet, it could be. I asked personnel if I could take leave, but they said once I was assigned to a ship, I wouldn't be eligible till I came back from my first deployment."

Times were always rough with her family, but she wouldn't really open up about it to him. Not that he could blame her—he had a penchant for saying the wrong thing at the wrong time.

"Sorry, Anna. Hey, you don't have to make any decisions today. When does the *Sweetwater* leave dock?"

"About a week and a half." She sounded pained.

"Come down, I'm sure between the three of us, we can figure something out." He switched gears. "You see all the ships out there? The people? Come on, take a day to think. It's been your dream forever to get off the planet, and skipping the launch won't do any good."

"Okay, one day. If I can't figure this out... I'm going to have to resign my commission and go back home."

"Great. Remember what Armstrong said: Never make a big decision without stepping back first, perspective is the difference between a mistake and a masterstroke."

"God, Ryan, where did you hear that, and since when do you know quotes?" she said incredulously, the old bubbly Anna starting to peek through the clouds.

"Like I said, I've been watching a lot of vids. You'd be surprised what you can learn by watching bios. They did a whole series—"

"Okay, stop, I'll meet you down there, but if it's just a bunch of political speeches, I'm leaving." She blew out a long breath. "Thanks, Ryan."

After she hung up, he glanced down at the time and started putting on his shoes. It was still a while till the party got started, but he wanted to get the lay of the land and figure out where the VIP tables were. While he wasn't a political junkie, rubbing elbows with the right people might help grease the wheels.

Smoothing his hair, he gave his dress uniform a final inspection. Satisfied, he straightened his jacket and set his combination cap in place.

Staring into the mirror, he noticed slight lines around his eyes and perhaps one on his forehead. He felt like he was aging quickly—too quickly. Something else he noticed when he arrived at the Academy: the cadets from the corpo or political classes looked younger than the average person he knew. Medical rejuvenation procedures, anti-aging medications, and supplements were the norm in their circles while the average life expectancy of someone from Ryan's social group had fallen from a high of ninety, decades ago, to a low of about sixty-eight. Hard living, dangerous working conditions, and poor nutrition had taken their toll.

He never really paid attention to such things when he was young, given that he was too busy surviving the camps or finding his next meal, but when the contrast was that stark, he couldn't help but notice.

Had he not been chosen for the Citizen Officer Corps, his destiny would have been working in one of the many labor factories or maybe construction jobs that the government mandated to its able-bodied lower-class citizens. The thought of slave labor wages and dangerous working conditions wasn't his idea of a good time, but that was all anyone knew. Well, that or going into a life of crime. That was as good as it got for someone like him, or at least that's what he thought.

Snapping back to reality, he brushed his hands over his coat, readjusted his cap, and walked out.

*

Ensign Marcus Batista stifled his second big yawn of the night as he sat as his station on board the ISA destroyer *Rio de Janeiro*.

The ship patrolled the busy commercial lanes between the Earth, Moon, and the Forge. Lately this job became exponentially more difficult as the upcoming launch of the *Cosmic Explorer* clogged the lanes with every type of ship imaginable. To help, the *Rio*'s much larger cousin, the battleship *Buenos Aires*, had taken up station nearby, away from her normal route patrolling a much higher orbit above the Earth.

Weighing in at nearly 12,000 tons and hosting a crew of three hundred, the *Rio* was not a small ship by any means, but compared to the hulking battleship, she was slim and fast.

Ensign Batista was assigned as the third rotation, second communications watch, on board the bridge of the blocky warship along with several of his classmates from the Academy class of 2183. He initially considered a posting on the *Buenos Aires*, but frankly, he wasn't interested in all the politics or ladder climbing he would be subjected to on the South American Union's flagship. He'd been keeping up with some of his other classmates assigned to the battleships, and they had only now gotten around to the selection process for spots on the bridge. The way they described the cutthroat competition made him glad he put in a request to be assigned the smaller ship, even though his family seemed disappointed with his choice.

That made him think of his chance encounter with Ryan and his friends. He still couldn't shake the feeling something was off. What that was, he couldn't imagine, but if nothing else, the feeling had become stronger during the *Rio*'s last patrol.

A chime broke his train of thought. The new incoming message notification popped up on his management screen. He mentally ran through the process he'd been taught during his training with the first shift coms officer.

Opening the message header, he looked at the sender: *ISA Fleet Command Lunar Space*.

That was a new one to him; normally at this time of the ship's day, it was just routine ship-to-ship messages. Next, he traced his finger across the screen and looked for the recipient: Captain Rafael Santos. That got his attention— this was the first command traffic message he'd handled. He refocused, trying to remember how to route the message to the captain's inbox. He snapped his fingers, remembering the instructions and looked for the priority designator...

"Zero?" he said aloud, puzzled.

"Lieutenant Silva?" He glanced over his shoulder at the equally bored lieutenant in charge of the third watch, sitting in the captain's seat.

The man straightened and cleared his throat. "What do you need, Ensign?"

Marcus pointed at his screen. "We have a message for the captain, but the priority is zero. Do I route it to his inbox?"

Before he knew it, the lieutenant was next to his station looking over his shoulder, reading the header. He reached over Marcus and punched the coms control. Several moments later, a weary voice came over the com.

"What can I do for you, Ensign?"

"Captain, Lieutenant Silva here, we have priority traffic from Lunar Command for you—I'm sending it to your PDD now."

He reached down and swiped the message to the upper right of the screen, then hit the confirm button. After about thirty seconds, the captain answered back, obviously walking quickly.

"Wake the first watch. Who's manning the helm? Hayes?"

"Yes, sir."

"Tell Mr. Hayes to spin up the reactors, I'll be there in two minutes."

Marcus stared at the lieutenant. "Uh. What should I do?"

Lieutenant Silva, looking a bit worried, ignored his question, instead tapping the message and bringing up the body of the communique. Marcus read silently along with him:

To: Captain ISA Rio de Janeiro | All previous orders rescinded. Redirect to Sector 2-Gamma, Hesperus AO. Possible distress beacon detected from ISA patrol ships Guardian and Sentinel. Render any and all assistance. Immediate action required. | ISAFCLS

Marcus looked up at the lieutenant. "The Asteroid Belt?"

"I'm not... I'm sure it's nothing. They probably just need a bigger stick to help deal with some troublesome spacers. They were sent to look for the mining ship *Bison* from the reports this morning," he said, sounding more like he was trying to convince himself.

"Monitor your console till you are relieved, Ensign. *Rio* can handle whatever's out there."

The lieutenant turned and walked back to the command chair. Marcus wasn't convinced it was as simple as the lieutenant made it sound. He brought up the fleet notices that came across during the morning shift, and right there at the top were several new reports of missing ships in the vicinity of the asteroid Hesperus. He tried to remember how many had gone missing at this point. Four or five maybe? That didn't sound like nothing.

The day crew, composed of the most senior and experienced officers, made their way onto the bridge. Lieutenant Commander Perez, the ship's primary communications officer, walked up to his station. He glanced up and met her eyes, which made his heart jump and caused him to grin like an idiot. Despite the short notice, her uniform was crisp and fit her curves as if it were tailored to accentuate them. Her dark hair, wound into a regulation bun, framed her perfect face. The glow of the consoles played across her skin; a warm bronze that made her sharp hazel eyes burn even brighter.

He knew there wasn't a chance in hell that an ensign straight out of the Academy would catch her eye. Especially a guy ten years her junior, from a small lesser-known family, but that didn't keep him from dreaming.

He tried to keep his infatuation private, but somehow all the other watch standers knew. His best friend, who'd transferred to the *Rio* at the same time, called it a week after he started training with her, and he was merciless. The punk actually told him to throw caution to the wind and confess his feelings. Marcus couldn't begin to picture how that conversation would go, telling his direct superior that he'd basically fallen for her the moment she stepped onto the bridge.

"You are relieved, Ensign," she said with a slight smile as he sat there momentarily lost in thought.

"Oh, I'm sorry, ma'am." Marcus stumbled over himself, nearly tripping as he scrambled to vacate the station. He nodded and mumbled something unintelligible before finally clearing the way. "It's nice to see you, ma'am." His face turned bright red as he made his escape, practically sprinting away before she could say a word.

"Captain on deck!" someone shouted, followed almost immediately by the captain's reply.

"As you were." This signified that the crewmembers ignore protocol and keep working.

Captain Santos walked to Silva, who started to relay the information that he collected thus far.

Marcus passed the captain and stopped right outside the door to the bridge, leaning against the cool bulkhead with his eyes closed, trying to figure out exactly what was wrong with his brain.

"Nice to see you?" he whispered, admonishing himself and holding his fist to the side of his temple. After waiting for a few more moments, he walked away from the bridge. His stomach was doing flip-flops and not just from being mortally embarrassed. He had to find out more about what was going on out there.

The feeling that something was off had morphed into the sinking feeling he always got when something bad was going to happen.

CHAPTER 7

Ryan made his way through the huge doors of the Forge's primary meeting hall, making a beeline toward the massive domed window that dominated one side of the room. As early as it was, the space was already filling with partygoers. The aroma of roasted meat, fresh bread, and something sweet he couldn't identify wafted over him, making his mouth water. He made his way to the window and spotted David chatting up a woman in a silky green dress with her back to Ryan, clearly enjoying herself.

"That dog," he said as he admired her curves for a couple seconds before straightening his jacket and giving his breath a quick sniff. He sauntered up behind her, giving his best smoldering voice. "Ma'am, is this person bothering you?"

As he rounded on the woman with his Mr. Charming smile, he finally noticed it was Anna.

"Oh shit, my bad, Anna!" Both she and David started cackling with laughter. Anna laughed so hard she doubled over, which just accentuated her bust.

"Why, I do declare!" She straightened, pretending to wave a fan under her face in a loud southern accent. "You are an absolute brute of a man! Why ever are you bothering me, sir!" This caught the attention of a nearby table.

Ryan's face started to burn. "Ha ha, yuck it up, both of you. It was an honest mistake—you do look great, Rodriguez... you steal that dress?" Anna punched him harder than he expected, making him flinch and rub his arm.

"No, you jerk. I was going to wear this to the new officer's ball after we graduated… figured I'd wear it now, just in case." A pang of regret crossed her face for a moment before she caught herself and pointed a finger out the window at the night's honored guest.

"Check it out," she said.

The *Cosmic Explorer*, which was attached to the framework of the Forge directly across and above the hall, had been lit with huge spotlights arranged for the ceremony. Anna picked her flute of champagne up from the table and tipped it at the ship. "She's all dressed up too."

The ship gleamed. It was primarily a flat silvery grey color due to the steel panels that lined the outside of her hull. A dark blue accent stripe was added strategically along the sides, accentuating its sleek bow. All along the ship, wherever there was an access door or antenna boom, bright red accents had been added, making the areas pop. They even painted its name in white lettering outlined in red about halfway down from the top of the ship near where the bow rounded out into the main body. To top it off, all its navigation lights were lit, adding to the grandeur of the scene.

Ryan was the first to break the silence. "She is a sight to behold." A server walked past just then, and Ryan deftly grabbed four new flutes from the tray. Quickly downing one, he passed two to his friends. Holding up a full glass, he spoke solemnly. "There are good ships and there are wood ships, the ships that sail the sea. But the best ships are friendships, and may they always be."

He slung back the glass and emptied it with a flourish.

"More quotes." Anna snorted at him before downing her glass.

David just shook his head and finished his drink. "What?" Ryan said, looking at the two. "That was a good toast."

"You made that toast two times last night," David said, causing Ryan to cock his head.

"You don't actually remember, do you? HA!" Anna laughed. "The last time was at the Hyperion, you told some blonde from Security that you made it up just for her, remember? You said you liked the 'cut of her jib.'" she imitated Ryan, using exaggerated air quotes.

The memory snapped back into focus for Ryan. "Ahhhhhh! Sheila…" he said, taking a deep breath, looking far away, hamming it up for Anna. She answered with another punch in the arm.

"Owww!"

David decided to throw Ryan a lifeline and pointed to the bottom of the *Explorer*. "Did anyone ever figure out what those bumps are for?"

On the top and bottom of the ship were two oddly shaped but smooth bulges that didn't seem to house any type of sensor or weapon any of them had seen before. Further, they were hinged on some kind of frame that blended into the body of the ship.

David finished his drink. "One of the guys I worked with last week said that nobody on the construction crew knew what they were. They came up in one big piece and were fitted onto the end of those arms."

Ryan snapped his fingers. "Sensors. A guy I met on my last watch said they were huge deep scanning sensors."

David looked at him skeptically.

"Seriously, I guess he designed 'em or something. Though, he might have been crazy."

A glint of silver drew Ryan's eye to the window. Emerging from the left side of the station, a sleek shape glided behind the Forge's towering scaffolding. From this distance, it looked no bigger than a heavy shuttle, but Ryan recognized the outline immediately, it was one of the Columbia-class battleships. Trailing behind were three identical vessels, their formation a striking sight even at this distance.

"Look, they must be practicing for something," Ryan said letting the subject drop and pointing to the silver craft.

Anna reached over and grabbed a fancy embossed sheet of paper from the table near them. "It says 'Flyby performed by ISA Columbia, Buenos Aires, Seoul, and Yangtze.'" She made a low whistle. "That is a lot of firepower."

"I saw gaggles of Seoul and Yangtze crew on the way over here. Half of 'em were already drunk," Ryan said. "How are they out there maneuvering right now?"

Anna only shrugged, which caught Ryan's eye before he forced himself to ignore her low-cut dress. He turned to David. "The short version," he said, seeing his friend gear up for a long explanation.

"Uh. Duty stations," David said grudgingly.

"What's that supposed to mean?"

"They are down to one duty station for the party, the rest are here."

"Thanks, buddy. As Admiral Hayes says: *The more you say, the less people remember.*" Ryan looked over at Anna, wagging his eyebrows.

"Brevity is the sign of a weak mind… or so my family says." David sipped from his flute before remembering he didn't care for the bubbly.

A triple chime in Ryan's ear caught his attention. It was a familiar sound announcing a schedule reminder, so he assumed it was for the party. He brought up his wrist to mute it on his PDD when he saw the entry: *Watch standing duty, ISA Cosmic Explorer: 20:30 to 0:800 FUT*

He furrowed his brow and clicked the entry, not even remotely understanding what the PDD was referencing. When it opened his calendar, he groaned out loud.

"What's up, late for a date with Sheila?" Anna said.

Ryan shook his head. "*Shiiiiit…* I have watch."

Anna walked over, trying to get a glimpse of the small screen. "What, when?"

David leaned over and tapped the share button on Ryan's PDD, sending the message to the private group they had set up. He tapped on his own PDD, which he had modified with some less than legal software to examine the headers of the message. After a few moments of swiping he turned to his friends.

"Do we know this person?" he said, sharing a file photo of a young clerk.

Both shook their heads while David continued his search.

"Now if I cross-reference that with….oh." David stopped and glanced at Ryan before sharing another photo, this one from the man's personal social account. In the background of that photo was none other than Percival Slaunder.

"That's bad," David said.

Ryan was crestfallen. Beyond outright refusing the order, he would be stuck standing security watch on the bridge of the *Explorer* till tomorrow morning, missing the entire launch day celebration. As icing on the cake, he noticed another entry had appeared on his schedule. This one was much more concerning.

"Do either of you have a meeting with the political liaison tomorrow morning?"

"No," David said.

"Nothing," Anna said, looking at Ryan with obvious worry. "Ryan…"

"I know. Shit." Ryan hung his head, pinching the bridge of his nose. A visit to the political liaison was never good. In conjunction with his sudden assignment to stand watch during the biggest celebration in years meant trouble for him.

The more reasonable side of his brain knew it was mostly his own fault for taking so many stupid chances, for thinking he could actually land a spot on *Columbia*, and for crossing Slaunder. By this time tomorrow, he might be on a shuttle headed back to Earth.

"He got me," he said, defeated. "I figured he would try to knife me in the ribs, but this…" He slammed his fist on the table, making the silverware bounce.

He hung his head before finally looking at his friends, giving them a weak smile. "Drink a dozen for me, compadres, I guess I'm on duty tonight." He turned amidst the protests of his friends and walked away from them, feeling truly alone for the first time in years. Was this the reason he hadn't been given an assignment? The thought swirled in his head.

Slowly walking away from the table, he decided to angle his way over to the huge bar that had been arranged for the celebration. He was so mad at Slaunder but also at himself for not realizing that the guy would never let go of his grudge. He wasn't sure what he could have done… maybe apologize? Throw himself at his feet and beg? It burned his guts knowing that he didn't have any means of fighting someone with Slaunder's connections.

Ryan was in a dark mood, maybe the darkest since the months after his mother's death. He flagged down the bartender. "Double whisky… actually make it a triple, not like anyone will care." The bartender didn't respond, just poured with a practiced hand and slid the glass across to him.

Immediately downing it, he held up his finger for another. After chugging the second and then a third, he walked over to where the servers were staging the passed hors d'oeuvres and grabbed an entire tray, walking out like he owned the place.

"Fucking fuck." He blinked back his surging emotions.

His pace picked up as he left the room and made a beeline to the main elevator bank. Waiting by the lift, he ate one of the little meat-filled pastries. It tasted like ash in his mouth. The doors to the lift opened to disgorge a load of guests, mostly enlisted service members in their dress blues. He stopped short when he spotted none other than Slaunder at the back of the car.

He grinned like a cat who just cornered a mouse. Strutting forward, he pushed Ryan back and stood in front of the elevator till it closed behind him.

"Where you going, grub? You're going to miss the party," he said.

Ryan was never one to be at a loss for words, but this time he literally couldn't think of a thing to say. He stood gaping like a fish as Slaunder grabbed one of the pastries from his tray, circling him like a predator sizing up his prey.

"What nothing to say?" He sniffed the pastry and scrunched his nose before tossing it to the floor. He walked behind Ryan then leaned in close to his ear. "You thought you could screw with me? Make me look like an idiot?" Ryan could feel the hot breath hit his ear. "I'm going to make sure we run into each other again, and this time there won't be anyone around to save your sorry ass."

He walked away before tossing one last bomb. "Have fun at your hearing tomorrow."

Ryan stared blankly, his guts twisted into knots.

The elevator opened once again, and this time a load of civilians dressed in suits and evening gowns exited, excusing themselves as they walked around Ryan. He finally stepped on just before the doors closed, cutting off the lively sounds of a party in its beginning stages, and with it, his future in the ISA.

Now quiet, except for the hum of the elevator fan, he threw the tray with all his might against the far wall.

It pinged off the wall with a metallic clang, rebounding and landing on top of his foot. Emotions flaring once again, he lashed out with a kick, accomplishing nothing more than a bruise on his shin as it bounced back and hit his leg side-on.

He hung his head, heart thumping, pastry flakes littering the front of his uniform. Taking a deep breath, he brushed them off with the back of his hand and straightened his dress coat. When the display built into the door indicated that he was approaching the dock, he cleared his throat.

"I need another drink."

The ding of the elevator sounded his arrival at the *Explorer*'s dock. The entire area was devoid of life as he made his way up the gangway arm. The thick outer door to the ship was already open, nested inside the body of the *Explorer* to make docking connections easier, only the rounded corner of the meter thick hatch was visible as Ryan stepped into the recessed entry.

At the inner hatch of the ship, the automated systems chimed as they scanned his identity, and a green strip of lights surrounding the top of the door illuminated as the hatch swung open. He stepped on board, expecting a guard to challenge his presence, but was met by only an empty hallway and the smell of fresh paint and plastic. A small security station was built into the wall sporting a thick armored window, but it too was empty.

He walked down a short passage that opened into a massive corridor stretching the length of the ship, vanishing as it curved toward the bow.

"Now what?" Ryan said aloud, having never stepped foot on the ship. He referenced the orders on his PDD again, noticing that there were attachments, one of which had instructions on where to go once on board. He took a deep breath as the drinks he downed earlier started to take effect, a familiar feeling of heat forming under his collar, slightly relaxing his mood.

According to the map, each deck had two main passageways running along the port and starboard sides in gentle arcs, spanning about two-thirds of the ship. Markings on the walls indicated these corridors also served as munition and cargo lanes, with an overhead monorail system for moving heavy loads. Every fifty feet or so, large recessed airtight doors broke up the passage, outlined by bold yellow and black safety stripes.

The layout made the trip swift, it took less than a minute to make it through the empty passage to a large, armored hatchway that led to the protected bridge smack dab in the center of the ship. While the automated systems verified his access, he braced his arm against the wall. The heavy outer door slid aside, revealing an inner pressure door, which also started to cycle back, embedding itself into the wall. His head was swimming from the drinks, his mood still foul. How had he been such a fool? He knew his life was ruined, whatever chance he had at something better was gone.

Entering from the rear of the bridge sent a chill up Ryan's spine. The lights were dimmed, but the air smelled crisp and new. A small raised dais held the captain's seat, flanked by the navigation and first officer's stations, as was standard on larger ISA vessels. What wasn't standard was the sheer size of the space. Unlike the cramped simulators, this bridge felt expansive, with no exposed wiring or pipes cluttering the ceiling. The light-colored stations were trimmed with stitched acoustical panels, their surfaces smooth and rounded.

Along either side of the back wall were several more workstations, each with a nicely appointed chair—most likely science and auxiliary stations, he thought. Finally, along the outer wall on each side of the captain's dais were two consoles where he supposed the weapons and communications officers sat. It was all familiar but at the same time foreign, futuristic to the point it looked like a movie set rather than the working bridge of an ISA vessel.

The last dominant feature at the front of the bridge was a floor-to-ceiling screen, which, like every ship and simulator he'd ever seen, would show all the crucial shipboard information and displays that the captain would rely on during a deployment.

For a moment he forgot his troubles, his impending dismissal, even Slaunder. He'd never been so close to his dream as he was at this moment.

He felt like a kid again, being the captain in some vid, boldly walking onto the bridge, waiting for the guard to announce his arrival. "As you were," Ryan called out to the empty space, walking to the captain's chair and plopping himself into the seat with the beginnings of a smile. It quickly soured as Slaunder's words echoed in his ear.

"Whatever," he mumbled, leaning back in the seat, welcoming the warmth and buzz of the drinks as they worked their magic. He let out a wry chuckle when he realized he would be following in his mother's footsteps. At least he'd graduated; that was more than he could have ever imagined and something people like Slaunder could never take away from him.

He shifted in the seat, testing its feel as his fingers brushed over the small physical controls embedded in the armrests. Above them, faint holographic icons flickered to life, hovering in neat rows, waiting for touch commands. The layout was mostly standard, like the sims he'd played. Left-hand controls for ship systems and status displays, right-hand for sensors, weapons, reactor, and propulsion. But one control on the right caught his eye. Larger than the others, it had no corresponding holographic icon. The flat red button sat caged behind a clear protective cover, marked with a symbol printed directly on it: several wavy lines stacked over a circle.

Ryan leaned in, frowning as he studied the button in the dim light. "Huh," he muttered.

The lingering buzz from the drinks made his head swim. "Too friggin' dark in here," he grumbled. Figuring the bridge was still in standby mode, like in the simulators, he pushed up and made his way to the executive officer's station in front and to the right of the captain's chair. "XO should have controls for the bridge," he said to himself, studying the panel. He tapped the screen, which blinked to life, displaying a general status overview of the ship's systems.

"Bridge, bridge, bridge..." he said, tapping around, finally finding the entry for bridge subsystems.

"Power," he said, his finger hovering over the button. "What are they gonna do—fire me?" He punched the button in triumph. Lights all around

94

him went full bright. The screens at every station hummed to life, booting up all the various displays. He could also hear air circulation ramp up in the background and a low hum as power coursed through the space.

Plopping back into the captain's chair, he studied the now backlit chair controls. He tapped the "display" button on the left-hand side, and the huge front viewscreen turned on showing the default view from the external bow cameras. His eyes kept lingering on the mystery button.

"Now how do I find out what this one does?" he said, a little too curious for his own good, flipping up the clear plastic cover.

"For which button would you like an explanation, Lieutenant Junior Grade Anders?" a female voice sounded out, coming from directly behind him.

Ryan jumped out of the seat, spinning around with his hands balled up in fists. He scanned the room, finding nobody there.

"Hello?" he said tentatively.

"Hello. Which button would you like an explanation for, Lieutenant Junior Grade Anders?"

Again, he spun around. The voice sounded like it was coming from someone inches away from his ears.

"Lieutenant Junior Grade Anders, are you in distress?" Ryan started to think maybe the voice was in his head.

"Who… is talking to me?" he finally said aloud.

"My apologies, Lieutenant Junior Grade Anders, I am Aurora, the ship's AI—you activated me when you powered up the bridge systems. I was merely trying to answer your query but require more information."

Ryan laughed. "Oh god, I thought I was finally losing it." He spoke loudly, looking around for some kind of indication that the AI heard him.

"You can speak normally; I am tied into your PDD and the bridge microphones."

Ryan plopped back down into the captain's chair now that he knew he wasn't going insane. "You don't sound like you're speaking through my PDD."

The AI answered back quickly. "No, my default mode is to transmit directly into your auditory system using transitional radio frequencies. This provides a more robust and redundant means of communication while on the ship. If my transmitters were damaged in a particular space, I would utilize your earpiece."

Ryan whistled. "Fancy—I've never seen that kind of tech on a military vessel." He paused before continuing. "As a matter of fact, I've never seen an interactive AI on a ship… well, in simulations."

There was a short pause before the AI answered back. "Lieutenant Junior Grade—" Ryan held up his hand and interrupted, which again surprised him, as he hadn't said anything.

"Call me Ryan, or Anders, the rank thing is unnecessary."

A chime sounded and the AI replied, "Noted, Mr. Anders." Ryan sighed, deciding to let it go with "Mister."

"The *Cosmic Explorer* is designed for unique missions not previously undertaken by the ISA. Exploration has, to this point, been under the purview of government research and civilian organizations. It was deemed necessary that my AI Core be installed on board this ship to support some shipboard operations as well as a large contingent of scientific personnel and their equipment."

Conversing with the AI felt so seamless to Ryan. So natural that he could swear he was talking to another person, albeit one who was hung up on formality. Having used a number of "smart" AI systems over the course of his Academy education, this one was by far the best.

"Mr. Anders, you have an incoming communication from Ensign Marcus Batista, aboard the *Rio de Janeiro*."

Ryan was taken aback. This was the second time in as many weeks he'd heard from the enigmatic ensign.

"How did you—"

Before he could finish, Aurora spoke. "I am interfaced with your PDD to provide assistance in the case of a missing or disabled communications officer."

"Oh, okay… ummm, can you put him through?" He wasn't sure he liked the AI messing with his personal calls or his PDD. A short ding announced the call being answered. Again, it wasn't in his earpiece but transmitted into his ears.

"Hey, Marcus! I was meaning to call you," he lied. "What's happening over there on that tug?" There was a noticeable delay before Marcus answered back, more intense than Ryan ever remembered him being.

"Ryan, god, I'm glad I got a hold of you, nobody else is answering." Marcus sounded almost scared.

"Yeah, the party—" Ryan started to say before Marcus cut in, stopping Ryan short.

"Hey, can you do me a... oh, sorry, man. Listen, the *Rio* is headed out of port, and we're hauling ass, the delay is affecting all coms even with the repeaters."

"Ryan, ah..." He paused before blurting out, "I have a feeling something bad is happening."

"If you're talking about my personal life, then yeah, things are bad," Ryan said with a sigh.

There was a pause before Marcus chuckled nervously. "No. I just... can you check around and see if anyone has news about ships going missing near Hesperus? As far back as you can find. I'm getting worried that the *Rio* is headed into trouble. It's probably nothing, but two ISA patrol ships dropped a blank distress buoy and haven't been in contact since. Uh, keep that part to yourself."

Ryan sat up straight. "Okay, let me see what I can find. I'll send it direct to your PDD. Hey, Marcus... stay safe, brother."

"Ensign Batista has ended the connection," Aurora said, breaking the silence.

Ryan remembered the report about the mining ship but that was about it—with the launch of the *Explorer*, everything else had just been background noise to him. It then dawned on him: the oddball engineer and his conspiracy theories about asteroids and secret bases.

"No way..." Ryan said to himself.

"Aurora, can you help me find some information?" he called out, unsure what the AI could do beyond helping him figure out what the buttons were for.

"Certainly, Mr. Anders, I can help with many different types of queries, but as a watch stander, your access to certain information paths has been restricted."

Ryan sat, tapping his fingers against the chair. "So, I'm guessing you were listening to that conversation?"

Aurora replied quickly, "Of course, I would not be able to assist you in the performance of your duties if I wasn't privy to any and all communications to and from the ship."

Ryan figured as much, shrugging off the intrusion. "Okay, whatever you can find out about missing ships near Hesperus, far back as you can go."

The AI paused for a few moments, obviously processing the information. "From unofficial reports, I have compiled a list of ships either missing or destroyed at or near the asteroid Hesperus or in nearby orbits. I cannot confirm Ensign Batista's report of ISA patrol ships, but twelve civilian vessels have been reported missing or have been presumed destroyed based on recovered debris."

Ryan's mouth hung open. "Twelve? How have I not heard about this all over the news?"

Aurora seemed ready for the question. "I have reviewed the available data from military and civilian networks and surmised that early reports were not given sufficient attention based on assumptions that craft were destroyed in accidents or mishaps. Further, if we assume that Ensign Batista is correct, analysis of each ship's movements, planned routes, and eventual disappearances show a compelling pattern. Please keep in mind that my neural net is not trained for tactical simulation, so I can only offer you broad assumptions."

"Sure, whatever, so what was the pattern?"

"The patterns show a definite bias moving from the outer system sunward. The first reported incident that fits the pattern was three months ago. A Frontier corporation deep space mineral probe lost contact near the Jovian moon Thebe. Subsequent disappearances—"

Ryan interrupted. "Hold on. So the ships weren't all near the asteroid belt... wait... the disappearances are moving toward the sun..." He realized something. "Then the *Rio* might run into trouble before they get to Hesperus..."

"Correct. The pattern of disappearances is clearly moving, but it does not show a constant speed, so I cannot predict where the *Rio de Janeiro* will intersect its path."

Ryan rubbed his chin, thinking.

"Mr. Anders, you have an incoming call from Ensign Rodriguez."

Ryan waved his hand. "No time. Aurora, I want you to summarize what you found along with a list of the different craft that have disappeared and send it to Marcus... um, Ensign Batista... can you do that?"

There was a long pause before Aurora replied, "I have sent the information to Ensign Batista's PDD and received confirmation of receipt. Would you like me to forward my findings to ISA Fleet headquarters as well?"

Ryan nearly choked. "Uhhh, no, please.... I'm not sure I should even be talking to you right now."

"Noted. I will limit our findings to the ship."

Ryan breathed a sigh of relief and sat back into his chair. "Thanks." He couldn't stop thinking about Marcus and the *Rio*. Now he had a bad feeling too.

CHAPTER 8

Ensigns David Kim and Anna Rodriguez sat at their assigned table, uncomfortably far back from the large stage that dominated the event. A nearby screen set into the wall simulcast the third speaker of the night as he droned on about the storied history of the ISA and its roots in the Orbital Security Convention, giving the whole thing the feel of a corporate shareholder meeting. The tables near the exit where they'd been seated were populated by people like themselves: politically vulnerable and unconnected.

At the tables nearest the stage sat the top brass of the ISA, battleship captains and planetary government leaders. The next group farther back had their assistants, executive officers, smaller ship captains, and politically powerful families. Between them and the back of the room, the bulk of tables held the mildly powerful: wealthy merchants, celebrities, sports stars, and the like. As for the military, depending on where you stood in the hierarchy of the ISA determined your proximity to the stage.

David sighed, wanting nothing more than to leave the event, but Anna had told him about her mother, and he wanted to be there to support her. He wished something livelier would happen; the slate of speakers was just awful. The current speaker, an ambassador from Earth, was trying to engage the crowd with a rousing remembrance of those lost during the troubled times before the OSC was signed, but it fell flat with most of the people in the room, inciting just a smattering of applause.

David looked around, rubbing the back of his neck, noticing that Anna seemed to be having just as good of a time as he was, her head resting on her hand, eyes glazed over. Next to her was Ryan's empty seat, a card with his name still displayed on a small metal stand. He shifted in his seat trying to get comfortable, thinking absently about his friend whose career now hung by a thread.

David really enjoyed himself when Ryan was around, and despite his protestations to the contrary, he liked being pulled out of his comfort zone. Visiting seedy bars, engaging with all types of people up and down the social ladder, taking crazy chances. Anna was quite the opposite, caring, nurturing, but strong and brash. She would kill for her family and friends and had supported him in the most unexpected ways. He probably wouldn't have made it through the Academy without their support. The thought of life in the fleet without his two closest friends seemed so dull and pointless. Anna at least would accompany him on his first assignment, and he hoped his friend would survive long enough for the three of them to serve together again. No matter what happened, they were his family now. That would never change.

He shifted in his seat again, glancing behind the two other people that shared the table. With a good view of both large entryways at the rear of the room and nothing better to do, he decided to amuse himself by silently critiquing the stream of guests as they filed in.

While the first entrants of the night were a parade of polys and corpos who must have spent a fortune on the most lavish outfits, the crowd quickly morphed into the standard march of drab, unimaginative faire. Black suits, little black dresses, and fleet uniforms seemed to be all they could muster. It was all very boring, since even among the rich, no one wanted to take risks at these events for fear of looking foolish and hurting their political credibility.

Though a point of shame in the Kim household, David loved fashion. That was until his father had gotten wind of it and put his foot down. From that point on, Mr. Kim made it his mission to make David a man's man, pushing him into sports, engineering, and finally the military.

David absently swirled his neglected drink, listening to the ice clink against the sides of the glass.

He wondered how different things would have been if he hadn't been selected for the Academy. His attention snapped back as a woman entered the Dome like a force of nature.

She moved through the entrance nearest them with the kind of effortless poise that only came from a lifetime of refined upbringing. Her gown was a study in contrast—white satin that draped like liquid over her curves, its every fold catching the ambient glow of the low overhead lights, while the black lace bodice sculpted her frame with corset-like precision. The intricate lacework, obviously hand-embroidered with what looked like obsidian beading, traced delicate filigree patterns over her décolletage, giving the illusion of inked calligraphy against her porcelain skin.

The gown's hem skimmed the polished floor, parting just enough to reveal sleek black pleated silk d'orsay pumps, their delicate sheen catching the light with every step.

She was a vision—exquisite, untouchable, and utterly aware of it.

"My god, now that is a statement piece," he thought, tugging at the collar of his own boring and quite itchy dress blue uniform.

He gave her another long once-over when he finally noticed who it was. He nudged Anna under the table with his foot to get her attention and nodded toward the new entrant.

Anna looked, her face hardening. "Come on…" she whispered, standing. David followed, drink in hand, feeling like the night had just gotten a lot more interesting.

They both walked to the back of the room, then over to the woman who had paused inside the doorway, clearly looking for someone.

"Lieutenant Miller," Anna said in a deadpan voice.

Elizabeth looked toward the approaching duo. "Ensigns," she said, annoyance creeping into her voice.

Anna marched right up to Elizabeth, arms crossed, feet planted. "It was you, wasn't it? Do you know where Ryan is right now?" she puffed.

"I have no idea what you're on about," Elizabeth said, scanning the crowd.

"What the hell is wrong with you? I get that you think you're better than everyone else, but putting him on duty tonight of all nights? The meeting with the political officer? You won't even see him again after next week so why bother."

David saw both of Anna's hands ball into fists and her neck turn a deep shade of red. He was about to step in between them, but he could see his friend slowly regain control. She could be hot-tempered but definitely wasn't stupid.

"Listen... Anna." Elizabeth said, a frown forming. "Whatever Anders has gotten himself into, I can assure you that I had nothing to do with it."

"We know about the flag you put on our applications. Don't try to deny it."

Elizabeth cocked her eyebrow. "Well, I'm surprised you found out about that. I'll have to talk to my contacts and find out who was being... indiscreet." She waved at someone behind them. "Yes, I did put that flag on your request," she admitted openly. "That, however, was only business and that business has been concluded. I don't have any idea about a meeting with a political officer, nor do I wish to involve myself."

She stepped around Anna but paused. "If you're looking for answers, I'd talk to Ensign Slaunder. He seems to have quite the grudge against your friend. Oh... cute dress," she said, finally walking away and embracing another woman.

"Uhhh—I hate her," Anna said, watching Elizabeth and the other woman find their seats near the front of the room.

"Do you think she was telling the truth?" Anna said, leading David away.

"I think it fits you fabulously, and the color is perfect," David said, nodding.

"About Slaunder," she said, giving him a slap to the arm.

"Maybe? Why would she lie?"

Anna sidled up to the bar and ordered them both shots of tequila.

While they waited, she raised her arm and tapped her PDD before grunting in frustration and letting it drop.

"Ryan isn't answering."

She tapped her fingers on the bar's polished surface. "What do you say we get out of here; this party just went from dull to soul sucking." She looked in Elizabeth's direction with disgust before an evil smile formed on her face.

"You want to go up and tell him?" she said as the bartender slid both drinks to her.

"What? That Slaunder is trying to get him kicked out? I'm sure he already knows that."

She handed one to David, who hesitated, trying to decide whether drinking a shot was worth it.

"We might get a look at that ship too." Anna sweetened the deal.

The ambassador finished his speech to a round of applause and finally left the stage. A chime rang and white coated servers entered the room from side entrances, rolling silver covered trays to those up front. The smell of a finely cooked meal wafted around the room. A second larger round of servers entered, this time rolling less ornate carts to the rest of the room.

David looked at Anna. "Sure, but maybe after dinner?" he said, closing his eyes and taking a big whiff as a serving cart rolled past them.

"Yeah, after," she said, feeling slightly guilty.

*

The ISA destroyer *Rio de Janeiro* made it quickly to its maximum speed at just under 20 percent the speed of light. Deep in the bowels of the ship, the engineers kept a worried eye on the fusion reactors that powered the quantum, or "slip" drive as it was known in the fleet.

The drive was a marvel of human and AI ingenuity, allowing even the largest vessels to travel at incredible speeds. Officially called Quantum Field Manipulation Propulsion, the system relied on a specialized AI to exploit the phenomenon of virtual particle pairs. Its generator created a powerful quantum field around the spacecraft and selectively manipulated one of the particles, forcing it to transition from a virtual state to a real one. The energy for this transition came directly from the zero-point energy of the quantum vacuum, creating an imbalance that, in aggregate, was fantastically powerful and capable of pushing a ship to previously impossible speeds.

The vibrations and low thrum of the slip drive could be felt throughout the ship, but at the current speed, it was especially noticeable in the communication center where Ensign Marcus Batista manned his duty station. Four other specialists of different rank worked nearby, monitoring the ship's internal and external communications. He wasn't officially on duty now that he had been relieved by the primary watch, but he just received a data packet from Ryan and needed a larger terminal to review it. As he read the summary, the feeling of dread that had been tickling the back of his mind fully settled over him.

At first, he found it hard to believe Anders compiled the data so quickly. He'd been a decent study in the Academy, but the guy was far from a brain. Marcus assumed he had a lady friend in intelligence or something by the way it was compiled in fleet standard format. Something he wouldn't put past the guy who had quite the reputation when it came to fraternization. His boldness was one of the things Marcus liked about him.

"Holy shit." He breathed as he read the names of twelve different vessels that had disappeared within the past month. "No, fourteen if you count the missing patrol ships." Bile rose in his throat. That gnawing sense of unease he'd dismissed as nerves now settled in like a weight on his chest. It reminded him of what people said just before lightning struck—hair standing on end, a charge in the air, the dreadful certainty that something was coming and there was no way to stop it.

Did fleet intelligence really think this was some kind of pirate attack? He turned his chair towards the only other person he thought might believe him.

"Hey, Javi?" he whispered loudly. Ensign Javier Rojas, a skinny kid whose uniform always seemed a little too big for him, sat nearby, picking something out of his fingernail, waiting for the duty lieutenant to give him something to do.

"What's up, Marco?" He looked up, giving his shoulders a little stretch. Marcus motioned him over after seeing the duty lieutenant otherwise occupied. When he slid over, Marcus lowered his head towards him, speaking in a low, hurried tone.

"Javi, remember when we left port and I told you I had a bad feeling about those ships?" He tapped the screen in front of him. "I started digging. We're in trouble."

Javier's casual expression vanished as he scanned the message. His brow furrowed.

"What is this? Where did you get it?" He looked up sharply. "Is this from Fleet Intel? Why the hell do you even have this?"

Marcus glanced over his shoulder, then back. "Remember that guy from the other class, Anders? I sent him a message after we left port. Told him to check into the missing ships."

"Ryan Anders?" He looked incredulously back at the document.

"I know, he must have a contact in fleet intel."

Javier chuffed "I bet he does."

Marcus waved him off. "It all checks out, Javi—read it."

Javier kept reading. "Sunward—Marcus you know what this means? Whatever is happening out there, the *Rio* is gonna run right into it while we're in slip."

Marcus knew exactly what he meant. When ships were traveling using the slip drive, their forward sensors were effectively blind and vulnerable to any objects larger than small rocks. Traveling at speeds approaching 20 percent light imparted an enormous amount of energy into anything it hit. Since space wasn't nearly as empty as people assumed, careful courses and parallel slip fields were set up to shunt away debris, but an enemy could use this to their advantage if they knew the path a ship was traveling. Due to this vulnerability, warships always disengaged their slip drives well outside an engagement zone, but Captain Santos had no idea that the danger was so close.

Marcus looked at Javier. "What should we do? They would never take this seriously if it came from some unofficial source."

Javier crossed his arms over his head, stretching his shoulders one after the other. He looked back at the message and nodded his head. "You know, that really does look like a fleet message… just missing the headers."

Marcus looked again. Javier was right: whoever Anders had gotten the data from must have worked in the intel division; he had the same thought when he first read it. The phrasing, layout, everything.

"Damn, you are a genius, my friend," he said, opening the message queue and finding an actual message from fleet intel that came in shortly after they left their station. He stripped out the message and pasted in the data Anders gave him. Then using a trick Lieutenant Commander Perez had shown him, he edited the raw data stream to change the time received.

"You sure you want to do that, mano?" Javier said, looking around.

"Yeah, bro, I've never been more sure of anything," Marcus said, finishing the edits. "Here goes nothing."

He commanded the message to be included in the data stream that just came across the communication array and closed his eyes. Javier slid back to his station and pretended to look busy, waiting for the fallout if they recognized the message as bogus.

From behind them, the duty lieutenant started relaying the normal message traffic to his subordinates before stopping cold. Marcus and Javier glanced at each other as he contacted the bridge.

"Bridge, coms, immediate message from fleet intel inbound."

Marcus could hear Lieutenant Commander Perez's silky smooth voice answer back, "Roger coms, captain has the message, stand by."

Several minutes later, Perez called back. "Coms, Captain Silva wants to know if we've had contact with ISA vessels or listening stations in the vicinity of our target?"

The duty officer, Lieutenant Commander Garcia, tapped the display panel at his workstation before answering back. "Negative, bridge, we are showing zero response to pings on the datalink. Last contact was with ISA listening post 2306... fifteen minutes ago."

Marcus tapped his display and brought up a sector map. Listening posts were basically low observability spy satellites that monitored ship traffic in their local areas. Post 2306 was behind them. Two other listening posts were in front of them, flanking the area where the ship was headed. If they were both offline, the ISA was blind to a huge swath of space, and the *Rio* was headed right for it.

The captain must have come to the same conclusion because Marcus noticed the slight feeling of vertigo induced by the ship changing course at speed. He checked the clock—they'd been running full speed for a little over two hours. On their original course, they would reach the missing ships in less than an hour. He didn't know what the captain planned to do, but at least the entire bridge was now aware that this wasn't just some simple communication problem. Marcus stood and nodded to Javier before leaving the coms room. He was feeling just a little better, so he decided to go back to his bunk. He'd done all he could do, and now it was up to the captain and the *Rio*.

*

After sending the data on the missing ships, Ryan tried a dozen different methods to coax the ship's AI into giving him access to the onboard computers. Trouble was coming, and he was determined to help Marcus with whatever information he could find. The problem was that the most useful data was likely locked inside the military network.

After the frustratingly pleasant Aurora told him once again that he only had limited access to such systems, he decided to take another look around the bridge.

He noticed a nondescript door on the back wall near the entrance. With nothing to lose, he tapped the open control, jumping when it made a loud beep.

"Watch standers are not allowed inside the captain's duty cabin, Mr. Anders," the AI announced.

"Oh," he said, stepping back, he remembered that the duty cabin, just a few steps from the bridge, served as the captain's secondary quarters, a place to work or rest during long shifts.

"How am I supposed to do my rounds and make sure everything is secure if I'm not allowed to check?"

"Matters pertaining to security are not within my purview. If you would like access to the cabin, please activate the security subsystem on the first officer's control panel."

Ryan stepped up to the display, where a control had been helpfully highlighted. He hesitated, wondering if tapping into the security system would only land him in deeper trouble. Then he shrugged and pressed it.

A while later, he was still waiting. "Aurora, that didn't do anything."

"The Valkyrie subsystem is currently activating, please stand by."

Ryan was never surprised by the strange names that the military assigned to its systems. Acronym soup was something he'd become very familiar with during his three years at the Academy; in fact, whenever he encountered an unfamiliar one, he would try to guess what it stood for.

"Variable Autonomous Land... Labor... Link? Hey, Aurora, what does Valkyrie stand for... and what does Aurora stand for while you're at it?"

"Aurora is not an acronym. My designation was given to me by the head of research, Kazuki Sato, at Frontier Software, Mars."

Ryan was surprised by that revelation. "Frontier Software? I didn't know they did military AI research?"

"They do not. As I said before, my neural net is not trained for tactical or military simulation. My primary function is to monitor and assist the crew of the *Cosmic Explorer*. It is Valkyrie's primary function to assist with strategic and tactical planning, maneuver, target acquisition, shipboard security countermeasures, and a host of other classified tasks."

Ryan was taken aback by the answer. "Wait, hold on a second... Valkyrie is an AI too?"

"Correct," the answer came back in a completely different voice. It was neither male or female, but hard-edged and mechanical. It had a tone Ryan could only describe as slightly menacing.

"Oh, uh, hello, Valkyrie?" he said aloud.

"Greetings are unnecessary. Please state your query."

"Okay... Aurora? You still there?"

The pleasant female voice responded. "How can I assist you, Mr. Anders?"

He exhaled, relieved she was still listening. "Yeah, so what's the deal with the... other one? Is that another full AI?"

"Command authorization is required for access to classified materials," Valkyrie growled, making Ryan wonder if it was possible to piss off an AI.

"Mr. Anders, I have an Ensign Anna Rodriguez and Ensign David Kim requesting access to the ship. I do not have them on the watch stander list."

Ryan was surprised that his friends had decided to join him. "Uh, yeah, please grant them access."

There was a tone, then the AI replied, "They have been granted temporary access, but I cannot assign them privileges to any ship systems."

"That's okay, I'm sure they won't be here for long. Thanks, Aurora."

"You are welcome, Mr. Anders," Aurora said, with a cheerful inflection.

He cocked his head, looking around. He knew that Frontier made cutting edge models for luxury cruisers and robotics; he even interacted with a cognitive therapy AI once as part of his induction screening process before he was accepted to the Academy. They seemed to possess at least a simulated emotional component, but he never mistook them for anything other than a program. Aurora seemed different to him, more sophisticated. Valkyrie, on the other hand, seemed like your run-of-the-mill program, only… angrier if that was possible.

The door at the rear of the bridge slid aside, and the sounds of his friends filled the space, warming Ryan's heart in a way he hadn't expected.

"Heya, Ryan—look what we brought you." Anna, still resplendent in her green dress, came marching in with David in tow. She held out a fancy brown takeout box with a black logo on the side.

He could smell the familiar scent of steak, potatoes, and something savory.

Instead of grabbing the box, he surprised her with a huge hug. He then turned to David and gave him an even bigger one, lifting him off the ground.

His friends glanced at each other before mutually deciding to ignore the strange behavior.

"Glad to see you two," he said, returning to form, grabbing the box in both hands and burying his nose in the folds of the lid and taking a huge breath.

"Oh my god, Anna, you are the best—I'm starving." He unfolded the built-in lid and snapped the printed flat fork from the side of the container. "Oooh, gravy…"

"Anna said we needed to come here and save you. The party kind of sucked anyway," David said.

Anna waved him off. "Ryan, you will never guess who we ran into at the party…"

Ryan popped a small roasted potato into his mouth, his cheek puffed out like a chipmunk, chewing and speaking at the same time he raised an eyebrow. "Who, Slaunder?"

"No, it was Elizabeth. Wait what do you know? She mentioned him."

Ryan continued to eat. "Saw that dickhead on the way out." He swallowed and looked at his friends with a contrite expression. "Hey, I'm really sorry I dragged you guys into this, it was my stupid mouth."

"To hell with them, all of them," Anna snapped before David could say a word. "We'll get through this, Ryan. With any luck, once we ship out, they'll be nothing but a bad memory. Some people hate you just for breathing."

Ryan forced a smile, deciding not to bother telling his friends what Slaunder had planned for him. Anna had a way of getting protective, and the last thing she needed was to end up on that shitlist.

"Hey, look at me, I'm not worried," he said, flashing them an exaggerated grin before turning back to his takeout box.

They all knew it was bluster but chuckled nonetheless.

"Oh, and sorry for not answering your call earlier. I was talking to Marcus."

"That guy gives me the creeps," David said, earning him a dirty look from Anna.

"He's nice!" she said. "Sure, he's a little weird… what did he want?"

"They left their patrol station and hauled ass for the asteroid belt a couple hours ago. Marcus was pretty upset, said he thought something bad was going to happen."

Ryan went on to explain the mysterious disappearances of the ISA patrol ships, the possible distress call, and figuring out how a dozen other vessels had gone missing previously. When finished, his friends stood in silence.

"That doesn't sound good." Anna tsked softly. "What do you think, David?"

David squinted his eyes at Ryan, ignoring Anna's question. "Wait, tell me again, how did *you* figure out those ships went missing?"

Ryan looked sheepishly at his friends "Did I say I figured it out? It was actually Aurora…"

"Who's Aurora?"

*

In the forward birthing compartment of the *Rio de Janeiro*, Ensign Marcus Batista sat tapping on his personal tablet. It was still considered "night" in the compartment, so the lights were all set to a dim red. This allowed people to move around but not bother those who were sleeping like second shift.

He'd been reading the available reports of the ships that disappeared and cross-referencing the names Ryan sent him. In the doorway of the birthing, a shapely shadow blocked the white hallway light, which caught his attention. He looked up as the woman beckoned him to join her. He put down the tablet and walked over, finally noticing that it was none other than Lieutenant Commander Perez. His heart skipped a beat as he joined her outside the hatch, eyes blinking as they became accustomed to the bright white light.

"Commander… uh, what can I do for you?" he asked in a low voice, careful not to wake anyone. She didn't answer right away but instead raised the tablet she carried and turned the screen toward him.

"Care to explain this to me, Ensign?" she said in an equally low but quite stirring voice. He looked and immediately saw the raw header information for the message he'd fabricated, a look of utter panic crossing his face.

"What were you thinking?" She said. "I showed you that trick so you could correct mistakes and look good for the captain, not fabricate messages." Her voice creeped up in volume, and he cringed.

"Ma'am, I can explain." She turned and started walking away, pausing when he didn't immediately follow.

"Come on," she said, motioning to him.

Walking down the passageway, they stopped in front of a closed hatch with a loud fan blowing behind it, obscuring their conversation.

"Explain," she said, hand on her hip, leaving him momentarily distracted.

Marcus knew he was in big trouble, but that seemed less important than the fact that he was alone with Perez, away from the bridge. A subtle trace of her perfume, sharp yet faintly sweet, reached his nose and it was intoxicating.

"Ummm, oh, I'm so sorry ma'am, I know it was wrong, but we are in real danger here, I swear."

She looked confused. "Where did you get this information? Was it made up? You know what happens when the captain finds out. If he finds out I taught you how to change these messages, both of us will be in serious trouble."

He tried to remember everything she was saying, but she was talking quickly, and her skin was so... perfect.

"Ah, I didn't make it up, a friend sent that to me, and I knew if I tried to bring it up, they would laugh me off the bridge." He solemnly put his hand on his heart. "I would never tell them you showed me how to edit messages, they would have to torture me."

She looked at him earnestly. "Marcus. I appreciate that, and just so you know, I would have believed you." Marcus's world stopped when she said his first name.

"Tell me where you got the information and maybe I can soften the blow. I've known the captain since the Academy, and if we can verify it, maybe we can limit the damage to a slap on the wrist."

Marcus sighed. "From a friend. I called him when we got our orders for the belt. I think he knows someone in Fleet Intel, and believe me, he doesn't have the brains to fake that kind of report. That, and..."

She looked at him as he paused. "And? What, Marcus?"

He finally decided to come clean. "I get these feelings," He said in a rush. "These hunches or whatever you want to call them. My grandmother was convinced it was a gift from, you know, from god or something, but I..." He knew he was rambling and decided just to cut to the chase. "I can tell when something bad is going to happen." He winced and waited for her to laugh in his face, but that never happened.

When he had the nerve to look at her, she was deep in thought.

"My mother called it *pressentimento*," she said softly, looking him in the eyes. "One of my cousins had it too."

Marcus stood frozen, struggling to find words. She believed him. And she knew someone else like him. All this time, he had been alone with this burden, marked as a freak, feared and resented. Now, for the first time, someone understood... She understood.

Perez paused for several long minutes, chewing her thumbnail, obviously contemplating her next move. She brought up her wrist and tapped her PDD.

Marcus couldn't hear the other side of the conversation, but he quickly figured out she was calling the captain.

"Sorry to bother you, sir, I know you're trying to get something to eat, but I reached out to one of my friends at fleet HQ and she's been getting some strange reports from this area as well. Nothing concrete, but I thought you should know. Okay, thank you, sir."

She cut the connection. "Okay, we'll wait to see what happens." Pointing a perfect slender finger at him, she spoke seriously. "Don't make me regret this." Perez pondered something else. "I want you to come up to the bridge just before we leave slip. If you get another one of your feelings, come to my station and tell me you have a message from ops, that should give us enough time. I'm not sure what to do, but I'll think of something." She turned and started to walk away before stopping. "I'll have to tell the captain eventually, you know."

He sighed. "Yeah."

CHAPTER 9

Three hundred and seventy million miles from Earth, a blurred smear and spike of ultraviolet light heralded the arrival of the ISA Destroyer *Rio de Janeiro*.

Her captain Rafael Santos altered his planned course and brought the ship in high above the orbital plane of the solar system to give them a little breathing room in case someone was lying in wait.

Whatever they were facing, be it communications problems, pirates, or just bad luck, they had a job to do, and Santos would see it done quickly. A quick, clean resolution might also strengthen his case for the open XO spot on the cruiser *Bogotá*.

The buzz of conversations on the bridge picked up for a moment as all departments reported in.

Each station was manned with *Rio*'s most senior and experienced officers, who went about their duties with practiced ease. The executive officer, a stout man named Stratton, sounded the all-clear. "AI reports nothing on the scopes, Captain. Detailed analysis is still coming in, but I think we're clear. Engine room reporting slip field generator shutdown. Reactors idling at forty percent."

The captain sat at his station near the center of the small bridge. The *Rio* was an older destroyer and lacked some of the creature comforts of the newer models, but he liked being right on top of the other officers, especially at times like this. "Thank you, Commander, all ahead 1/3. Coms, are we picking up any beacons?"

Lieutenant Commander Perez was already running through several diagnostics. "Negative, Captain, no beacons, I'm checking the array now."

Santos sat nervously shifting in his chair from time to time as all available information was gathered and processed by the onboard systems. He stared at the large primary viewscreen affixed to the wall at the front of the bridge. Whatever information was gathered by the sensors would be displayed there, but for now, all the contacts were grey, shown as low confidence echoes or sensor shadows. Waiting was always the hardest part for him. Information gave him the power to make decisions, and right now he felt powerless.

Just as he was about to ask for a status, Lieutenant Singh, the navigation and sensor officer sitting to his left, called out, "Captain, I have something on the scopes bearing two-eight-five, minus seven five, thirty-seven hundred kilometers. Computer reports a high confidence debris field."

The captain saw the contact appear as a solid outline on the bridge screen at the same time. He touched the alert on his chair display, bringing up the field. The AI classified the material composition as steel. Definitely manmade and from the size and total mass of the fragments, it was probably a ship.

"Anything lurking out there?" he called out.

"Negative, Captain, nothing showing on active or passive scans," Commander Stratton replied.

Santos nodded. "Very well, bring us in slow, I want to get an analysis on the debris. If it is a ship, I want to know which one."

The *Rio* changed course, pitching down and to the left, as the thrum of the maneuvering engines could be felt in the deck plates.

Lieutenant Commander Perez sat intently scanning every frequency for any signs of communication. When she couldn't locate any of the navigation beacons, she brought up the raw data showing the frequency patterns from each main array and was struck by just how quiet it was.

She glanced over her shoulder at the back door to the bridge and caught the eye of Ensign Batista, who had just arrived. He shrugged and shook his head, indicating that he wasn't feeling anything, so she turned back to her console and ran one more check on the array, increasing the sensitivity to maximum. This wouldn't have been possible anywhere near other ships, as the powered signals might damage the equipment, but it was still dead silent.

The *Rio* closed within a thousand kilometers of the debris, and the ship's scanners started to resolve a clearer picture. A cloud of metal fragments, some recognizable and some not, were displayed on the main screen. The AI systems automatically matched them to parts of a Vanguard class ISA patrol craft. The small, short range patrol ships were manned by close to a hundred crew and weighed in at about a thousand tons.

"Mr. Singh, what do these mass numbers mean? Where's the rest of it?" Santos questioned.

"Working on that, sir, the computers are reporting lower than expected mass on identified parts. No recognizable weapon signatures. AI's best guess is slip drive malfunction, but low confidence. Material fingerprint is showing match to… ISA *Guardian*." Lieutenant Singh's voice momentarily wavered.

Santos nodded, sounding more resolute. "I want detailed scans of the debris. If this was really a slip drive malfunction, then where is the *Sentinel*? Run another full sweep of the area, I want to know where the rest of the ship is. This can't be everything."

It dawned on Lieutenant Commander Perez what was happening with her equipment. "Captain, I think we're being jammed."

Captain Santos swung around in his chair. "Are you sure?"

Perez looked up from her console. "The computer doesn't see it, but I'm not getting anything, no background signals, not even long range nav beacons. Either everything in the system suddenly went dark or they're being blocked somehow."

"Captain, sensors are offline," Commander Stratton said quickly. "Nothing, sir, not even the debris field. They still have power, but nothing at all, no returns."

"Take us to condition Charlie, XO," the captain spoke sternly. A split second later, an alarm sounded around the ship.

Perez keyed her console and made her announcement to the ship's crew. "All hands to duty stations, all hands to duty stations, set condition

Charlie throughout the ship, stand clear of all blast doors and locks. Ready countermeasures and prepare for maneuver." She repeated the announcement again before monitoring the readiness state of each compartment of the ship. As the indicators changed from red to yellow and finally green, she waited for the XO to give the captain the all-clear; if he failed to do so, she would step in.

"Captain, the ship shows ready at condition Charlie," the XO called out a second later.

"Thank you, XO. Mr. Singh, what was the status of the search before we lost sensors?"

At the back of the bridge, Ensign Batista had been quietly watching the events play out. He jumped as the armored door behind him sealed shut automatically when Perez called for condition Charlie. He silently chided himself, as he was now trapped on the bridge. His supervisor would notice he was gone from his duty station soon. Hopefully he would rightly assume that Marcus had gotten trapped on the bridge and wouldn't report him missing.

He still didn't feel anything other than his normal nerves, so he was pretty confident that they weren't in any immediate danger but couldn't be sure.

Minutes ago, he was starting to worry that maybe he was wrong about the whole thing, but when they discovered the destroyed patrol ship, his mindset shifted and started worrying that maybe he was right.

He peeked out from behind the hatch and scanned the room, his eyes landing on the small, windowed ports at the rear of the bridge to the right of where he stood. Those were the hatches to the emergency escape system. Found in various parts of the ship, they served as lifeboats in the event of an emergency. You could seal yourself into one and the craft would automatically blow the outer doors and fire escape thrusters, moving you away from the ship.

He kept trying to remember his training on how to activate the pods but couldn't quite focus. He wanted to run to Perez and drag her to one of the capsules right now....

"Oh god," he said out loud, realizing that his heart was now nearly pounding out of his chest. A feeling of dread and doom washed over him. Before he could consciously react, he was walking across the bridge.

Perez noticed someone approaching her station and looked up. Ensign Batista hovered over her with a panicked look on his face. He opened his mouth but didn't say anything. She knew right away he had sensed something was happening.

"Thank you for the message, Ensign," she said aloud. "Please wait at the back of the bridge, I may need your assistance." He didn't move right away, so she stood up, gently pushing him toward the back. She then quickly moved to the captain's chair.

"Captain, we need to get out of here," she said in a low but urgent voice.

Captain Santos looked confused. "What? Why?"

She glanced over toward Marcus, who was looking toward the starboard side of the ship and slowly backing away as if he'd heard a wild animal. Thankfully, nobody else on the bridge seemed to notice his odd behavior.

"Captain," she said, putting her hand on his arm, something she would never do while she was on duty. "We need to move the ship now; we are in danger." He looked confused, but something in her eyes made him react.

Santos knew he wasn't particularly skilled when it came to ship-to-ship combat, having been promoted mostly due to his familial connections, but he'd learned long ago that listening to the people he trusted helped him survive in the cutthroat political arena. Here maybe it was even more important, and Perez had his implicit trust.

"Get back to your station, Yara." He motioned towards her seat, then spoke loudly. "XO, sound the maneuver alarm, we're getting out of here."

As the new alarm sounded, Perez hurried Marcus to one of the empty observation chairs at the rear of the bridge. He was wild-eyed, but when she touched him, he calmed down and followed her instructions, buckling into the seat. She made it back and strapped herself in just as they started moving. The pseudo gravity systems were at maximum, but she could feel the ship accelerating faster than it could keep up. More and more g-forces were leaking through.

Several seconds into the acceleration, a bright flash dimmed the viewscreen, and alarms started to sound.

Santos yelled over the blaring sound, "Evasive maneuvers! XO sound general quarters…someone kill the bridge alarm."

Lieutenant Singh called out, "AI has the helm and is maneuvering."

The ship pitched up and rolled while the XO tapped his panel furiously, looking up in shock.

"Captain, looks like we took a hit, no source, no bearing."

The alarm went silent, and there was a low groan from the structure as the ship continued to twist and turn.

"Our starboard sensors are showing red. External cameras on that side aren't functioning either; the mast may have been damaged."

Lieutenant Singh, who sat forward of the captain to the left, called out, "Logs showed cascading failures of the starboard array before they went dead. We're also starting to see a slow pressure loss along several spaces near the mast. AI is still chewing on the data."

The captain nodded, contemplating for a precious few seconds.

"Where's my target, Mr. Stratton?" he said, gripping the arms of his chair, trying to wrap his head around the tactical picture. He could see the zigzagging course the AI had plotted, and a large red zone marking where the shot might have come from.

At the back of the bridge, Marcus's brain was in a fog. He wasn't sure how, but he was strapped into a chair. Holding his breath and bearing down seemed to clear his thoughts for a moment, allowing him to focus. He could see the members of the bridge furiously trying to locate the threat. He took a gulping breath and held it for as long as he could, feeling that whatever attacked them was still out there, like a big cat prowling in the darkness just beyond the light of the fire.

It was there, and it was terrifying.

He sensed that if he slipped up, made just one mistake, it would pounce and kill them all. Unbidden, he swung his head up and to the right toward the danger, a small yelp escaping his lips as he cowered in his seat.

Nearby, Lieutenant Commander Perez, who was relaying messages to the bridge from one of the damage control parties, heard the sound and glanced over at Marcus. She followed his eyeline, momentarily confused by what he was looking at.

Then it hit her—he was looking toward the danger. "Captain! Target bearing… zero-three-zero, plus four five."

The captain looked confused. "Explain, coms…" he started to speak when the display screen flashed white, followed by an ominous rumble in the deck plates. Alarms started a renewed wail, and the lights dimmed on the bridge momentarily. Everyone could feel the ship lose maneuvering power as the random motions all but ceased and the rumble of the engines and thrusters noticeably decreased.

"We've lost main propulsion; maneuvering thrusters are still responding but degraded," Singh said.

"We've lost sensors aft of frame 130… I think the entire section has decompressed!" his XO reported.

A representation of the ship flashed up on the captain's screen, showing a large flashing red area stretching from around the middle of the ship back to nearly the engine compartment at the rear.

"I need more information, XO, what the hell hit us?"

The XO shook his head and looked dumbfounded. "I still have nothing on active or passive sensors. The only thing the AI is reporting was a surge in photons and heat a millisecond before the hit." He paused, looking worried. "I don't know, Captain."

Santos could feel panic rising in his stomach. "Coms, you saw a bandit right before we were hit, explain yourself."

Perez turned, looking back at Marcus, his head lolling around like he'd been punched. "I can't explain it right now, but I think Ensign Batista can… sense them before they fire."

Captain Santos turned his chair to look back at the young ensign, who returned his gaze slowly. His red-rimmed eyes were wild, catching flashes of light from the indicators around the bridge.

He then looked to his left straight at the bulkhead and tore at his restraints, teeth bared like a wild animal. Perez also noticed and yelled something to him. He turned towards her as she pointed in the same direction.

"Captain, bandit nine o'clock!" she repeated.

"Main propulsion is back online!" the XO said, pulling his attention back into focus.

"Ahead flank! Emergency topside thrusters, get us the hell out of here, Mr. Stratton," the captain said, his voice nearly cracking.

The ship bucked forward immediately while the topside thrusters pushed the ship downward, its superstructure groaning under the huge loads imparted by the emergency burn. All thrusters were firing wide open, well past their safe design tolerances, dumping tons of specialized propellant into their chambers.

"Put us in slip, random heading!" the captain yelled over the waterfall-like rumble of the engines and thrusters firing full out. It was a risky move, going into slip blind, but Santos knew they didn't have a chance against this unknown enemy. He was fighting with both hands tied behind his back.

The reactors spooled up and the slip drive fields started to form as the hair on the back of his neck stood up. The screen pulsed a white light again, signaling the now familiar signature of the enemy weapon.

"Near miss!" the XO called out triumphantly "AI estimates a track now based on the new readings… bandit bearing two one zero, plus three seven, no range, but based on early data, best guess is two hundred kilometers plus or minus."

The captain's eyes widened. "Two hundred! He's right on top of us—full countermeasures, continue evasive."

The ship was gyrating wildly as the computers pushed the ship in random directions while the large main engines burned a line through space. Active and passive countermeasures fired from multiple launchers along the sides of the ship, providing a screen of electronic noise and physical objects in an attempt to fool the enemy's sensors.

"Full spread of missiles, XO, and have another volley in the tubes ready on my mark."

The XO looked toward the captain. "Sir, we don't have a solution, still no reading on the bandit."

"Best guess, XO… he doesn't know we can't see him; just send them in his direction and give us some breathing room. How long till slip?"

The XO sent the firing plan to the tactical officer, then switched his attention to the quantum drive projections. Thumps sounded from somewhere behind them as missiles leapt from their launchers. The bridge screen showed a split tactical view with all available sensor data, now including a flight of twelve small missiles heading quickly behind them.

"Approximately ten seconds to slip, the computer is recalculating based on the new maneuver package. Weapons are away and tubes are reloading, chaff and flares deployed, decoys are offline."

The captain cursed his luck; one of the best countermeasures they had was a rack of decoys—small powered buoys that emitted an identical electromagnetic and thermal signature to the ship.

Onscreen, clouds of chaff were being emitted behind the *Rio*, the metalized strips of polymer shooting out much like large bullets from launchers. Volatile binders vaporized at a predetermined distance, shedding the strips in a cloud, which could confuse missiles and attenuate laser-based weapons.

"Five seconds," the XO said while flares fired in sequential streams on either side of the stern. The hot burning rockets flew in random directions, spewing a mixture of elements meant to mimic the ship's thrusters.

"Four, three, two, one, slip drive engaging," the navigator said. The quantum fields fully enveloped the ship just as Marcus let out a primal scream. A sudden wrenching threw the crew sideways as chaos engulfed the bridge. Sparks flew as several of the high-power lines criss-crossing the space overloaded and exploded. The XO's harness failed, sending him tumbling end over end through the air before smashing into the nearby bulkhead with deadly force. The lights flickered for several moments before the bridge went completely dark.

*

"So let me get this straight," David said, looking around the bridge of the *Cosmic Explorer*. "There are two different AI cores on this ship?"

Ryan nodded. "Yep, wild, isn't it?" David looked at Anna, who didn't seem to understand the significance.

"Wild isn't the half of it Ryan, do you know how much it would cost to put two full AI cores on one ship? I know you don't, so stop nodding."

Ryan immediately stopped nodding and asked aloud, "Aurora, how much does your AI core cost?"

Aurora spoke, startling both David and Anna. They whirled around, trying to pinpoint where the voice was coming from. "I am not at liberty to discuss costs associated with this project, Mr. Anders. For access to this information, you would need command clearance."

Ryan looked around at his friends expectantly. "Cool, right? Piped right into the old noggin," he said, tapping the side of his skull.

David regained his composure. "Mr. Anders?"

"Lieutenant Junior Grade Anders was getting annoying."

David rolled his eyes and continued. "Anyway… it would cost like a billion dollars each. I bet the cores cost more than this ship."

"Even patrol ships have AI," Anna said, running her finger down one of the panels, noticing just how nicely the ship was constructed.

David sat down at the navigator position. "Not the same. Other ships have assistant level AI. They do things like balance the reactors, run the slip drives, even help route coms, but these…" He motioned around the bridge at nothing in particular. "Full general AI, and two of them? One could probably run a ship even without a crew. Two? Well, I'm not sure why they would even put two in… redundancy, maybe?"

"We don't know if it's two full AI," Ryan said aloud before lowering his voice. "Valkyrie might be… less."

David looked up before addressing the ship. "Um, Aurora?"

"How can I help you, Ensign Kim?"

He thought for a second before continuing. "Hi. Uh, why are there two discrete AI cores on this ship? Wouldn't one be enough to run all the connected systems?"

Valkyrie's strange voice answered back startling him, "No information about special projects may be accessed."

Ryan looked at David. "See what I mean? Anyway, from what Aurora told me, her mission is to do research or something. Maybe Val runs everything else."

"Val? You already gave it a nickname?" Anna said.

David ignored the banter; instead, he tapped the screen in front of him and it came alive. "Whoopsie," he said with a little giggle. It had a red band around the perimeter, signifying that it was locked, but David could tell it was fast. He couldn't remember seeing a higher quality monitor outside a tech show. Anna had the same idea and plopped herself down at the tactical station.

"Wow, this is amazing," she said, touching the controls. "Can you imagine—"

An alarm started to sound, startling the three of them. "I didn't touch anything," Anna cried, jumping up and looking around.

Aurora spoke. "A fleetwide alert has been issued. Ensigns Kim and Rodriguez will have to depart the ship."

Ryan held up his hands. "Whoa, what alert? Why do they have to leave?" It was Valkyrie that answered back.

"Unauthorized personnel are not allowed on ISA craft during heightened levels of readiness. Please remove the unauthorized personnel from the ship. Noncompliance will be noted."

Aurora then spoke, "Apologies, Mr. Anders, a fleetwide alert was issued raising the readiness condition to Bravo. No further information was made available."

Ryan thought hard for a second, trying to remember what Condition Bravo meant before David helpfully filled in the blanks in his particular way.

"According to fleet regs, Condition Bravo means they need to close down unnecessary access to ships in port and set increased security watches. While underway, they wake the captain and all senior members of the crew." He looked quite pleased with himself as he finished.

"Thanks, Dave. Guess you two better get going before… it gets upset."

Ryan waited for Valkyrie to say something, but when it kept quiet, he just shrugged. "Keep in touch, guys, I don't know what's going on, but I'd feel better if you two were close." They nodded and headed out the back of the bridge.

"Ryan, don't play with that AI too much, you might go blind," Anna said with a smile before they stepped out.

The two made their way across the outer hatch into the gangway just as a group of five armed security officers stepped off the elevator. Dressed in black tactical gear and wearing helmets, they had patches signifying they were assigned to the Forge. At the front strode a compact but commanding woman, around 5'6", with the energy of someone used to giving orders and expecting they be followed. Her dark chestnut hair was pulled into a tight ponytail, just visible beneath the back of her helmet.

Armed with submachine guns and pistols, they passed by the two ensigns without acknowledging them, finally taking up stations around the hatch to the *Explorer*.

Anna and David stepped onto the elevator, watching the soldiers until the doors closed.

The team leader touched the coms panel inside the inner hatch, which buzzed several times before they received an answer.

"Hey, you must be Sergeant Martinez. The ship just told me you were coming."

The sergeant looked at her PDD and saw she was speaking to the watch stander, Lieutenant Junior Grade Ryan Anders.

"Yes, sir, I have my men posted at both access points to the ship to provide security. I'll be here at the personnel gangway if you need anything."

The young lieutenant seemed a little unsure of himself. "Uhhh, okay, well, thanks, Sergeant, I'll be here." The line went dead.

"Take a seat, guys, you know the drill," Martinez told her four teammates.

She leaned against the inner bulkhead and started fishing for information about the alert on the Forge message boards.

Her unit, called a Special Reaction Team, had pulled the short straw and was the only one on duty during the launching ceremony. The team was kept on ready status whenever high-profile dignitaries were on the station just in case they needed to evacuate, but their primary focus was high-risk law enforcement actions. The Forge employed nearly nine thousand civilian workers in manufacturing, shipbuilding, and station operations. This was in addition to the nearly three thousand military personnel working in the ISA headquarters on the lower decks. As with any large community, there was money to be made in all manner of illicit activities.

Which was why pulling guard duty on a ship in drydock came as somewhat of a surprise to her. After about twenty fruitless minutes of searching, she closed down her PDD in frustration, not finding a single entry on the boards.

"What's up, Sarge?" Corporal Johnson, her second in command, said, stretching his arms behind him and repositioning his plate carrier, which covered his chest. At twenty-five, Johnson was on the young side, his dark skin glistening with a sheen of sweat as he adjusted the straps, but he was sharp and one of the best tech specialists on the Forge.

She unbuckled her helmet and slid it off, smoothing her hair with the other gloved hand before setting it back on her head. "Pulling guard duty seem kind of strange to you, Johnson?"

He gave her a huge toothy grin. "I just figured you pissed off Colonel Gill and got us some extra special duty." The other three behind him laughed.

"Funny, Malik, maybe you want some extra, extra special duty," she said in her best team leader voice. He hammed it up even more, pretending to fend off an imaginary blow.

Her PDD chimed an alert into her earpiece, drawing her attention to the wrist mounted screen that showed the priority message. She keyed the private team channel so the two members at the rear cargo ramp could hear her.

"Okay, guys, listen up. Looks like they're cutting the party short for the ambassadors."

She let her arm drop. "Johnson, head down to the Dome, Ace and the rookie will meet you there. Chico will stay on station at the cargo ramp." A double-click on the com channel signified that Chico understood his assignment.

"Ambassador Omandi wants to wait in his quarters till his ship is ready to head back to Mars, make sure he gets there in one piece."

Johnson, now deadly serious, nodded. "Roger that."

"Lata, Cooper, you're with me. We'll escort Ambassador Stanton to his shuttle standing by in bay five. Nguyen, hold down the fort till we get back."

Nguyen, a large brick of a man, nodded, turning toward the gangway cradling his oversized assault shotgun.

"Okay, let's move," she said, leading the way to the elevator at a jog. "Remember, they're ours till they're safe—no mistakes."

A chorus of clicks responded back.

CHAPTER 10

T he party inside the Dome was in full swing. After some dry opening remarks, the presenter invited the captains of its largest most powerful vessels up to the stage. Three senior captains stood from their tables and gave a small wave to the crowd, slowly walking past the diplomats and political elites to stand by the presenter.

On cue, a formation of battleships passed across the view of the impressive dome. Flying behind the *Cosmic Explorer*, they appeared near the bottom of the window and crossing diagonally up and over the top of the station.

The lead ship, the ISA *Columbia*, seemed incredibly close to the station, eliciting gasps from the crowd. Originally christened the NAF *Columbia*, she was the first battleship ever created in space, back when the Forge was a fraction of its current size. Later, after the OSC was signed, she served as the template for every other battleship that followed.

Columbia represented the North American Federation and was emblazoned in the red, white, blue, and green colors of its members, painted in stripes across the bow of the ship. The three ships that followed her, the *Seoul*, the *Buenos Aires*, and the *Yangtze*, represented their own countries or political unions. They formed an echelon close behind the Columbia, firing tons of colored flares into space, making an impressive spectacle. It was a truly awe-inspiring sight and represented the bulk of the ISA Fleet's firepower. The only battleship not present at the celebration was the *Britannia*, which was orbiting near Mars, guarding the red planet. Since Mars had officially signed the OSC, their own ship *Olympus Mons* was in the early stages of construction on the far side of the Forge from where the *Explorer* was berthed.

Elizabeth Miller watched the flyby from her table, making a mental note that the captain of the *Columbia* wasn't at the celebration. She'd been chatting with her tablemates off and on for the last hour, nursing her drinks and having a terrible time. She absolutely hated these types of social events but was aware that nobody got command in the ISA by just being good at her job, and nobody got to a real position of power without being able to fake their way through endless parties like this one.

She realized that her tablemate Lieutenant Jameson was speaking to her.

"I'm so sorry, Emma, what did you say? The flyby was spectacular, don't you think?"

Giving a polite nod, Jameson covertly motioned to a slender woman in a simple black dress a few tables over. She was maybe twenty-five with a chic brunette pixie cut.

"That's June Armstrong," she said in a conspiratorial tone, just loud enough for her to hear over the background conversation and clinking silverware.

"She was assigned a very cushy spot on the *Explorer*. Her grandfather is the captain of the *Columbia*, you know."

Elizabeth feigned surprise but knew exactly who she was. "Oh... I see. I'll have to make an excuse to talk to her." She smiled as the other woman giggled, taking a sip of her drink.

Unbeknownst to the lieutenant, Elizabeth had a contact in security who alerted her the moment June arrived on the station. Excusing herself, she set a folded napkin neatly on the chair and rose, her head throbbing from nearly an hour of idle chatter.

She crossed the room toward the bar, weaving between the tables. The faces she passed weren't all strangers. Some she greeted with a polite nod, others with a faint, knowing smile, each acknowledgment was calculated, a reminder that she remembered them... and that they should remember her.

A small crowd gathered in front of the bar even with the presentation still going on stage. There seemed to be more people here than at the tables, making it difficult to navigate.

"God, this party is the worst," a woman next to her said, putting a clutch under her arm. Elizabeth cringed at the thought of making small talk, but when she glanced over, it was none other than June Armstrong.

She put on her best smile. "You're telling me. If I have to endure one more conversation about budget forecasts or interplanetary tariffs, I might excuse myself into orbit."

The bartender finally glanced their way but addressed only one of them. "What can I get you, ma'am?"

Elizabeth's practiced smile didn't so much as twitch, but inwardly she burned at the snub.

"I'll take one of the Cosmics," June said, ordering the sparkling, violet-hued drink named in honor of the ship.

Elizabeth resisted the urge to roll her eyes. "Oh, me too, they're so good," she said, faking an enthusiasm she certainly didn't feel.

June turned to her, her pale amber eyes flashing in the light. "Everyone says they're too sweet, but I love them," she said, offering a hand. "Hi, I'm June."

Elizabeth shook her hand, a little off balance since she expected June to drop her very well-known last name like a bomb.

"Elizabeth," she replied in kind, still smiling. "So, what do you do around here, June? I don't think I've seen you before."

June grabbed the first drink the bartender served and passed it to Elizabeth. "I just came aboard the station; I'm assigned to the *Cosmic Explorer*."

Elizabeth took the drink, still feeling off balance. "Oh, thank you. Uh, the *Explorer*, really? Me too."

June lit up. "I'm working on the bridge, assigned to communications. What about you?" Elizabeth waited a moment for June to get her drink and held up her glass. After they clinked the glasses together and took their first drink, she answered.

"Me too, I'm working the third watch, but I'm hoping for weapons if the opportunity arises."

She waited for June to turn her nose up at the mention of third watch, as it wasn't the most glamorous posting to say the least, but once again she was taken aback as June lit up with a huge smile.

"Elizabeth! We should hang out. I was getting so worried that I didn't know anyone on the crew, but now…" She held up her glass, and Elizabeth returned the gesture. "Now I have a friend!"

Elizabeth drank, feeling conflicted. June actually seemed like a decent person and not the nepo baby she expected. She hadn't mentioned her political connections once and incredibly gave Elizabeth her drink first, which wasn't something she would have predicted, or something she herself would have done. Regardless, she decided to play her cards close to the vest with the woman, as June's wholesome demeanor could all just be a facade to gauge Elizabeth's intentions.

She smiled big. "June, I have an idea! Have you gotten your room assignment yet?" June grinned back as they both started tapping at their PDDs, comparing notes, but before they got very far, a group of armed soldiers dressed in black tactical gear marched into the room.

A murmur ran through the crowd, drawing their attention as they made their way to the VIP tables near the stage. Elizabeth switched gears and checked PDD for alerts but didn't see any news on the Forge network.

"Oh, they're taking the ambassadors," June said, standing on her tiptoes and craning her neck to see around the crowd. They both watched as the Earth Ambassador and his staff were escorted out of the gathering followed by another group surrounding the Martian Ambassador. Elizabeth moved to follow them.

"Where are we going?" June said, taking a sip of her drink. Elizabeth had left hers on the bar, thankfully. The cloyingly sweet drink started to give her an even worse headache.

"I want to see which way they're headed… if they go left, that's the way to the VIP quarters, if they go right, that's toward the shuttle docks."

June looked a bit confused but nodded, watching.

"Ambassador Stanton went right. Omandi went left?" June said, questioning.

Elizabeth was searching her PDD again, speaking offhandedly. "SOP during a threat—get the high-level personnel to safety before announcing it to the masses. Shoot, nothing posted yet."

Staring at the captain's tables, she saw what she was looking for. "There… look." She pointed.

June didn't understand what she was saying at first, but then the three captains all stood, and started to make their way out of the room. As they and their entourages got to the door, a general alarm started to sound.

*

On the bridge of the *Explorer*, Ryan called out over the alarm, "Aurora, what's going on!" He turned when he heard the thunking sound of the blast doors behind the bridge closing.

After several moments, Aurora spoke. "ISA Fleet Command Lunar Space has raised the security level. Valkyrie has placed the ship into alert condition Charlie. Unknown craft have been spotted headed towards this station. ETA twenty-three minutes."

Ryan couldn't believe what he was hearing. The Forge was the headquarters of the ISA Fleet and had the best sensors in the system. A meter-long asteroid couldn't make it past Jupiter's orbit without the extensive surveillance network setting off alarms.

"How fast are they moving? How'd they make it past the sensor net?"

"The ships are traveling at significant speed. It is unknown how they penetrated so far in-system without being detected. The alert was triggered by Lunar optical tracking stations."

Ryan chewed on that bit of information. The incoming ships must have some kind of top-notch electronic warfare capabilities; those tracking stations were designed to detect asteroids, not ships. "Whoever they are, they picked the wrong day to stir up trouble. Half the fleet is out there." He chuckled, thinking about some pirate skiffs slipping into the teeth of the four *Columbia* class battleships. "Well, I guess that means the party is over…" He stood up from the deceptively comfortable captain's chair. "I need to get back to the Forge. Wonder if there's any more of that steak left over." He stretched.

Aurora interrupted his musings. "Mr. Anders, all ISA Fleet personnel are being recalled, but per fleet regulations, your temporary assignment aboard the *Cosmic Explorer* supersedes your normal duty station."

"Great." Ryan plopped back down into the seat.

He tapped his fingers on the arm of the chair before deciding it wasn't all bad. At least he wasn't on the station, where a crisis like this would mean donning a hot pressure suit and leading a damage control team. He tapped the chair's display to life and selected a flashing icon. To his surprise, the information loaded instantly. "Hey, Aurora, what gives? I can get to the alerts."

"Yes, Mr. Anders. Due to the ship being placed in condition Charlie, you've been granted command access automatically as the highest-ranking officer on board."

"Command access?" Ryan smiled wide, then jumped out of his seat, practically running to the rear of the bridge. As he approached the captain's duty cabin, the control turned green, and the door smoothly slid open.

"Ha!" he exclaimed in triumph. He walked through the door into a small but well-appointed cabin. It was about four meters wide and about five meters long with a small desk and chair along one wall, with a couple other chairs and low table arranged nearby. At the rear was a small, overstuffed couch that looked plenty comfy enough for a nap. Along the left side of the room was a built-in refreshment station, mirror, sink, and wardrobe. Curious, he opened the wardrobe and saw an emergency pressure suit hanging within. The suit, designed to protect its wearer from decompression, had a green testing tag banded to its collar. To his surprise, behind the pressure suit was a dress uniform jacket.

The last person to inhabit the cabin must have been a captain from the shipbuilding and testing division of the Forge. "Probably did her space trials," Ryan said, taking off his own formal jacket and putting on the newly found one. It was finely tailored, replete with four gold lace rank stripes topped by a blue star on each sleeve and two rows of gold buttons down the front. He wondered how long the owner had been looking for his jacket.

Ryan straightened up, pulling the jacket down tightly over his shoulders, and posed in the mirror. It was a bit tight across the chest, indicating that it was made for a slimmer man, but otherwise, it was a great fit.

"Not bad!" He nodded to himself.

"Mr. Anders?" a voice behind him nearly made Ryan jump out of his shoes. Whirling around, he saw a soldier dressed in a black combat uniform complete with tactical helmet with a deadly-looking shotgun slung across his chest. The huge man, an Asian American in his mid-twenties, stood just inside the doorway.

"Sir," he said, snapping off a sharp salute. "I was told by the computer that you were in here. My name is Private First Class Nguyen. I'm with the Forge Special Reaction Team."

Ryan blew out a breath "Sorry, PFC...."

He didn't seem fazed by Ryan's lack of recall. "Nguyen, sir, Alex Nguyen. My squad leader told me to ask you if Chico and I could post ourselves inside during the alert."

Ryan cocked his head. "Chico?"

Nguyen thumbed over his shoulder. "Sorry, sir, Private Morales. He was assigned to the cargo hatch. Sergeant Martinez said there was no point guarding a locked meter-thick door from the outside."

Ryan understood, looking vaguely up at the ceiling. "Ah. Sure thing. Ummm, Aurora, can you let Private Morales inside and show him the way to the bridge?" They both waited a few seconds before the reply came back.

"Mr. Anders, Private Morales is on board. I am directing him to the bridge."

Nguyen stretched his bulky frame. "Mind if we wait in the chow hall, sir? I haven't eaten in a while."

Ryan shrugged. "Knock yourselves out, I'll be here." Nguyen saluted and walked away after Ryan returned the gesture. He wondered if all the members of their team were as formal as the private. He also wondered how he knew where the chow hall was or even if it had food.

"Aurora." He peeked out the door to make sure Nguyen wasn't nearby. "Where's the chow hall?"

*

On the bridge of the ISA *Columbia*, Captain Benjamin Armstrong finished wrapping up the flyby and ordered his helmsman to take them back to their assigned parking orbit. The other three battleships did the same, albeit much more slowly. He made a mental note to speak to the captain of the *Seoul* tomorrow as his crew had overshot their assigned position and was slowly maneuvering to correct.

"Damned sloppy," he said under his breath.

The party on the Forge was in full swing, and he debated allowing third shift to debark and join in the fun. Like other ISA vessels, *Columbia* normally had three full shifts of personnel to rotate through each duty station. While one slept, another would be on standby, and the primary would be actively running the ship. It wasn't the most judicious use of manpower, but the fleet found that splitting into three duty rotations per day allowed them to train the maximum number of people on the job, and the rapidly expanding fleet sorely needed bodies.

He had let second shift debark before the flyby, as they were off duty, but cutting the number of people to one shift felt wrong. Just about every other ship was running on fewer than that—mostly skeleton crews, and that rubbed the sailor in him the wrong way. Perhaps, he thought, he was just old-school in his thinking, but then again, he had been in the ISA, and the North American Federation Space Command before that, for the better part of forty years. Hard lessons were not so easy to forget.

"Helm reports secure from maneuver." The call came from his navigator as the hum from the maneuvering engines faded.

"Thank you, Lieutenant. Coms, any update from headquarters on the alert?" His communications specialist tapped the panel and spoke over his shoulder.

"Negative, Captain, we are still at Condition Bravo systemwide." Something flashed onscreen, drawing his attention. He typed in a few commands. "Sir, immediate message traffic from Lunar Command, reads: *All ISA vessels, alert, incoming unknown ships have breached the Hotel defense zone and are considered hostile. Stand by further instructions.*"

The captain sat upright in his chair. "Stand by? How the hell did they get past the ARGUS net?" He looked to his executive officer, a younger square-jawed commander named Simpson, who was swiping his screen rapidly.

"Captain, looks like they might be jamming active sensors. Fleet reports optical tracking only. On your screen now." He touched a control that sent the grainy optical images to the captain's display.

Armstrong rubbed his short white beard as he examined the pictures. He could barely recognize the outlines of two or three contacts. The combat AI circled several more with a 60 percent chance of up to five different contacts.

"XO, how do we know these are ships?"

The XO must have had the same question and sent another analysis to his screen. "Fleet says they maneuvered to bypass a small asteroid designated 74KA2 before returning to course. I…. I've sent size estimates to your screen."

Captain Armstrong heard the trepidation in his XO's voice as the course and size estimates popped up on his display. His eyes widened as he read. The largest ship, if it was a ship at all, measured almost four times larger than the *Columbia*. It was gigantic, nearly a kilometer wide if the estimate was to be believed and surrounded by at least four or five other possible vessels each nearly the size of his own ship.

"Battle stations," he called out, catching everyone off guard.

He had worked with most of these men and women for years, and he wasn't disappointed as their training kicked in immediately. The call went out ship wide with only a moment's hesitation, klaxons sounding throughout the vessel. Each station on the bridge was abuzz with activity.

"XO, break orbit and make best speed to intercept." The ship lurched forward as the executive officer relayed the commands to the helmsman before turning to face him, keeping his voice low.

"Captain, we haven't received any orders from fleet yet. Breaking orbit without authorization…"

Captain Armstrong absently stroked his beard, interrupting his second. "XO, where do you think the ISA brass is right now? My guess is that they are running back to headquarters as we speak. At the rate those bandits are closing, they'll be on our doorstep before we get clearance, and the last thing we want to do is trade shots with them right next to the Forge."

Commander Simpson nodded as he processed the captain's words. He was probably right; launch parties were one of the rare occasions that drew nearly all of ISA's top brass. Captain Armstrong had to fight hard not to attend himself and was only granted the dispensation due to his age and proximity to retirement.

"Shouldn't we at least link up with the other battleships first, or our escorts?" he asked, confused by his normally by-the-book captain flying out alone to meet a numerically superior enemy.

Armstrong knew the younger commander had a point. In any other scenario, he would have gathered his screen of smaller destroyers and cruisers before sailing out to meet a threat. A lone capital ship could be swarmed by fighters, missiles, or smaller craft from close range, but he didn't see much choice.

"The same thing applies to the rest of our ships, XO. You saw how long it took the *Seoul* and *Buenos Aires* to return to station. I'd be surprised if they had more than half a duty station on board right now, the only people manning those ships are a handful of officers and enlisted." He stroked his beard again. "If the bandits truly are a threat…" He let the words hang in the air.

The XO rocked back in his seat. He could see now what the captain was so concerned about: while a small crew could pilot a ship with the help of the onboard AI, it could barely fight. It certainly wouldn't be combat effective.

"Aye, Captain," he said gravely, returning to his screen to check their progress.

"Helm, as soon as we are clear of traffic, I want every ounce of speed you can wring out of the fusion drives. Push her to the limits, Mr. Hopper."

As the navigator entered the commands, Armstrong watched the point of intercept recalculate. They were too close to use the slip drive, as the chances of overshooting a moving vessel was too great and they only had one chance. It was the best he could do given the circumstances.

"Tactical, load the 120s with birdshot, we're only going to get one pass at these bandits. Once I call the shot, reload with slugs."

Commander Owens, the tactical officer, called back, "Birdshot on the merge, then slugs, aye." He tapped his control screen, queuing up the needed shells.

The *Columbia* ramped up speed quickly, but it was still too slow for her captain.

"Coms, I know fleet is trying, but I want you to transmit a directional signal to the bandits. Tell them to stand down and heave to or we will fire on them. Repeat on all frequencies as many times as you can."

The XO turned to the captain with a smile as the communications officer called out his affirmative.

"Sir, the *Duma* and *Razorback* are with us." He motioned to the forward viewscreen, which showed the two destroyers moving into formation ahead of the *Columbia*.

Captain Armstrong keyed his com. "*Duma, Razorback*, glad you could join us."

On the viewscreen, two smaller windows near the bottom came to life, showing views of the relatively cramped utilitarian bridges of both destroyers. The *Razorback*, with a young captain sporting a thick mop of blonde hair, answered first with a distinct Southern U.S. drawl.

"Great to sail with you again, Captain. *Razorback* is ready to rock and roll."

The other captain, whom the computer helpfully tagged as being from the African Union, spoke with a thick Kenyan accent.

"Captain Armstrong, it is a pleasure to make your acquaintance. The *Duma* and her crew stand ready."

The captain smiled. "Gentleman, please extend my gratitude to your crews. I intend to take the bandits head-on and would appreciate a forward screen to pull away any torpedoes or smaller vessels."

Both captains nodded and simultaneously called out, "Aye aye."

CHAPTER 11

The ship's AI, parsing through all the data sent from the Forge, indicated that the enemy fleet maintained a loose arrangement, holding a straight-line course. To Armstrong, this suggested either an inexperienced commander or one so confident in their superiority that tactical maneuvering seemed unnecessary.

Duma and *Razorback* accelerated ahead to either side of the *Columbia*, the destroyer's engine flares shining brightly behind them until they were just points of light.

The bridge display returned to normal as the other captains signed off. Forward view from the hull cameras expanded back to fill the screen with some at-a-glance tactical information on its borders. Time to intercept ticked away at the bottom.

"XO, do we have returns on the bandits yet?"

"Negative, Captain. Our sensors are still blind. Computers aren't detecting interference, but there's no way this is natural—they have to be using some kind of jamming. Optical is just now getting a basic fix, but the resolution is barely usable."

Armstrong tried to remember the last time he ran drills with active sensors down. Five, maybe ten years ago? Even then, it was a damage control exercise and not a tactical one.

"If we don't pick them up, we'll have to improvise... Ideas?"

The XO was swiping his screen furiously. "Sir, the only entry I could find refers to using the forward LIDAR array for clearing navigational hazards.

AI estimates that as long as we have external cameras, we can fire weapons with eighty-two percent accuracy, but that's based on stationary or straight-line targets. Factoring in distance and maneuver, it drops to… less than two percent."

Captain Armstrong didn't like those odds. Assuming the enemy could lock on to them, it would be a one-sided fight. Luckily, *Columbia* was designed to take a pounding.

"We'll make do then."

Commander Owens, the tactical officer, swiveled in his chair. "Sir, targets have detected us. They are accelerating and turning to intercept. Time at the merge will be"—he tapped his screen—"five minutes."

"Have they started evasive maneuvering?"

"Negative, sir, they continue on a straight intercept course."

Armstrong felt a glimmer of hope as he reviewed the weapons inventory from his own display, stopping at one particular entry. "XO, load all forward tubes with Hedgehogs, hard set range to target at one point seven nine, maximum yield. Let's give them an old-fashioned barrage."

The XO barked orders to the tactical station, nodding in agreement with the captain's decision. With their sensors compromised, there was no room for elaborate tactics—Hedgehogs were the best option. Typically used against hardened targets, asteroids, or even small planetary bodies, these massive bombardment munitions were propelled by outrageously expensive fusion boosters. Just before impact, they would detonate, unleashing a deadly spread of tungsten-alloy spheres the size of desks. Now, with the enemy on a collision course, the weapons might actually prove effective. The captain had also wisely ignored the proximity fuse and was ordering them to be set to explode at a specific range since there was no guarantee the fuses would pick up the stealthy ships. *Columbia* only carried four of the weapons—they would get exactly one volley.

"Magazines are cycling Hedgehogs into position." He spoke calmly, noting that the shells would be ready only moments before they reached maximum firing range.

One by one, the bridge crew grew quiet as they waited in anticipation. The hum of the air circulators and random chimes emanating from several stations filled in the gaps along with the ever-present low frequency white noise of the main engines.

"Weapons ready," tactical finally called out.

"Nothing from the bandits... no launches, no emissions. Still tracking directly towards us," the XO added.

Captain Armstrong silently watched the range counter tick down. The Hedgehogs were his longest-range weapon, as they were basically autonomous fusion powered craft. His other weapons wouldn't come into effective range for several more minutes.

"Coms, any reply?" He knew the answer before the communications officer said a word.

"Negative, sir, still silent on all channels."

"Computer reporting optical change... they could be opening tubes." The XO's face went slack. "Captain, they—" he started to say something but never finished his sentence.

Ahead of the *Columbia*, a massive explosion bloomed in the black, causing the main viewer to automatically dim as the *Razorback*'s telemetry winked off the screen.

A stunned silence momentarily filled the bridge before everyone snapped back to their duties.

Armstrong knew the ship had been destroyed, but there was little he could do at this distance other than watch and wait. He observed his crew as one by one they came to the same realization. Most had never been in battle, much less witness firsthand the destruction of a vessel.

Surprisingly, it was Commander Owens, the tactical officer, who broke the silence. "*Duma* is coming into weapons range..." His voice cracked before he cleared his throat.

"*Duma* is launching countermeasures; they have torpedoes away. Looks like they emptied the magazine."

Captain Armstrong wondered if the *Duma* had actually attained a target lock or if they were still as blind as he was. He contemplated ordering the other ship to stand down and withdraw, but right now he needed every gun to slow these bastards down.

"Fire tubes one and two," he said as he silently sent out a prayer for the crew of the lost destroyer.

He continued counting down, tapping his armrest to keep time. The huge flares of the first two Hedgehogs flew past the forward cameras, vanishing rapidly into the distance. "Fire three and four." Again, the large torpedoes flew out of view. He felt a pang of regret as he thought of the *Razorback*'s young captain—the son of his wife's best friend, once considered a possible suitor for his own granddaughter.

More time ticked away; his resolve never faltered. "One-twenties, Mr. Simpson, birdshot, full spread."

The massive 120-centimeter guns roared, unleashing what ISA ship crews called buckshot or birdshot, depending on the projectile size. These specialized shells scattered hardened steel spheres into an enemy's path, turning their velocity into a deadly hazard. Birdshot in particular was often used as a missile screen—easily avoidable by any ship with decent sensors but nearly impossible for fast-moving missiles to evade at close range due to their limited ability to maneuver. Armstrong hoped that even if the Hedgehogs missed, they would distract the enemy just long enough to make the birdshot screen inescapable. Damaging missiles, sensors, thrusters, and packing enough punch for a lucky shot to kill a vessel. In ship-to-ship combat, survival often came down to a battle of time, acceleration, and pure luck.

Round after round fired, the ship moving slightly to cover a preprogrammed area wide enough to encompass the flight path of the enemy ships. Finally, the guns went silent.

"Fire control reports full coverage of the enemy's course," the tactical officer reported.

His communications officer solemnly called out the news. "AI confirms, *Razorback* is presumed lost with all hands, no emissions or lifeboat launches detected."

Without warning, the *Duma*, too, erupted into a blinding sphere of light, its existence snuffed out in an instant, leaving only the lingering glow of its destruction against the void.

"Damn," Armstrong said, his voice barely audible above the background hum of the bridge.

*

Anna and David watched as the party around them dissolved the moment the alert sirens blared. Instead of rushing to join the crush of bodies clogging the passageways and elevators leading out of the Dome, they decided to wait it out near the now-abandoned bar. Getting to their duty stations would be impossible until the bottleneck cleared, so they figured a few extra minutes wouldn't hurt.

"What are you two doing?"

Anna glanced up and groaned. "What does it look like, Elizabeth? We're waiting for the crowd to thin out so we can actually get to our stations."

"You need to go. Now." Elizabeth's tone was sharp, her expression tense. "This isn't a joke."

Anna waved her off dismissively. "I'm sure it isn't. Thanks for the concern."

Before Elizabeth could respond, David let out a sharp gasp, cutting the brewing argument short.

"Oh my god."

He grabbed Anna's shoulder and turned her toward the massive dome window.

They all followed his gaze. Far off in the void, a dim speck of light flared violently, becoming momentarily brighter than all the surrounding stars. It expanded in a brilliant orb—then, just as quickly, it vanished into the darkness.

"Was that a ship?" Anna said in disbelief.

Elizabeth and June ran to the window followed closely by Anna and David. The four of them stood, mouths agape as another explosion lit up the same section of space.

The alert changed from a long, low warble to a stuttering triplet, signaling something new. A whooshing sound and bright flash of light caused them to shield their eyes as a half dozen huge missiles leapt from launchers somewhere above them on the station. The missiles boosters pushed them away at incredible velocities.

Anna looked at Elizabeth, who was already on her PDD calling someone, and from this side of the conversation, it didn't sound good.

"Alex, what happened?" She paused, listening. "What, but they... Okay, okay. Good luck."

She terminated the call and looked at the others standing around her. "My contact in the security office says we're under attack. Two destroyers were lost. The *Columbia* is intercepting..." She paused for a split second before continuing. "...alone."

June seemed to shrink, her confidence momentarily deflating. But after a brief pause, she straightened, lifting her chin. "They won't get past *Columbia*... Her captain is the best in the fleet."

Anna and David were confused, but Elizabeth gave a subtle shake of her head.

"Ensign Rodriguez, Ensign Kim, meet June Armstrong, granddaughter of Captain Benjamin Armstrong."

Anna thought it strange that Elizabeth was making introductions until she put two and two together. Her expression softened and she held out her hand, giving it a firm shake.

"Hey, look, one of the other battleships is moving out," David said hopefully.

The others craned their heads to the left to see the huge rear engines of the *Seoul* light up the surrounding area. Several large personnel shuttles seemed to be chasing it down as it started to accelerate. Nearby, space was jammed with swarms of shuttles and small craft trying to get to the many ships stationed nearby.

Elizabeth looked around, seeing that the crowds had died down in the surrounding passages near the Dome.

"You two get to your duty stations. If the Forge comes under attack, the Dome is the last place any of us wants to be."

Everyone nodded in agreement and followed her toward the elevators, only to be surprised when she slipped down a side passageway instead.

"Where are we going?" Anna said, but Elizabeth kept walking, finally coming to a halt in front of a bank of yellow and black striped lockers set into the walls of the passageway.

"We need to take some precautions first." She pulled down a red handle, which popped the cover off the damage control locker.

Inside were several items useful in emergency situations. Breathing masks, flame retardant clothing and hoods, heavy gloves, and emergency pressure suits with helmet mounted lights. She grabbed one of the vacuum sealed pressure suits and ripped open the bag. While she unrolled it, she kicked off her high heels.

"Isn't this a bit premature?" Anna said but followed suit nonetheless. Elizabeth unzipped the back of the suit and stepped into it.

"If we decompress, it will be too late." She tucked her dress into the back of the suit and grabbed the long pull connected to the zipper negotiating it up and over her shoulder to make the seal. The helmet was attached to the neck in a single unit and hung behind her head, allowing her to snap it on in seconds if she needed.

"Anna, help June. I'll try to get an update."

Anna made a face but turned and helped June, who was struggling to open the tightly wrapped suit, her long nails preventing a good grip. In the background, they could hear another volley of missiles roar from the station.

*

Aboard the battleship *Columbia*, Commander Simpson, the executive officer, said a short prayer as the missiles launched from the now-destroyed *Duma* closed in on the enemy contacts.

"Captain, I'm detecting explosions…" he reported, eyes locked on the display. "It looks like *Duma*'s missiles were set on timed detonation."

Armstrong knew the torpedoes didn't stand a great chance of hitting anything due to the extreme range they fired at and the loss of the *Duma*'s active optical tracking, but secretly he hoped for a miracle. His volley of Hedgehogs would soon reach position, and any extra damage to the enemy would be welcome. The main screen changed view automatically as the enemy fleet entered enhanced optical range. What were just blurry blobs now resolved into optically enhanced targets. Still no more than black and white shapes, the captain was glad to finally see his enemy.

"The Forge has launched loitering munitions," the tactical officer said with a tinge of doubt in his voice. The captain waved his hand, acknowledging the report. "Thank you, Commander."

They all knew that without a firm target lock, the missiles would just fly a pre-programmed course until they self-destructed for lack of a target.

"Do we have an ID on the bandits yet, XO?" Armstrong said, absently stroking his beard.

"Negative, sir. No known identification." He tapped a couple keys on his console and a new wireframe picture of the targets constructed by the AI popped up in the lower left corner of the main display. The targets were oddly shaped. More like large, five pointed crystals with the tip of the craft angling back to spikes flared out to the rear. Since the AI couldn't see behind the craft, it was just a flat plane.

Nobody speculated aloud, but Armstrong couldn't help but think they were so... alien, or at least made to look that way. He let out a breath, sitting back into his chair, not quite believing that this might be the way Earth's first contact with an otherworldly species played out.

A vague memory crossed his mind, something he had overheard years ago, back when the ISA was still being formed. He closed his eyes, forcing his shoulders to relax, pushing the immediate chaos aside to make room for the thought. He ran through the events of that day, trying to conjure the feeling of the conversation, the faces of the people speaking, until the words finally came to him.

He remembered a private meeting with his old friend, Admiral Casey. She had repeatedly warned that the fleet needed to be prepared for "unknown forces," like somehow an enemy would appear that could rival the might of Earth's newly unified governments. At the time, he'd assumed she was referring to the Martian Confederation's military buildup. But then she'd slipped and said "alien forces." Now, he wasn't so sure what she had meant.

"Computers report *Duma*'s volley a miss," the XO said, his voice dropping slightly. "Hedgehogs are entering range; they will reach their target in three.... two... one.... Mark—"

In an instant, the space in front of the enemy fleet erupted into a firestorm as the first two Hedgehogs detonated, showering their load in wide cones of hot metal followed seconds later by the final two.

The display compensated for the explosions ramping down the brightness until the ships could be seen once again. This would be the most crucial time, as any deviation by the enemy craft would render the shots ineffective.

"Any change in target aspect?" he said aloud, knowing his XO would tell him the minute it happened, but he was growing impatient.

"Negative, Captain, they're entering the field now."

Flares of light could be seen peppering the enemy craft. More and more sparks lit up the noses of the alien vessels, reaching a white-hot crescendo. The bridge crew exclaimed as one in triumph. Their captain, however, sat stoically, hands gripped into tight fists on the armrests.

"XO?" he said, waiting.

Commander Simpson looked momentarily flustered, eyes darting to his display. "Sorry, sir, stand by."

He consulted the tactical officer before turning back. "Computer reports three enemy ships falling out of formation. Remaining ships are still on course for intercept in thirty seconds."

Armstrong sat upright, forcing a smile.

"Good job, people. Now let's finish this," he said, not wanting to break the mood on the bridge, but a niggling doubt crept into his mind.

He swallowed hard and unfurled his hands, which had started to sweat. In his estimation, a full barrage of Hedgehogs would have decimated the *Columbia* several times over. Even a few hits at this speed would have disabled the great battleship, so the fact that only three of the smaller ships had fallen out of formation meant they must have defensive capabilities well beyond the ISA vessels or had gotten incredibly lucky.

"Slow us down, XO. I want that birdshot to hit them before we get in range. I don't think these fellows are too sharp, so I want continuous fire on the one-twenties with slugs into the merge. Let's see if we can make him flinch."

As the XO confirmed his order, the main centerline guns and every forward secondary turret that had a firing solution started spitting out solid slugs of hardened steel. The smaller guns of the *Columbia*, which didn't have a clear line of sight, targeted the outlying enemy craft.

On the main bridge display, the picture of the enemy was growing clearer, and with it, the strangeness of the craft was becoming apparent. No weapons emplacements, antenna, or engines could be seen on the view... no portals or bays either. The ships were clearly metallic, based on the computer analysis, but human they were not. Thankfully, all the ships, even the biggest ship now had distinct pockmarked craters scattered across their hulls, the worst of which were even venting gas.

Armstrong noticed a peculiar extension below the nose of the largest of the craft. They looked like some sort of spikes or towers. Touching a button on his control panel, he zoomed in closer just as they started to swivel around, moving like insect antenna until one by one, they stopped—pointed directly towards them.

"Evasive maneuvers!" he tried to call out, but *Columbia* wrenched sideways so hard that it threatened to snap his restraints. The lights flickered as he heard a strange sound pinging through the hull of the ship, like rain falling on a metal roof or gravel hitting the wheel wells of his old Ford.

Columbia's guns fell silent.

"Report," he said as the ship recovered, oscillating wildly as the thrusters fought to get the ship back on track.

"Sensors are showing decompression all along the starboard hull, decks twenty through twenty-five, frames three hundred to three-fifty." The XO paused, adding a relieved, "Minimal casualties."

Again, the captain heard the strange sound patter across the hull before the *Columbia* was pushed sideways, this time less intense and at a different angle from the first.

"Decompression starboard lower decks, aft of frame three-fifty. We have coolant leaks in engineering!" the tactical officer called out.

Just then the weapon counters hit zero.

Flares showed again across the hulls of the enemy ships as they encountered the thick cloud of birdshot. One of the smaller vessels at the periphery faltered, and the computer showed it slowly falling out of formation before being hammered by the massive slugs of the main guns and exploding into fragments and bursts of light. A cheer went out from the other members of the bridge once again.

"Merge in ten seconds!" the XO called out.

Captain Armstrong studied the tracks of the three lagging enemy ships about twenty seconds behind the main formation. They were still flying straight on but ever so slowly spreading apart from one another. He decided to split the difference and make his turn late.

The *Columbia* blew past the main enemy fleet, which now only consisted of the largest vessel and one of the smaller ships. He waited.

"Time plus two… plus three…" the XO said. The display now showed the backs of the remaining enemy fleet.

"Hopefully everyone remembered their training," Armstrong thought to himself.

"Sound the deceleration alarm." Pausing a second as the klaxon started to wail, he then added, "Reverse course, full emergency burn!"

The ship groaned as the huge fusion-powered thrusters flipped the ship end over end. Its bow pointed back towards the enemy formation, the large fusion engines flaring to life. A dull roar could be heard on the bridge as everyone was pressed back into their seats.

"Second enemy formation." The XO gasped for air. "Passed."

A low groan could be heard from somewhere deep within the superstructure, alarming Armstrong, who knew every noise the ship had ever made.

"M…main guns," the captain managed to groan out as the g-forces threatened to render him unconscious. The XO blew out his breath several times, gulping air.

"I think… we took… damage to the…."

Alarms started wailing just as the thrust from the main engines ramped down noticeably.

Before Armstrong could ask why they had slowed, the ship abruptly started to veer to starboard, slamming everyone hard into their restraints. Thrusters automatically attempted to compensate, trying in vain to point the ship back towards the original heading to no avail. Explosions ripped through the bowels of the already damaged sections of the ship, causing cascading power failures, taking the remaining thruster and computers offline and plunging them all into spinning darkness.

Captain Armstrong tried to see what was happening but could barely think as they spun violently out of control. His world softened into a grey haze before a calm washed over his body like a wave. His thoughts no longer concentrated on fighting, just on his family.

CHAPTER 12

Located near the bottom of the Forge, the ISA Space Combat Center was in a state of near chaos as the first reports of the *Columbia*'s encounter came in. Inside the huge space, many of the combat information stations had three and sometimes four people milling around them as more and more senior officers who were attending the party made their way down to the control hub.

First, a wave of moans as the smaller ships were destroyed, followed by cheers as the quick one-two punch of the *Columbia* hit home. Everyone in the control room of the Forge knew Captain Armstrong was one of the most experienced tactical minds in the ISA, but when the *Columbia* was sent into a flat spin on the back side of the encounter, the officers were at a loss. No external explosion, missile, or beam were seen by the optical sensors of the Forge. The other battleships were still in various states of readiness, loading their crews by shuttle craft. Only the *Seoul* was moving slowly out to intercept the enemy craft, it being the only other battleship that had more than a bare skeleton crew aboard. The data gathered by the optical tracking stations was being reviewed by ISA intelligence, but answers were not likely to come by the time the ships arrived.

Elizabeth and her three compatriots were slowly making their way down a stairwell, trying to get to their assigned duty station, but crowds of people trying to do the same made it slow going.

"My feet are in a puddle of sweat already," Anna said, looking sideways at Elizabeth, who was leading them down yet another flight of stairs in the poorly ventilated space.

"Would you rather be doing this in five-inch heels?" Elizabeth said, tired of the other woman's complaining as she tried to pick up the pace.

David, for his part, was tiring of the two sniping at each other. He leaned against the wall as they ran into the back of another large group of people jamming the stairwell and noticed everyone was headed the same direction—down. Most of the civilian and military quarters, control rooms, engineering spaces, as well as their duty stations were toward the bottom of the Forge.

"Hey, why don't we just go up?" he said, wiping the sweat from his brow with the back of his gloved hand, his jet-black hair now plastered in clumps across his forehead.

Anna looked around, especially at the plug of humanity that was still flooding into the stairwell below and realized what he meant—there was one place they could wait out the alert.

"The *Explorer*! Great idea, David, let's go," she said, turning on her heel and trudging up the stairs, followed closely by David.

June shrugged, a look of worry still marking her brow as she waited for Elizabeth to make her decision. Finally, after seeing that Anna and David were making quick progress upward, she relented. They quickly passed the doorway leading to the Dome level and made their way up ten more flights before bursting out into a cool passageway somewhere near the construction docks.

A passing trio of maintenance workers dressed in grease-stained coveralls looked at them questioningly before hurrying on to their destination. Nearby, a window looked out towards space, the view partially obscured by one of the *Explorer's* mooring points. A mechanical arm stretched out from a floor above them, looking like a crane that was attached to the side of the ship with massive clamps.

David walked to the window, eyes scanning for any sign of combat near the station. Two of the battleships still hadn't moved from their positions as a dozen shuttles queued up near the docking ports, waiting to offload crewmembers. Smaller warships slipped out of view, heading toward the area where they'd seen the explosions earlier.

June was tapping her PDD in frustration, looking worried as no new updates had been posted.

"Hey, guys," David called to the group, motioning for them to join him.

Anna was the first to the window and craned her neck to the right, face pressed up against the glass like David.

"What are we looking at?" she said, noticing nothing.

A flash of light lit up the side of the structure in that direction, then another. As the four of them tried to see what was going on, one of the battleships started to move, then the second, nearly running down a shuttle that was frantically moving out of its way.

"Well, that's rather foreboding," Elizabeth said, her breath fogging the glass. A new alarm none of them had ever heard outside drills started to sound, low and fast.

"Shit, collision alarm!" David said. More flashes lit up the scaffolding of the Forge until they heard a low stuttering sound like a jackhammer far off in the distance. The window lit up in a blinding white light, causing everyone to squint. Elizabeth blinked rapidly, trying to clear her vision when the entire structure of the Forge slipped sideways a few centimeters, causing them all to instinctively reach out to steady themselves. Anna found herself on the floor.

"Ow! What the hell."

Outside, a shower of large debris wheeled across the docks in front of the stunned group, hitting scaffolding and creating sparks as several impacted to their left with loud clangs.

The maintenance workers who passed by earlier came running down the hallway toward them yelling, but the three were screaming over each other, so nobody could make out what they were saying. Anna and Elizabeth noticed a subtle change at first, before David and June both held their hands to their ears, jaws working back and forth.

As the workers, red-faced and puffing from their run, approached at full speed, the strip of green light over the door to the stairwell turned red. The three stumbled to a stop a few feet later cursing and out of breath.

"Come on, lady, didn't you hear us?" one of the workers with a bushy mustache said, hands on his knees, puffing.

Elizabeth choose to ignore him, turning back to the window. June spoke up, still trying to equalize pressure in her ears.

"We couldn't hear you; everyone was screaming at once."

Another worker with stained hands answered. "The door to the stairwell… we're all trapped here now." He panted.

Anna spun around. "What? Why?" she said, looking at the red indicator over the door.

The first man spoke again. "Pressure loss somewhere, this floor is locked down."

Seeing Anna's concerned look, he added, "We should be safe. We just need to sit tight till the alert is over."

Elizabeth wheeled from the window and walked toward the stairwell. "We don't have that much time. We need to get to the *Explorer*… now." She pointed out the window, drawing their attention to the debris spinning wildly outside.

The two men who spoke looked concerned but dismissed it out of hand. "Lady, that isn't going to happen. These doors are controlled by central. There is no way we are getting out of here till they let us."

The third man, Anna noticed, was several years younger than the others. His disheveled brown hair and the streaks of greyish dust on his face gave him a scrappy, unpolished look. But it was the expression that caught her eye— one she knew all too well. It was the same look she wore whenever an officer was talking out of his ass.

A rumble shook the station. Strong enough that even the stoic maintenance men couldn't hide their concern, it spurred Anna to speak.

"What's your name?" she said, eliciting a shy grin from the man.

"Steve, ma'am."

"Steve, did you have something to add?" He looked at his two compatriots before returning to glance at Anna.

"Actually, ma'am, I was thinking that the doors could be opened using a maintenance override. We just need a twenty-three BN... uh, that's a piece of test equipment."

The first man spoke up. "Yeah, sure, and get us all fired for doing it during an active lockdown—keep that shit to yourself, kid."

Elizabeth walked to the man who was clearly the most senior of the three. "Listen, Mister Leblanc," she said noticing his name tag, her accent tightening into something cool and authoritative. "My name is Lieutenant Miller, I'm assigned to the *Cosmic Explorer* as well as Ensign Armstrong here." She dropped the name, watching him come to the realization about whom June was probably related to.

"We have classified information that needs to get to its captain. I can't share the details of course, but it has to do with what's going on out there," she lied, motioning to the window.

"Now, you can either help us reach the *Explorer*, or I'll be forced to report this lack of cooperation to the Logistics Division chief... a Mr. Brenner, wasn't it?"

She gave him a tight, expectant smile.

"Your decision, of course."

Anna watched the exchange and saw the man's face drop at the mention of whoever this Brenner person was.

"Uh, yes, ma'am, er, Lieutenant," he muttered, clearly not thrilled. Turning to the other two workers, he snapped out orders. "You check the nearest supply locker, see if there's a twenty-three BN lying around. Steve, go check that damage control locker, see if they have a crowbar, maybe we can force this thing open." He stalked off down the hall, cursing under his breath, as the other two went through the nearest door.

Elizabeth turned back toward the window while the others looked on.

"Forgot to mention this classified information to us," Anna said dryly.

Elizabeth rounded on Anna. "You still don't understand, do you? That bright light and shaking... that had to be the *Seoul*."

*

In the smoke-filled darkness of the bridge of the *Columbia*, Captain Armstrong slowly regained consciousness. His mind tried to reason out what happened until a fit of coughing wracked his lungs, sending shooting pains down his chest. He unbuckled his safety harness and stood on wobbly legs.

Moans of the other bridge members signaled that they were still alive. A thought came to him as he tapped his PDD, the light nearly blinding him and making his head pound.

"XO," he weakly said before following it up more strongly. "XO, report!" He coughed again, shining his light around the area.

The XO lay nearby with a gash across his forehead that bled down the front of his face. Captain Armstrong moved over to his old friend and checked his pulse. Thankfully it was still there, fast, but there, nonetheless. Several others, lying crumpled on the port side of the bridge, hadn't moved.

"Computer lights," he called out, but everything seemed to be offline.

"Captain," a voice called out from beyond the light of his PDD. "Emergency power is still active. I can hear the air scrubbers." He recognized the tactical officer's voice.

"Owens?" he replied. "Can you get us some light?"

Just then the emergency lighting flickered on with a spark from an overhead panel and the fresh smell of burnt electronics.

The entire ship was probably in the same predicament, he thought, especially those farthest from the axis of spin. He eased himself down in his chair and tapped his display, which thankfully popped to life. Looking at the time, he realized that they had been out of commission for the better part of fifteen minutes.

"Blast it," he said to himself, thinking of the alien fleet heading towards the thousands of people near the Forge, and the billions on the Earth and Moon.

He pulled up the damage control screen.

The Columbia was a mess. A full third of the compartments had decompressed, and much of the structure was damaged. The spine of the ship was still intact but bent, throwing the engines badly out of alignment which had caused the spin. Armstrong's jaw clenched as he skimmed the casualty reports. He forced himself to look away, pushing past the pain in his chest.

Now wasn't the time. The ship had to get back on its feet.

"Captain, medical says they're on the way," the tactical officer said weakly, holding his side.

"Thank you, Mr. Owens." He keyed the panel on his chair several times before it responded. "Engineering? Engineering, report?"

The back door to the bridge creaked open as the med techs used the manual controls to override the seal, cranking it just wide enough to slip through. One of them made a beeline for Armstrong, but he waved her away.

"See to the XO," he said, pointing toward the wounded officer.

"Crewman," he called out to one of the men who was helping widen the opening. The petty officer stepped onto the bridge and hurried over limping.

"Captain?" he said, holding his obviously painful leg.

"I need you to get to engineering, Mr. Tremblay," he said, reading the other man's name embroidered over the pocket of his blue coveralls. "We need power and we need it now. They're probably in worse shape than we are, so take one of the med techs... call the bridge when you get there, I need the chief engineer." He pushed the man into action.

"Sir, the XO is in bad shape." The woman who had tried to treat him was at his side. "He needs immediate attention." The captain looked at his friend laid out on the floor nearby and shook his head.

"Do what you can, Corpsman, but I need you to get as many of the bridge crew functional as you can. Stims, pain meds, whatever you need to do, you got me?" He looked at her seriously. "Those ships are headed to our home... our families. Do you understand?"

The color seemed to drain from her face as she slowly nodded. "Yes, sir." She pulled an injector from her bag and gave the captain a shot in his arm. Immediately Armstrong's vision cleared.

"That will give you maybe twenty minutes before you crash hard, sir," she said, turning his head from side to side, inspecting him. She then rushed to the nearest crewmember, administering a cocktail of stabilizers before sealing a deep wound with a dermal fuser, its emitter hissing softly as the tissue knitted itself shut.

He tried to help where he could, his own pain keeping him from doing much.

"Tremblay to the bridge." His PDD relayed the message as he hobbled back to his chair.

Captain Armstrong tapped the control, relieved. A jittering video stream of the crewman he had sent down popped up onscreen.

"Mr. Tremblay, good work. How is it down there? Have you located the chief?"

"No survivors, Captain. I found some others from third watch on the way down here; they're trying to get the reactors back online."

Armstrong tried to keep his composure. "Very well, Mr. Tremblay, good work."

The primary lights on the bridge came to life along with most of the control stations. On his screen, a familiar face came into frame, but Armstrong couldn't quite remember her name. Her voice was slurred and she had a gash down one side of her cheek and a large bruise on that side of her face as well.

"Captain…" She struggled. "Reactors one and five are cold. Two through four are up and running. I would try to keep them under… eighty percent since we don't know how damaged they are."

She turned away, talking to someone offscreen before walking away shouting something. Armstrong noticed the AI was operating again.

"Computer, status of the drives; can the ship move?"

The computer sluggishly responded.

"Affirmative, Captain Armstrong. Damage control diagnostics report slip drive fully functional. Fusion engines are also functional but operating at reduced capacity. Portside maneuvering thrusters are offline. Starboard docking thrusters are offline. Emergency thrusters are offline. I advise caution using fusion drives, as hull damage has offset the center of thrust."

Armstrong rubbed his beard, eliciting a wince as he read the detailed report. "Weapons status?"

The computer paused before replying. "Main battery autoloaders have sustained heavy damage; secondary batteries are fully functional. Missile batteries are fully functional."

He looked around solemnly, taking in the scene. Several officers were still unconscious and being treated by the medics, and people were trickling onto the bridge: a mix of personnel from second and third watches. Everyone was nursing wounds and looking scared and unsure about what to do.

"Listen up," he called out louder than he should have given the pain he felt. "I know we're all hurting here, and the ship is pretty bashed up. We've lost shipmates, friends." He looked at each of the people on the bridge in turn.

"But we can't stop fighting." He stood, ignoring the pain shooting through his ribs. "Those ships are headed directly to the Forge, directly to our people." He paused, still seeing uncertainty in the faces of his crew. "They gave us a bloody nose for sure, but we just took on five of their ships and we're still here." He straightened his jacket as some of the newly arrived crew nodded in agreement. "Now, I intend to link up with the other battleships and show them what the ISA is really made of."

Several people called out in agreement, lifting the spirits of the others in the process.

"Let's get strapped in. Corpsman, take some volunteers and get the injured to sickbay," he said as they started to move the unconscious people onto stretchers.

"Navigation, glad to see you're with us," he said, not remembering the person sitting at the console who must have been from third watch. "I want you to spin up the slip drive, Lieutenant, make best speed for the second enemy formation. Keep the fusion drives at low power; our back is bent, and I don't feel like another spin."

"Aye, Captain."

"Everyone, buckle up!" he said, fastening himself painfully into his seat. The navigation officer whose arm was tightly wrapped with a sling against her chest tapped a couple controls with her good hand.

"Slip drive is spooling, Captain, fifteen seconds." The familiar sensation started as the hair on the back of Armstrong's neck stood up. The navigator finished her countdown as the ship shuddered unusually but seemed to enter slip without issue.

Armstrong looked at the calculations. Given the last recorded speed of the enemy, they had arrived at the Forge several minutes ago unless they were interdicted en route. He prayed they weren't too late.

"Commander Owens, are you with me?" he called out to the woozy tactical officer who was clipping into his seat.

"Yes… Yes, sir," the man called back, tightening his harness.

He thought hard before he made his next command. "Computer, unlock emergency protocols and load specials in all tubes on my authorization."

The other crewmembers looked at him as the computer chimed its confirmation and the AI's voice spoke into the sudden silence.

"Nuclear ordnance requires dual confirmation." The captain looked at Owens.

"Commander, if you would." When Owens hesitated, he continued. "The XO is unconscious; you are the next highest-ranking member on the bridge."

The officer looked around, then spoke. "I confirm." The computer chimed again, and the border around his screen changed to a red and black crosshatched pattern indicating that live nuclear ordnance was available.

"Thank you, Mr. Owens. When we exit slip, I want a staggered spread from the launchers. Two waves… three seconds apart. Target the enemy ships farthest from our own, understand?"

The tactical officer nodded, his expression resolute. "Yes, sir."

*

Lieutenant Junior Grade Ryan Anders stood, arms crossed, and tapped his chin with his finger while studying the onscreen menu. When he found out that the ship's galley was not only functional but had top-of-the-line food printers, he rushed down to test them out. The two privates who were supposed to be guarding the ship beat him to the punch and sat nearby, wolfing down their second helping of meatloaf.

He grimaced, looking away from the macabre scene; printed meatloaf was literally the worst thing ever. It reminded him of biting into an apple made of undercooked meat. Shuddering, he tapped the display and decided on a good heaping of french fries. As the printer started whirring, the ship's AI voice sounded in his ear.

"Mr. Anders, please report to the bridge." He looked longingly at the printer's timer and then sighed, turning and walking out the door.

"What's going on, Aurora?" he said, walking up a ladder towards the command deck. Valkyrie, the ship's other AI, answered him instead.

"Unknown craft have been intercepted inside the exclusion zone. Please return to the bridge for a full briefing."

Ryan quickened his pace down the passageway from the officers' mess and entered the bridge through the armored doorway at the rear before calling out.

"Aurora?"

The voice of the first AI answered back. "Yes, Mr. Anders?"

Ryan's stomach growled.

"Aurora, I'm getting whiplash from this dual AI back and forth. I'm not sure how this is supposed to work, but can you just answer for the both of... you?" There was a pause before Aurora answered.

"Negative, the combination of functions, while possible, would require ranking command authorization and is not recommended. The separation of function is for the safety of the crew and has been deemed twelve percent more efficient in simulations."

Ryan scoffed. "Oh, twelve percent, why didn't you say that in the first place... Wait, I have command authorization, don't I?"

"Yes, Mr. Anders. You have authorization, but the requested function can only be unlocked by the captain, not provisionally designated personnel."

Ryan plopped into the captain's chair, girding himself before speaking to the testy tactical AI. "Okay, Valkyrie, I'm here."

The AI wasted no time with pleasantries as it outlined the tactical picture unfolding in space, starting with the destruction of the two ISA escort ships and finishing with the *Columbia*'s limited success.

When he saw the estimates of *Columbia*'s rate of spin, his heart dropped, and he wondered if any of them had a chance to survive.

"Jesus, over a hundred Gs…" He breathed. "At that rate, it would have turned everyone to paste."

Valkyrie must have taken it as a question. "Incorrect. Survivability increased exponentially toward the rotational axis."

"The bridge?" he asked.

"Survivability amidships calculated at over eighty-nine percent."

He crossed his arms, stroking his chin.

"I don't get it," he muttered. "Why would Armstrong only take a few escorts? There are still three other battleships out there, plus a flotilla of cruisers, destroyers, patrol ships… That should be an easy win for the ISA."

But something still felt off.

"Who could they be? Pirates would be hard-pressed to take on two destroyers, much less a battleship."

The only other possibility that came to mind was the one Miles Carter, that conspiratorial engineer, had rambled on about: the Rogue Five terrorists.

"Could that wacko actually be right?" Ryan muttered.

"Apologies, Mr. Anders. Which wacko are you referring to?" Aurora asked.

"Never mind." He waved the question away. "Where did these ships come from?"

"Based on limited sensor data, it is likely the vessels are of alien origin."

Ryan nearly choked. "What… like *alien* alien?"

"Yes, Mr. Anders. Given their shape, composition, unknown weaponry and propulsion, there is a high probability that the craft are not of human origin."

Before he could speak again, a new alarm sounded through the ship. Ryan had heard it so many times in the simulators that he knew it by heart: Battle Stations. His mind was running wild at the thought of aliens attacking. Maybe it was all just some big misunderstanding, a trick, a simulation, a gag?

"Hold on, what did you say?" Ryan had missed something the computer was saying over the incessant alarm.

"The *Seoul* has been disabled by enemy fire and is drifting," Valkyrie reported matter-of-factly. "Unknown craft are on a bearing which suggests their next target is the Forge itself." There was a short pause. "I have initiated lockdown of the ship and suggest you contact ISA headquarters to request a relief crew."

Ryan jumped to his feet, barely able to comprehend how another battleship had been disabled by the small enemy force. He rubbed the back of his neck, trying to decide what to do, his breathing rapid.

"Sure, yeah, I'm sure they'd get right on that," he said, feeling lightheaded, his hands shaking. "The ship isn't even finished yet. Maybe call 'em up and tell them to install some weapons in the next five minutes since we're fucking defenseless!"

Valkyrie spoke again, causing Ryan to jump. "Main battery is offline, defensive cannons and countermeasures are online, vertical launch array one is fully operational, array two is offline. I suggest undocking the ship, as any hit to the truss could damage the engines or field array."

Ryan laughed bitterly. "How the hell am I going to do that? I'm not the captain, remember... we don't even have a crew, and what can we do against an enemy that just disabled two battleships?"

Aurora spoke this time, oblivious to his meltdown. "I'm afraid all non-priority channels to ISA headquarters are busy. Valkyrie has submitted a request to the personnel department on your behalf."

Ryan turned, looking around. "What? Why? Don't do that... Can you cancel that... like unsend?"

A sudden flash of light came from the forward viewscreen. Before he could ask what had happened, a shockwave hit the Forge, knocking him off his feet and landing him right back in the command chair.

"The *Seoul* has been destroyed," Valkyrie spoke again matter-of-factly. "Enemy vessels have arrived within the Forge exclusion zone. All ships in the vicinity are moving to engage. Forge defensive batteries are active, but unknown countermeasures are preventing electronic detection and weapons lock."

"Christ..." he breathed, the weight of it all hitting him at once. The two soldiers he'd left in the chow hall ran in through the rear door, grabbing his attention.

The enormous Private First Class Nguyen was in the lead and spoke. "Sir, sorry for the interruption, my team leader just contacted me saying she was on the way with classified cargo. She'd like to store them on board the ship until the alert is over."

Ryan, still reeling, nodded. "Classified… yeah, whatever you guys need. Valkyrie, can you give them access?"

Aurora answered instead. "I have granted Sergeant Martinez and her team access."

PFC Nguyen turned and radioed his team leader while Ryan sat, trying to come to grips with what was happening. He sat motionless, mind reeling. He felt like a kid again, trapped in the refugee camps, cornered by thugs with murder in their eyes.

"Incoming communication from Ensign Rodriguez."

Ryan kicked himself for having nearly forgotten his friends. "Put her through. Anna?" He waited impatiently to someone speaking in the background before she answered.

"Ryan? Are you still on the *Explorer*?" She sounded nervous, somewhat scared.

"Yeah, I'm here, Anna, what about David, is he with you?" He could hear banging and cursing in the background.

"We're here with Elizabeth and a couple others too. We're trying to get to you, but we're trapped five decks down next to the stairwell. The whole station is in lockdown."

He could now clearly hear David and a man in the background talking about a door.

"Elizabeth? You mean Miller?"

"Yeah, long story. Ryan, what's happening?" she said, her voice wavering.

"Stay there, Anna, I'll try to get you help." He paused for a moment. "Anna, there are enemy ships incoming."

She paused. "Yeah, we figured that out, big guy. Please hurry." She broke the connection.

"Sir," Private Nguyen said, finishing his call. "My team is inbound, shouldn't take them long to get here."

Ryan's eyes narrowed. Something clicked. "Private, the station has gone into lockdown—you might want to pass that along to your team if they don't already know."

Nguyen nodded to his buddy, who started contacting his team via his PDD. Ryan continued. "Some of my fellow officers are trapped five decks below us outside the stairwell and I need some way to get to them here."

"Sir, my team can override any of the locked doors. Just give me the word and I'll go get 'em personally."

Ryan smiled. "If you wouldn't mind, I'd be grateful for the assistance. Their names are Ensign Rodriguez and Ensign Kim."

The private stood tall. "Yes, sir." He snapped a sharp salute. "Morales, wait for the sarge; I'll be right back." He turned on his heel and walked off the bridge.

Ryan was a little taken aback. He half expected the private to tell him to work it out himself, but Nguyen was treating him like a high-ranking officer and not some junior lieutenant.

Leaning back in his chair, he reached out to check the situation around the Forge when he noticed his sleeve.

"Aaaaahhhhhh shit…"

He was still wearing the coat he'd found in the captain's duty cabin. Alongside the rest of his dress uniform, which he donned for the party. He was pretty much impersonating a ship's captain. It was an honest mistake, and he was about to call out and correct the private, but he was already long gone, and his compatriot had left the bridge as well.

"Guess I'll come clean later," he said to himself, keying the display.

CHAPTER 13

Near the docks, people were chaotically cramming shuttles to the point of overload as they tried to get back to their ships. Sergeant Jessica Martinez and her team received word that the Earth Ambassador's shuttle just cycled out and was headed back to safety.

She put her fingers to her lips and issued a short, sharp whistle, which got the attention of her team over the din of the cavernous bay. The wait had been an orderly affair until the battle stations klaxon sounded and the entire structure shook. A shuttle that was docked had a seal failure, and the inner doors slammed shut, nearly cutting several passengers in two. Now it was a free-for-all with officers pushing their way to the front and rich corpos yelling threats of lawsuit after being told they would have to wait.

"Corporal Johnson, what's your status?" she said, releasing the com button.

"Ma'am, we just left the ambassador's quarters and are headed to the main stairwell."

Due to a slow loss of pressure in the secure wing, she had ordered Johnson to escort the ambassador to the shuttle bay for evacuation, but the chaos was only ramping up. After surveying the crowd, she knew that given enough desperation, even an armed tactical squad like hers wouldn't stand a chance against so many people, so she redirected him to the only other place she could think of.

"Roger that, let me know when you get to the *Explorer*. That section is in lockdown, so use your override key, but be careful. We don't know which spaces are depressurized at this point, and I can't get through to Central."

When Johnson double-clicked his transmitter, she turned to speak to Specialist Lata and Private Cooper.

"Everyone stays alert. The last transmission I received before the call to battle stations said possible bandits incoming. We'll link up with Johnson at the *Explorer* and hunker down there till the fleet can sort this out." Both women nodded.

"Let's move." She took the lead.

Snaking her way through the chaos took shouting and a bit of shoving, but for the most part, the people who saw the black-clad and armed soldiers moved aside quickly.

They made their way through the passageways until they finally neared the stairwell directly below the construction docks. A nervous crowd of people was milling around, mostly civilians and Forge workers with a smattering of ISA enlisted in their dress uniforms.

When she approached, she could see they were being held back by Thompson, otherwise known as "Ace" to the team, and the rookie Kyle Wilson. Corporal Johnson, her second in command, was next to the stairwell door with the ambassador and a well-dressed, professional-looking young woman.

"Make a hole!" Wilson yelled, seeing his sergeant approaching. The crowd parted and allowed the three armed SRT members to the front.

"What's going on, Wilson?" Martinez said, scanning the crowd, trying to assess their intent. Lata and Cooper joined Ace and the rookie to keep the crowd back.

"Ma'am." The pasty, freckle-faced young man put his fingers up to the front of his helmet. "The crowd started forming as soon as the station went into lockdown. All the main passageways out of this section are sealed. Stairwell is locked too, and Johnson's having a hell of a time trying to override the seal."

She nodded and walked over to Corporal Johnson, who was being dressed down by the curiously bedecked Martian Ambassador.

"Ambassador, what seems to be the problem?" she said, using her best command voice, cutting him off mid-sentence.

The ambassador turned on her, looking down his nose. "…and you are?" he sneered.

"Sergeant First Class Jessica Martinez, Forge Security, sir," she recited, standing a little taller.

"If that means you are in charge of this… person, please let him know I want to return to my quarters until this unpleasantness is over."

Martinez nodded sympathetically as he spoke, pausing when he finished. "Ambassador Omandi, your quarters have been deemed uninhabitable due to a pressure loss in that section. You are being moved to a secure location. It shouldn't be long, and it's for your protection." She looked to the young woman who she figured was his handler or assistant, who took her pause as it was meant and used the opportunity to interject.

"Ambassador, I just received a report that the environmental controls were damaged in that section and temperatures have dropped ten degrees. Maybe it would be better if we went with them."

The ambassador looked horrified and gripped himself as if a cold draft had blown through the passageway, but before he could reply, a low frequency vibration rumbled through the station followed by a shudder through the deck plates.

Everyone grew silent for a moment, looking at each other before another rumble, then a third.

Martinez locked eyes with Johnson. "Corporal, what's the hold-up?"

He opened his mouth when the massive station lurched sideways several inches before the lights cut out. Screams and shouting from the civilians pierced the darkness. Several long seconds later, the emergency lights popped on, flooding the area.

Johnson pushed himself away from the bulkhead, then straightened the strap on his weapon. Only the members of the tactical team were still on their feet.

"Sarge, my override isn't working. I tried a dozen times, but I think the pad might be broken." She walked past him and touched her PDD to the control pad, passing her credentials into the system, which seemed unaffected by the power outage. She thought she heard something and pressed her ear up to the sliding metal door. Trying her credentials again, this time she commanded the door to remain open and unlocked. While it didn't move, she could definitely hear the clicking sound as the mechanism locked open.

"The door is stuck," she said with certainty. "Johnson, Lata, put your ass into this door and get it open. Blow it off the hinges if you have to. We need to get moving now."

*

On board the *Explorer*, Ryan assessed the situation and it didn't look good. There were shuttles and small ships everywhere, criss-crossing the space beyond the scaffolding, trying desperately to escape the area. The first indication he had that the enemy had arrived was the battleship *Seoul* exploding in a brilliant flash. After the initial explosion, what looked like fireworks started to detonate within the hull of the enormous ship, one after another until a massive secondary blast rendered it asunder.

This caused a general panic that Ryan found both fascinating and horrifying. A small civilian shuttle was thrusting hard past the scaffold, trying to get past a slower ship when it lost power and clipped an antenna array, sending the craft spiraling away into the dark of space shedding parts.

Ryan wasn't sure what caused the next flash, but a large passenger liner's engines exploded, throwing the craft hard to starboard, slamming into an ISA patrol ship before both detonated in a flash of quickly spiraling debris.

"Oh shit."

In nearby space, the enemy had arrived, and with them came a deafening silence as nearly all communications ceased.

The largest enemy vessel, a behemoth nearly a quarter the size of the Forge itself, led the way. Its strange weapon, showing no light, no smoke, sparks, or any emissions at all, swiveled under the bow of the ship, turning toward random vessels. The larger heavily armored ships of the ISA fleet would take one or two hits before going silent or outright exploding, but the civilian shuttles and passenger vessels would just vaporize in a blinding flash.

The smaller alien craft, nearly the length of a battleship, followed a similar tactic. It targeted nearby ships and destroyed them, pausing for some unknown reason before continuing its grim work.

Ryan pushed back into the captain's chair. "What's happening, Aurora?" Panic seeped into his voice.

"The enemy has arrived."

"I know that! What do we do? Are they coming here?"

It was Valkyrie that answered this time. "Analysis of the enemy movements indicate that this station may be the primary target. Standby, estimating time to eliminate all friendly ships."

"Never mind that! What the hell—" His breathing became fast and shallow.

"Incoming communication from Ensign Rodriguez," Aurora interjected.

"Yeah, yeah, put her through." Ryan waited for a few seconds before he heard the connection being made.

"Ryan, are you there?"

"Anna, where are you? I sent a guy down to get you through that door, he should be there by now."

A flash of light drew his attention to the main viewscreen before the nearby tactical panel started rapidly beeping. He watched in horror as an ISA auxiliary ship with half of its bow missing and venting gasses slid sideways through space. He followed it as it grew bigger until it impacted the station somewhere below him. A low rumble shook everything almost immediately. He noticed one of the massive loading arms that transferred raw ore from the visiting freighters to the station break loose, striking the side of the Forge and puncturing one of the floors. Gasses and odd-looking objects spewed out in a great misty jet. Ryan turned his head away, realizing what the objects were, unable to get the image of the person-shaped debris out of his head.

"Anna… the Forge took a hard hit. As soon as that soldier gets there, you need to get up here fast. The *Buenos Aires* is intercepting now, but the size of this enemy ship…"

He punched up the rear cameras, expanding the window to the entire front viewscreen as Anna relayed the news to the people around her. The *Buenos Aires*, flanked by what looked like a cruiser, came into full view from the left. Their engines lit up the surrounding area as both pressed on toward the enemy, which itself was still powering forward on a direct course for the station. The battleships' massive forward batteries were pumping out shots, pounding the largest enemy vessel, while the cruiser's lighter weapons and beams impacted the smaller one.

At first, Ryan didn't understand what was happening as the rounds impacted in great blueish white sparks of light. He zoomed in on the biggest ship and realized that the enemy must have some kind of energy shielding protecting it, vaporizing the slugs as they hit home. The shielding in one section turned an almost blinding white, after being hit with a lucky one-two punch of huge hundred-twenty-centimeter steel slugs. This seemed to allow follow-on projectiles to finally get through and smash into the hull, sending sparks and bits of metal flying off into space. From the scarred and battered front end, the behemoth must have entered the system with some substantial hits, courtesy of the *Columbia*, he assumed.

Slewing the camera back to the *Buenos Aires* and her escort, he was just in time to see the cruiser go silent, a massive gash gutted the nose of the ship. All the lights strobed and went dark. It was still on a straight heading toward the smaller of the two enemy ships but had already passed behind the side of the station.

His eyes darted back to the *Buenos Aires*. He could see that it was still at max thrust. In the many gaming sessions he and his friends had played at the Nebula bar, he knew that they would have a tough time keeping the main guns on target unless they started slewing the bow right away, moving into a slide before pointing its main engines on a reciprocal course. The *Buenos Aires*'s main engines, however, were still burning bright as it flew past the enemy ship, showing off its vulnerable rear.

Ryan had to close his eyes when the ship's engines disappeared in a flash, taking many of its crew with it. A cascade of explosions ripped through the hull of the battleship, cracking off large chunks of armor and equipment. A spray of escape pods announced the end of its battle. From somewhere deep within the wreck, what must have been its primary magazine touched off a titanic explosion.

"Holy shit, Anna, the *Buenos Aires* is gone…" A pulse of energy washed over the station before a massive section of the doomed ship's armor spun into view heading right towards them. "Brace, brace!" he shouted into the com before the chunk of armor collided with the Forge, shaking it to its core.

Ryan held on for dear life before the lights flickered, and his com connection dropped.

Valkyrie's vaguely menacing voice broke the silence. "Lieutenant Anders, the Forge is no longer supplying power; I have switched to internal emergency batteries. I recommend startup of all fusion reactors."

Ryan was trying to regain contact with Anna to no avail. "Yes! Start them up." He swiped his PDD in vain before seeing that he lost all links to the station.

"Negative, Lieutenant Anders, unable to start up main reactors without auxiliary power."

He threw up his hands. "Aurora?" Ryan called out, feeling frustrated and helpless.

"How can I help you, Mr. Anders?"

"This is ridiculous, do you know how to start up the reactors?"

Aurora's rich female voice assured him that it did and started reciting the instructions.

"Auxiliary reactor startup can be accomplished by engine room personnel…"

Ryan waved his hands in frustration. "No, no… I need *you* to do it, I'm all alone here, and if you hadn't figured it out: I'm not an engineer! This is an emergency, please start up the reactors."

Aurora paused before speaking again. "Mr. Anders, certain precautions have been put into place to prevent AI manipulation of critical systems." Aurora paused again, this time long enough for Ryan to think it had gone offline. "I have analyzed the current predicament and concur. Neither you nor Private Morales have the skills necessary to perform the operation. Due to extenuating circumstances, I can make recommendations to bypass the AI lockout."

Ryan ran his fingers through his hair. "Thank you! That wasn't so hard… now what do I have to do?"

*

Ensign Anna Rodriguez pushed herself up from the floor. The only dim light was coming from the window nearby. David and Elizabeth moaned, disentangling themselves from one another. Something hit hard moments after Ryan had told her to brace. She looked at her PDD and saw it was offline with no signal.

"Ma'am, are you okay?" The young mechanic she had spoken to earlier stood over her with his hand extended. He had lost his hard hat but otherwise seemed unscathed. She took his hand and stood.

"Thank you, Steve," she said, ears still ringing from the thunderous noise of the impact.

The young man cocked his head right, noticing a low din of voices approaching. Several beams of light pierced the dark hallway as the two older maintenance workers emerged around the corner. Following them was a gaggle of other people dressed in civilian clothing, some nursing wounds no doubt from the earlier shaking.

"Look who we found locked in one of the other sections?" the older man, Leblanc, said, extending his arm and stepping out of the way.

"Dad!" The young engineer ran up to a grey-haired man and embraced him.

In all, there were over thirty other people who gathered around, asking questions and speculating about what was happening. When asked, the two older maintenance technicians turned the crowd to Elizabeth for answers.

"This lieutenant knows what's happening, supposed to have top secret intelligence, right?" Everyone looked to Elizabeth, who was, for the first time, at a loss for words.

Luckily for Elizabeth, at that moment, the locked door behind her slowly slid to the side with a piercing metal-on-metal sound. The two flashlight-bearing supervisors swung their lights up and were met by the weapon light of PFC Nguyen. The large man stepped through the doorway, holding up his hand to shield his eyes.

"Take it easy with the lights, fellas, I'm the rescue party." He smiled, deep voice booming in the now quiet space. "I'm looking for Ensigns Rodriguez and Kim?"

Anna answered for them. "We're both here."

Nguyen bowed his head, motioning toward the now open door. "The captain has requested your presence on the *Explorer*, ma'am." He nodded to David. "Sir."

They both scoffed, looking at each other. "Sure—take us to the captain," David said, motioning for Anna to go first. The supervisor Leblanc grabbed Nguyen's arm. He turned slightly, a deadly look from the huge man making Leblanc immediately drop his hand.

"What about us?"

Nguyen held up his finger as he keyed his com set, still looking pointedly at Martin.

"*Explorer*, do you read?" The silence that greeted his transmission told him the station relays must be offline. He looked at his PDD and confirmed zero signal, so he switched to point-to-point mode, hoping it would penetrate five decks. "*Explorer*, this is Nguyen, do you read?"

"…go ahead.." a staticky, garbled Anders replied back. Nguyen tapped his PDD, filtering out the noise.

"Cap, I found your friends, but there are some civilians here, looks like they need a place to hole up."

The reply came back clearer this time. "Sure thing, bring 'em up, the more the merrier, I guess. *Explorer* out."

Nguyen motioned for them all to follow Anna and David while he took up the rear.

The stairwell was dimly lit. Several emergency lights flickered, but the majority of them lit the way well enough. Nguyen looked over the railing down into the seemingly unending spiral of the emergency stairs. To his surprise, lights were making their way up from several decks below.

Nguyen keyed his com set. "Sarge, is that you in the stairwell?"

"Negative," Corporal Johnson replied back, static on the edges of this transmission. "Sarge was playing hero and saved the ambassador from a piece of debris. She's out of commission. What's your twenty?" Nguyen looked over the rail.

"I'm about six floors above you in the stairwell. Escorting some officers and civilians to the *Explorer*." He looked up, checking their progress.

"Roger that, we'll rally on the *Explorer*, tell them to prep a med bay for the sarge."

*

The twisted and battered *Columbia* raced across the starfield like a greyish bullet on its quantum field drive.

Columbia's captain sat strapped into his chair, wheezing through what must be broken ribs. The corpsman injected him with a cocktail of meds, dulling the pain to a manageable throb. Right now, it was only a minor annoyance as he plotted his next move. The interception of the three lagging ships of the enemy formation would take place in a matter of minutes. Unsure just how damaged they were and what they would do when he engaged them, Captain Armstrong had decided to use his most potent weapon. Nearly banned from use by the Orbital Security Convention, the nuclear warheads were restricted use weapons, only to be employed in the most dire of circumstances.

Armstrong knew that without an atmosphere to amplify the effects of the weapons, he would need sheer numbers to destroy the enemy ships. A near miss would probably be ineffective, so he would have to get into knife fighting range to ensure a hit, which posed its own problems.

His executive officer was carried off the bridge by the medical teams, and from their expressions, he didn't think the man would make it—yet another blow to his already scarred soul. He grimly pushed aside the thought and concentrated on the approaching task. The communications array was heavily damaged, so they weren't able to transmit to fleet HQ, but they had intercepted some communications from Lunar Command that warned the Forge was under attack. Shortly after that, all signals in the area went dark.

Commander Owens, the tactical officer, turned slightly, still strapped into his harness, his broken arm tied tightly to his chest.

"Exiting slip in one minute." He paused. "Sir, shouldn't we make for the Forge and bypass these stragglers?"

"Negative, Commander, they still have a flotilla of ships, but we don't know if the addition of these will throw a wrench into their battle plans. It's best that we take care of them here, far away from the Forge." He stopped short as a wave of vertigo washed over him. Clamping down on the armrests to steady himself, he continued. "What we desperately need is more data. We hurt them, but so far, we haven't killed a single one. We need to know if specials will do anything before we, or someone else, goes slinging them around the Station."

"Aye, sir."

Armstrong cleared his throat. "Make ready to fire the missile batteries. We need to get close, Mr. Owens; I want direct hits."

As Owens nodded his agreement, Armstrong remembered the damage the *Columbia* sustained and quickly spoke to the navigation officer.

"Helm, I want you to keep an eye on our yaw rates; that twist in our spine won't allow us to use much thrust from the mains. Compensate with everything we have, but keep her nose straight."

The navigation officer acknowledged as Armstrong shook his head again, trying to clear his thoughts. He would have never forgotten such a detail before. He assumed it must be his busted ribs or the medication... or both. He blew out a deep breath, wheezing as the counter hit zero.

The virtual particle field surrounding *Columbia* collapsed as they dropped out of slip. The aftereffects of the field caused a rippling blue light to dance across the hull as the ship's speed immediately dropped to near zero. As a byproduct of the field manipulation, the forces that would normally be associated with such a maneuver also ramped down exponentially, only giving them a short jolt as they entered normal space. Luckily, they stopped almost exactly where the AI had predicted. Armstrong patted his armrest in silent thanks to his ship, damaged as she was.

Three of the enemy craft were in a loose staggered line. The ship closest to them was venting atmosphere, obviously more damaged than the other two, which were much farther ahead.

The AI constructed a best guess estimate of the state of the lagging enemy ship, and it was more than Armstrong could have hoped for. It looked very badly damaged indeed, and the other ships steamed forward without care or cover for their limping comrade.

"Helm ahead full! Make for bandit Charlie. Tactical, hold fire on missiles, I want main guns only on that ship."

Commander Owens glanced back. "Firing range in ten seconds, Captain, autoloaders are still down; we'll have maybe two volleys at most."

It had slipped Armstrong's mind but didn't change anything in his estimation. "I know, Commander, target the first volley at those arms coming off the rear of that ship. Let's see what pulling their feathers will do."

The first wave of four massive slugs leapt from the nose of the *Columbia* and closed the distance quickly to the trailing enemy vessel. The first of the metal slugs overwhelmed the weakened energy shielding, allowing the next three to tear the crystal-shaped spine completely away from the ship, sending pieces spinning through space in all directions.

"Hit!" Owens shouted before wincing in pain. "Computer reports negative acceleration from bandit Charlie, looks like they're drifting." He looked back at his captain, who didn't seem surprised. "How did you know?"

"A hunch, Mr. Owens. The other two only have minor damage to those structures and are quite a bit faster. This one was already missing several of the…spines."

Owens's panel flashed a priority message. "Sir, small objects have separated from bandit Charlie."

Armstrong checked the report himself, pulling up the image. Small dartlike spines were spilling out the rear of the damaged ship.

"Could those be missiles?" Armstrong asked, watching the flood of small, slow objects.

The computer finished analyzing the tracks, and they were clearly headed toward the *Columbia*.

"Spin up the point defense guns, don't let them get near us."

"Aye, Captain, portside point defense guns are coming online. We have limited maneuverability, but computer says we can outrun most of them."

The *Columbia* limped past the now derelict vessel, its computers bringing the point defense grid to life. Deep within the ship, the primary array surged to life, channeling hundreds of megawatts into an X-ray generation chamber near the reactor core. Within microseconds, the high-energy beam was relayed through a series of diffractive waveguides, passing through precision-tuned intensifiers along the outer hull. The result was a barrage of tightly focused X-ray pulses that caused the closest darts to flare in waves like dying embers before vanishing in cascading showers of ionized gas and molten debris.

"Coms, I want data from every sensor and camera on this ship ready to transmit the minute we get in range of another ISA ship or buoy." He held up his hand, knowing the long-range transmitters were down. "Short range transmitters should be able to handle the load if we're close enough."

"Aye, Captain," a young, unfamiliar officer called back.

Armstrong gripped the armrests and set his jaw. "Make best speed to bandits alpha and bravo, ready the specials."

*

Ryan tugged on the small, knurled knob of the circuit board under the tactical station, grunting in frustration.

"Are you sure this is the one? Everything under here looks the same."

"Yes, Mr. Anders, if you counted correctly, the board you are currently struggling with is the AI lockout controller."

Ryan stopped pulling for a second. "Very funny... Are you sure this is the only one I need to remove? Seems like one kick to this panel and you AI are running the ship."

"Mr. Anders, AI controllers and processors already run most ships. The lockout controller is merely a safeguard to protect certain systems from automated manipulation such as life support and power controls."

"Oh, is that all." He rolled his eyes. "Okay, I got it." He finally yanked the board out of the slot. "Now what?"

"Now put the system into testing mode by manually moving switch bank thirty-eight A from its configuration to…"

"To test, got it," he said, seeing the bank of half a dozen micro switches.

"Now reinstall the board and I should have access to the reactor controls."

Ryan slid the board back into place and waited. "So… how long?"

The lights flickered, and the bridge sprang back to life. The deck plates thrummed as the reactors flooded the ship with power. The scene outside displayed on the main screen caused Ryan's jaw to drop. Clouds of debris were all that remained where masses of vessels once maneuvered. The scaffolding of the Forge had taken more hits, and their crumbling and twisted remains were everywhere like the skeletal branches of trees.

He spotted flashes in the distance to the right. Using his chair controls, he directed the computer to enhance the image. Sighing in relief, he saw that the battleship *Yangtze* was still in the fight, chasing the enemy squadron, along with a motley crew of smaller vessels that took flanking positions.

Scars ran down the sides of the big ship, and it bled atmosphere from holes along the starboard side, but the massive engines were still thrusting, and her captain seemed to be furiously fighting the ship with everything at their disposal. Beams and missiles reached from the ship to the sides and rear of the huge enemy vessel with traces of light and explosions flashing in the darkness.

Turning his attention to the enemy, he saw they were drawing ever closer to the station and all but ignoring the remaining defenders until the *Yangtze's* main cannons managed a lucky hit on one of the extended spines on the rear of the ship, blowing a substantial chunk off the structure. The huge craft pivoted on its axis slowly, promising nothing good for the damaged battleship.

Farther from the fight, pinpoints of light were scattered across the black of space, brightly flaring as fleeing ships made their way at whatever speed they were capable of toward the overpowering white of the Moon and the blue marble of the Earth.

"Reactor field stability at twelve percent and increasing. The *Cosmic Explorer* will have full power in approximately thirty minutes."

"Thirty minutes! You can see them shooting out there, right? Those ships are headed right towards us." When there wasn't any answer, Ryan looked around the bridge. "Umm, Aurora?"

"Apologies, Mr. Anders, I am analyzing power flows and equipment readiness throughout the ship; several noncritical subsystems are showing above average—"

"Are you kidding me? We need to run—who the hell cares about that garbage! Get the ship moving already. We're sitting ducks here!"

"Mr. Anders, the *Cosmic Explorer* has several construction mooring points attached, which cannot be automatically disconnected. Would you like me to submit a request to the Forge construction office to have the ship released?"

Ryan jumped out of his seat and paced across the floor below the main viewscreen, heart racing. Glancing at the screen, he could see the enemy craft were definitely making a beeline to the station.

"Are there any other ships docked nearby? Shuttles, fighters, yachts?" His voice sounded desperate even to himself. A part of his brain was telling him to run, but he knew there was nowhere to go.

"Mr. Anders, Private Nguyen has requested that the medical bay be prepped for an injured member of their team."

"Sure, can you do that?"

"I can prepare the bay, but a trained medical professional is required to operate the equipment."

The Valkyrie AI growled in his ear, making Ryan jump. "I am monitoring a large group of unauthorized personnel approaching the main gangway. Arming antipersonnel countermeasures."

The large viewscreen, which to this point showed the fleet's vain attempt to stop the enemy ships, split down the middle. The right side showed a security feed from the main gangway—the door Ryan used previously to enter the ship. Walking toward the camera was a large hodgepodge of people led by two ISA officers that Ryan immediately recognized.

"Stand down, Valkyrie. Aurora, authorize access for all of them, that's Anna and David."

"Negative, Lieutenant Junior Grade Anders, non-ISA personnel will not be allowed access to this ship," Valkyrie said, sounding deadly serious.

"Help me out here, Aurora. There is no way I'm leaving them out there with those ships coming."

After a short pause, Aurora spoke. "Fleet regulations do allow emergency transport of refugees on board ISA vessels during periods of conflict. Have you designated the non-ISA personnel being led by Ensigns Rodriguez and Kim as refugees?"

"If you had lips, I'd kiss you. Yes, those are refugees."

Valkyrie spoke again, and this time Ryan could swear it sounded disappointed and angry. "Direct all refugees to the hangar bay. Any deviation will be met with force."

"Anna, David, do you read me?" Ryan spoke, knowing Aurora would route the message to their PDDs if they were in range. Onscreen, he could see the pair clearly now. Several black-clad members of the SRT group were making their way forward, including the burly soldier he'd sent down to retrieve his friends.

"Ryan! Yes, we're at the door. We have quite a few people with us," Anna said, sounding relived. David waved at the camera.

"Anna, listen, can you and David escort them to the hangar bay? Aurora, I know you're listening. Send them directions, please."

"Yes, Mr. Anders."

"Good. Anna, make sure they don't go anywhere else, I'll explain later. Then bring David and the tac team up to the bridge. We need a plan to get the hell out of here."

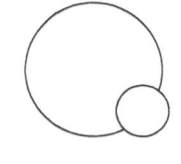

CHAPTER 14

The countdown flickering on the primary screen of the battleship *Columbia* was quickly ticking down. Over the painfully long minutes it took to close the distance to the last two lagging enemy ships, Captain Armstrong had come to one inexorable conclusion: he and his vessel were dying, and it would be a race to see which one crossed the finish line first.

He was having a hard time keeping his vision clear as the effects of the medication the corpsman gave him started to wear off. His wheezing had grown louder, and painful ribs wouldn't allow more than a shallow breath, but he didn't dare call the corpsman back for another shot as it muddied his thoughts, and right now everything hinged on a clear head.

He didn't think the *Columbia* stood much of a chance against the behemoth enemy vessel attacking the Forge, even if she were undamaged, but the last encounter showed him that the smaller ships could be beat, and if that gave the Forge and the people on board even a slim chance of survival, he would take it, whatever the cost.

His ship, the first and oldest of her class, wouldn't last long even if they survived the upcoming battles. Her back was twisted, and her systems heavily damaged; the only thing in her future was a trip to the salvage yards on the Moon.

A loud bang emanated from somewhere in the structure of the craft.

He patted his armrest as he would an injured animal. "Hold together, old girl, just a little longer."

"Captain, engine three is showing signs of overheating. Cooling loop might be damaged, but internal sensors are still dark. I'm compensating with engine two, but I'll have to pull throttles back to sixty percent."

Armstrong wiped his eyes and took as deep a breath as he could manage, realizing that his mind had started to wander. He turned his attention to the nervous young woman with the bandaged arm and shoulder sitting at the helm.

"Thank you, Lieutenant... Uh, Carmine?"

"Yes, sir, from third watch."

"You're doing a fine job, Lieutenant, keep up the good work and be ready," he said, coughing, eliciting a concerned look.

"Tactical, ready the first salvo," he said, turning back to the onscreen timer. "Still nothing from the enemy?" he asked mostly to ensure they weren't missing something obvious.

"Doesn't look like they can see us, Captain," Commander Owens, the tactical officer, said, shaking his head in disbelief as the *Columbia* slowly closed on the partially damaged enemy ships. "Launchers are standing by for your order, engineering reports autoloaders are still down, and we have maybe one shot on the forward guns, secondaries and point defense still fully operational."

An alert chime sounded. "Stand by. Computers report bandit two is altering course."

The trailing enemy ship started to spin on its axis, moving its bow to starboard. Armstrong could see the enemy weapon under the nose of the ship was slewed hard over, trying to come to bear on the *Columbia*.

"Collective fire, missile batteries one and two! Helm hard to port!"

As the ship knifed hard to port, the armored doors protecting the huge missiles of the vertical launch system slid aside with a scrape and low thud that bridge members felt through the deck. The missiles roared from their launchers, tracing white lines across the topside view, their main boosters firing wide open while thrusters pushed the nose over.

Each of the eight missiles reached their minimum safe distance and flashed, seemingly turning into a blur of light, reaching out nearly instantly with the turning ship. A split second before connecting with the rearmost craft, the missiles' particle fields collapsed, returning the warheads to normal space. First one, then another warhead ignited into a massive flash of light and radiation. Three direct hits collapsed the energy shielding, allowing the last five to slam into the side of the turning craft before igniting.

Returning to normal view after the detonations, the screen in front of Armstrong didn't show wreckage as he had hoped; instead, it showed the starboard side of the craft lit and glowing from within like hot metal pulled from a forge. A mishmash of deep craters adorned the side of the craft, but it seemed otherwise unaffected.

"Reverse our turn…" Armstrong wheezed, which devolved into a fit of coughing before he could get it under control. "Target the center crater and fire the 120s, two rounds only." He gasped, wiping the back of his mouth with his hand.

Two shudders ran through his chair as the primary guns accelerated their massive slugs along the centerline of the ship. It took only a few seconds before they connected dead center on the side of the craft, punching holes directly through the ship and sending gouts of flame and debris out the other side.

"Enemy ship is breaking up!" Owens shouted as more alerts sounded. "Final target is making a turn to starboard. Computer estimates ten seconds before we're in its firing arc."

The tactical officer's face fell. "VLS will be ready to fire in…. one minute forty-seven seconds."

"Push the engines to the limit, Lieutenant Carmine," he called out to the navigator. "Translate up with everything we have, try to stay above him."

Thrusters all along the belly of the ship started firing at full, pushing the warship above the line of fire of the enemy's main gun. Armstrong could see that it wouldn't be enough as the computer showed the other ship maneuvering in response.

"Secondaries are coming into effective range." Owens strained, being pushed into his seat.

"Concentrate fire on his starboard flank, set the missiles to fire the second we have five in the chamber," Armstrong said in a rush, his vision dimming due to the forces pressing him into his chair. He could feel the pseudo gravity fields working, but the damaged system was only taking the edge off.

Along the sides of the ship, the secondary batteries of the *Columbia* opened up, throwing a mixture of slugs and high explosive rounds at the enemy ship. The energy shielding started to splash blue as the fire ramped up, it intensified toward a brilliant white as more and more guns joined the broadside before finally stabilizing into a luminous skin that outlined the entire craft, pulsing as each new round struck.

"Secondaries are redlining," Owens reported as the pace of fire slowed automatically to keep the secondary guns from melting down. "That shielding is absorbing everything… we're just not getting through."

Armstrong cursed, straining to remember anything, any trick he had learned over his long career of driving ships to keep up the fight.

The enemy finished his turn, now pointing directly at the *Columbia*.

"Stand down the secondaries, Mr. Owens, report? Why isn't he firing?"

"AI says possible damage to power grid or weapons malfunction. Low confidence."

"Helm, turn us into him, sound the collision alarm." The low tone of the collision alarm blared, and the nose of the *Columbia* started to move directly toward the enemy.

Commander Owens silently wondered if the old man was giving up and intended to ram the enemy ship. Without an effective weapon, the enemy would just absorb the hits until there was nothing left to throw at them. He scrambled for a possible counter beyond sacrificing themselves but came up empty. The captain had pulled more rabbits out of his hat than he thought possible up to this point. He clamped down on his doubts, putting his trust in the man who had gotten them through this far.

Armstrong suppressed another fit of coughing. He imagined that a collision between the two ships would most likely destroy them both, but he didn't intend on stopping here. The giant enemy ship was probably tearing through the fleet at this point, so he had to do something desperate to even the odds and get past this one.

"Roll the ship ten degrees and ready the…" He tapped his display, showing the working thrusters. "Portside thrusters." He remembered, adding, "Port docking thrusters as well, Ms. Carmine."

"Aye, Captain," she responded as the two ships grew ever closer.

"Let's test their mettle now, shall we." He wheezed, actually managing a short chuckle as the two ships grew closer and closer.

The screens all around the bridge flashed messages about the imminent collision, warning them to take evasive action, but the captain ignored their incessant chatter, silently counting in his head.

"Now Ms. Carmine, full thrust."

As the two ships closed in, the *Columbia* translated upward just enough to avoid a head-on collision. But as their hulls drifted dangerously close, the *Columbia's* forward port flank breached the enemy's energy shielding. Blue, crackling flame danced across her side as massive sheets of meteoric steel were sheared away, atomized in an instant and erupting into light and energy.

The roaring thrusters died on the spot as the space-facing sides of their fusion engines simply vanished.

Seconds later, overcome by the sheer mass of the human ship, the enemy energy shielding failed, allowing the two hulls to briefly meet.

*

The *Cosmic Explorer's* passageway was abustle with the sounds of people. Anna and David led a mixture of ISA personnel, civilians, and Special Reaction Team members through the ship with the assistance of the AI.

Making their way down the main port passageway, they arrived at the hangar doors. Anna turned and waved her hand in the air.

"Ladies and gentlemen, my name is Ensign Rodriguez. I have been instructed by the… captain to have you wait here in the hangar bay while we prepare the ship."

As she continued, PFC Nguyen, the huge man who escorted them up the stairwell, waved for David's attention. "Sir, our corpsman says she needs to get

the sergeant to medical and is requesting assistance from the ship's doctor."
Concern colored his deep voice as he motioned to the unconscious woman.
Two of his soldiers carried her between them on an emergency litter. Her
head was bandaged, and she looked pale.

"I don't think we have a doctor yet—"

"Excuse the interruption, Ensign Kim. I've scanned the identification
documents of the refugees you're escorting and compiled a list, which I've
sent to you and Ensign Rodriguez. That is all the information available, as I
cannot access the Forge personnel system at this time. However, there may
be someone who can assist Specialist Lata," Aurora said through his earpiece.

"Thank you, Aurora," he said as he scanned over the list of names and
departments.

"Not much to go on."

Elizabeth nudged her way forward, June still sticking close to her side. "We
need to get to the bridge and talk to the captain."

"They need a doctor first, but there isn't any crew on board yet. Just the
people here." David pointed to his PDD.

Elizabeth looked annoyed, grabbing his arm and scrolling the list in one
swipe. "Here," she said, flagging a name. "This guy works for BlueSpace, a
medical subcontractor." She let his arm drop. "Let's get moving."

David glanced up at an anxious Nguyen. "Maybe we can get you some
help."

Anna had just finished, so David turned to the crowd behind them and
raised his voice. "Excuse me, is there a Mr. Ravani here?"

A hesitant hand came up as the rest of the civilians around him stepped
aside. He was a stout man in a well-worn suit a size smaller than it should have
been. His black hair was thinning and unkempt. "I'm Ravani." He paused,
looking at the others. "Did... did I do something wrong?" The man looked
around as if he was searching for an escape route.

"No, sir, we need your assistance." He glanced up at the crowd again. "If
there is anyone else with medical experience, please come forward." He waited
a few more seconds before he turned back to Ravani.

"Sir, would you go with these people and help in whatever way you can. They have an injured colleague and need medical assistance."

Visibly relieved, the man bowed his head. "Oh, of course." He nervously followed Nguyen to the stretcher.

Nguyen motioned to the corpsman. "Lata, get the sarge to medical. Take this guy with you, I guess he's a medic?" he said, looking questioningly at Ravani.

"Something like that," the man said noncommittally, drawing a distrustful stare from Nguyen.

He knelt beside the stretcher and gently lifted one of Sergeant Martinez's eyelids. His brow tightened as he checked the bandage around her head, stopping when he uncovered her ear. "Look, I'll give you my CV later. She needs treatment—right now."

Specialist Lata, the corpsman, knelt, lifting the bandage and noticing a trickle of fluid and blood seeping from the sergeant's ear. "Shit, he's right. Which way to medical?"

Her PDD sprang to life, showing that the medical bay was nearby.

"You're with me," she said to Ravani, hoisting the stretcher off the deck with the help of Private Cooper. The three moved quickly down the passageway.

A low rumble made everyone go quiet for a second.

"Excuse me, excuse me..." An exasperated voice came from the back of the group. "Move aside, I say!"

Heads started turning back as a strangely dressed man in what could only be described as a cross between a business suit and ceremonial robes pushed his way through the crowded passageway, trying not to touch or even look at the others. He was followed by a well-dressed young woman in a suit who had the look of someone who was used to apologizing for the older man's behavior. Close behind the two were several members of the tactical squad, keeping a watchful eye on the crowd.

Corporal Johnson, who was pacing the older man and obviously in charge of his security, opened his mouth before being shushed to silence.

"Ensign... Rodriguez," the gentleman said, with a strange lilt in his voice.

"I am Ambassador Omandi of the Martian Emirates. I have been illegally detained by these ruffians." He pointed at Corporal Johnson and the other members of the tactical team who were escorting him. "...and dragged all around this awful place. I demand that you escort me to my ship. I wish to depart this dreadful station." He pulled his robes around him tighter.

Anna exchanged glances with Johnson, receiving a knowing look that anyone who had to deal with the ridiculous demands of the privileged understood. She wasn't a politician, but the past three years at the Academy had given her plenty of practice putting self-entitled snobs at ease.

"I am so sorry, Ambassador!" she said with as much contrition and mock exasperation as she could muster. "I am sure we can get this all worked out right away. Would you like to talk to my superior?" She gave a quick glance at David, who almost immediately understood and nodded in agreement. "I'm sure he can answer all of your questions and put you in touch with your ship."

"I should hope so." The older man sniffed, pulling a handkerchief from under his robes and holding it to his nose.

"Right this way, Ambassador." She passed Corporal Johnson, who was careful to keep a straight face. She led the man out of the hangar by the hand like a countess who had just fainted.

"Oh goodness, your hands are so cold. I'm sure we have dignitary quarters on board where you can freshen up."

"Thank you, my dear... come along, Emily. You see, we just needed to take control of the situation."

David watched Anna lead the man and his assistant down the passageway. She was trailed closely by four armed guards, a dazed June Armstrong, and a very testy Elizabeth Miller.

A huge hand landed on David's shoulder, threatening to unbalance him.

"Fuckin' corpos and pollys, am I right?" the huge PFC Nguyen said before remembering that David was an officer. "Oh, umm, sorry, sir." His deep voice rumbled like a thruster.

David looked at him before realizing that he probably thought he belonged to one of those groups. "I'm from L.A.," he said, defusing the situation, immediately eliciting an ear-to-ear smile from the man. "Damn, I knew I liked you, sir."

"Call me David."

*

On the bridge of the *Explorer*, Ryan was going through the feeds of the various external cameras that ringed the ship on his personal display, muttering to himself. "I don't see a single shuttle, even the runabouts are gone. Who took those things? They can barely make it to the other side of the station." As he continued searching for an escape route, the screen went white, and he could feel a low shudder roll through the ship.

"Mr. Anders, the battleship *Yangtze* has been destroyed," Aurora said matter-of-factly.

Ryan looked up at the main screen in time to see an expanding cloud of debris where the final battleship had met its end. Seconds later, the massive enemy ship pushed through the debris field without bothering to navigate around it, causing flares of bluish white light to spring to life along its forward energy shield. Watching the massive ship slowly growing larger hit him like a cold slap in the face.

He leaned back, crossing his arms over his chest. Ryan had been in plenty of scrapes and close calls growing up in the camps: held at knife point, beaten, robbed. Before today, he thought he would handle his death with a devil-may-care attitude. He told Anna and David once that it was "no big deal" and that "everyone dies" in his usual blustering way, promising to go out with a bang. Now, the certainty that he had maybe twenty minutes at most before that leviathan made scrap out of the Forge took his breath away.

He could only think about himself, his friends, and, oddly, his father, whom he hadn't given much thought to at all over the years after his mother passed.

"If every ship the Earth has wasn't enough to stop them..." The words hung in the air.

The rear door to the bridge slid open smoothly with a burst of chatter spilling into the dead-quiet room.

"Right this way, Ambassador." Anna's voice snapped him out of his doom spiral of thought.

He stood and turned, wanting to see his friends at least one more time. Anna entered first, speaking with an older man in peculiar clothes. At his side was a striking young woman in a business suit, her expression sharp and watchful. David came next with a group of armed security officers trailing him, while a few stragglers tried to make their way around the small gaggle of people.

While he didn't have the heart to tell Anna about the impending destruction, his expression must have given it away. Her smiling face dropped a bit before she noticed something that made her give him one of her "you're in big trouble" faces.

"Excuse me for one moment, sir," she told the older man who was looking around the bridge like a tourist. Anna, nearly stomping, walked to Ryan's side. Keeping her voice low and back toward the new arrivals, she looked him in the eye. "What the hell, Ryan?"

"Hey, I sent a guy, the computer wouldn't let me off the ship, I swear."

"What? No, not that... thank you, by the way..." she said, stumbling. "I mean this!" she said, pointing at his new coat.

"Ohh, yeah, funny story."

"Captain, I must congratulate you on this ship," the older man said, appearing at their side. "Amazing piece of technology, I must say—much more refined than those other ISA vessels. It's positively Martian in its design!"

"Thank you, uhhh—"

"Forgive me" Anna interjected. "Ambassador, this is my... superior... Ryan Anders. Ryan, this is Ambassador Omandi of the Martian Emirates."

Omandi frowned at the interruption. "Excuse us." Omandi guided Ryan away from the others. "I'm not sure how you deal with these kinds of things, Captain, but on Mars, that breach of etiquette would be severely punished."

Ryan wasn't sure what the man was talking about and couldn't care a lick. He walked away from the ambassador, leaving him gaping like a fish out of water, and grabbed Anna by the arm. He led her away from the increasingly crowded bridge into the captain's duty cabin.

"Anna, I'm sorry."

"It's fine, Ryan. I mean, what were you thinking? You're going to be lucky if they don't arrest you."

"No, Anna." He paused, trying to make her understand. "I'm sorry for everything. Maybe if I wasn't such an idiot, we would have already been off this station. Who knows, maybe we…"

"What is it?"

"The fleet is gone."

She saw sincerity in her friend's eyes for the first time.

"The *Yangtze* bit it; the enemy is headed here." He looked at the floor. "We don't have much time, and the ship is stuck. We… I don't think we're going to make it." He looked at his friend earnestly.

Anna stared at him, her hair plastered to her head, its former meticulous styling gone. The emergency pressure suit, rumpled and streaked with dirt, stood in stark contrast to the green velvet dress underneath, which was soaked in sweat.

Her chest tightened. She couldn't stand it. After everything they had fought for, not just the Academy, but all they had worked for in life, he was ready to give up without even trying. Fury coiled in her stomach.

"Anders!" she shouted, forcing his eyes up to hers. "Listen to me." She leaned close, letting every ounce of anger and disbelief pour into her voice.

"You were the best at this back at the Academy. All those impossible scenarios, the ones meant to break you, you figured them out." She poked a finger into his chest. "*That's* who you are. *That's* what you're good at. We can't just lie down and let them take everything. You need to fight. So, figure this shit out!"

Startled by her outburst, Ryan looked at his friend, the raw anger in her eyes, the dark hair, hands on her hips. At that moment, all thoughts of fear fled.

"God damn, Anna." He gave her his best shit-eating grin. "Your brothers must have been so glad when you left home."

She slapped him on the chest, relief crossing her own face. "What are we going to do?"

"I'm serious, we are literally stuck. Aurora said that there are two construction mooring points attached, and they can't be automatically released. Someone is going to have to go outside and release them manually. Damned if I know how to do that."

"Shoot," Anna said, chewing her lip before her eyes lit up. "Oh! Aurora gave us a list of the civvies we have in the hangar; we have construction crew on board!" She pulled up her PDD, swiping several times before sending it to Ryan.

He pulled up his own screen, reading the names and divisions. A huge smile crossed his face, hope springing up in the back of his mind.

"YES!" He grabbed her shoulders and meant to kiss her on the cheek, but either he missed horribly or maybe she turned into him, but the kiss landed directly on her lips.

He could feel her warmth, the musky but sweet scent of her sweat. She closed her eyes as her shoulders slowly relaxed in his hands just as the door to the cabin opened, revealing a gobsmacked David.

"What the fuuuuuck?"

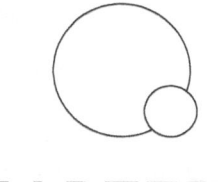

CHAPTER 15

A rumble and shudder rolled through the *Columbia* as its hull impacted that of the enemy ship. The sound grew louder and louder until a deafening silence washed over the bridge as their paths diverged.

Lieutenant Carmine, the navigation officer, opened her eyes, momentarily stunned by the fact that they weren't dead. She looked to Commander Owens, who seemed equally surprised.

"I have decompression alerts all along the port side," Owens said, regaining his composure.

Captain Armstrong nodded as if he had expected the report.

"What's the bandit doing?" He wheezed, suppressing another cough.

"Computer reports enemy ship… damaged. Looks like it lost one of its spines."

"Perfect, what's our status?"

"Momentary power loss when the reactors went into flux mode. We only had three missiles in the tubes before the loader went down," Owens said.

Armstrong clenched his teeth. "Alright, hold fire. Helm, turn us toward them, I want to hit them with a one-two punch. Owens, we need a clear line of sight on that damaged section of their hull." Armstrong shifted his weight, trying to turn his torso to relieve the stabbing pain.

"She's trying to keep the damaged side away from us, Captain." Lieutenant Carmine slapped her panel in frustration. "Half our thrusters are down. They keep pulling away."

The enemy was befuddling. During the engagements to this point, they'd shown almost no capacity for space warfare, instead relying on brute force to achieve their goals. They didn't practice any fleet support beyond rudimentary maneuvers and disregarded any protective measures. Now, suddenly, this ship had started to show signs they were adapting to the *Columbia*'s attacks.

"This is new," Armstrong said.

*

Ryan hastily pulled back from the kiss, face beet red. "Um, oh hey, Davey, uh, hey, just an accident… accidental kisses happen," Ryan stammered.

Anna crossed her arms, looking at Ryan. "Didn't seem like an accident to me."

Ryan cleared his throat before mumbling, "Time is, uh, ticking…" before practically running out the door, leaving his two friends alone as it automatically closed behind him.

The two looked at each other before suppressed smiles turned into full-blown giggles.

"Wow, so you two…" David said, eyebrow arched.

"There isn't anything happening between us. I don't know why he kissed me," Anna said, watching David closely, trying to read his reaction and hoping it didn't make things awkward between the three of them.

David held up his hands. "Even if there was, Anna…"

"Tall, dark, and emotionally unavailable? Yeah… hard pass," she said.

"Yeah." He smiled as they both broke down, the pressure of the last few hours released in a cacophony of laughter and hugs.

*

The cabin door thudded shut behind Ryan. His face felt like it had reached supernova temperatures, and he was almost certain he heard muffled laughter behind him, making it so much worse. As he stepped onto the bridge, he realized his abrupt entrance had drawn every eye. The room fell silent. Worried faces turned toward him in unison.

Nearby, the four members of the tactical squad had snapped to attention. Behind them he saw Elizabeth recognize who he was and do a double take of his captain's coat.

He cursed himself for forgetting to remove it once again. No doubt this would cost him dearly if they made it out of this situation alive.

"Did you receive word from command, Captain?" Corporal Johnson said, hopeful.

The others around him lit up at the suggestion.

"Uh, negative." His thoughts kept returning to that kiss. He shook it off, angry at himself for letting it go on for so long.

The ambassador put his hands on his hips, opening his mouth in what had to be a reprimand of Ryan's earlier brusqueness. His chest puffed up, and the young woman with him cringed as if she knew he was about to melt down.

"Captain, I must protest. From the moment this situation started, I have been more than patient, putting up with the ISA's heavy-handed and frankly incompetent handling of this crisis, but this will stop now." the ambassador demanded. "I hereby formally invoke my right—"

Using his best command voice, Ryan rounded on the man. "Sir, if we don't get this ship moving in the next few minutes, we're all dead. You get me?" he said pointedly, staring at the older man, who looked shocked.

They both stood staring at each other.

The door to the captain's duty cabin opened, breaking the uncomfortable silence. Anna and David walked out, looking at the scene before deciding to make their way to the back of the gathering.

Glad for the interruption, Ryan gathered himself. "Listen up! All communications with ISA are still down. We have enemy craft incoming, and we don't have much time."

"Valkyrie?"

"Standing by." The menacing voice startled everyone who was unaccustomed to the strange, disembodied voice.

"Please display a tactical overview on the main screen. I'd like to show the severity of our situation to the ambassador," he said, gambling that the temperamental AI wouldn't tell him to screw himself.

"Confirmed."

The screen came to life, the bulk of which showed the enhanced image of the gargantuan enemy mothership, its pockmarked bow and flanks making the alien craft look even more menacing. The top left side of the screen showed a representation of the Forge, the top of which had sustained several impacts. Pressure loss was annotated near the midpoint of the structure near where *Explorer* was birthed. The data showed it wasn't updating due to the loss of communications. Below that was an overhead map view of nearby space, including the *Cosmic Explorer*, the station, and the enemy vessel. Projected course lines predicted the enemy was coming straight for them.

"Time to weapons range?" Ryan said, secretly hoping that they had time.

"Extrapolation of enemies' primary weapon engagements show a ninety-six percent chance that the Forge and *Cosmic Explorer* will be within range in approximately seventeen minutes, plus or minus ninety seconds."

"What are we to do?" wailed the cowed statesman, who wrapped himself ever tighter in his robes. "We must flee!"

"Corporal Johnson?" He pointedly ignored the cries, instead looking to the young dark-skinned tactical specialist who accompanied the ambassador onto the bridge.

"Sir?" The corporal snapped to attention.

"Corporal, there are two booms locking the *Explorer* in place that can't be disconnected remotely. Now, the good news is that we have people from the construction division aboard who can probably help us. I need you to go down to the hangar bay, form two teams, and disconnect the ship."

"Yes sir!"

Ryan could see the young man visibly relax. He was the same way under pressure: if he had something to do, he wouldn't panic.

"Ensign Kim, can you help Corporal Johnson? Ask Aurora, give him whatever support he needs?"

"Sure thing, Ry… Captain," David said, giving Ryan a sheepish grin.

Ryan walked to Johnson, looking him in the eye. "We're all depending on you to get this done, whatever it takes."

"Yes, sir, we can handle it," he said, jaw clenching, looking resolute.

Turning to his teammates, he barked, "Morales, stay with the ambassador, the rest with me." He and David left the bridge with purpose, the two other SRT members following closely on their heels.

Ryan turned to the remaining people on the bridge.

"I'll be frank with you all. The fleet has been destroyed, and there is nothing standing between us and the enemy. Right now, as far as I can tell, the Forge is still on emergency power, so we're on our own." He let the thought hang in the air for a second.

"Until Corporal Johnson and his team can get us detached, we have to prepare as best we can."

Ryan surveyed the group. He had always been good at reading people—a necessity in the camps when your life could depend on picking the right side in a fight.

Elizabeth looked circumspect, and he assumed she was calculating the best way to take advantage of the situation.

The woman with her was terrified, her hand over her mouth, almost in tears.

The ambassador held his arms wrapped tightly around him, his eyes wild. His assistant closely behind was watching him, her own outward demeanor stunned, but she never shifted her stance. Curiously the rest of her body language told him this wasn't the first time she'd been in a scrap.

Anna chewed her lower lip the way she did when she faced a tough situation.

The only truly calm one in the bunch was Morales, who stood by the doorway to the bridge, weapon slung across his chest, prepared to defend the ambassador.

With so much doubt and fear in most of their eyes, Ryan racked his brain trying to think of some job he could give them to take their minds off the real possibility that they could be dead within minutes.

"Ambassador, I humbly apologize for earlier. We do the jobs we've been assigned the best we can." Ryan smiled laying it on thick. "Obviously you're handling this better than most." He feigned being deep in thought before coming to a conclusion. "This isn't something I would ever ask someone as…

esteemed as yourself, but as you can see, these are desperate times. May I ask you to return to the hangar bay and take charge there? I don't want all those civilians to panic, and you're the only one on board who might be able to calm their nerves."

Omandi, now the focus of the group, quickly put on his mask of authority.

"Of course, Captain." He dipped his head. "Men like us have to make decisions under pressure. No harm done."

He made a show of considering the request. "Well, I am obviously well versed in speaking to the masses, and clearly nobody else could calm those poor, scared people." He uncurled his arms, smoothing his robes.

"Emily, I think a short but rousing speech should do the trick. Perhaps an anecdote about the early settlement of Mars?" He turned, walking away from the bridge, bouncing ideas off his assistant. Morales, his lone protector, spun on his heel and followed the pair down the passageway.

Ryan waited for them to be out of earshot before turning to Elizabeth and her friend, holding up his hands in surrender. "Miller, you can have me arrested later, but for now, these…" He pointed at the gold stripes on his arm. "…are the only way we're getting out of here."

"You can't be serious, Anders." Elizabeth hissed "I will not allow this."

"What?" June stammered in confusion before turning to Ryan. "Captain, I need to get in touch with the *Columbia*, it's urgent."

"I'm sorry, Miss…" Ryan looked at the woman who by all appearances was just another civilian in an escape suit but somehow seemed familiar to him.

"Armstrong…" She stopped short before composing herself and standing at attention. "Lieutenant Junior Grade June Armstrong, Communications specialist. I've been assigned to the *Explorer*." Her shoulders slumped. "Sir, I need to contact the *Columbia* immediately."

Ryan recognized the name as almost anyone who followed the captaincy of the ISA would. The Armstrongs were well regarded as strong leaders almost exclusively because of the *Columbia*'s old man. Ryan didn't give it much beyond a passing thought.

Elizabeth stepped forward. "I don't know what kind of game you're playing at—"

"Aurora, what is the status of communications?" Ryan asked, cutting her off.

"Unknown jamming is still preventing any long-range communication or data links. Intra-ship and short-range channels are still somewhat effective."

"Can you locate the battleship *Columbia*?"

"Negative, Mr. Anders, optical sensors can no longer locate the *Columbia* due to the station's current position."

Ryan switched gears. "Last update?"

"Long range optical sensors detected *Columbia* intercepting the enemy fleet unsuccessfully at 22:41 local time and sustained damage. At 23:15, it recovered and continued pursuit. No further updates were possible when power and communication to the station was interrupted."

June wiped the back of her dirty hand across both sides of her face, blowing out a sigh of relief. "He's still fighting."

After a moment, Ryan held out his hand, which she took hesitantly.

"My name is Lieutenant Junior Grade Ryan Anders. Nice to meet you, June."

"Obviously, I'm not the captain." He gave her one of his best "oops" grins. "I was just standing watch and found the jacket. I put it on as a lark right before all of this happened…" He waved his hand toward the screen. "I swear I didn't mean to fool anyone."

Elizabeth scoffed. "I find that highly unlikely."

"June, without the jacket, those guys who rescued you would have told me to buzz off and you'd *all* still be trapped in that stairwell." He looked at Elizabeth.

"If I read that situation correctly, I think the ambassador was about to take charge… and now that I mentioned it, Elizabeth here will realize that I'm right, and we don't want or need some puffed-up politician calling the shots."

He could see Elizabeth out of the corner of his eye bristling, but as she contemplated his words, she grudgingly accepted the truth of the situation.

The Martian ambassador might not be able to take control of the ship, but he could exert considerable influence over the decisions a captain could make.

"I suppose that is… accurate."

"You see! That wasn't so hard," he said. "I know I'm done once this crisis is over, but right now we have probably less than twenty minutes to get free of the station or we go down with it."

A thought occurred to him. "June, you said you were a communications specialist?"

"Yes, sir."

"We're the same rank, you can call me Ryan." He smiled. "Can you take the communications station—keep trying to raise the fleet or Lunar Command? Anyone who can help us out?"

"I can do that," she nodded before walking to the station and taking a seat.

Elizabeth met his gaze as he turned to her. "Don't even think about ordering me around." She said.

Anna strode forward. "Why don't you just admit he's doing the best he can. I don't see you doing anything to help us get out of here"

Ryan held up his hand to calm his friend. "Elizabeth, can we call a truce for just one second? The only way we make it through this is working together. I'm willing to do that—are you?"

"Perhaps," she said, putting hands on her hips. "Computer?"

"Her name is Aurora," Ryan said helpfully.

"Aurora?"

"Yes, Lieutenant Junior Grade Miller."

"I outrank Anders, do I not?"

"Yes, Lieutenant Junior Grade Miller. As your date of service precedes that of Mr. Anders, you do outrank him."

"Computer, please note, as I am the highest-ranking member of the ISA aboard, I will be taking command."

"What the hell!" Anna gasped, taking a step toward Elizabeth.

Before anything could happen, Aurora cut in. "Negative, Lieutenant Junior Grade Miller. As my designated watch stander, Mr. Anders's authority cannot be supplanted by someone of the same rank, regardless of time in service."

"That is ridiculous, I am intimately familiar with fleet regulation and of my standing within the ISA. If you contact headquarters, they will clear this up." She held her chin high.

"Negative, all communications with fleet command have been lost."

"Elizabeth," Anna said warningly. "Kinda sounds like you're trying to take over the ship."

"Lieutenant Junior Grade Anders, do you require assistance?" The unexpectedly forceful voice of Valkyrie boomed over the bridge speakers as well as all of their earpieces, causing everyone present to wince.

"I don't know, Elizabeth; do I require assistance? Are you trying to take over?" Ryan held his hand to his chest in mock distress. He waited for her to fume a bit.

"Valkyrie, I think Elizabeth… sorry, I think Lieutenant Miller and I will be working together, as it is the best chance we have at survival. Isn't that right, Lieutenant?"

She crossed her arms, realizing that he had her checkmated.

"Lieutenant, I feel like I should warn you that Valkyrie sometimes acts independently, so you may want to say something."

"Fine," she said through clenched teeth. "No, Computer—I will not take command of the ship."

*

The *Columbia* was in trouble. With damaged thrusters and limited options, she was slowly losing ground in the fight to bring her weapons to bear before the enemy could fire on them.

"Turn zero-four-seven and increase to Flank, make them chase us."

"Zero-four-seven increasing to Flank, aye," the navigator called back.

"She's stopped her turn," Owens said, studying the display intently. "Enemy vessel is changing course to pursue." The seconds ticked by. "She's going to take up position directly behind us. Enemy closing to estimated weapons range, sir."

"Steady as she goes, Commander." An idea flitting around the edges of his mind started to coalesce into a plan.

"Captain, computer says we don't have the turn rate to get our main guns on target before they close the distance and fire."

"Get me an estimate on the enemy weapons traverse rate—how fast can it track us?"

"Approximately thirty degrees per second based on our last encounter. They nearly have a shot," Owens said.

"Steady..." Armstrong said, looking pale but determined.

"Target their starboard flank, ripple fire the remaining missiles."

The huge missiles jumped from their tubes on chemical boosters, thrusting for all they were worth to clear the hull and target the damaged side of the enemy ship.

"Helm, hard to starboard... Get me a clear shot at their flanks." He struggled to take a breath.

All the remaining port thrusters flashed to life, brilliantly illuminating the front of the ship, sending a roar through the superstructure as they were pushed to the absolute limit.

"Enemy is trying to match our turn... she's struggling," Owens called out.

"No good," Lieutenant Carmine growled in frustration. "We can't turn fast enough with all those missing thrusters..." It looked like she was going to put her finger through the glass of the console if she mashed the screen any harder.

"Five seconds. Enemy is in weapons range, recommend evasive maneuvers!" Owens whipped around to plead with his captain, seat straps digging into his hip, wondering if the injured man was still conscious.

"Sir, we have to turn away, we won't get a shot."

"Emergency power on the mains, override the lockout!" Armstrong yelled over the thrusters.

"Now, helm, now!"

As Carmine slammed her hand on the override, the full power of *Columbia*'s engines roared to life, lurching the ship forward, but with the computer no longer artificially limiting the engines, the bow accelerated like a centrifuge to starboard due to the ship's twisted spine, threatening to send them into another deadly flat spin.

"All stop, reverse our turn," Armstrong managed to gasp as the ship turned at the razor's edge of control.

Suddenly quiet, after a momentary pause, the starboard thrusters sputtered to life before fully engaging. Lieutenant Carmine struggled to keep her eyes on the yaw rates as they tried to reverse their turn. The ship bucked and rattled like a land crawler with bad servos.

Without thinking, she swiped over the safety overrides and initiated an emergency burn on the starboard engine to add its own counter thrust to stop the developing spin.

Nearby, the missiles had reached their optimal firing position, power cells dumped their charge into the sacrificial generators, which in turn created a wave of particles across the body of the second stage; as the fields collapsed, the warheads instantly accelerated.

A moan escaped Armstrong's lips; his insides felt like they were being torn apart by the sudden reversal of forces. He could taste blood and started to cough, which worsened the pain he felt. The world started to go grey before returning to color as the engines finally overcame the forces of his risky plan.

Outside the ship, brilliant explosions chained on the outside of the enemy vessel as one missile after the other struck home, exploding into short-lived nuclear fireballs and dropping the enemies' weakened shields.

"Main guns!" Armstrong managed to say around his wracking cough, which bloodied his lips.

The final two rounds from the *Columbia*'s forward guns flew toward the enemy before the fireballs fully dissipated.

On the bridge, it was quiet save for the captain's wheezing breath and a damaged ventilation fan, which scraped with a rhythmic beat as it malfunctioned.

Commander Owens said a small prayer as the huge metal slugs made contact.

He gave a wild, nearly feral cheer as a massive explosion enveloped the enemy ship from within, sending fragments spinning off in all directions.

"Sound the all-clear," Armstrong struggled to say.

"Aye, sir!" Lt. Carmine touched the control that sent a chime throughout the ship.

The remaining crewmembers of the *Columbia* unstrapped from their harnesses and hugged each other. Moving slowly, often limping, each one finished their short-lived celebrations, then moved back to coordinate the grim work of repairing the ship, locating the dead, and preparing for the next battle.

Captain Armstrong, now completely unaware, slumped down into his seat, consciousness slipping away in relief.

*

After calling an uneasy truce with Elizabeth Miller, Ryan set about trying to raise Corporal Johnson, whom he'd tasked with disconnecting the *Explorer* from her moorings. Time was running out, and external cameras showed both construction docking points still firmly attached to the ship.

"Why can't we hear anything, Aurora?"

"Mr. Anders, as I explained earlier, we have limited range on our point-to-point communications due to enemy jamming."

"We were able to contact Private Nguyen earlier... he was farther away."

Elizabeth, who'd made herself at home at the XO's station, glanced over her shoulder, giving Ryan an incredulous look.

"What?" he said.

"You'll figure it out." She went back to configuring the panel to her liking.

Anna stationed herself at the tactical console on the starboard side of the bridge. Still locked out of everything important, Ryan logged into the station himself, so she was able to at least monitor some of the lower security functions like cameras and interior sensors. Elizabeth and June were both officially on the crew roster, so they had no issues accessing any of the ship's functions normally assigned to them.

June turned to Ryan in triumph. "Captain... I mean Ryan, I have Corporal Johnson."

"Finally! Corporal, what's your ETA? How soon can we detach?"

"Captain," a static-laden reply came through. "The first mooring point is detaching now." He said something unintelligible.

"Hold on," June said, tapping her controls.

The signal resolved stronger and clearer. "...don't think our coms can punch through to the second team. Any word from them?" Johnson said.

"Negative," Ryan replied, looking down at his display and cursing himself for not putting up a countdown clock to the enemy ship's arrival. A low clunk sounded somewhere in the distance, followed by what might have been a vibration in Ryan's chair as the aft mooring point detached itself from the ship.

"Corporal, double time it to the second mooring point. We have... Shit, computer says the enemy is already in range." He cringed, waiting for the enemy to hit the station. Several seconds later when nothing happened, he looked around at the others.

"Maybe they think the station's already dead?" Anna said, putting up one of the exterior cameras on the main viewer.

A flash of light from the bridge screen caught his eye. "What's that?" He pointed.

The top of the station, which acted as somewhat of an umbrella between them and the sun, winked, then grew brighter, almost twinkling.

"Can you zoom in on that?" he said, but Anna was on top of it, commanding the cameras to focus on the area, which was growing brighter by the moment.

"The top of the station is coming apart," Elizabeth said in awe, watching the millions of solar collectors seemingly turning to dust along a rough line starting at the edge nearest the incoming ship. As the line of disintegrating panels reached the center of the station, a massive jolt ripped through the structure.

Screeching metal and a grinding, torturous sound transmitted through the remaining docking point as the enemy weapon punched a hole in the structure, leading to secondary explosions, which flashed on the screen.

"They must have fired on us." She was tapping keys so fast, it reminded Ryan of a concert pianist. A slew of different submenus and popup screens were flashing across her display as she cross-referenced the multitude of different sensors on board.

"Computers can't classify the weapon…. Valkyrie says best guess is probably a particle accelerator of some type from the damage. It looks like it's vaporizing sections of the station."

Ryan knew they were out of time. He looked at the final mounting point on the screen that connected to the mid hull of the ship just forward of the main gangway. The picture oscillated slowly as the arm strained to dampen the movement imparted by the explosion.

On the open channel, he could hear Corporal Johnson cursing and telling his men to double-time it.

"Corporal, we're out of time, the station is taking fire. I want you to fall back to the *Explorer*."

"Sir, what about the other mooring point? We can—"

"Negative, Corporal, we'll get in touch with the other team from here and tell them to hurry. Who'd you put in charge?"

"Ensign Kim, sir."

"What!" Ryan was about to ask why but then remembered he was the one who sent David to help.

"Never mind, I'll see you on the bridge, Corporal." Ryan ended the transmission.

"Why would David go out there?" Anna said, worry coloring her voice.

Onscreen, another slash of light opened up far above them as the enemy weapon gouged a new furrow across the top of the station. This time a gout of molten, glowing liquid sprayed in all directions from somewhere deep within the station. The liquid mass was blowing out in a spray from the now decompressed section.

"They must have hit one of the forges," Elizabeth said, still tapping her display. "Computer analysis confirms. Some sort of particle weapon."

A thought bubbled up in the back of Ryan's mind that they might have to leave without David if they couldn't call him back, but just as quickly as it came, he squashed the thought.

"Anna, we have point defense... any chance one of them has a clear shot at the mooring point?" Ryan said, trying to get back on task before the enemy hit something more volatile than liquid iron.

"Ryan, we need to get David back to the ship!"

"I know that, Anna, but we're all done for if we can't get loose. June, keep trying to reach the second team, broadcast a message for them to get their asses back here, okay?"

"Aye, sir," June said, fiddling with her controls before recording a message.

"Anna, does point defense have a shot?" Ryan could see Anna was angry, but he didn't have a choice. David would make it back in time; he was sure of it.

"From what little information I can access, one of the secondary batteries on that side has a shot, but the gangway is blocking most of it. I'd have to do a structural analysis to see if it would decompress the whole deck if it got hit. Portside PDC six maybe has an angle on the attachment point at the station, but we'd be dragging that arm if it didn't work. We're just too close."

"There may be others on the station who could help," Elizabeth said, looking over her shoulder.

Ryan looked at her distrustfully.

"Not everyone evacuated, Anders. If June can contact them, they might be able to help detach us and find David."

He had to admit that he hadn't thought of that. His natural inclination was to never ask for help, to always go it alone. It was so ingrained he hadn't even considered the possibility.

"Coms, can you put out another call to anyone who receives the message? Just tell them that the station is taking fire and we're going to evacuate on the *Explorer*. Also let them know we're trying to get free, and we need assistance removing port forward mooring clamp."

She nodded and started recording the message to broadcast.

Another shudder ran through the ship, pulling his attention back to the bridge viewscreen. Large chunks of the top of the station were cartwheeling away.

"I'm seeing large amounts of atmosphere," Elizabeth said matter-of-factly. "Computer says the core of the station has sustained damage; a depressurization event is likely."

"Damn." He blew out a deep breath and looked up at the ceiling. "Come on, David, you can do it, buddy."

CHAPTER 16

Ensign David Kim led his team down four decks to locate the second mooring point. His team included two of the black clad soldiers, a construction supervisor, and an engineer. They took a meandering route through the station, bypassing some locked doors and stairwells, but the biggest problem they faced was that none of them actually knew its exact location. The engineer, who was no older than twenty in David's estimation, had been there once with a friend and swore he knew exactly where it was before they left the ship.

"This is it!" the engineer said as they entered yet another nondescript room, eliciting eye rolls from both of the trailing soldiers.

The young man swung his handheld damage control light left and right, cutting swathes through the darkness to reveal a spiderweb of large industrial hydraulic equipment. The exposed parts of the walls themselves were covered in a series of large quilted thermal blankets that had been painted over many times, indicating that they were at least at the outermost wall of the station. There was all manner of control and monitoring equipment attached to the mechanism.

When his light landed on a particular console, he turned, flashing the light in David's eyes. "That one!"

Using his hand as a shield, David turned. "Private Thompson, can you call the ship and give them an update? We'll get it detached."

"Yes, sir," said Thompson, a lean dark-skinned woman about David's age. She motioned to the other private, Wilson, who passed her a high powered but bulky handheld com set they had brought with them.

David and the two engineers inspected the equipment. The small console was attached to the support structure of the mechanism and was running on backup power. The young engineer fiddled with the controls hesitantly. David watched over the man's shoulder as he logged into the system and started down a rabbit hole of menus.

"I'm not sure what any of this means," the man said, wiping the back of his neck with a handkerchief.

The supervisor shrugged. "Yeah, none of this is familiar…. I worked in ore refinement for a while, and they use Compton Control firmware… this looks like Frontier."

The young engineer tapped through submenu after submenu while the supervisor gave him questionably helpful advice.

"Excuse me, Ensign, we can't get through to the *Explorer.*"

David turned to Thompson, who held out the com set. On the screen, the indicator showed no connections detected. He pondered their route through the station, assuming that the section they were occupying must be more heavily constructed due to the mooring point.

"Private, can you take the com set and go back to that room we passed with the window? That may allow for a more direct line of sight."

Private Thompson nodded hesitantly and glanced at Private Wilson before answering. "I'm pretty sure we can get there, sir."

David could see her confusion, but that didn't surprise him, as most people would have gotten turned around. Their small group had criss-crossed their own path no less than three times by his recollection, though none of them noticed since each path came from a different direction. One of the reasons David scored so highly in the Academy navigation simulations was an uncanny ability to fix his point in space and intuitively discern the best paths to take to a given destination. Even now, he knew without a second thought that they were on deck 20, frame 56, ring 7, which meant nothing to most who just used their PDDs to navigate.

He tapped a few commands on his own PDD, bringing up an offline map of their deck, noted the room they passed earlier, and drew a direct route to the place before sharing it with the private.

"Oh, thank you, sir," she said sheepishly before handing him a smaller radio. "Take my com. We can act as a relay between you guys and the ship."

He nodded his thanks as she gathered the other private and left the room.

David turned back to the task at hand when he started to feel a bit lightheaded. The engineer and supervisor both made noises that made him think it wasn't just him.

Seeing David's reaction, the supervisor bounced at the knees. "Gravity just lightened up. Backup batteries must be running out of juice. Makes your head swim, doesn't it?"

"We had better hurry. I don't do well in zero g," David said to the two who went back to puzzling the interface on the mooring clamp control station. A shudder rolled through the station followed by a series of smaller but still pronounced vibrations.

After being nearly knocked from their feet earlier, David held on to the frame of the device with white knuckles. It didn't help that the station had been making a regular litany of deep bangs and screeching, tearing metal sounds since the first hit.

Now this newest series of sounds had him even more concerned as it seemed to be growing closer.

"Got it!" the young engineer said in triumph. "It's cycling. Oh, wait." He pressed the "commit" button again. On the small screen, a charge number slowly ticked up from 15 to 25 percent before stopping. "Damned thing keeps resetting. Don't worry, I can just keep hitting it. Must be damaged or something."

A dense haze of what David thought to be smoke passed through the beam of his light. "Did something short out?" he asked.

The supervisor noticed as well, cursing. "No, sir, we need to find a damage control locker; that was decompression," he said.

David was starting to feel the change. He experienced the same in the high-altitude training simulator at the Academy, so he knew it wasn't that bad yet.

"Here, let me do that," David said to the young man pressing the button. "You two find Private Thompson and Wilson and get back to the ship. I'll follow as soon as the clamp unhooks."

The display read 83 percent, so he estimated another five minutes at the most.

He flicked him the same directions he gave the two privates. "Just follow the directions. Use the handheld to call when you get there—it should have enough power to reach me. Go."

Both men nodded and left.

David stood alone among the looming machinery, his handheld light casting a small, flickering pool around him. He kept tapping the onscreen button, faster now, regretting that he'd sent the others away. The darkness and silence closed in around him. He stabbed the button again, willing it to move faster.

*

June Armstrong tried everything she could think of to contact the *Columbia*. It didn't amount to much, as the strange interference the alien ship was causing meant their communication options were severely limited. They were left with old-fashioned radio frequency point-to-point methods, and even those weren't completely immune to the alien influence. The last known optical tracking data from Lunar Command said her grandfather was still in the fight, but the ship was heavily damaged after its first encounter.

She couldn't help but think that the man who had helped to raise her was unstoppable. She thought back to when he would arrive at their family ranch in southern Wyoming. His gruff exterior would slough off and he would meet her, arms open wide with a huge smile, calling her his "June bug." They would ride horses, fix the farm robots, and generally annoy her father, who had a less than perfect relationship with the man whom he thought should be president of the North American Union by now, and not some lowly captain.

She said a silent prayer and tapped the status update for the communication satellites and stations one after another, hoping beyond hope that one would miraculously connect.

She glanced over at their impromptu leader, Ryan Anders, who was bickering with her new friend Elizabeth Miller.

"Acquaintance," she thought. Friend might be a stretch.

The minute she met the woman, June knew she was putting on a show for her. You didn't need to be an Armstrong for very long to know that almost every person wanted something. Career help, money, connections to higher-ups: it was the reason she had no real friends beyond her close family. She learned to judge people through that filter, but Elizabeth didn't seem all that bad. She came from a prominent family, and June thought, once the usual wrangling took its course, that they could at least commiserate together, maybe one day become friends after some clear lines were drawn. Her apparent kneejerk disdain for the lower classes was off-putting, but her own father felt the same way, so it wasn't a deal breaker.

Anders, on the other hand, was a mystery. She saw the same spark of recognition in his eyes at the mention of her last name, but he brushed it aside like so much dust off his shoulder. He had admitted, if you believed him, that he had somehow mistakenly impersonated a starship captain, a violation serious enough to get him drummed out of the ISA with a permanent black mark on his record. It would ruin him, but he didn't seem to care a whit about the repercussions. Instead, he focused on keeping them alive and saving the ship.

Static filled her ears as an alert popped up on her workstation. Her heart leapt for a moment until she realized it was the radio frequency receiver. The computers tried to filter the signal automatically, but it was weak and garbled. June removed the filters and instead applied a different set of algorithms to the signal, relying on boosting amplitude within the 30–3k range, then sending the signal through an AI filter gate, which would recognize the patterns within words and strings of words to finally translate the broken signal to a recognizable voice.

Private Thompson's voice finally broke through "…do you read me?"

Using a reversal of the process, the computer predicted the best frequencies to amplify and return a strong signal.

"I read you, Private Thompson, this is Lieutenant Armstrong on the *Explorer*."

Remembering that with all the interference she would probably need to signal she was finished speaking, she quickly added, "Over."

"...couldn't make out your message." A whining static moved over the frequency before being damped down by the filters. "... have located the mooring point, and Ensign Kim is working to get the ship unhooked. Over."

The static was now much less pronounced as the computer's algorithm adjusted.

"Stand by, Private."

June turned, coming face-to-face with Ryan, who'd heard her make contact.

"Oh, sorry, Mr. Anders." She decided to follow the ship's AI in addressing her captain-not-captain simply as "Mister." "Private Thompson reports that their team made it to the mooring point and are attempting to disconnect the ship."

A look of relief swept his face. "Excellent. Tell them we're taking fire and to do whatever they need to do to get the ship detached. They have..." He glanced at the onscreen timer. "...maybe three or four minutes tops before I want them to drop what they're doing and get back to the ship. Detached or not."

So far, they'd been lucky, as each successive hit on the top of the station hadn't seemed to do any catastrophic damage, probably due to the fact that shooting the forges was like shooting a molten iron asteroid. If the enemy decided to move down the superstructure, it wouldn't take long for the situation to become dire.

June turned back to her station and started relaying his orders.

"Ryan, Corporal Johnson's team is back on board. He's headed to the bridge as ordered."

"Thanks, Anna," he said, walking back to the captain's station. He noticed Elizabeth's evaluating stare.

It was something she'd done since the Academy, and it always felt like he was being sized up by an alligator trying to figure out if he would make a good meal.

"Anders, sensors are showing large discharges of atmosphere from the top of the station," she said offhandedly.

"Uh, thank you, Lieutenant," he said, deciding not to use her name since it seemed to piss her off.

He brought up the information she shared on his own display and ran some projections as the minutes ticked away.

"Aurora?" he said quietly.

"How can I assist you, Mr. Anders?"

"Based on these numbers, how long does David's team have to get back?"

There was a short pause before the AI replied. "Insufficient information. I can only provide a window of eight to ten minutes before pressure loss in their section would render them unconscious without supplemental oxygen."

"Okay, that's what I thought." He looked over at Elizabeth and cleared his throat, then speaking at normal volume. "As soon as David gets that clamp free, we need to be ready to detach the main walkway and get outta here. Can you do that from there?"

Elizabeth made a show of tapping an icon at the top of her screen and holding her hands toward it like he was an idiot. Displayed was a customized navigation screen worthy of one David would have configured.

"Uh, thanks."

"Enemy ship is changing course," Anna said, putting up the enhanced image on the main display. The large alien ship had stopped firing and was starting to veer away from the station.

"Guess they decided we weren't worth the ammo," Ryan said hopefully.

"Ryan, look!" Anna said, pointing to the screen. In the wake of the turning ship, a cloud of smaller dart-like objects detached from its stern and were accelerating towards them.

"There must be a hundred of them…" Elizabeth shook her head, hands flying across her screens. "They might be missiles. Twenty seconds to impact!"

Ryan didn't know what to do. In the simulator, he would have cut and run, dumping countermeasures or ducking behind a big object. Tied to this station, they didn't have a chance.

"PDCs!" he yelled, remembering they had at least some defensive capability.

"I don't have access to fire control!" Anna said hopelessly from the tactical station, tapping on her display.

"Valkyrie, activate point defense!" he said, looking around wildly, hoping the AI was listening.

"Point Defense online, prioritizing targets... firing," the growling computerized voice announced.

Outside the *Explorer*, fore and aft point defense pods extended from the hull of the ship from behind hidden armored hatches. The small turrets swung with robotic precision, glowing a soft maroon color and moving with incredible speed as they targeted dozens of the objects in quick succession. The invisible beams made contact with the surface of the darts, initiating a series of bright, flickering flashes before a split second later, they exploded.

"There are too many of them," Anna said. "Computer predicts... seven impacts on the ship. We need to move!"

"Aurora, can we break free? Just use the thrusters and snap that thing off?"

"Negative, Mr. Anders. Forcefully detaching the ship would cause catastrophic damage to the hull. The clamp locations are—"

"What about using the secondaries?"

"No clear line of sight from portside ventral cannons. Passenger walkway fully obscures the target," Valkyrie answered, causing Ryan to pause in momentary confusion.

He snapped his fingers. "Maybe I could get us a clear shot. Helm," Ryan said, forgetting momentarily that the helm station wasn't manned. "Uh, Lieutenant Miller, can you use the stern thrusters to twist the ship?"

She pulled up her screen. "You heard the computer, that might kill us all."

"We just need some upward deflection. Do it!"

"Secondary cannons are coming online automatically," Anna called out.

"Command has to come from your station, Ryan—I have no control." She sounded frustrated.

"Aurora, what do you think? Aurora?" Ryan asked, biting his lower lip.

"Ten seconds to impact," Elizabeth said, urgency finally creeping into her voice.

"Give us a nudge, just enough to put the nose down a degree or two. As soon as we're free, get us out of here, Elizabeth," Ryan said, wincing as he heard the grinding of the *Explorer* pushing against the mount holding her fast. As the nose dipped, a confirmation button appeared on his screen.

"Taking the shot." He moved his finger to the firing button.

June whipped around in her seat at nearly the same moment, speaking over Ryan. "I have the second team on coms."

Ryan's finger stopped just short of the screen as a resounding thud sounded through the ship.

"We're loose!" Elizabeth called out as the ship wobbled beneath their feet.

"Get us out of here, Elizabeth!" Ryan yelled, but the ship was already moving, the big breaking thrusters mounted under the nose of the ship lighting up the side of the station as they nimbly moved backwards out of the line of fire.

Seconds later, they could see the darts fly through the spot they occupied only seconds before, continuing down and presumably out into space. Ryan gripped his armrests tightly, waiting for an explosion as the shower of projectiles landed in various places around the Forge.

"What happened? Why didn't they blow?"

"No idea... looks like they just punctured the outer hull of the station," Anna said, bringing up the midship external camera with the best view. A deep, ragged hole in the hull above the docking arm sparked and spewed the last puffs of atmosphere and debris into space.

"Shit, David," Ryan said, noticing the proximity to the final docking arm.

"Damage control doors would have closed automatically. Just the damaged compartment would have depressurized," Anna said. "Look, the damage control drones must be independently powered." She pointed as three small shadows approached the hole before the familiar blue arc of light from welders shone on the hull, beginning their work patching the hull.

"Where's that enemy ship?" he said, remembering the danger was far from over.

"Last update showed it turning away and accelerating; we should have a view in a couple seconds as soon as we clear the station."

"They had us beat, why leave the job unfinished? They didn't stop pounding those ships out there till they were scrap."

"If someone hands you silver, don't complain it's not gold," Elizabeth said over her shoulder, eliciting an eye roll from Anna.

"Analysis of the enemies' flight path shows a reciprocal course out of the system," Aurora said helpfully.

"Where the… Aurora, where were you?"

"Apologies, Mr. Anders, my protocols do not allow me to participate in offensive or defensive actions."

"Great," Ryan said, still unsure what the hell good having two separate AI systems was.

"Previous estimates gave only a thirty-eight percent probability that the objects were missiles. New data suggests a seventy-one percent probability that the objects were in fact boarding craft."

Everyone looked at each other with surprised expressions. Anna, mouth covered by her hand, was the first to speak. "Oh no, David!"

"June, get the second team back online, tell them we'll have to circle around and figure out a way to pick them up." Ryan's heart was still pounding from the near miss.

"They said they were almost back to the ship when we detached, I lost them after that," June said, listening to the recording, trying to clear up the transmission with filters.

"Sir," a familiar voice called out from behind him.

Ryan turned to see Corporal Johnson walking onto the bridge. He stopped near the command dais and snapped off a salute. "Anything from the second team?" he asked, looking at the screen.

"We got word they were almost to the ship when we had to cut loose. We're going back to grab them, but…"

"Sir?"

"Corporal, there may be some sort of alien invasion happening on the station… what kind of weapons does your team carry?"

*

"Rook, you okay?" Private Thompson called into the darkened and smoke-filled room. Something hit the station dangerously close to the compartment where Ensign Kim told them to make contact with the ship. She reached across and pressed the rubber-clad button on her shoulder, the light energized slicing a beam of white through the smoke.

"I think so," was all Private Wilson could croak out. His head was foggy, and the air tasted sharp, like an electrical fire. "What the hell was that?"

Thompson stood over him, offering him a hand, which he gladly took. "I think something hit the station."

"Yeah." Wilson rubbed his ear, trying to see if the ringing would get any better. "Maybe you should call the ensign. I'd love to get out of here before we get killed."

The corner of Thompson's mouth curled as she got ready to give the rookie a hard time when a screeching metal sound came from somewhere nearby. It echoed down the passage and seemed to be coming from every direction.

"Shit, is the station coming apart?" Wilson said, putting his hand out to brace himself.

The sound came to an end when another started: it was almost a moan but not quite. It was low, a deep base that made their ears itch.

Wilson opened his mouth to say something when a bloodcurdling scream rang out. At first Thompson thought perhaps someone had gotten hurt, but it was so—primal, so guttural, until it stopped abruptly, leaving the room in silence once again.

Both of them looked at each other. Without thinking, each had their weapons at the ready position, safeties off.

"What the fuck was that?" Wilson said as another scream echoed down the passage, this time closer.

Thompson kept her weapon trained on the hall and used her other hand to grab the bulky handheld radio. "Ensign Kim, come in."

*

David peeked around the corner of the passageway, peering into the darkened and now haze-filled hallway that led to one of the outer stairwells. He'd finished cycling the docking clamps right before a tremendous crash rocked the section he was in—seemingly right on top of him. Deciding that either the *Explorer* hit the station, which wouldn't surprise him given the fact that Ryan was in charge, or things were starting to really come apart, he decided to make a beeline toward the ship.

Hurrying to the nearest access ladder, he was brought up short by a metal-on-metal clang somewhere down the passage. "Hello?" he called out, shining his flashlight into the hazy corridor.

He wanted to hurry back to the ship, but the thought of someone lost or maybe injured made him hesitate. He pursed his lips and turned away from the ladder.

"What am I doing?" he mumbled his hand shaking slightly. An eerie quiet settled over the station. David's instincts were straining against his better nature, urging him back to the ship before the station fully decompressed or split in half. He shook the thoughts from his head and ventured farther down the passage.

A red light was blinking on the panel of a nearby door, the small display showing it was locked. He wondered if the noise he'd heard came from within. He reached out to see if he could bypass the lock when something moved behind him—instantly locking his muscles and causing him to sharply inhale. His body refused to do anything besides quiver as something dark approached.

"Just my luck," a voice said from the dark, followed by a wry chuckle.

David's shoulders relaxed and he turned slowly, the beam of his light casting enough illumination to show a smallish, bedraggled man in a dirty tuxedo.

"Slaunder," David yelped, finally exhaling for the first time in what seemed like ten minutes. "Why are you here?"

"I ask the questions, grub," he said, reaching out and snatching the light from David's hand. "What are you doing in this section? That door is off limits... or did you already know that?" His eyes narrowed as he looked David up and down. "Are you trying to break in?"

"N-no, I thought I heard something. I...I just wanted to see if someone needed help..."

Slaunder paused, waiting for David to stop speaking, then laughed. "I'm just fooling around." He slapped his arm and pushed David away from the door. "You grubs are always so nervous."

He pulled a key card from his pocket and waved it in front of the panel, unlocking the door with a loud click. Slaunder tossed the card aside and slid the door open, letting the light sweep across piles of goods in boxes and barrels scattered through what looked like a secure storage area.

The light finally fell on a black duffel to one side. A rack of vials caught David's eye as Slaunder inspected the bag he had found. Just as David realized the vials were probably illicit drugs, Slaunder swung the light into his eyes.

The Forge groaned worryingly, causing both of them to look around.

"Sounds like the station is on its last leg. Too bad you and your friends will go down with it." He hefted the bag over his shoulder. "My father made sure there was a private escape pod back at our offices, but... sorry, company personnel only." He chuckled with glee.

"An escape pod won't get far with the fleet gone," David said. Slaunder had been nothing but trouble for him and his friends, but he couldn't let him die in space waiting to be picked up. "You can come with us, Ryan and—"

Slaunder moved faster than David expected, grabbing his arm painfully. His sour, hot breath caused him to recoil. "Where is he?" Slaunder hissed, his voice low. "Where's Anders?"

David swallowed hard. "On the ship, on the *Explorer*."

A distant scream caused David to freeze again. He couldn't tell how far away it was, but it was close enough to echo down the passageway making him shiver in Slaunder's grasp.

"Take me," Slaunder said, slapping David across the face, regaining his attention. "Take me to the ship, grub." He spit the words into his face, reaching into his bag.

A thudding and high-pitched screech of metal, this time much closer, caused both of the men to look down the dimly lit passage. Slaunder pushed David away from him roughly into the wall, causing him to trip over his own feet and land in a pile.

Then David heard the sounds of something… else. It made the hair on the back of his neck stand on end, his breath caught.

It was a low throaty sound, almost a moan. His mind tried to classify it. It wasn't the sound of metal, or the groaning sound of a partially compromised atmospheric seal. It was—biologic, something that set the most primal parts of his brain alight. It sounded positively demonic.

Without thinking, he backed away slowly, still on the ground, pushing himself with his feet, his hands feeling behind him. Whatever was making that noise chilled his blood and scared him beyond words.

Slaunder stood, pointing the handheld light down the corridor. Something was coming closer, a scraping, wet sound that sent shivers up his spine. He let the emergency light clatter to the floor and reached into the bag, pulling out a pistol and spilling several stacks of bundled cash onto the floor in the process.

David stood on shaky legs, his breath coming in uneven gasps. He continued to back down the hallway, straining to see what was making that awful noise until he hit a closed and locked door.

A dim emergency light mounted at the far end of the hall provided just enough backlight for him to make out the shadow of something as it rounded the corner. It was hunched over, maybe three-quarters the height of a person but bulbous on top with skinny legs or appendages below. Its movement was jerky as if it weren't acclimated to the simulated gravity of the station, looking almost drunken. Still no more than a far-off shadow, it put out its arm to brace itself on the wall as it rounded the corner. At least David thought it was an arm until it uncoiled with a meaty thump on the ground in front of it. Another appendage that was seemingly wrapped around its upper body uncoiled like a python and joined its fellow in front of the thing.

David froze, unwilling to even breathe, waiting for several moments until it launched itself off its two front limbs with a throaty chattering bellow. It crashed down the hallway at breakneck speed, lightning fast and covering the distance so quickly, he didn't have a chance to react. Slaunder screamed in primal fear, which caused the creature to trumpet its own oddly melodic yet terrifying sound in return, lashing out several thickly corded arms striking the quivering man.

David's mind didn't register anything for a moment except that Slaunder dropped his bag, then to his horror he realized that his arm and part of his shoulder still held it. The rest of Slaunder screamed.

The creature closed the distance blindingly quick and took only a moment to tear what remained of Slaunder into bloody gurgling pieces, then paused before making a wet moaning noise.

Something grabbed David by his pressure suit and yanked him backwards through the previously locked door so hard, his teeth drew blood, clacking together on his tongue as his chin hit his chest.

Darkness, metal, and his own screams were all he could sense as the dim light of the hallway disappeared. The red eyes of monsters were everywhere, eliciting another scream from him before a thunderous clanging sound nearly deafened him. He felt himself being dragged up a stairwell backwards, his heels smacking the tops of the steps, body limp in fear. David kept his eyes clamped shut as tightly as he could and hugged himself with his arms, sure he would feel the monster's teeth sink into his soft, meaty parts any second.

Instead, he just heard... laughter?

A light snapped on, nearly blinding him even through his eyelids. David dared to open one eye and was met not by some otherworldly nightmare but a group of smiling, dirty, and bloodied soldiers.

"Oi, you gonna lie there all day?" the leader of the group said, eliciting chuckles from the others standing over David. The man's crimson and brown uniform was somewhat tattered, and he had several jagged wounds across his face and neck that were sealed over with a jelly-like substance.

"Wh…who are you?" David squeaked.

The man reached down and grabbed David's hand before hoisting him effortlessly onto his feet with an electronic whine.

"Name is Chief Huatare, Martian Special Services," he said in a strange accent. "These here are my troopers." He motioned to the other soldiers.

A heavy clang of something hitting the hatchway below them caused several of the soldiers to snap down some sort of high-tech goggles over their faces, which whined as they powered up, showing three red glowing dots where their eyes would be. David noticed none of them had actual weapons except for the chief, who held an odd-looking handgun. The others were carrying makeshift clubs, pipes, and one had a jagged piece of metal that was vaguely sword-shaped with cloth wrapped like a handle on one end.

"We can deal with formalities later, but we need to make stride. Do you know the way to the ship?"

Another bang, this time with the sound of metal bending, echoed up the stairs.

David tried to tamp down his fear enough to think. After several tries, he resolved the picture in his mind. "We're right underneath it, two more floors up to deck twenty-five. Just a couple passages beyond that."

The radio in his pocket crackled to life. "Ensign Kim, come in."

He fumbled, tearing it out of his pocket, turning the volume slider down. "Thompson, is that you?" he whispered.

The chief looked expectantly at David, clearly wanting to get moving.

"Roger that, sir, we're still up at the…" She sounded distracted by something, speaking away from the microphone. "Wilson, stay back here… no, I don't give a shit what you saw."

The chattering of weapon fire erupted through the microphone before the radio went dead.

The chief snapped down his own goggles and jammed the light into David's hand. "Too many of them, we need to bounce."

"Inna," he called to one of his soldiers, who David noticed was a lithe young woman a couple inches taller than his modest 5'8." The left side of her hair was cut tight to her scalp, and the other side was worn straight, almost to her shoulder, colored a turquoise blue, and cut at a severe angle toward the back of her head. At first glance hidden beneath smudges of dirt and shadow, the woman had some sort of deep red geometric tattooing on her face and neck that looked almost tribal.

"Roch," she said in the odd Martian way of elongating the *o* sound.

"Stay here, when the thing comes thro'gh, drop some wreckers down there."

She clasped her hand and slammed it against her chest plate, her fitted power armor whining with each move. She turned to the railing behind her and stood overlooking the floors below. Propping up her impromptu sword against the metal railing, she pulled out what looked to be grenades from a pouch on her thigh.

David was taken aback, wondering who would give Martian soldiers, or any soldier for that matter, a grenade on a space station.

He wanted to try contacting Thompson again, but the chief took off, headed upwards, his boots clanging on the metal stairs, followed by five other Martians. David had no choice but to run after them, glancing back at the woman who armed both devices.

David pumped his legs as hard as he could. The metal-on-metal clang of the Martian boots hitting the stairs above him echoed caused him to cringe. He used his arms to help propel himself upwards, but he knew that he wouldn't be able to keep it up much past the two flights of stairs they needed to travel. Even now he gasped for breath in the thin atmosphere, which didn't seem to bother the Martians.

As they arrived at the doorway to deck 25, two of the leading soldiers continued clanging up the stairs, heading upwards.

"Wait… this is…"

Chief Huatare held up his hand to silence David as one of the other Martians, this one with a very distinctive geometric tattoo encircling his bald head, pressed a small metal disk about the size of a bottle cap to the door.

After a couple seconds, he announced that it was clear, standing back and touching the manual release. It clicked, then swung open with a hiss, as another Martian silently moved into the hallway beyond, wielding his club.

The chief whistled, which caused the two clanging soldiers who ran up the stairs to immediately stop and reverse course, this time on softened footsteps. He moved quickly out the door, motioning David to follow him.

Two soldiers moved left toward the direction of the *Explorer*, and the two who came back down the stairwell exited and moved toward the other end of the hallway. David could see they were all on high alert, but none of them seemed as scared as he felt.

He whispered to the chief, "What's happening, what was that thing down there?"

He swept the light around, noticing small bits of junk scattered everywhere on the floor. Some kind of cards, a picture, pieces of foam-like material.

"Dunno, damned quick whatever they are, we lost half our troopers tryin' to find a way to the ship." He touched his belt, then his chin with two fingers. "Stumblin' through the dark, we hear you screamin'."

David had only just recently met his first Martians. He didn't know much about them other than they were famously temperamental and xenophobic. The entire planet seemed to keep to themselves. Only in the last few years since signing on to the OSC treaty had more of them found their way into the fleet.

"You from da bar!" the Chief exclaimed with a wide smile.

"Oh... that was you guys?"

"Good fight!" The Chief tossed a casual slap at David's shoulder, which felt like one of Anna's punches.

"Your friends alive?" he asked casually, no different than if he were asking about the weather.

"Uh, yeah, Ryan is running the *Explorer* right now..."

"Anders!" The Chief laughed. "Good. You in contact? I don' wanna get shot and… no coms." He held his odd-looking PDD up. "Receive only."

Twin whumping sounds from the closed doorway behind them made him jump.

The chief bobbed his head slightly. "Better hurry, doors don't help much."

CHAPTER 17

As its quantum field collapsed, the ISA battleship *Columbia* stumbled into normal space with a shudder dangerously close to the humanities' largest space station known as the Forge.

"How did you know?" its stunned navigator said, mouth agape.

Captain Armstrong let out a weak, wet-sounding cough, his breathing somewhat strengthening thanks to another half dozen injections he'd been given by the corpsman after he passed out.

"Report?" he said, ignoring the question, knowing in his heart he had just taken the biggest risk of his career, trusting the mass of the station would be great enough to collapse the slip field before they smashed into it, killing not only his remaining crew but the thousands who called the Forge home.

"I don't know how you did it, sir, but we're ten kilometers from the station. No enemy ships that we can see on optical, active sensors are still down."

"They're still here somewhere," Armstrong said, trying to clear his thoughts. The drugs he'd been given temporarily returned his consciousness and the ability to breathe, but his mind was foggy like he'd just woken from a long nap.

"Remember your engineering, people," he said to his bridge crew, sounding stronger. "The drive field will collapse when it's near a large enough mass. That station is just big enough to interfere with a quantum field as strong as ours. Simple mathematics." He spoke with a confidence he didn't feel.

As the *Columbia*'s computers chewed through the optical data from the remaining exterior cameras, a picture of the surrounding area populated the main viewscreen.

The navigation officer gasped as more and more data began to fill the screen.

Tactical notations showed two massive debris fields and labeled them "ISA *Seoul*" and "ISA *Buenos Aires*." Scattered all around were smaller fields of twisted metal with either "unknown" or "unknown vessel" designations. Dozens more were floating nearby, tagged as possible civilian vessels and shuttlecraft.

Armstrong leaned forward in his seat despite the dull pain wracking his chest. "Do a full sweep, is there anyone left?" He didn't want to believe it, but given the state of the fleet when he'd left orbit, it was an outcome that he had considered. He hoped they would rally, but given his own meager victories and the state of his ship, things were looking bleak.

"No... nothing, sir." Commander Owens spoke softly as he queried the system. "Wait, computer is showing one vessel hidden in the debris hugging the station. It's the *Cosmic Explorer!*"

"I thought the ship wasn't finished?" Lieutenant Carmine said to herself while she ran sweeps with the communication array.

"Computer reports RF emanating from the *Explorer*, very weak, but I think it might be communications."

"Nicely done," Armstrong said. "Try to hail them, Lieutenant."

*

Elizabeth Miller slowed the ship using the aft docking thrusters and tried to guide the vessel back into position near the walkway that previously connected the ship. Upon closer inspection, they realized that it'd been damaged by a secondary explosion caused by the impacting enemy darts, making a safe docking nearly impossible. Frustration kept bubbling up, making her want to smash the panel each time she fought to keep the ship going in a straight line, but her clumsy attempts kept causing oscillations that she would have to counteract. She thought about asking the AI for assistance, but just when she would be ready to ask, Ryan would make a comment about moving more quickly, which served to anger her further.

Watching the slow progress from her station, June Armstrong could see the woman struggling, but knowing the type of person Elizabeth was made her bite her tongue. It wouldn't do any good, as there wasn't another person remotely qualified to dock the vessel. A rush of static from the communications array brought June's attention back to her console.

The second team was still trapped on the station and worryingly hadn't tried to contact them since the darts hit. She queried the computer and much to her surprise, the source of the static was coming from behind them, not the station. She touched the console controls feeding the pattern into the matrix, and her heart leapt when it returned: Quantum Field Dispersion Flux.

Ryan was bent over his display speaking to Corporal Johnson in the hangar bay, trying to coordinate some sort of rescue effort. "We'll try to get as close as we can to the walkway, Corporal. The computer says the structure might be too unstable to dock." The main display showed the image of the tactical team leader clearly. Behind him, several of his teammates and civilians were rigging up some makeshift pully system. "Make sure you have enough emergency suits with you for the team on the station."

"Roger that. A couple of the civvies down here rigged up a line that we should be able to tie off and bring them across. Just give us the word and we'll be ready."

They would probably have to use their emergency pressure suits to make their way across the distance. Ryan didn't have much faith in getting the *Explorer* docked after he watched Elizabeth maneuver the ship. Not that he could do any better.

"Sounds great, Corporal, tell them thanks from me. Any word on Sergeant Martinez?" Ryan questioned, steeling himself for bad news.

"I just checked in with our medic. She says the sarge is stable for now but needs a real hospital when we can manage it."

"As soon as we can get out of here, she'll be our top priority," Ryan said. "Oh, the specialist said you got some help… uh, Mr. Ravani?" Ryan snapped his finger, remembering the name Anna mentioned.

"Yes, sir, I guess the guy's pretty good with what they have in the med bay. Specialist Lata said it might have been different if he wasn't there."

The large private who'd been on the bridge earlier walked up, standing partially off camera.

"I'll send word soon."

"Thank you, Captain." Johnson nodded just before the picture reverted to a duplicate of the navigation display Elizabeth was using at her station.

"If you don't tell them, I will." Elizabeth glanced over her shoulder at Ryan, who still wore the captain's coat.

"As soon as we're out of this mess, you can escort me to the brig personally, but for now, the last thing we need is a muddied chain of command. Anyway... the ship says I'm in charge, and the person that's in charge of a vessel after it leaves port is the captain... I looked it up." Ryan smiled, sitting back in his chair, eliciting a growl from Elizabeth, who returned to the painfully slow maneuvering process.

"Mr. Anders, I have something you should see," June said, swiping the signal analysis she'd run to his console.

"Thanks, June.... Uh, what is a 'Dispersion Flux'?"

"I think there might be another ship in the area. It came in from behind us.... Well, that would be to port now."

Anna, who had very little to do since her rights aboard the ship were so limited, quickly touched her controls and brought up several portside views, displaying them on the leftmost portion of the bridge screen. A mass of floating debris and twisted metal moved randomly in frame. Clouds of ice particles further obscured the view, but a distant object stood still just at the periphery of one camera.

"....*plorer*, come in." The signal was so laden with static, June almost dismissed it as more background noise. She hurriedly applied the same filters she'd made earlier and saved as presets on her console.

"*Cosmic Explorer* ...ome in."

"The ship is hailing us!" June said, relief flooding her voice.

Ryan smiled genuinely for the first time, imagining that a flotilla of ships from Earth had scared off the giant alien dreadnaught. "Hell yes. Open a channel and put it on the overhead." He beamed.

"Unknown vessel, this is the *Cosmic Explorer*. We receive you." June's voice surged with relief.

"*Cosmic Explorer*, this is the battleship *Columbia*, stand by for *Columbia* actual."

June looked at Ryan, tears in her eyes as she responded, "Roger, *Columbia*, *Explorer* is standing by."

Several seconds later, a gruff but soft-spoken voice came over the bridge.

"*Cosmic Explorer*, this is Captain Armstrong of the *Columbia*." He paused, drawing a stuttering breath. "Forgive me for breaking protocol, but is that Lieutenant June Armstrong on the com?" His voice exuded a sense of authority, but when he said June's name, it faltered slightly.

June looked to Ryan, who nodded before she answered. "Yes, sir, it's so good to hear from you, Grandpa... I'm sorry, Captain," she said, wiping her face with the back of her hand, smearing the soot and dirt that covered just about everyone who had escaped the station.

"You don't know how much it warms my heart to hear that you're safe. I wish we had time to talk, but I want you to connect me directly to the captain, we have some things to discuss." He paused before adding, "Love you, June bug."

"Love you," she managed to choke out before Ryan's personal com beeped, signifying a private connection between himself and Captain Armstrong.

"Who am I speaking to?" The old man's voice seemed tired and far away.

"Lieutenant Junior Grade Ryan Anders, sir."

The line went quiet; only the occasional artifact from the AI filters chirped in his ear intermittently. Ryan was about to ask June if they'd lost connection when Armstrong spoke again.

"I... I don't. How... how did you manage to take control of that ship, Lieutenant?"

"Sir, I was on watch during the attack and.... well, I guess it just sorta happened."

"I see…" Armstrong said. "My coms officer tells me that she can set up a low-speed datalink over this channel. Aurora, are you there?"

"Yes, Captain Armstrong," the ever-present Aurora said.

"Compile a full report and send it to me on this channel. We're moving the ship as close as we can to cut through some of the interference."

"Report has been compiled; handshake received. Sending now," Aurora's said.

"Lieutenant, give me a few minutes. *Columbia* out."

When the com cut out, Ryan looked up, noticing that everyone else was staring at him.

"He's gonna call me back," he announced, pointing to his ear.

He eased out of his chair and walked to the tactical station as the others turned their attention back to their tasks.

"Hey, you doing okay, Anna?"

"If I could do something… anything but scanning these stupid cameras, I'd be doing great." She blew a stray lock of hair from her face, pushing back from her console and crossing her arms. "I'm really worried about David. One of those missile things hit pretty close to where he was supposed to be." Her face was lined with worry as she chewed her lower lip.

"David's fine, the guy's a cockroach. You can step on him, but the only thing you're gonna get is a roach crawling up your leg." He smiled, trying to put her at ease.

"God, Ryan, you always know exactly what to say to make someone feel better."

"Thanks," he said proudly before he noticed her deadpan look. "Oh."

"Why don't you put some of that Anders charm to work and go ask June how she's doing… the poor thing."

"Maybe you should… you know… girl to girl?" Ryan gave her his most disarming smile, which had the opposite effect on her.

Anna nearly belted him again as he danced out of the way.

"I'm busy, and she might appreciate the guy pretending to be the captain giving her some encouragement, asshole," she said under her breath.

Ryan quickly moved away from his friend. He had no idea what he did to make her angry but decided it wouldn't hurt to see the pretty young lieutenant.

"Hey, Lieutenant, how are you doing? Must be great hearing from the *Columbia*, right?"

June nodded, wiping her face with the back of her hand. "I'm fine, Mr. Anders," she said, regaining her composure. "I hoped…. I'm just glad they're okay."

He nodded to June. "I'm glad too." he said, unsure what else to say.

Elizabeth looked over her shoulder and cleared her throat. "Ryan, we're about in position, do you mind looking at these numbers?"

"Duty calls, keep your chin up." He smiled and retreated, drawing a disapproving look from Anna.

Elizabeth's calm demeanor made Ryan raise his eyebrow. He'd half expected her to jump on the com and tell the *Columbia* to come arrest him when the call came in, but now she seemed rather professional.

"What's up?" he said, walking over to the executive officer's station.

Keeping her voice low, she pointed at her screen, which contained data Aurora had compiled about the *Columbia*. "Ryan, they're in really bad shape. Frankly, I'm surprised that the ship is still in one piece. She must have taken several direct hits. They're leaking atmosphere, and what little information is coming through the sensor array shows they've been exposed to high levels of radiation. Even our degraded sensors are showing hot spots all over their bow."

Ryan sat down at his own station and studied the analysis for several minutes. He let out a low whistle when he finished, glancing at June out of the corner of his eye.

*

"Mr. Anders, Captain Armstrong for you," June said, catching him off guard.

The beep in his ear signaled the private communication. As it connected, he stood and walked into the open door of the duty cabin, deciding to ask the storied captain if he needed assistance.

"Captain Armstrong?"

"Lieutenant Anders, I've read the reports, and it seems I owe you a debt for getting my granddaughter off that station."

"Well, that was really the tac guys, sir, and I have to level with you, I may have led them to believe—"

"Take the compliment, Lieutenant," he interrupted. "I see you also have the Martian ambassador on board... that will come in handy if we can get you away from here."

"Sir?"

"No doubt you've seen the state of the *Columbia* by now. We're still trying to get an accurate count, but there aren't many of us left over here and the ship is in tough shape." A weak, wet cough told Ryan the captain was probably not doing much better.

"The enemy probably moved to intercept us when we destroyed their escort. They didn't expect us to bypass them and come straight here. Damned foolish but had to be done." He rambled, his voice trailing off before seemingly remembering Ryan was still on the com.

"Lieutenant, I've sent you a detailed tactical plan, but the long and short of it is the *Columbia* will screen your retreat. You will make best possible speed to Mars where you will hand over the *Explorer* to Captain Windsor of the *Brittania*. The *Explorer* contains highly sensitive information that cannot fall into enemy hands."

"Sorry to interrupt, sir, but I don't think I'll be able to do that. Before the alert, I could barely turn on the lights. I had to bypass some, uh, safety systems to start up the reactors."

"I see." Armstrong's voice seemed a bit stronger with maybe a hint of annoyance. "Aurora?"

"Yes, Captain Armstrong," the soft voice answered.

"Make a note in the ship's log. I am awarding Lieutenant Junior Grade Anders with a temporary battlefield commission to Captain effective immediately. Until such a time he hands over the *Explorer* to Captain Windsor or another commissioned officer in the ISA, you will give him full access to the ship's systems."

Ryan dropped into one of the not-so-soft chairs in the duty cabin.

A tone sounded before Aurora answered, "Noted. Valkyrie's tactical system has also been updated."

"Nearly forgot about that…" Armstrong said under his breath. "You still with me, Ryan?"

"Y…yes, sir?" Ryan let out the breath he was holding. "Sir? Are you sure… I mean, sir, I need to confess: I think I was about to be kicked out before all this… maybe someone else might be better—"

"Cut the shit, Lieutenant. I've read the highlights and Aurora is very, very thorough. I'll be frank with you, if there were anyone else on that ship I could trust, they would be sitting in that seat."

Armstrong paused. Ryan could almost hear him deciding on his next words.

"Anders…" he started before his voice softened. "Ryan… You don't know it, but…" He paused for several seconds before he started speaking again with conviction. "Ryan, I've been following your career since the beginning. I admit… with that chip on your shoulder… I didn't have much hope, but you're stronger, braver, and smarter than you think you are. You have a real knack for command, and the last few hours proves it. You have heart, son, just like your mother."

"My… wait, how do you know her? What do you mean?" Ryan felt a flood of emotions as his mother's face flashed into his mind unbidden.

"Ryan, I knew your mother back when she was in the Academy. I don't expect you to understand this, and I am sorry for the way everything unfolded." He sounded wistful and far away. "She was amazing, an incredible woman, stubborn as anything, but—"

"Sir," he interrupted, temper flaring. "I have no idea what you're talking about, how the hell did you know her?" Ryan felt panicked. He had butterflies in his stomach and started to feel a little dizzy. He stood from his chair and punched the panel at the back of the cabin, closing the door. He turned and leaned against it, the coolness of the metal coming through his uniform.

"Ryan, I made a promise that I said I would never break, but... things being as they are."

"I don't know what you're saying, sir!" He desperately tried to make sense of the man's words.

"I'm your father, Ryan."

Ryan's vision blurred as tears welled up in his eyes, his breathing coming fast and hard as he slid down, hitting the floor with a thump.

"My father? No, my father is—"

"Ryan, I'm sorry we don't have time. I've wanted to tell you, I really did, but your mother forbade me—"

"No, don't you say a thing about her!" Ryan's mind was on fire, and he was breathing so hard he was seeing white spots around the periphery of his vision.

"Ryan—"

"I don't know what kind of game you're playing, but my mom met my father—"

"After she dropped out of the Academy." Armstrong's voice was firm. "Lieutenant, I know this is hard to process, and I would never think of doing this in such an indelicate manner, but we don't have time for this dance. Whether or not you want to believe it, I am your father. I was an instructor at the Academy, and after she became pregnant... well. Well, I knew my career would be over if it came out that I had an affair with..."

"A grub, sir?" Ryan felt the familiar flames of his anger.

"Someone not from my social standing." Armstrong ignored the comment and continued. "I am ashamed to say that I was weak. When my family found out, they pressured me to break off the relationship and convince your mother to terminate the pregnancy. They held her commission over her head, and mine. Chloe... your mother was braver than I ever was. She broke up with me and left the Academy the next day. A week later she was married with a new name."

"Yeah, that turned out great," Ryan spat, remembering the many times after his mother's death that his father berated him, told him how worthless he was, how he was no son of his. How right he turned out to be.

"Your mother's only request was that I never contact her again and that under no circumstances was I to ever be involved in your life. She has... had quite a temper." His voice was thick with emotion.

Ryan couldn't deny that he'd inherited not only his looks but his temper from his mother. She could be volatile one second, screaming and throwing things, and the next minute be the sweetest, most genuine person in the world.

Captain Armstrong said something he couldn't make out before he came back clearly.

"Ryan, we have to go. The enemy ship is almost here, and you have to get *Explorer* to Mars."

Ryan wanted to ask a million questions, deny Armstrong with every fiber of his being. He felt like his mother's memory was under attack, but he couldn't find any words.

"She was a truly amazing woman that I never stopped loving... I see all of that in you. You are your mother's son." Armstrong's voice broke slightly before he regained control, his emotion drained away, replaced by the tough-as-nails captain.

"Captain Anders, I expect you to do your duty and get that ship to Mars. When you're ready, Aurora will brief you on any other questions you might have... Oh..." His voice softened slightly. "Do an old man a favor, take care of June. I don't suspect I'll see either of you again."

He didn't know what to say beyond a simple, "Yes, sir."

"You both make me so proud. *Columbia* out."

A soft knock cut through his stunned consciousness. "Ryan, the enemy ship just arrived, *Columbia* is accelerating. Looks like they're headed out to intercept," said Anna's muffled voice.

Ryan stood, wiping his eyes with the back of his hand before turning to open the door, locking eyes with Anna.

"What's going on?"

"Come on, Anna, let's get out of here," Ryan said, brushing past her.

"Anders, I think that's as close as we're going to get to the station." Elizabeth rubbed circles of smudged soot on her temples, displaying just how taxing maneuvering the ship had been on the impromptu navigator.

"Good work, Elizabeth," he said, sitting down in the captain's chair.

"My chair," he thought to himself, trying to will away the conversation he just had with Armstrong before his well-built defenses kicked in. He pushed it to the back of his mind.

He resolved to save his friends and everyone else on this ship.

"Coms, connect me to Corporal Johnson," he said without pause, trusting June to route the message for him, his eyes lingering on her profile, trying to see if he could spot something familiar.

"Aye, Mr. Anders."

As he waited for June to make the connection, he wondered if he should speak to her... question her about the old man. Was he a liar? A political sycophant? A legend? What kind of person was he? Did he have a kid in every port? Did she know about... about his mother?

"Johnson here," came the crackling, barely audible, answer to Ryan's ear.

"Corporal Johnson?" Ryan said, thinking the static must be getting worse as the corporal gathered his men by the main entryway to the ship.

"Go ahead, sir," June said, tapping her console trying to clear up the signal.

"We're as close as we can get. The dock is depressurized, so be careful, those aren't EVA suits."

"No problem, sir, we do drills in emergency suits all the time."

"Roger that; as soon you're ready, the computer will cycle the door. Any word from our people?"

"Negative." He paused before adding, "We'll get everyone back."

"Good luck." Ryan signed off feeling even more troubled than he'd been. David and the others were over there because he asked Johnson to disconnect the *Explorer*. True, he didn't have much of a choice, but he could have made the trip. David was smart, but on the failing station with all the dangers he would face...

"I should have gone," Ryan thought.

CHAPTER 18

Ensign David Kim slowly made his way down the passageway, following the six members of the Martian Special Services. They had reached the portion of the station that connected to the hallway leading to the main gangway where the Explorer was supposed to be docked. This was their third attempt, as the previous two had ended at emergency doors locked firmly in place. The small handheld tactical radio was tucked into his pocket and connected to his PDD, leaving his hands free to climb.

A crackling in his ear sent a shiver down his spine, causing his limbs to spasm momentarily and drawing curious glances from the Martian team as they came to a halt.

He smiled awkwardly as he regained control of his body and signaled that he was hearing something.

The crackling grew louder until it formed a voice.

"Bravo team, do you read me?" Lieutenant Johnson's signal finally broke through the static.

He looked around, wondering if he should speak before finally deciding to cover his mouth with his hand and whisper as softly as he could into the PDD.

"We read you..."

"Ensign, glad we found you. *Explorer* had to detach, but she's parked about a hundred meters away from where it was docked. We're running a line for you and the others. Can you put Thompson on the com?"

"We got separated. I'm with the Martians."

"The what? Sorry, sir, I must not have received correctly..."

David decided not to muddy the waters any further. "Corporal, I was separated from the rest of the group, and it took me a while to get back. The emergency doors are closed and I'm trying to find a way around them."

"Roger that, Ensign, I'll keep trying to raise the rest of Bravo team. Can you make your way to one of the external airlocks near the gangway? We're running a line back to the ship."

"Uh, did you say airlocks? I'm not sure we can do that. Can't they just dock... uh, you know, the ship should be able to dock to another gangway."

"Negative, sir, my orders are to get you here as fast as possible. We don't have much time before the enemy ships make it back, and this is the closest we can get."

David knew the corporal was right. He desperately thought of alternatives, but the other closest gangway was over ten minutes away during the best of times. Then taking into account docking the ship, it would just take too long. As if punctuating his thoughts, another shudder ran through the station followed by a low groaning sound.

"Okay, Corporal, we should be at the gangway in five minutes," David said, defeated.

"Yes, sir, we'll be waiting. Johnson out."

David looked up at the Martian soldiers after closing the connection. They patiently awaited his signal with grim looks. Not quite knowing how to respond, he gave them a weak smile and a thumbs-up. The thought of doing some sort of spacewalk to get to the ship made his stomach turn.

Chief Huatare nodded and motioned the group forward, swiftly moving through passageway after passageway. When they rounded yet another blind corner, the Martians came up short and spread out. The lead man signaled to the chief, who leaned around the corner before making a counter signal with his hand, sending several of the soldiers forward on power-assisted strides.

He signaled to David to come.

Before he reached the junction, he could smell something foul, something unrecognizable.

In the silent hallway, he strained to hear anything, but he only picked up a soft ticking sound, like water falling and striking a hard surface. When he peeked around the corner, he was immediately confused. There was something covering the walls and floors of the passageway. In the darkened place, everything was muted and shadowed by his harsh light, but when he took a longer, harder look, he nearly vomited. There, on the floor in front of him, was a pile of gore, mixed with bits of fabric and white bone. In that pile, staring back at him, was half a face, undeniably human and so horrific that David just stared.

The chief's face was in front of his now. His finger at his lips signaled silence. He guided David past the horrifically pulverized shapes until they were on the far side of the scene. They turned the next corner and stopped.

"Can you fix it?" Huatare said to him, putting something into his hand.

David stared at him for a second before he motioned to the object. David looked down; recognition sparked somewhere in the back of his mind. He threw it back at the chief without thinking, rubbing the slightly sticky feeling on the front of his legs as he backpedaled away from Private Thompson's damaged radio. The image of the half face flashed into his mind, finally realizing what he recognized as Thompson's dark skin and blank eye.

His hands shook. His breath came in short, sharp bursts. The grisly scene threatened to overwhelm him, but a sudden sound snapped him back to reality.

The long, low warble of the thing, the creature who had committed such horrors, was near.

The entire team coalesced out of the darkness and moved forward as a unit. David didn't realize it, but he was being carried along by the chief before he could get his legs under him. They padded up the hallway nearly silently. Only the soft whine of the servomotors would give them away if not for the near constant moans and creaks of the station.

David's legs grew steady as they approached the third and final corridor near their destination. The hallway started to look increasingly familiar even in the emergency lighting with its familiar grey doors and painted wall navigation markers.

He was about to tell the chief that they were near the airlock, but the Martian team reacted in unison. From the swiftness of their response, he assumed it wasn't good as they spread out and hugged the walls.

He concentrated on trying to be quiet; his breath came in small fits and starts as he attempted to be completely silent, but compared with the Martians, he might as well be crashing cymbals together.

After standing silently in the dark corridor for several minutes, scanning the way ahead with his strange three-eyed goggles, Chief Huatare made several odd hand signs toward the other members of his team, sending them into action before looking directly at David at the rear of the group. He made an odd gesture with his pinky, then waved at him, pointing down the way they'd come.

David had no idea what the grizzled man wanted and shook his head.

The chief then used two fingers like legs and bounced them across his other flattened hand in big arcs before pointing to a nearby door they'd just passed.

David made an exaggerated nod and walked slowly toward the door, assuming they would follow him as soon as he made it into the room.

When he arrived, he placed his hand near the panel, bringing it to life, and looked back over his shoulder to see if he should open it. Only the woman called Inna stood nearby. She stretched her arms backwards and rolled her muscled shoulders. Noticing his gaze, she looked over at him and winked before setting her makeshift sword onto the deck silently before her.

About twelve feet farther toward the intersection, the chief was down on one knee, his handgun drawn and aimed toward the passage. In front of him, four of the other soldiers separated into groups. The first was nearest to the chief, flanking him to either side, standing like baseball players at home plate, their makeshift bats hoisted over their shoulders, both waiting for a pitch to be thrown. The second group was nearest the intersecting passage. The two soldiers were kneeling low, sides pressed against the wall. Neither of them looked like they were ready to strike but had their clubs held close to their sides, waiting in ambush.

After making a gesture that drew his attention, the Martian woman near David drew a short, ornate-looking knife from behind her lower back and handed it to him, handle first. Unsure what to do, he grabbed the knife.

She motioned him to open the door and step inside as she turned to face the passage.

As he followed her instruction, the beep from the door control and subsequent sliding of the door mechanism sounded like a klaxon in the hushed hallway. Somewhere in the far passage, a croaking, scraping moan answered, making David tense in fear before sickeningly familiar wet, thudding sounds touched his ears. Quickly stepping into the room, he turned and desperately motioned for the rest to follow, but the Martians seemed unconcerned, perhaps even eager.

He grasped the handle of the blade tightly, struggling to remember his basic combat classes. There was a day dedicated to hand-to-hand and knife fighting during their overland escape and evasion course, where they learned some basic techniques, but he hadn't paid much attention, as he assumed that he would spend his days on a ship… in space… not trading blows with an unknown enemy with a sharpened stick.

A scream brought him out of his rumination with a start, but it wasn't the approaching creature. It was Inna, the Martian woman.

She belted out another scream as she stomped her left boot onto the deck with a thud. Chest pushed out, arms back outstretched, sword still at her feet.

The rest of the Martian team let out a cry in unison as she finished her second scream. David wasn't quite sure what they were doing, but whatever it was nearly made him slam the door. Only after furiously looking around the room and realizing he was in a storage closet did he turn back to face the group. Outside, more screaming made him wince as it reverberated through the corridor. A grating change from the near silence of only a few moments before. He could just make out what they were yelling, their heavy accents and strange pronunciations making it difficult.

"We arr the flaem!" She whipped an arm around and slammed it into her chest plate.

"Born oh dust, forged in bloo-id!" the answer from her teammates came again, louder and more pronounced.

David could see each of the Martians was breathing hard, as if they'd just run sprints. Chests heaving, a wild look was in each of their eyes.

"We rize, we strike, we DIN-eh fall!" She stomped her right foot down. The power-assisted thud sounded through the plates.

"We arr the redd! We arr the flaem!" came the answer.

Just as he thought another round of screams were coming, a shadow flew into view, thick, meaty tentacles stopping the bulk of the creature from overshooting the corridor and launching itself down the hallway containing the Martians and David with a sickly roar.

In the illumination of the emergency lights, David finally got a clear look at the thing, and it wasn't the formless monster he'd pictured in his previous encounter. The creature looked vaguely bipedal with shorter, odd-looking lower limbs splayed out into three large tentacle-like toes. Its arms were elongated, nearly twice the length of its torso, ending in thin, spindly claws, each tipped with sharp-looking black points, giving it a praying-mantis-like gait as it moved. Its head was more of a suggestion with a rounded bulb protruding from its thickly muscled torso. David couldn't see eyes, but where the top of the rib cage would be in a human, a slobbering wet orifice opened and closed repeatedly as if tasting the air. The creature's body, which seemed to be comprised entirely of sickly grey corded muscle had no clothing or pressure suit, but the smack of its forelimbs on the ground sounded like it was encased in some sort of hard shell as it bounded down the corridor.

A sharp crack and flash sounded as Chief Huatare opened fire. The snap and arcing blue flash of the strange pistol caused David's ears to ring and his vision to darken. As each of the rounds smashed into the creature, it barely seemed to register other than to emit its warbling cry and to move even faster, making a beeline to the chief; rivulets of dark fluid ran down the muscled frame from each of the wounds.

The two Martians who'd been pressed against the side of the corridor both swung their clubs in unison, not aiming for the head area as David would have but swinging into the thick legs with a thud. The first club smashed into the right tentacled foot of the creature, tripping it up before the second hit near where the knee of a person would be on the other leg, causing it to stumble and slow.

The thing's right arm-like appendage flicked out so swiftly, David's brain didn't have time to register the movement. Only as the second Martian flew backwards into the wall of the corridor, landing with a sickening thud and leaving behind a dark red stain, did he realize it had made contact.

The chief's pistol cracked rapidly at the closing nightmare, finally stopping as panels on both sides of the receiver flipped open, allowing hot gasses to escape with a hiss. Both of the two flanking Martians sprang forward on power-assisted legs, nearly matching the thing for speed. Instead of broad swings, the two used their clubs like shields, deflecting the lashing tentacles and leading the way. Each crashed precisely into either side of the creature inside its swinging arms, slowing it in a shower of sparks as their armored feet screeched backward across the deck, struggling to impede the beast.

David hadn't seen Inna make her move, but she flashed by him so fast that he swore he could feel the wind of her passing tug at his clothing.

Her piercing scream filled the corridor as she launched herself into the air, legs straight together, back arched, with both hands grasping her makeshift sword behind her head. David was stricken by how time seemed to crawl as the woman hurtled towards the chief, who still had his back turned, until at the last second, he dropped to one knee. His head bowed and clenched hand, still holding the pistol outstretched before him as if in prayer, allowed the mad woman to sail directly overhead.

As she swung, the sword drew a bright line of sparks across the ceiling before coming down like a guillotine, digging a deep V-shaped furrow nearly a quarter way through the body of the alien before she smashed into the thing's chest with her expertly turned shoulder.

The creature and three Martians fell to the floor in a heap of flailing tentacles and swinging arms. The chief and one of the others from the first attack joined the fray, knives drawn, punching and slashing with abandon, each screaming some sort of battle cry at the top of their lungs.

David ducked his head back instinctually as the chief came sailing past him, flung from the pile by a thick tentacle, his armored foot nearly decapitating him as he sailed by.

His tumble finally came to an abrupt end ten feet past the doorway with the sound of scraping armor and a harsh grunt. Another Martian on the pile paused mid-swing, making a gurgling cry as his head snapped back at an odd angle before rolling off the pile and landing on the deck, his now glassy eyes coming to rest on David.

An otherworldly warbling scream reverberated through the passage as Inna wrenched out her now bent sword from the monster and slashed across one of its flailing limbs, severing it cleanly near the body. It spurted some sort of greenish fluid over the side of the corridor and Inna herself. Another tentacle, this time a leg, shot out and wrenched the sword from her grasp, probably dislocating her shoulder as her power-assisted armor sparked, adding its own reddish fluid to that of the creature.

Arm hanging limply, but without missing a beat, she lashed out pushing one of the remaining Martians away from an arcing blow that would likely have killed him instantly. Instead, the thick appendage slammed into the wall of the corridor, leaving a deep dent. The last Martian, who David recognized from his bald and tattooed head, drove his hand, elbow deep into the gash that Inna had cleaved with her sword, pulling gore and sinew from the thing like a hunter gutting a fresh kill. With a screech, one of its limbs wrapped around the soldier's arm and tore it from his body in a shower of sparks, blood, and screaming.

Inna retreated as the alien turned its focus on the howling Martian. She dragged the man she'd saved earlier from the fight with her remaining powered arm, his expression showing he was probably severely concussed as his head lolled to either side.

The crack of a newly reloaded pistol signaled Chief Huatare's reengagement from David's left. He ran forward, limping, firing the weapon rapidly, covering

Inna's retreat while grabbing the man's other arm and helping her move him away from the fight.

"This way!" David screamed to the soldiers, waving his hand wildly as the alien beast finished dismembering their unfortunate teammate, his bare headless and limbless torso falling to the floor like a wet bag of clay.

The monster stepped forward on one gore-covered leg. Its remaining arm thumped to the ground in front of it, and the sucking orifice opened greedily, showing rows of needle-sharp yellow teeth, which unsheathed from the flesh around the mouth before retracting again as if promising horror they hadn't yet seen.

As the two Martians pulled their injured comrade toward the doorway into the storage room, David noticed the interior control pad was dark. He jabbed his finger onto the screen, eliciting no response. In a full panic now, he reached outside the door and slapped his hand on the outer pad. The squawking tone that answered told him that, like everything else on the station, it seemed to be malfunctioning.

A tentacle lashed out, striking Inna's leg and knocking her off her feet. Before she could react, it coiled tightly around her already injured arm, yanking her toward the creatures dripping maw. She cried out as her arm twisted. The full weight of her comrade now fell onto the chief, whose bad leg buckled under the strain, sending them both crashing into a heap.

David looked on in shock, wishing he could do something, anything, when he realized he was still holding the ornate blade.

He let out a bloodcurdling scream and launched himself at the thick limb of the monster, driving the knife deep into the muscled appendage, causing a gout of greenish fluid to spray out of the wound. Still screaming, he pulled the knife and struck again and again, wrapping his legs around the corded thing, forcing it to release the woman.

Only then did David realize it was retracting the limb with him on it, straight toward a nightmarish, tooth-covered orifice.

The warble coming from the thing sounded gleeful to David's ears. The horror of what was about to happen to him struck almost as quickly as it stopped in a flash of light and heat.

A thunderous roar and pressure wave knocked David from the thing's limb and dashed him against the bulkhead, causing him to fall to the floor stunned. The creature slammed into the opposite side of the passage before shrugging off the blast as if it were nothing more than an inconvenience.

In the haze of the passage through his spotty vision, Inna's face appeared over him smiling, her white teeth stained dark with blood. Her left eye was nearly closed, face puffy from swelling on one side, with a line of fresh blood running from a head wound. She grabbed the front of his suit with her good arm and hoisted him to his wobbly feet just outside the doorway they'd tried to take cover in. Behind her, the chief stood between them and the beast, legs outspread, his pistol sounding off rapid shots before discarding the empty weapon and drawing a huge, wicked-looking blade from behind his back.

Inna looked at David approvingly. "When we meet the Red Father, I will tell him to take pity on you."

David looked down at his bloody hands, realizing that he would likely be dead soon, torn limb from limb or worse by the seemingly unstoppable beast.

As Inna turned to join the chief, her legs buckled and she went down on one knee, coughing up a spray of blood, barely catching herself with her arm before she collapsed, face down onto the deck. David was at her side before he could stop himself, unsure what he would do other than to shield her for the briefest of moments, all feeling of fear gone.

A wave of crackling gunfire roared from the passage where the beast had emerged. Errant rounds pinged off the walls and deck, forcing David to duck while shielding Inna. The creature slowed, shuddering as bits of flesh flew from its back. Undeterred, it moved forward, out of the line of fire and towards David and his group, singularly focused on destroying its prey before turning on the newcomers.

Its lone arm flung out, aimed at the chief with deadly precision, the thick appendage flying at him like a battering ram. Standing firm in front of David and Inna, he flipped the knife in the air in one smooth motion, reversing his grip while leaning forward. He bent his knife arm across his chest and braced the pommel in his opposing hand, taking the full brunt of the blow.

The monstrous tentacle-like arm impacted the knife, its own momentum driving the blade through the thickened skin and nearly severing itself in half as the chief turned his body away from the blow, absorbing or deflecting most of the energy with his armor.

Howling, the creature flicked the damaged limb back before lashing out again even faster, this time slamming the chief in the hip, sending him sideways spinning through the air.

Now with a clear path to David and Inna, it stalked forward with its injured limb whipping back, spewing dark fluid, ready to deliver a killing blow.

Spilling into the corridor, a group of soldiers dressed in black tactical gear renewed their fire at the creature. The chatter and bright muzzle flashes of their submachine guns filled the corridor with strobes of light. One soldier strode boldly forward, nearly as wide as he was tall, the booming report of his weapon providing a bass beat to the others. He unloaded his assault shotgun, cutting the three-pronged limbs out from under the thing before delivering a seemingly fatal shot to its lower back from close range.

As it fell near David, twitching, its puckered mouth opened and closed a few times before becoming still.

Slowly realizing that he wasn't dead, David opened his eyes and cautiously looked at the twitching creature before managing to breathe out a slow sigh of relief.

"Holy shit, that thing is hard to kill!" PFC Nguyen lifted the visor on his helmet and hefted his oversized shotgun onto his shoulder.

David looked up at the sound of the familiar voice and opened his mouth to reply, but the words wouldn't form. A sharp pain lanced out from his lower abdomen. To his horror, some sort of sickly green proboscis had penetrated his outer pressure suit and tangled in his clothing, pulsing and writhing like a snake trying to burrow into his gut. Without thinking, he grabbed at the thing, ripping it away from his midsection and tossing it to the floor, stomping on it several times. His shocked mind followed the now lifeless coiled tube back to its source: the sucking orifice of the monster.

He recoiled in horror, stepping away from the wriggling tendril on the ground, and used his hands to brush the front of his suit, frantically looking for bits of the thing still attached to him.

"Damn, did it get you, sir?" Nguyen said, stepping up to David.

"No, I... I don't think so... I think my suit stopped it."

Slapping him on the shoulder, Nguyen gave a big toothy grin. "Looks like you're the only one left standing. Good job!"

"I wouldn't be if not for the Martians."

He hurriedly knelt down to the now unconscious Inna, looking her over.

"We need to get her to a doctor!"

"Medic!" Nguyen shouted, turning to his comrades, who were checking the bodies of the fallen.

*

On the bridge of the *Explorer*, Elizabeth watched as *Columbia* flew over the station, trailing a cloud of icy particles and atmosphere from its many battle scars. She noticed Ryan, who'd finished his communication with the ship, was now sitting back in his chair looking stunned and perhaps... sad?

"We're still getting some information over the datalink. Enemy ship is closing fast. If *Columbia* can't stop them, we'll have less than five minutes before they can fire on the station again," she said, gauging his reaction to the news. He was obviously in distress, and she could guess what might have happened. She figured a low-level officer from a questionable background taking command of a ship could not have gone over well, even in times like these. Whatever transpired, Elizabeth decided she needed to act.

"What did Captain Armstrong tell you?" she asked, turning in her chair. "Ryan?"

He made no indication that he had heard her question, so she stood, moving to the side of his chair. "Lieutenant!"

"What? No, uh, yeah, it went fine."

"I need to know what the captain told you. If he relieved you of duty, I'm still the highest-ranking officer here,"

Ryan's focus finally snapped back into place, his temper flaring.

"Give it a rest, Elizabeth. He didn't relieve me, he promoted me."

Ryan looked around the bridge noticing the silence. Anna was standing with her hands on her hips and a skeptical look on her face and June, who seemed to be as distracted as he was, had even turned looking puzzled.

"What?" Elizabeth said. "Why would the captain promote you over... a more senior officer?"

"You mean someone with your connections?" he asked, eyebrow raised.

She ignored him. "Aurora?"

"Yes, Lieutenant Junior Grade Miller?"

"Was Anders promoted?"

"Yes, Lieutenant, Captain Armstrong of the *Columbia* promoted Ryan Anders to Interim Captain of the *Cosmic Explorer* effective immediately."

Elizabeth stood gaping.

"You gotta be shitting me," Anna said from behind him in disbelief. "How the hell did you convince him to do that?"

The color left Ryan's face at the question. The change was so slight, anyone but Anna would have blown it off as nothing.

"Actually, it's just a temporary and—"

"Mr. Anders... Captain, Corporal Johnson is reporting in," June said, unsure again how to address him.

"Thanks, June," he said, grateful for the distraction.

"Elizabeth, please return to your station and prepare the ship, we need to get out of here." He turned to the equally stunned Anna, smiling. "Aurora, please assign Ensign Rodriguez to the tactical station... she is now officially part of the crew."

Anna's PDD beeped, and Aurora's smooth voice spoke in her ear. "Ensign Rodriguez, you have been assigned to the *Cosmic Explorer* as Tactical Officer, effective immediately."

"I heard," she snapped, turning back to her station.

"Captain." Corporal Johnson's voice was much clearer now, and for the first time, Ryan didn't cringe at someone calling him by the rank—not very much, anyhow.

"Go ahead, Corporal," he said, trying to brush past the discomfort.

"Sir, we have Ensign Kim and are transferring him across to the *Explorer* now."

Something in the way he said that filled Ryan with a sense of dread.

"What's going on, Corporal? Is he hurt?"

"Negative, Cap, he's banged up, but he should be fine. We picked up some other stragglers too, but the rest of Bravo team are gone, sir."

Ryan looked at the main viewscreen. Elizabeth had put up a countdown for the enemy ship's estimated max firing range. It had just ticked under one minute.

"Shit, I'm sorry, Corporal." He paused only momentarily. "Time is running out, let the bridge know when you're secure down there and come up for a debrief."

"Yes, sir, Johnson out."

"Elizabeth, you have it in you for some fast maneuvering?"

She had just sat down at her station with a frown. "Fast?" she asked incredulously. "Do you see all the debris out there?"

"Elizabeth, you did fine getting us back to the docking port. We just need to move, the faster the better."

"Fine." She threw up a hand, waving him off. "I'm far better suited to XO than navigator." With a reluctant sigh, she touched the control interface and pulled up the thruster checklist.

Ryan thought about what she just said. He disliked her immensely, and he was pretty sure she would have him arrested if they weren't in this situation, but he had to admit that she would probably make a pretty good executive officer. She had an attention to detail that most engineers would covet and didn't seem to have any problem telling her superiors if she thought they were wrong. If they were going to fly the *Explorer* to Mars, Elizabeth would fight him every step of the way if he didn't make the chain of command crystal clear. Plus, it wouldn't hurt to throw her a bone so she wouldn't try to murder him in his sleep.

"You're right," he said.

"I'm always right." She scoffed and went back to her checklist.

"Aurora?"

"Yes, Captain Anders."

"As Captain, can I promote members of the crew?"

"Yes; however, battlefield promotions are provisional based on ISA approval."

"Good. Please note in the ship's log I am promoting Lieutenant Junior Grade Miller to Commander and assigning her as XO of the *Cosmic Explorer*, effective immediately..."

Anna whipped around in her chair and gave Ryan a death stare.

"...aaand please note that Ensign Rodriguez, Lieutenant Junior Grade Armstrong, and Ensign Kim are all promoted to full Lieutenant." He gave his best smile as Anna flipped him the bird and turned back to her station. "Ah, and please assign Ensign... er, Lieutenant Kim to the helm as our navigator whenever he gets here."

"The promotions and assignments are noted," Aurora answered smoothly.

"This doesn't change a thing, Anders. You still don't belong in that chair." Elizabeth bit off the words, her face flush as she clearly forgot what she was doing and hammered her fingers on the controls of her display.

Ryan sat back and smiled, taking a few moments to pat himself on the back. He had never seen Elizabeth so uncomfortable as she was at this moment, which was exactly what he hoped. Growing up, he'd seen similar tactics used by the smaller gangs who were constantly combining or absorbing others in power plays. He supposed it was a tactic used by leaders throughout history now that he really thought about it. Marriages or alliances with former enemies to bring them together... or to keep an eye on them.

June said a few words to someone on the com before turning. "Captain, Corporal Johnson reports the outer hatch is secure and everyone is back on board."

"Commander?"

Elizabeth ignored him, as she finished feeding in her commands and sent them to the navigation computer.

The thrusters started to fire, slewing the bow away from the station before slowly accelerating away, putting some distance between them and the approaching enemy.

"Heading?" she said sitting back, clearly stressed.

Ryan thought about it for a second. "Get us away from all this debris and keep us in the shadow of the station for now. I need to fill everyone in on what Captain Armstrong is planning."

On board the station, lights flickered on as primary power was restored, deck by deck the lights revealing to its inhabitants the outright carnage and horror of the past hour. Unaffected by light or darkness, the creatures that boarded the station continued their grisly work, sensing the cloistered survivors and smashing their way through doorways and bulkheads alike to bring them to a horrific end.

CHAPTER 19

As the battleship *Columbia* left the crippled space station in its wake, Captain Armstrong took in a long, slow breath. He could still feel the broken ribs scraping together when he did so, but the strong medication he'd been given pushed back the pain until it wasn't as noticeable.

"Commander, has the *Explorer* started moving yet?"

"Just now, sir," the tactical officer said, doubt seeping into his voice. "They're pulling away from the station… slowly."

"We'll just have to buy them as much time as we can," Armstrong said, for the first time not speaking of victory over the enemy. At this point, he knew his crew accepted that victory was beyond reach. Most of his ordnance had been expended or taken offline by the battering the ship sustained. The enemy didn't seem to be much damaged beyond the punch in the nose he'd given them on their first pass. It showed signs of battle with the rest of the fleet, but it wasn't leaking atmosphere or maneuvering slowly. The only positive he could see was that they didn't seem to have any other weapons beyond the main gun, which he found bizarre. What he thought were torpedoes actually turned out to be small boarding craft according to the report he received from the *Explorer*. As long as they could move, that didn't seem to be a problem.

He surveyed his displays, paging through the various ship's systems, weapons inventory, main drive, and thrust arrays. Nothing was in the green besides the life support system and the escape pods. From the reports trickling in, fully half the crew was either dead or seriously wounded. Most of the remaining were injured in some way but still manning their stations.

He looked at the situation map, which fused together every remaining sensor and computer projection, straining to come up with something, some tactic to keep the enemy away from the station and the *Explorer*.

"Lieutenant Carmine, how much speed can we manage before intercept?"

"At maximum sustainable thrust… just over thirty kilometers per second."

Armstrong silently dismissed the idea, having never taken it seriously. The thought of ramming his ship into the enemy ran against his very being, but the numbers didn't lie. Even with the mass of the *Columbia*, he wasn't sure that the tactic would damage the huge ship. Its energy shielding was an unknown quantity. Even with his biggest, fastest weapons concentrated on a single point, they barely punched through. A blunt impact spread over a large area might just cause the ships to glance off of one another, no doubt destroying the *Columbia* in the process.

"If I only had a dozen more hedgehogs or a big…" A thought caught his attention. "Commander Owens, are the probe launchers still functioning?" He swiped through several menus, but probe launch control was completely unfamiliar to him.

"Uh, sorry, sir, it's been a while… yes, yes, sir, probe launchers are still active with… ten buoys loaded."

Armstrong snapped his fingers. "Work with Lieutenant Carmine, see if you can reconfigure them to broadcast RF. If we stagger them, we just might have the range we need to get a message to Lunar Command."

"Roger that, sir…" Commander Owens said, then paused. "Sir, Lunar Command only has point defense and a couple squadrons of patrol craft and light fighters. Maybe some of the destroyers escaped, but I'm not seeing anything with teeth out there."

"Launch the probes as soon as they're configured," Armstrong said, hurriedly punching in projections to his console. The AI systems on board were old, but they came up with the answers he needed quickly. He might just be able to pull off one last miracle.

Minutes later, several doors opened just aft of the cargo bay. Magnetic rails extended from the side of the ship and started to spit out the probes. Each one a small, pulsed plasma drive topped with an electronic package and array of antennas. They moved away from the ship: a bright line of manmade stars flying toward the Moon, each one blasting at maximum thrust.

Brushing hair from her face, Carmine sat back. "Final probe is away…. It was messy, but I've programmed them to spread out and maintain contact with each other… hopefully there will be enough of them."

"Fine work, the both of you," Armstrong said, still consumed by his calculations. He knew he should share his plan, but time and distance were working against him. His foggy brain wasn't helping either, but if they were able to make contact with Lunar Command, they would only need to be in the correct position to make it work.

*

Ryan Anders, now Captain of the *Cosmic Explorer*, stood behind his station, arms draped over the chair, drumming his fingers on the hard plastic shell. After explaining the orders he'd received from Captain Armstrong, the small group, which now included his newly rescued friend David Kim and Corporal Johnson, were all speaking over one another.

"*Columbia* is in no shape to fight that thing, they won't last two minutes," Elizabeth said, swiveling her screen so Ryan and the others who were gathered around his chair could see the wireframe model surrounded by yellow cautions and red flashing warnings. "How can they delay that ship long enough for us to get out of range?"

"Commander," Ryan warned.

"I'm just trying to be realistic," Elizabeth said, switching to a softer tone. "I'm sorry, June, from the reports we received, they've already done so much, but in their current state…" She let the statement hang.

"The *Columbia* wouldn't have made it this far if it weren't for her captain," June said at the edge of tears. "I know they can do it."

"I don't know, Ryan," Anna said, crossing her arms. "Elizabeth has a point. You saw what they did to those other battleships. Maybe if we just made a run for Earth instead? We're faster and more maneuverable."

"David, what about you?" Ryan asked. His friend wasn't a tactical genius, but he'd been a very persuasive voice in the past when he and Anna disagreed with each other about a plan of attack, often seeing a line in the middle they'd overlooked.

David finally seemed to take notice of the attention. "Oh, whatever you think."

Ryan watched him for a moment before deciding that if he was going to be Captain, he needed to make some sort of decision.

"Okay, listen, the enemy already made the mistake of underestimating Armstrong, so let's not be the ones to count him out?" He cast a nod in June's direction, which seemed to buoy her spirits. "We take the ship to Mars and hook up with the *Britannia*. She is the second-best ship in the fleet, and her captain was taught by Armstrong." Honestly, he made that last part up, but he didn't know what to do, and Armstrong was very clear that he wanted Ryan to get the ship to Mars. Regardless of what he thought of the guy, that seemed the right thing to do in the face of the seemingly unstoppable alien ship.

Surprisingly, the others seemed to take his word as final and dispersed slowly back to their stations. Albeit with a few daggers coming from Elizabeth.

"Hey, how are you doing, buddy?" He turned his attention to his friend, who was standing next to Corporal Johnson.

"Never better," David said somewhat distractedly, his face smudged and splashed with dried blood. After receiving the abbreviated report from Corporal Johnson, Ryan wanted so badly to hear about the encounter in detail but restrained himself through sheer force of will and a healthy dose of self-preservation after glancing at the countdown clock.

"Think you can handle the helm?" Ryan said, clasping his friend's shoulder. He felt guilty not offering him a break, but they would have to make the run for Mars soon, and they were seriously short on qualified crew.

"Yes… of course," David said, wincing before catching himself and smoothing out his pressure suit.

"Maybe Elizabeth can—"

"I said I'm fine," David snapped at Ryan, who let his hand drop from his shoulder. "I'll take a break after we get away from here."

"Okay," Ryan said hesitantly, thinking that his friend seemed hot to the touch—possibly running a fever. He also looked more pale than usual. Johnson told him that David had stayed out of the majority of the fighting and got a little banged up at the end. "Go ahead and take your station."

David walked away before Ryan turned to Corporal Johnson, who seemed to be watching him as well.

"Corporal, when you have a moment, I'd appreciate it if you could ask your medic to check on Lieutenant Kim?"

He nodded before lowering his voice. "Might be shock, sir. It was a pretty bad scene down there, Private Nguyen practically had to carry him back to the ship."

"What about the others?" Ryan said hopefully.

Johnson shook his head. "We couldn't find any sign of the engineers from Bravo. I don't know if the squids got to them or if they're still hiding somewhere in the station."

"Squids," Ryan said before he realized the corporal was talking about the alien. "Oh, got it."

"Privates Thompson and Wilson were both confirmed KIA."

That news hit Ryan like a slap. "I'm, I'm sorry, Corporal." He didn't know what else to say, but he felt awful. It was his decision that sent them down there, and now there were two deaths, maybe four, squarely on his shoulders. Johnson just nodded stoically, hands behind his back.

"How is your sergeant doing?"

"Specialist Lata has her in a medically induced coma. She's stable for now. I guess the doc has been asking to meet with you along with the ambassador and half the civvies down in the hangar. The Martian chief who saved David too."

He had absolutely no desire to meet with the pompous ambassador but wanted to personally thank the chief who saved David. Ryan supposed he would have to eventually speak to everyone, but only once they were out of danger.

"Corporal, with everything that's happened, I'm hesitant to ask, but I'm going to need to keep the ambassador out of my hair and make sure we don't have any problems with the civilians."

"I can do that, sir."

"I know you can." Ryan nodded. "Your team is the only reason any of us are here."

"Not my team, sir, I'm just in charge till the sarge is back on her feet."

"Yeah, same here. Armstrong ordered me to get to Mars, and I hope I can count on your support to get that job done."

Johnson stood tall. "Yes, sir, you can count on me and my team."

"I think we need to make things a little more formal before someone gets the bright idea that they would rather be in charge," Ryan said with a smile. "Aurora, please assign the members of SRT as ship security."

"Yes, Captain Anders. I have made a note in the log that the members on board have been assigned as ship's security and given them appropriate access."

"Also, please note I am awarding a promotion to Corporal Johnson to Chief Petty Officer."

"Corporal Johnson is not a member of the ISA Fleet and therefore cannot be promoted as such."

"Is there an equivalent rank?"

"Warrant Officer would be recognized by both the ISA Fleet as well as ground forces command."

"Please promote him to Warrant Officer and assign him as Master at Arms of the *Explorer*."

"Noted."

The new Master at Arms snapped off a salute to Ryan, who was now very uncomfortable.

"At ease, Mr. Johnson," Ryan said saluting him back. "I'm sure they won't honor these promotions once we get to Mars, and if I can let you in on a little secret, mine will definitely be clawed back."

Johnson's eyes darted to him for a second before returning his straightforward.

"Let me know how you'd like to handle promotions on your team. From the debrief, I'd say they deserve some. Oh, and tell the Martian chief I'd like to see him when time permits."

"Yes, sir!" He saluted again before turning on his heel, then walked off the bridge.

"Don't let that go to your head... Captain," Elizabeth said, giving him a start, as he hadn't noticed her standing behind him.

"You either... Commander," Ryan said, turning to meet her gaze. "Hey, while we're both playacting, can you check in with David? He says he's fine, but I'd hate for him to pass out in the middle of flying us out of here. Maybe help him set up his station and keep an eye on him?"

Elizabeth scoffed but brushed past him on her way over to David's station.

*

"Sir, I'm receiving a ping from the probes! I think we have a connection," Lieutenant Carmine nearly shouted as she queried the ISA network for the first time since the long day began.

"Lunar Command is answering... low bandwidth voice to your com."

A chime in his ear gave Captain Armstrong a flicker of hope.

"Command, this is *Columbia* Actual." Armstrong started speaking before a crackling reply stepped over his signal, causing him to halt mid-sentence.

The woman answering his call had a noticeable French accent.

"*Columbia*, this is Admiral Lefevre. We were delighted... oh, I see, the delay."

"Admiral, forgive me, but as you can see, we're in the thick of it and don't have much time. I'm sending targeting instructions now." He pointed at Commander Owens, who nodded, turning to his console.

"I need you to fire the Warden guns without delay."

Armstrong impatiently waited for the reply. After the *Columbia* left the station, the enemy immediately turned in pursuit. They had a good lead and they were thrusting for all they were worth, but his ship was still hobbled by the damage she sustained.

"Captain, surely this would make no difference. My officers tell me we still have no targeting data, and without a firm target, the guns will not fire."

Armstrong started speaking before she finished. "They do have a target, but I don't know how long I can keep this course. Use my signal to target the *Columbia*, and fire the guns, Admiral!"

Several long seconds crept by before a quiet reply crackled to life. "Understood, godspeed, Benjamin... Lunar Command out."

Commander Owens deflated slightly as he finally understood his captain's tactic. Theoretically, the Warden asteroid guns could knock a battleship out of space with ease, as each of the slugs were gigantic: meant to use their mass and speed to deflect dangerous asteroids. In practice, they'd only ever been fired a few times in tests and only at targets with a flat trajectory.

He considered the tactic for a moment and dismissed it out of hand. The chances of everything coming together perfectly were so low as to be laughable. The ship was barely holding together, and its captain was seriously injured. Running was the only clear option now: if he could just convince Armstrong.

*

Due to their limited firing arcs, only one of the four Warden guns was in position to answer Armstrong's call. A deep rumble could be felt by anyone within several kilometers as the systems that powered the gun were fed copious amounts of energy. A huge concrete dome made from lunar regolith slid slowly to the side, uncovering the firing port and the business end of the nearly ten-kilometer-long rails, which would accelerate the thirty-meter-long nickel-iron rounds to a brisk 80 kilometers per second.

Armstrong previously consulted the information stored in *Columbia*'s data banks about the guns and their capabilities. This showed him that, once fired, the projectiles would take nearly twelve minutes to make the journey from the surface of the Moon to their position. Moreover, since they weren't guided, he would also need all of the dense nickel-iron slugs to effectively be traveling in a straight line. To do this, he had to keep the ship perfectly straight and at a fixed speed as if they were a target asteroid. When he could verify the firing of the cannons, the shipboard AI could calculate the exact point in space where the slugs would be at any given time. Then if they were extremely lucky, he could lead the enemy by the nose and place them in their path.

"This is never going to work," Armstrong thought to himself, rubbing his tightening chest, cursing the waning ability of the medicine to hold back his symptoms.

"Put us right between the Warden firing position and the enemy ship, Lieutenant Carmine. Let me know the minute we have a fix on the projectiles; hopefully, the *Columbia* will shield the launch and the bastards won't see them coming."

"Aye, sir."

Owens directed the long-range optical array to the known coordinates of the closest guns. Each grainy image was stabilized, and a helpful overlay pointed out each feature of the gun covers. All but one of them lay unmoving. Finally, a black dot appeared, showing the port had opened. Moments later, small plumes of dust could be seen, disturbed by the electrostatic forces of the launch.

"Computer confirms the gun has begun its firing sequence."

"Steady as she goes, Lieutenant." Armstrong settled in. It was going to be a long wait.

*

Ryan stood next to David as he finished configuring his console with Elizabeth's help.

"Okay, move us out slowly, take your time," Ryan said, trying to be helpful but only gaining a sideways look from his friend and Elizabeth. "Maybe I'll go take a seat." He backed up.

He could hear the thrusters firing in short bursts as David got the hang of the controls. The nose of the ship moved, slowly at first but then gaining speed and confidence.

"She moves like a ballerina," David said wistfully. "Her low-speed thrusters and engines must be twice the size of a ship like the *Columbia*."

"Correct, Lieutenant Kim, we also carry much less mass than a traditional

ISA ship, as our armor and structure are made of a new alloy," Aurora helpfully added.

"Nicely done, David," Ryan said as the *Explorer* deftly sidestepped a large chunk of debris.

Elizabeth walked back to her station and sat, nodding at Ryan's expectant look.

"Good," he thought; at least his friend was getting back to normal. He didn't trust Elizabeth that much, but her read on David put him at ease.

"I think the Forge has restored power," Elizabeth said. "Still no signals, but we might be able to get through from this range."

"Finally, some good news. Maybe things are starting to turn around after all. If the *Columbia* and the Forge can coordinate fire, that last ship doesn't stand a chance," he said hopefully. "Coms, try to hail them."

"Yes, sir, I've been trying, but no response so far. I don't think they're listening to RF as a matter of course," June said.

"Elizabeth, sorry, XO, any ideas?" he said, smirking at Elizabeth.

"Communications are still unavailable... Captain, but we may be able to form a datalink with the station AI by reconfiguring the main communications array."

"Work with Lieutenant Armstrong and make it happen." he said.

Elizabeth frowned but he could see she had already started the process.

*

The pressure in Armstrong's chest seemed to settle a bit over the last few minutes as they made a wide turn to close on the enemy dreadnaught.

"Well, I suppose we should get on with it," he thought to himself, sitting up straight and smoothing his uniform jacket.

"Ready the secondaries," he called, bringing up the weapon statuses and reviewing them one last time. "Portside cannons and point defense systems."

"Aye, sir." Owens glanced over at the captain, who seemed to be somewhat back to his old self. It was clear he was confident in his plan, but try as he might, he couldn't think of one thing that would make a difference in the upcoming fight.

"Secondary cannons and point defense stand ready."

"Missiles as well, we need to hold their attention."

"Sir, we only have short-range vipers loaded. Swapping out the—"

"That will do, Mr. Owens."

Owens was thoroughly confused now. The *Columbia*'s short-range missiles were designed to interdict small craft or missiles.

Owens readied the salvo for all the good it would do.

"Launchers are ready," he called out.

Armstrong cleared his throat. "Slow us down. I don't want to pass them too quickly; we need to make some tight turns, so make sure you're strapped in tight."

"Aye, sir," everyone answered back.

"Ten seconds," Commander Owens called out as the battleship *Columbia* closed with the enemy vessel.

"Start the turn to 030, give them a full broadside," Armstrong said, pulling his straps taut, wincing.

The *Columbia*'s port bow thrusters fired simultaneously with the starboard aft thrusters slewing the ship and redirecting its massive main engines. All along the port side, the large secondary batteries started pumping out shells. Complementing the guns, the point defense beams and salvos of small rockets flew out to strike the craft. The alien dreadnaught seemed to ignore the *Columbia*, continuing on course until the first rounds evaporated into its energy shielding, capturing its attention as round after round splashed into its side.

"There she is." Armstrong followed the track of the enemy ship as it changed heading. "Keep it up, Commander, don't let up for one second."

"She's coming around behind us," Owens said just before a rolling shudder and moan ran through the superstructure of the *Columbia*. The light started to flicker, and the roar of the maneuvering jets ramped up loudly.

"We're hit! Engine one has failed. We have decompression in the port aft engineering spaces, bulkheads are closing!"

"Continue evasive, Lieutenant. Mr. Owens, reset the main viewer and dispatch damage control when able."

The familiar moaning of the ship vibrated through his seat as the Columbia's computers, guided by the deft hand of Lieutenant Carmine, shifted the battleship's course at random. Each maneuver was calculated to throw off the enemy targeting systems, which normally had to lead their shots by several seconds to account for the vast distances between combatants. The enemy's main gun was fast, but not instantaneous, and that small delay gave them precious time to try to dodge out of its path.

Armstrong's straps dug into his shoulders and back as he watched the icons representing the immediate area resolve on the screen, centering on the Columbia, showing the closing enemy craft and more importantly the four projectiles that were launched from the lunar surface.

"Turn port to 280, up ten, increase to full," he tried to call out forcefully but only managed to wheeze out a horse whisper.

"280, up ten, accelerating to full aye," Lieutenant Carmine answered, glancing back at him.

"Computer predicts the enemy will be ready to fire again in thirty seconds."

"Damn, that's at least two more shots," Armstrong said, letting his fist fall limply to the arm of his chair. "What's the status of the Explorer?"

"She's in the lee of the station, I don't have eyes on her."

"Good, if we can't see her, neither can they." His voice started to trail away. "I just wish I had more time… I'd like to talk to my son." He smiled as the lights in the room started to dim before rapidly darkening to an inky pitch blackness punctuated by flashing pops of light.

"Captain?" Owens looked back, not quite making out what the captain just said.

"Captain!" he shouted as Armstrong's head lolled to the side and his body slumped over, only the acceleration harness keeping him in his seat.

The corpsman had warned Owens that the captain needed scans urgently, but there hadn't been time. He hadn't been too concerned, however, because like the rest of the crew, Armstrong seemed unstoppable.

Owens straightened himself and returned his attention to his console. They couldn't unstrap to check on him without serious risk of injury, and medical personnel couldn't make it to the bridge. He thought about ordering the ship to retreat, but even at Flank speed, he doubted he could put enough distance between them and the enemy.

"Lieutenant, contact the med bay and tell them the captain is down."

Lieutenant Carmine didn't look shocked, only concerned as she nodded and started relaying the information.

Owens, holding on to the sides of his chair, fought against the gyrations of the ship while he tried to think of something. Now that the enemy ship was chasing them, he doubted that anything other than a bigger threat would pull them away.

"Okay, in ten seconds we'll go full evasive and pop every countermeasure we have left. Get ready for a hard starboard turn." He looked at the thrust profiles of the *Columbia* now that she was down a main engine. "Damn it." He balled his fist on the console, looking back at his unconscious captain.

"Aye, sir, standing by," Carmine said, her voice full of trepidation and fear.

*

"Ryan, *Columbia* is engaging the enemy ship," Anna said, pointing to the main viewscreen.

On the screen, flashes of light bloomed as the optical tracking array locked onto the ships after they were far enough away from the station. The image was still fuzzy at this range, but the augmented outline of the *Columbia* was visible. It opened up with nearly every gun it had, judging by the sheer volume of fire. Shells, missiles, and beams lanced through space, followed by bursts of light as explosions peppered the strange crystalline vessel. Within seconds, a roiling fireball engulfed one side of the enemy ship.

"Enemy ship is turning to intercept."

"OK, his plan is working," Ryan said with a smile, giving a little fist shake. He glanced at June, who seemed to be sitting a little taller as she tapped her console.

A kernel of hope started to form before Ryan could tamp it down. He was no tactical genius like Captain Armstrong, but if he were fighting in the sim, he would try to drag that enemy ship closer to the station and give them a walloping. He was sure that would be Armstrong's plan as well now that the Forge had regained power.

"Captain, she did it... Aurora was able to communicate with the Forge central AI and instruct it to reconfigure the main coms array to broadcast RF. We should have voice now."

"Good job, both of you. Get me Forge control if you can, Lieutenant. We need to tell them Columbia needs help."

June tapped her screen. "Forge control, this is the *Cosmic Explorer*." She waited a couple seconds. "Forge control, come in?"

"They are receiving, Captain... no response from control. Maybe they had to evacuate? I could try the hangar, or maybe the administrative section?"

Ryan stroked his chin for a second. "We don't have time to guess, can you just broadcast to the whole Forge?"

"I think so, we can just relay it through the internal communication system. I'll have Aurora prioritize ISA responses." June glanced up at the screen, sneaking a peek at the *Columbia*, which was just disappearing behind the structure of the Forge as David maneuvered the ship.

"Okay, that should do it," she said.

"This is the *Cosmic Explorer* to anyone on the Forge able to receive. Please respond." He waited a few seconds before repeating his call.

"We're getting responses!" June said excitedly before tempering her expression. "Mostly civilian... a few ISA personnel, but nothing from command."

"Just pick one, we need information."

Over the bridge speakers, a desperate-sounding woman was patched in mid-sentence.

"...thank god, you have to send help. We haven't been able to contact anyone in command, and I don't think we can hold out much longer."

"This is Captain Anders of the *Explorer*, who is this?"

"Please come quickly, this is Lieutenant Jameson, we've got the doors locked but they found us!" A thudding sound could be heard over the connection in the background.

"Emma?" Elizabeth joined the connection to Ryan's confusion before he realized that she knew the woman.

"Elizabeth! Please send someone, we haven't been able to get a hold of anyone else. Please hurry!"

The thudding sound was pronounced as shouts and crying could be made out in the background.

"What's going on? Who's found you?"

The woman was clearly speaking to someone else in the room with her, but they could only make out snippets of the conversation as they spoke of fighting whoever was trying to break in.

David appeared beside Ryan, his face pale. He was breathing as if he'd just finished sprinting. "Tell them to run, the doors won't hold," he said at almost a whisper.

Ryan then realized what he meant—the squids.

He turned to June, who was speaking to someone else, trying to calm them.

"June, where are they? Can you pinpoint them?

She paused, tapping her console. "It looks like they're in a cargo area near the *Olympus Mons*."

"Is that in view of the enemy ship?"

"Negative, this side of the station." June added, "Sir, Aurora and I are talking to several other groups, everyone's reporting the same thing… I don't know how many people are still on the station, but only a few pockets here and there are responding to our hail."

He understood. While the military evacuated to their ships, many of the civilian transports were political or corporate craft. That meant a large number of the civilians that worked on board were probably still there. He couldn't remember how many of the darts had hit the station.

"Lieutenant Jameson, listen to me. You can't fight these things; you have to get out of there. Can you evacuate the people with you to the hangar deck?" Ryan said in his best command voice, talking over

Elizabeth, who was still speaking to the woman.

"Sir, we tried that. Half the station was showing low pressure warnings, and all the doors locked down automatically. We have over a hundred people in here, and some are critically wounded and can't be moved."

"Shit," Ryan said to himself, looking at Elizabeth, who shook her head.

"Maybe Aurora can open the doors?" Anna said, snapping her fingers.

"Good idea. Aurora, can you override the lockdown on the cargo deck where they are located and get them a clear path to the hangar bay?"

"Emergency authorization to perform such actions would need to be granted by Forge command level personnel."

"I'm guessing that doesn't include me," Ryan muttered. "Can you hack into the Forge network, David? David?" Ryan looked at his friend, who was staring blankly into the distance. He finally touched him on the shoulder, eliciting a shiver, bringing his eyes back into focus.

He looked angrily at Ryan, blinking several times, before recognizing he was being spoken to.

"No, can't hack that part of the network, you would need a tactical AI to brute force that. Valkyrie could probably do it. Yeah, do that easy."

"Okay, thanks, David. Maybe go sit back down buddy, you aren't looking so hot," he said as David wandered back to his station.

"Lieutenant Jameson, we're going to try to override the doors remotely. I know you have injured, but you don't want to be there if those things break in... get everyone ready to move. Anna, give Johnson a sitrep and tell his team to stand by for another rescue,"

Anna turned and immediately started relaying his orders.

Before he could speak, a sharp intake of breath drew his attention to June, who was staring at the main viewer. A brilliant flash lit the screen, followed by a rapidly expanding cloud of debris and gas venting from the Columbia's rear section. The ship had taken another direct hit from the alien weapon.

"Captain," June said, looking at him, pleading in her eyes. She didn't need to say anything, and he doubted she would ever openly ask, but she wanted him to help the *Columbia*.

CHAPTER 20

Commander Owens coughed and blinked rapidly, trying to clear his stinging eyes. Several power surges had caused some lighting and control stations to overload on the bridge before the automated systems cut their power. The acrid smoke had blown around, and he seemed to have inhaled half of it before the filters could take the sting out of the air. All around the bridge, many of the displays winked in and out before finally stabilizing. The *Columbia* had taken another hard hit as it struggled to stay one step ahead of the alien craft.

"How bad is it, Lieutenant?" He coughed.

"Looks like number four engine was hit… catastrophic failure… we lost most of the secondary engineering space."

"Damn it, secure from maneuver." He surveyed the bridge again. "How can we fight like this?"

They were running on the barest of bare-bones personnel. The captain was unconscious, and only he and the lieutenant were manning the bridge. The rest of the ship was in similar straits, with so many injured and killed that if not for the AI systems, the ship would have been dead in space long ago.

"Aye, sir," Lieutenant Carmine said before a timer appeared on the bottom of the main display at the front of the bridge, while ending the evasive maneuvering program that had been running right before the strike.

Owens stood down their weapons, as they were doing absolutely no good beyond goading the enemy into the chase. He hoped that the aliens would turn away once they stopped firing, giving them some breathing room, but they continued their single-minded pursuit regardless.

Columbia had little left in the way of armaments, and now their maneuvering advantage was gone with only two of four main engines still functional. Only thanks to the shipboard AI and Lieutenant Carmine's heroic efforts were they even able to fly in a straight line.

He glanced at the displayed path of the Warden gun projectiles; they would be in the vicinity shortly after the enemy took another shot if the calculations were to be believed. If he was going to follow through on the captain's plan, he would have to do it in less than a minute and had no clue how to execute it without telegraphing this to the enemy ship.

"They don't care," Lieutenant Carmine said aloud, breaking his chain of thought.

"What's that?"

"The enemy ship, sir." She stopped; her face lit up. "I can't believe I didn't see this before. It looks like they're just reacting to whatever we toss at them. They only change course when we do, and they just fire on whatever seems to be the biggest threat."

An icon appeared on his screen, which signaled a data share was initiated by the lieutenant.

"You can see the route of their ships in every engagement we've had. It's almost like they're following a preprogrammed path, then only reacting when they need to." She turned to face him. "Sir, I think they might be drones. Even our basic AI systems could outfight them if it weren't for their shields and jamming tech."

"But we've been treating them like humans."

"Exactly... at least I think so, sir."

Owens nodded his approval to the lieutenant. Turning his attention to his console, he cleared his throat. "Okay, let's make our turn to 225 down 20, increase to Flank."

"225, down 20 aye. Increasing to Flank," she said with some hesitation in her voice. The loss of the engine made "Flank" speed no more than half of what the *Columbia* was formerly capable of.

"Not sure if we'll make it that far, but we've got nothing to lose at this point," he said to himself.

After a full minute, they made their last turn, directly into the path of the huge projectiles.

"Turn 316, up 5."

"316 up 5, aye," Lieutenant Carmine answered back, and the ship groaned in response to the commands, causing the two to trade worried glances.

"Vessel is still following. Twenty seconds to enemy guns."

"Carmine, start your evasive program at five seconds..."

"We can't." The Lieutenant quickly followed up with a belated, "Sir."

Looking a bit embarrassed, she continued, "If we start evasive maneuvers, that might put them out of the projectiles' path. We need to dodge at the very last second."

She was right, of course, he thought. Even with their best optical tracking, they didn't have a perfect fix on the incoming projectiles. The random movements introduced by their evasive actions could cause the enemy ship to react in a way that would cause a glancing blow or a clean miss.

"Given the damage we've sustained, what does the computer say our chances are of moving out of the way in time?"

She looked up, locking eyes with him before finally admitting, "Factoring in the loss of the thrusters, fifteen percent... well, fourteen point nine three, to be exact."

Commander Owens sighed.

"Ten seconds to enemy guns," she said softly.

"Zero thrust on the mains, turn to 180 and let's hope this hit doesn't cut the ship in half. Sound the collision alarm."

The rumble of the main engines ceased, and the big maneuvering thrusters turned the *Columbia* directly toward the enemy, putting its thickly armored bow directly in the line of fire. Alarms sounded down the mostly empty smoke-filled passageways of the *Columbia*. In places where the crew was congregated, the damage control teams and medics moved to their acceleration chairs and strapped in.

"Any reaction?"

"Negative, sir. No aspect change. Enemy weapon should fire in five seconds." She cringed as the timer hit zero.

Decompression alarms started to blare once again as the computer displayed areas near the bow of the ship turning from yellow to red on the damage control display shown at both of their stations.

They both held their breath, only slowly letting it out after a few moments when they realized they were still alive.

"Report?"

"Decompression in a line starting from frame one back to twenty. Nearly straight through the bow down the centerline."

"Casualties?"

"None reported. Damage control teams are moving forward, but most of the remaining crew are in engineering and the CIC."

"Tell them to stand down, we don't need…"

Owens could feel a sudden sharp vibration in his feet as another alarm sounded.

"Fire in the forward compartments. I think the thrusters were hit!"

"I thought those spaces were already in vacuum." He rapidly switched to camera view and tried to find a working camera in the forward spaces.

"Sir, the projectiles!"

He glanced back to the tactical display on the main screen and realized they had precious few seconds before they would be struck by the slugs.

"Dodge!" he yelled out.

"All forward thrusters are down. ECUs are restarting…" she said as the ship wallowed, trying to turn using only the rear and midline emergency thrusters. "I'm getting power fluctuations all over the ship. Eight seconds until the mains are back online."

Owens looked at the computer projections of the ship's current state, and a sinking feeling came over him. They would be badly out of position with almost no ability to move the ship out of harm's way. The *Columbia* would be destroyed by the projectiles, and the enemy would have free reign across the Earth.

Proximity alarms started to blare over the fire warnings, prioritized by the computers as they recognized the danger of the incoming rounds.

His mind was blank. Nothing came to mind; no last-minute save or trick he'd learned popped into his head. He looked dumbfounded at the young Lieutenant Carmine, noticing that she reminded him of his own daughter, whom he would now never be able to speak to again.

Carmine was taken aback by the utter lack of reaction from Owens. He just sat there, staring blankly with his head cocked, as if he were trying to remember something long forgotten. Without thinking, she started to shake her head, unwilling to simply surrender to whatever fate had in store for them. She took in the tactical situation for several moments.

In her extensive studies at the Academy, she'd often read of fencing duels between nobles in old Europe. In some rare situations, one combatant would be outmatched and struck through, mortally wounded. Knowing that death was near, they sometimes did the unthinkable and stepped forward, impaling themselves further but allowing them to close the distance and deliver their own mortal blow.

Reversing thrust, she rolled the *Columbia* and initiated an emergency depressurization of the main hangar bay, overriding every warning and safety system still operating.

"If we're not going to survive, neither is he," she said through gritted teeth, touching off a chain of explosive charges that cut through the main hangar door's carriage assembly, sending the three-meter-thick armored covers tumbling off into space.

*

Newly promoted Warrant Officer Johnson, along with all the remaining members of his Special Reaction Team, stood around a large table in the medium-sized conference room he'd commandeered. The ship's computer directed him to the spaces set aside for the onboard security detachment, but besides easy access to the small brig and empty weapons storage lockers, he found they were too far away from where he needed to be.

Sergeant Martinez had taught him to always be as close to the action as possible. On the Forge, the SRT working and living spaces were all less than a minute away from the main docking bay, the security section, and central elevators.

"Sure could use you right now, Sarge," he said, privately hoping his injured leader would miraculously wake from her coma.

"What you mumbling over there?" Private Morales asked.

"Just praying for you Chico. God knows you need it."

All around the room came chuckles, even from Chico, who laughed somewhat nervously.

Since Lieutenant Armstrong gave them a heads-up that they would be heading back to the station for a rescue mission, his team was on full alert: eager to go but wary to tangle with the alien monstrosities.

With Private Thompson and Private Wilson both gone, and their medic, Specialist Lata, standing vigil at the bedside of the SRT's critically injured leader, the team was down to just Chico, PFC Nguyen, PFC Cooper and himself.

"They aren't so tough," Cooper said. She spun her combat knife across the back of her hand, whipping it in a full circle and catching it in her off-hand while it spun full speed in the air. "Gonna get some payback for Thompson."

"And the rook." Nguyen said setting his shotgun on the table with a thud.

Chico smiled. "I ever tell you, I found the both of them in that dive bar near the cargo elevators?"

"That place with the fake snake?" Nguyen asked.

"Yeah. I popped in and found Thompson hitting on the waitress. She said she was trying to get the rook laid, but you know Thompson. Wilson could barely see straight and was just staring at her ass the whole time."

They all laughed somewhat half-heartedly. When it died down, they went back to inspecting their gear in silence.

Johnson let them chatter as they stripped and cleaned their weapons and organized their kit.

Sadly, what they had didn't add up to much, and the *Explorer*'s small arms lockers hadn't yet been filled. Johnsons main worry was ammo. Their standard loadout was the Ross Mk. IV submachine gun. Not flashy and didn't hit as hard as the ISA ground forces' coil guns, but the caseless subsonic ammunition was designed to be fired within the thin walls of shuttles or space stations without risk of penetration.

"So how long 'til we get the word?" Chico said, absentmindedly oiling his weapon again.

"We were told to stand by, and we're standing by," Johnson said. "My guess is less than thirty minutes, but when have I ever been right? If we do go in, Alex, I want you on point with that cannon of yours."

PFC Nguyen nodded, grabbing the big 10-gauge shotgun and racking the action several times, its loud metal-on-metal clatter making a direct response unnecessary.

"Cooper, you have our six. From what the Ensign told me, those things are attracted to noise, so everyone make sure to tie all your shit down, okay? What's the count on ammo?"

"Four mags for the Ross, four for my sidearm," Cooper said, slamming the magazine home and holstering her pistol.

Chico sheepishly looked at his fellows. "I'm down to a mag and a half."

"Jesus, Juan, you selling those things?" Cooper said, laughing.

"Hey, that alien thing was crazy!" he cried before remembering to add, "Oh, and four pistol mags."

Johnson shook his head. "Here." He tossed one of his extra mags to Chico. "Nguyen, what do you have?"

The huge Private reached under the table and plopped a full bandolier on the surface.

"Fifty shells for this bitch and four mags for my pistol," he said with a grin, his deep baritone rumbling. "I'm not gonna get eaten like Chico."

Chico flung an oil-stained rag at the big man's head. "I'm gonna bag the next one I see, you just watch. You just got lucky and found a weak spot."

Nguyen moved his head out of the rag's path with ease. "Luck nothing, if it weren't for Big Betty, you'd all be stains on the deck," he said, causing the team to burst out in laughter.

Johnson chuckled along with the rest, but perhaps a bit more darkly than he would have liked. In his own estimation Nguyen hit the nail on the head. During the last encounter, it looked like their submachine guns didn't do much at all. Only the massive penetrator slugs of the shotgun, which were designed to tear steel hatches off their hinges, staggered and eventually killed the already severely injured alien creature.

Their laughter started to quiet just as the door to the conference room slid open, drawing the attention of the group.

A large, hard-nosed man stood there for a second, filling the doorway.

Nearly as big as Nguyen, the red-haired, red-bearded Martian chief strode into the room accompanied by the whine of power-assisted armor servos. His bulging and tattooed arm was hitched up to his shoulder, carrying a black canvas bag.

Close behind him, a thin woman with turquoise blue hair followed. Her face was still somewhat swollen from wounds she'd sustained during the battle on the station, and one of her arms was wrapped tightly with bandages around her shoulder and bicep, though it seemed to be functional, as she had the hand laid casually on the top of the hilt of what looked like a large, sheathed blade.

"Chief." Johnson turned on the pair. He was unsure how Martian ranks compared to the ISA's and had no idea the proper way to address the man, so he simply held out his hand. "The Lieutenant told me your team might be joining the mission. We're glad to have you."

The Chief walked up to the table and dropped the bag onto its surface with a metallic clatter.

Turning to Johnson, he eyed him up and down before breaking into a grin and clasping his forearm tightly.

"Roch," the Chief said loudly, slapping the other man on the shoulder with his free hand. Seeing confusion in Johnson's eyes, he explained, "Excuse me, Warrant Officer. 'Roch' means hello, welcome, yes. I say soldier-to-soldier." He pointed to himself, then to Johnson.

"Roach then," Johnson said back with his toothy grin, causing Inna to stifle a laugh at the mispronunciation.

"Glad to have you with us. Both of you." He glanced to the woman who stood behind the chief, finding the strange geometric tattooing over some of her face and the exposed skin of her neck and shoulders intriguing.

"Champion Inna," she said with pride banging her clenched fist to her breastplate with a clank of metal on metal.

The chief turned on her. "No, not Champion. Inna will now be my second. Guardian, I think. She fights like the winds of Tholus!" He raised his voice and his fist, bringing it down on the table, causing everything there to jump into the air.

Inna seemed stunned and elated at the same time.

The chief eyed Johnson. "She will lead when I am gone. Much like you?"

Johnson didn't know where the big Martian had gotten his information, but it wasn't a secret.

"Our sergeant is still kicking. She's just out of commission for now."

"Ah. Forgive me." He bowed slightly.

"No problem, Chief. Hopefully I won't screw things up too much by the time she's back on her feet."

"For the next fight, I bring a gift for our new cohort," the chief said, pointing to the bag on the table. "Your ship has... good makers," he added, as if testing the phrase.

Puzzled, Johnson reached over and unzipped it at the chief's urging. Inside were several sizes of long blades, each sheathed in black nylon, their handles long enough for two and a half hands, hilts wrapped in some sort of synthetic material.

Pulling one from the bag, he realized it wasn't just a lengthened knife but something akin to a Katana or maybe a cavalry saber without the guard. It was surprisingly light, and as he pulled it from the sheath, he noticed the blade itself was thick, almost like a machete with a rounded back.

"Thanks?" Johnson said, unsure if this was a tradition amongst the Martian ground forces.

"Nice." Cooper noticed, grabbing up one of the swords as the others gathered around.

"What are those for, Johnson?" Chico eyed the blades suspiciously.

Johnson hesitated, unsure what the chief wanted them to do with the things. He didn't want to lug some ceremonial "friendship" blades around just for tradition's sake.

Thankfully the chief spoke first. "For fighting the things. Guns are…" He waved his hand side to side in a "so-so" manner. "But they are fast, and strong, with fast arms… too fast sometimes to reload. If you are close." He gestured to Inna, who drew her blade, which Johnson noticed was a close match to the ones they'd gifted his troopers.

She whipped it up, into a one-handed guard position, pommel beside her temple. Then rotated the blade down and to the side in a quick arc, flashing it by so fast it whistled. The sword crashed into a steel conference chair, splitting the backrest in two. It finally came to a stop with a thunderous clang when it hit the flat seat, leaving a sizeable dent in the surface.

For a second, the stunned troopers looked at the small woman before bursting into further cheers and laughter, each scrambling to grab one of the blades.

"Wear it like so," Inna said, showing how the sheath was worn on her hip.

"Inna can teach your men," Chief Huttare said, becoming serious. "She had great success with a blade during fight."

"Thank you, Chief. I don't know how much use we will get out of them, honestly; we didn't take any swordsmanship classes in basic," Johnson said, still unsure how they would use them.

The Chief shook his head. "No fancy… if you are so close to use blades." He drew his own blade from behind his back with his right hand, then made a fist with his left and held his forearm up as if he were holding an imaginary shield in front of his body. He then rested the blunted back of the blade against the front of his forearm, making a cross.

"Hold like this… just… ah." He searched for the right word. "Protection.

Yes. They strike fast, almost faster than we can see. This can save *and* hurt." He sheathed his blade.

Chico whirled his blade in the air clumsily. "Those squiddies won't stand a chance against us."

"Quidee?" Huttare said, trying the new word and nodding. "Never expect they are less than we,"

Johnson thought about that for a second. "He's right. Never underestimate your enemy. You guys get with Guardian Inna and get some pointers. We'll have our primaries but doubt the pistols will do much, so swords might just be what the doctor ordered."

Nguyen stood with his big arms crossed, his face showing no hint that he would use one himself.

"Now who's gonna get eaten when he runs out of ammo," Chico said, laughing.

"I was gonna save this as a surprise." Nguyen reached into the small of his back and pulled the largest bowie knife any of them had ever seen, and thunked it down onto the top of the table.

"Twenty-four inches of high carbon steel, lasered to a razor's edge." He grinned ear to ear. "Figured I might need something a little more... stabby for a close encounter with our alien friends."

CHAPTER 21

Ryan was now officially starting to panic. He wanted nothing more than to fly the ship back to Earth as fast as possible and hide, but there were so many things pulling him in different directions. Should he fly out and help the *Columbia* like June wanted? Do as he was ordered and flee to Mars? Help save the civilians on the station?

To compound his dilemma, almost the entire ISA Fleet lay in tatters around them, meaning no help would be coming.

He was captain, and as captain, he had to make a choice—and none of his choices were good.

"Sir, I have Lieutenant Commander Compton for you," June Armstrong said, her voice wavering.

The name sounded familiar to Ryan before it occurred to him that Compton was the fleet officer who caught them trying to get assigned to the *Columbia*.

"Commander Compton, this is the acting captain of the *Explorer*."

"Captain, this is Commander Compton; I am requesting immediate evacuation of the Forge. We have sustained heavy damage, and an unknown enemy is moving unchecked through the station."

"We understand that, Commander, we're trying to contact Forge command right now."

"Captain, I was in communication with command until thirty minutes ago. They were taken out by these things. I believe I am the ranking officer on board, so once again, I request that you commence evacuation immediately.

Please transmit a request for assistance to any and all ISA vessels in the area."

"Yes, sir, we are on the way, but there aren't any others. The fleet was destroyed."

"I see." Compton paused before continuing, a deep weariness entering his voice. "We are on level four and we are making our way to the main hangar bay. We can hold there long enough to get the civvies off."

Ryan snapped his fingers several times, getting Elizabeth's attention. He gestured to his ear and made a pointing motion, which she gratefully understood, nodding and relaying a message to the other group.

"Commander, it will take us about… ten minutes to get docked; in the meantime, we're in contact with another group of civilians trapped near the Olympus Mons. We are attempting to override the doors and get them moving to the hangar."

"Thank you, Captain, we'll head that direction and try to pick them up on the way."

"Oh, Commander, some of our guys tussled with these things. Tell everyone to stay as quiet as they can. From what we can tell, they're attracted to noise."

"Roger that. Forge out."

The line went dead.

Bile rose in Ryan's throat. They'd barely escaped, but now, once again, he felt helpless to do anything else other than run back into the fire. He looked around the bridge, trying to gauge the others' reactions to the commander's orders, but beyond a nod from Anna, everyone seemed preoccupied with their duties.

He blew out a long breath. "Okay, Valkyrie, I need you to override the door lockouts on the Forge between the Olympus Mons and the hangar deck."

"Negative," the testy AI tactical system answered back.

"Valkyrie, that's an order. You heard the commander; people are going to die over there unless we do something," Ryan said, wondering how the hell the ISA allowed such a system to exist on a warship.

"Negative."

"Captain, the Valkyrie subsystem may not break into any secure ISA network unless such an action is deemed necessary by local command."

"How the hell am I supposed to do that... command is dead."

"I am unable to make such recommendations, as all tactical queries must be made to the Valkyrie subsystem."

"God damn it, that makes no sense," Ryan said, throwing up his hands. "Can't you do something... You could take over those functions, right? You seem more than capable of dealing with these things... and having two separate AIs is just dumb. No offense."

"Combination of functions, while possible, would require command authorization and is not recommended. The separation of function is for the safety of the crew and has been deemed—"

"Yeah, yeah, fifteen percent more efficient or whatever..." Ryan pondered for a second before throwing caution to the wind. "Do it—I have authorization now, so go ahead and combine functions. We can take a fifteen percent hit."

"Twelve," Aurora added.

"Right, even better. Do it, Aurora."

"Functions that carry inherent risk to the crew must be confirmed by two ranking officers."

"Anna, could you?" Ryan said exasperated.

Anna looked doubtfully at him. "There is probably a reason they kept those functions separate, you know... Fine, whatever. I authorize."

A chime sounded over the bridge intercom.

"Elizabeth?" Ryan said, drawing a questioning look from the distracted commander who was relaying orders to Emma and her group on the Forge. "I need your authorization so I can get the doors open."

"I authorize," she said, going back to her hurried conversation.

A final chime sounded before lights on the bridge flickered and the consoles all reset simultaneously.

"What the hell, Anders!" Elizabeth looked at him accusingly.

He shrugged again, but before he could say anything, all the systems returned to their previous states. Elizabeth hurriedly spoke into her com, sending instructions to her friend and the group of civilians.

"Aurora?" he said apprehensively.

"Much better. I'm here, Captain," Aurora answered back strangely, drawing looks from all around the bridge.

"Okay..." Ryan said. "Can you please unlock the doors between the Dome and the hangar?"

"Absolutely."

Elizabeth swung around. "She says the doors just opened. They're moving out now." She turned back to speaking with Emma.

"Great. June, can you contact the commander and route him to the survivors?"

"I have already taken the liberty of relaying your orders, Captain," Aurora said. The synthesized voice sounded somewhat different, but Ryan couldn't put his finger on why.

"Oh, great. Can you work with Lieutenant Armstrong on that? She is the communications officer."

"Of course, Captain," Aurora answered back almost before he finished.

He wasn't looking forward to his next order. Flying them back to the station and the danger it represented would probably cause David to revolt, but he had no choice.

"David, reverse course and get us back to the station? Keep it between us and the alien ship... I want to be in and out in a flash."

"Yeah, that's a good idea," David said so eagerly that Ryan cocked his head involuntarily.

The main engines went silent as the ship's thrusters swung the vessel around and onto a reciprocal course before relighting, the pseudo gravity field allowing just enough of the momentum change through to allow those on board to notice.

"David, you sure you're okay with that? I know it was a shitshow over there before, but Johnson and his crew..."

"Yeah, it's safer on the Forge than out here."

"Well, I'm sure Armstrong will pull a rabbit out of his hat sooner or later."

Ryan didn't know what to make of David's almost eager response. From the scene Johnson painted, he would have bet money that David would be triggered by a return to the station.

"Ryan, the survivors from the cargo bay have almost finished their evacuation," Elizabeth said, standing and stretching her shoulders. She gave a quick glance around before approaching Ryan.

"Your orders are clear—we need to get to Mars right now."

"But the *Columbia*..." He started, keeping his voice low. Elizabeth just shook her head.

Ryan's confident expression dropped. Elizabeth was right. Once the enemy ship finished with the *Columbia*, they would come here, and if they were still attached to the station, they would all die.

He stood. "Anna, can you join me for a second?"

Looking to ask David to join them as well, Ryan glanced over and noticed he was once again staring blankly into space, both hands hanging limply by his side.

"Uh, June, let me know if we get any further updates. Commander?" he said to Elizabeth before walking back to his cabin.

As they both joined him, he closed the door.

"We can't risk delaying any longer, we need to leave," Elizabeth said before he could even turn around.

"What? We need to rescue those people... that's your friend over there!" Anna said, aghast.

"I understand what you're saying," Ryan said, trying to keep an even tone. He knew in his heart that Elizabeth was right, but he had a hard time convincing himself to abandon those people.

Anna rounded on Ryan so quickly he almost took a step back.

"Are you kidding me? I get why she doesn't give a shit, but Ryan, you heard him. There are hundreds of civilians over there."

"What is that supposed to mean, *Lieutenant*?" Elizabeth said cooly.

"Oh, we can see how much your friends mean to you, and don't you even think of pulling rank on me," Anna said, waving her finger in the air, looking her up and down while squaring off on the other woman.

"If you had your way, we'd all be in the brig, and then where would you be? Hmm?"

"Whoa." Ryan stepped in between them. "She's right, Anna, a little decorum, please." He grinned at her, then turned to Elizabeth who was uncomfortably close. "You too, Commander, please step back."

As they both stepped away, he backed up himself. "It seems to me we have two options: Mars or the station." He looked at each of them while they just eyed each other. "Come on, you two are smart, and I'd like to stay alive."

They both tried to speak over each other.

"We need to go back to the station," Anna said, crossing her arms.

"We need to go to Mars. Armstrong's orders supersede Compton's," Elizabeth said, giving Ryan a stern look.

Ryan pondered the decision for a long moment, stroking his chin. "You're right, Elizabeth. Armstrong's orders do supersede Compton's."

"What?" Anna said.

"But..." Ryan held up his finger, forestalling her ire. "According to fleet regs, captains are given autonomy to carry out those orders as they see fit, especially when dealing with 'enemy action.'"

"Those rules were put in place because they assumed you could be months away from contact, not hanging in lunar orbit right next to ISA headquarters," Elizabeth said, crossing her arms.

"Rules are rules... and I make the final decision." Ryan realized he'd talked himself into a corner.

"Shit... alright, we're headed that direction anyway, and Compton did give us a direct order, which was probably recorded somewhere. The way I see it, if we don't go back to the station and the *Columbia* does survive, I'll probably be put in a hole somewhere for a very long time for running away and letting all those people die. The ISA hates bad publicity."

"Armstrong gave you an order too, so if they do survive, you'll probably be in that hole anyway," Elizabeth said before whirling on her heel and walking out the door.

"Just because the ice queen doesn't like it doesn't mean it isn't the right thing to do," Anna said crossing her arms.

"Great." Ryan took off his jacket and tossed it on the desk. "June, call down to Johnson, tell him we'll be docking in…" He looked at Anna.

"Twelve minutes."

"Twelve minutes if my calculations are correct," Ryan said, eliciting a backhand from Anna before she walked out.

"Yes, Captain."

As he turned to leave, he spotted himself in the small mirror over the bar. His hair was a mess, his shirt was ruffled, and his old rank insignia was still pinned to his collar.

"God damn it," he cursed, grabbing the jacket from the desk and putting it back on.

*

Aboard *Columbia*, time seemed to stop for Lieutenant Carmine as the computer tracks of the leading Warden projectiles merged with the *Columbia* on her display. Everything seemed hushed, the tick of a damaged fan, the odd hum of equipment she hadn't noticed before. Pain from her arm was getting worse by the moment as the drugs she'd scrounged earlier from the bridge med kit had worn off. She could just make out the warning klaxon in an adjoining compartment, the ones on the bridge having long since been disabled.

She closed her eyes tightly and her stomach sank.

A resounding crash of metal and sudden low thudding bang caused her to jump as the ship and everything attached to it found itself moving sideways. The straps dug deeply into her right shoulder and caused her to pitch over whipping her head away and downwards. Her hastily tied up hair came loose, flying into her face.

When she realized she was still alive, she opened her eyes and brushed back her hair, spying the damage control status of the ship before letting out a whoop of triumph and throwing her one good arm in the air. Her gamble had worked, and while the Warden projectiles did impact the

Columbia, she'd managed to thread the needle and they passed through the unarmored walls of the hangar deck.

"It worked!" she yelled, looking to Commander Owens.

Still strapped into his seat, his head lolled to the side and both his arms hung limply. A large chunk of a broken console lay nearby, having been damaged earlier in the day; it must have finally come loose.

The bridge viewscreen flashed brightly, causing her to squint. The external cameras still trained on the enemy ship showed two bright pulses of light. After the automatic filters kicked in, she could see two bright glowing spots side by side on the lower left of the enemy craft, heat being bled away into space, seemingly unscathed.

As it dawned on her that the projectiles hadn't damaged the ship, a new massive hole opened up on the bow of the alien craft, followed by another, and then a third. She sat silently as the layers of the craft were peeled back, open to space. Atmosphere, unknown fluids, and chunks of the structure exploded outward in a fan as secondary explosions rippled across the open decks.

Then larger cascading explosions started to tear great chunks off the ship, sending them randomly tumbling end over end.

She closed her tear-filled eyes in joy, finally allowing herself to hope.

Fired in pairs, the enormous projectiles tore the structure of the enemy ship apart. The last pair of these slugs entered the ship, finding nothing of consequence to stop their forward momentum until finally they reached what would be the engine room on a human vessel. As they intersected with the strange pulsing and whirling device and its associated energy field, entire sections of the slugs lost atomic cohesion and were instantaneously converted to their fundamental subatomic components. With that change, an enormous, nearly cataclysmic amount of energy was released.

In the blink of an eye, a wave of radiation and neutrons struck the outer hull of the *Columbia*, heating it from −100 to over 4000 Celsius in a fraction of a second, boiling the hull away like so much steam. The inner structure survived a few moments longer before the fragile encasement superheated and exploded outwards, caught up in the wave of particles, adding its own mass and the mass of its occupants to the reaction.

*

Having finally found a second to use the restroom in the captain's cabin, Ryan walked back onto the bridge of the *Explorer*. Elizabeth glanced over her shoulder at him, still speaking to who he assumed was her friend on the station. Anna stood next to David, arms crossed, concern creasing her face. She was keeping her voice low, but something was happening.

He meant to speak with his friend. David's odd behavior was starting to get worrisome. Maybe a little time to change and freshen up would help. His greasy and unkempt hair was a mess, and his skin seemed so pale he could see the veins underneath. He was barely paying attention to whatever Anna was saying, but Ryan could see he was sick.

Ryan started to walk over himself but decided to stop at June's station first to check in with her. She was looking forlorn but kept a stiff upper lip during the whole ordeal.

"Any updates?"

June looked up from the console where she was monitoring the exterior camera feed. Onscreen was an AI enhanced picture of the *Columbia*.

"Not really, sir, they were maneuvering hard for a bit, now they've changed course. Not sure where they're heading, but the alien ship is still chasing them."

"I wish there was something we could do, Lieutenant. This ship is amazing, but weapons are one thing we just don't have yet."

"I know." She let her hands fall in her lap. "I just wish…"

He waited for her to finish her thought, but she just went back to watching the camera feed. "Stay strong, the day isn't over yet." Ryan touched her shoulder before walking away.

Ryan didn't feel good about the decision to go back to the Forge, but between Compton's orders, Anna's vehemence, and his general inability to see any clear course of action, the decision was made, for better or worse.

Before he could make it the short distance to David's station, the lights on the bridge dimmed before snapping back on full.

"That can't be good," Anna said, hurrying back to her station.

Elizabeth looked like she was going to blame Ryan before every display on the bridge went black.

"Aurora, report? What happened to the displays?"

He was about to ask again when the main viewer flickered back to life, showing a terrifying sight.

With the Forge hanging in the foreground, what looked like a miniature sun shone behind it in the distance.

"What is…. holy crap, he did it," Ryan said, awed at first, then a wave of elation overcame him.

"He did it, Armstrong took down the alien ship."

Confirming his suspicions, Anna was the first to speak.

"Long range sensors are coming back online. I think jamming stopped." She showed a huge smile.

Even Elizabeth, showing an unconsciously large grin, spoke quickly. "Confirmed. I'm starting to get pings from the beacon network."

"I'm getting a flood of coms traffic. It's garbled but I'm trying to clear them up now," June added.

"June, please send a message to the *Columbia* congratulating Captain Armstrong," he said through a huge smile. "Also, if you could add that we stand by to assist in whatever way they need."

"Aye, sir," she returned, pride and relief smoothing the worried lines of her face.

"David, change course and get us above the station, I want to take a quick peek."

"Sure thing," David said. Even his sour mood seemed to lift for a second as he started to input the commands.

"Wait… Something's up with my controls."

An alarm sounded all around the ship, blaring over the speakers on the bridge as well as in the ear of everyone connected to the local network.

"Whoa," Ryan shouted over the ruckus. "What's happening, Elizabeth?"

"Backup systems kicked in, looks like both AI cores are in safe mode. Sensors all over the hull took a dose of radiation before going offline."

Elizabeth overrode the alarm functions on the bridge, returning relative quiet to the space. "Analysis shows energy off the charts at the point of detonation, but it isn't acting like any explosion I've ever seen... it must have set off a chain reaction of some sort... That first wave of radiation must have knocked out the AI; it was mostly visible light, X-rays, and gamma. Luckily, we're still mostly behind the station. Not sure what that slower wave is composed of; the computers are analyzing, but I need the AI cores."

"Dangerous?"

"No, but..."

"But?"

"That chain reaction is starting to throw off gamma rays, and a lot of them." Her fingers drummed the surface of her workstation.

"Output is growing too fast." She paused. "Yes, if it keeps going, it's going to be dangerous."

Ryan watched her expression go from curiosity to concerned. He sat back in his chair and put his harness on.

"Okay, give us some distance, David. June, tell Johnson's team to stand down and strap in."

"Maybe we should get back to the station, we'll be safer there than on this ship." David licked his lips, eyes unfocused and far away.

"Didn't you hear what Elizabeth said, David?" Anna tapped her console, pointing the powerful sensors of the *Explorer* at the site of the explosion.

"We need to get away from that."

Now that the network was back up and running, *Explorer*'s suite of sensors along with the sensors from the station analyzed the phenomenon. Constructing a three-dimensional model, they could see a bright ball of some type of energy spinning and pulsing. It was throwing off waves of energy in ribbon-like structures almost like mini solar flares. A hazy sphere of hot matter seemed to be moving outward slowly from the core. The main bridge display zoomed out to show the extent of the sphere.

"What is it?" Ryan said, cocking his head to the side, trying to make sense of the picture.

Elizabeth paged through several screens, trying to get a reading on the event, but the offline AI kept many systems from integrating properly.

"Whatever it is, it's moving very fast," she finally answered.

Her fingers danced on her console.

"We need to move the ship, now."

"Why? At this distance—"

"We need to move... the radiation output is increasing in intensity at the same speed as that wave... it's traveling with that wave, Ryan!"

"Shit. Go, David, go," Ryan said.

Whether it was the urgency in Ryan's voice or the sight of the evolving wave onscreen, David shook his head as if clearing the cobwebs. Without warning, the ship's thrusters fired at maximum, throwing the bow around 180 degrees, taking them all off guard.

"Oww!" Elizabeth and Anna said simultaneously.

The main engines then fired at military thrust, pushing them back so hard into their chairs Ryan thought for a moment he would break a rib, as he wasn't sitting straight ahead when they lit. Head pressed back into his seat, torso twisted, he could only move his eyes to look at the screen as the g-forces kept increasing.

"Okay, Jesus, David... keep it under ten Gs." Ryan could feel everything pressed backwards painfully.

The bridge lighting flickered along with random interference patterns on Ryan's screen. The main viewer went into some sort of test mode with a jumble of numbers and letters scrolling down the screen.

"Radiation on the outer hull is rising quicky," Elizabeth said, grunting. "We're not fast enough."

"Go to slip, get us out of here," Ryan gasped.

The quantum slip field started to form outside the *Cosmic Explorer*. More and more of the strange virtual particles popped into existence near the hull, drawn in by the exotic matter fields hugging the ship.

Ryan could feel the tingling sensation of the field run up the back of his legs, causing his hair to stand on end.

On the main screen, the slip drive status window popped up into the lower left corner, showing an approximation of the slip field overlaid on a wire frame of the ship. It was a familiar sight from the sims, but where there would normally be a bulbous and symmetrical field concentrated along the rear of the ship, a stunted and somewhat divided field was trying to form. Red areas of the field started to flash before growing ever wider.

"David, I think something's wrong with…" he started to say as a strange sound slowly grew in the background seconds before power flickered again, and a deep vibration started ramping up in intensity before stopping.

"Phew… we're in slip," David said. The g-forces acting on them slacked over the next several seconds, but he kept a worried eye on the slip diagnostics.

Ryan rubbed the back of his neck, trying to work out the kink that was threatening to form from the high-g maneuver. As he rubbed, he could feel a slight vibration in his chair.

"Shit, the field is destabilizing," David said.

The ship started to shudder, vibrating with increasing frequency before it abruptly stopped.

"We've reverted to normal space, and I'm getting alerts from the engineering section," Elizabeth said, looking pointedly at David.

"Damn it… main engines and primary power control networks for both reactors are down. Looks like that radiation spike really hit us hard. Overloads tripped the failsafe, but reactors are still online."

"Are we at a safe distance?" Ryan said, struggling with his nav screen, finally getting the computer plot to show them coasting half a million kilometers away from their last position.

"Unsure, rerunning my analysis," Elizabeth said.

Elizabeth held up her finger as she studied something onscreen. "Radiation levels are in the green."

A wave of relief washed over Ryan. "Okay, could be worse."

"I'm getting remote telemetry from Lunar Command," she said, sending the information to the main screen.

Hanging quietly in space, the Forge lay in ruin.

The only thing they could recognize was the core of the station, which was still somewhat shaped like it was before, but the entire top of the structure had been sheared away, millions of pieces of twinkling wreckage catching the sunlight in an ever-expanding cloud. What remained was a spinning, off-gassing, and burning wreck.

"All those people," June said, tears streaming down her face, her voice breaking.

Slumping back into his seat, Ryan ran both his hands through his hair. Knowing they had survived the alien threat made him feel thankful, but numbness spread through the center of his being. Everything he'd come to know over the past weeks, the places, the people, the routine of his life... everything was gone, and whether or not he wanted to admit it, he'd started to like the life he was building inside the ISA.

His mind played scenes like snippets of a show: walking the promenade with his friends, laughing at a ridiculous outfit displayed in the window of the shop they always passed walking to Nebula; Bob the bartender wiping a scratched and dirty mug with an equally dirty rag; dancing in the club till morning, then his mother's face, her meager funeral.

"What can we do?" Anna said softly.

Ryan was trying to find something, some words of encouragement, but thankfully, Elizabeth answered for him.

"Nothing."

"June, see if you can get in touch with Lunar Command. Tell them we are adrift and are requesting any available assistance."

Something on Elizabeth's screen caught her eye, causing her to do a double take.

After a few seconds, she spoke, still tapping her screen. "David, what's the status of the engines?"

She sounded concerned.

"Still offline. I don't know if we're getting those back without a repair crew."

"Slip drive?" she said, more concern.

"Offline as well. That we might get to reset, but we need to reroute commands through the secondary systems—I don't know how to do that yet."

"Do I have to ask?" Ryan said tiredly, looking at Elizabeth.

"Gamma radiation is starting to climb."

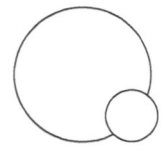

CHAPTER 22

"**M**y analysis shows a steady decrease in radiation; however, the source of that radiation isn't dissipating as fast as I would have thought. The aliens must use some sort of matter chain reaction to power their ships. Somehow, its destruction caused an uncontrolled release of a form of energy I'm not familiar with."

Elizabeth droned on like one of the guest lecturers at the Academy while Ryan rubbed his face with his hands, wishing he had thirty minutes to close his eyes. His eyes burned and brain hurt. A deep weariness lay over him like a wet blanket. He tried to remember how long he'd been awake.

"Two days?" he mused to himself, having no idea what time it was and how long they'd been going from one crisis to another.

"Ryan, are you listening to me? This is important information," Elizabeth chided him while she stood in front of the main viewscreen. She was using it as a glorified projection screen, and over the past minutes, she'd detailed everything she could glean about the energy discharge from the destruction of the alien ship.

He scratched the side of his stubbled face, wondering just how long she'd been talking. "Sure, yeah… so can't we just ride it out? If the radiation is going down, then we're out of danger."

Elizabeth looked at him like he had just eaten a turd.

"Of all people…"

She visibly calmed herself and started over. "Radiation is going down, but the sphere of… quasi matter or whatever we're calling it, is getting closer by the minute. The readings spiked… here… and here… and here." She pointed to the graph showing energy output on the screen. "I think it absorbed wreckage at those locations, or interacted with it in some way, and that must have started more chain reactions."

"Alright, so not great."

"No, not great, Ryan. If that wave hits the ship and spikes at this rate… the ship will be relatively untouched, but we will receive a lethal dose of radiation."

"Alright, really, really not great then."

"All surviving assets in nearby orbits are evacuating, including Lunar Command," Anna added, having taken over June's communications duties. Ryan told her to take a break after they all came to the sad conclusion that the *Columbia* and Captain Armstrong were lost in the explosion.

He wished he could take a moment; a pit churned in his stomach, and his chest felt crushed from the inside, but the universe had other plans, so he shoved the feeling down and pressed on.

"How long do we have?"

"Well, the hull of this ship looks like it was designed to take much more radiation than your standard ISA vessel, so there is that. I'd say that if the radiation buildup from the wave doesn't cook us first… about twenty minutes till it hits us."

"David, any luck getting the computers back up?"

"Huh, oh, ah… yeah, after they went into safe mode it looks like all it takes is a command to reinitialize them. They should be back online in ten or twelve minutes." He let out a series of wet sickly coughs, barely able to control them, as if he were dealing with a mild case of pneumonia.

"Take a break, buddy. When the computers come back up, I'll call for you, but maybe go see the doc, okay?"

"I'm feeling better," he said between coughs, causing Ryan to unconsciously hold his breath. He could tell Anna and Elizabeth were uncomfortable as well.

"Well then, how about you go grab a snack from the mess, and while you're down there, get us all something. We're running on empty."

"Sure." He stood without so much as a look back and somewhat unsteadily left the bridge.

"I'm worried about him," Anna said. "He's looking bad… and….and…"

"And he smells like the Thames on a hot afternoon," Elizabeth finished the sentence for her.

*

Outside the bridge, David stumbled down the passageway. He shook his head, trying to clear his thoughts, but the motion caused a stab of pain in his abdomen.

He couldn't think about food without his stomach flipping end over end, but if he hadn't left the bridge, he was afraid he would throw up or worse. Ryan would probably make a big deal out of it and order him to see the doctor, but right now he just wanted to be left alone. All he really wanted to do was to find a warm, dark room and sleep. He *needed* to sleep. Sure, he was a little woozy, but otherwise he felt fine, and everyone needed him right now, or at least that's what he kept telling himself.

He was at the hatch leading to the bathroom.

"How did I get here?" he thought to himself.

Before he could answer the question, he found himself inside, nearly running to the last stall before slamming the door closed and vomiting into the toilet. Closing his eyes tightly, he steadied himself after what felt like ten straight minutes of heaving. His chest was burning, his stomach tied in tight knots. When he finally regained his breath, he spit a few times and slowly opened his eyes. What he saw made him clamp his hand over his mouth and gasp, backing into the door of the stall with a bang.

The toilet was full of blood. Not your average amount, whatever that might look like, but a mess of deep red and black speckled gobs that strung together in a disgusting web of shock.

On top of everything else, the pungent smell that hit him nearly made him vomit again. He quickly reached over and hit the evacuation button on the toilet, making the lid close automatically and suction out the frightening mass.

"What the hell is wrong with me," he whispered, no longer feeling able to stay upright. David quickly unzipped the side of the emergency pressure suit he'd been given for the journey back to the ship. He pulled the thick plastic ring over his head, allowing the top half of the suit to fall to the floor. His black uniform jacket was torn beneath in several places and crusty along the front.

He felt his midsection with his hands, not feeling any particularly painful spots, reinforcing the thought in his mind that he was completely fine. The only curiosity was that he had a hard time feeling anything at all. A numbness spread along the front of his torso, which didn't raise any alarm bells, but he decided to take off his jacket just to make sure.

With shaking hands, he flipped each of the brass buttons loose from their holes, letting the jacket fall open. It smelled awful as he peeled it back, making him finally realize that the crusted mess was mostly dried blood which deeply stained the front of his ripped white shirt. He worked the buttons open and revealed a similarly stained t-shirt underneath.

He didn't want to look any further. David's mind was reeling from the sheer amount of blood he must have lost, and he incoherently wondered if his clothing was the thing keeping him alive. As if his guts would spill onto the floor the minute he lifted his t-shirt.

He gave one last shiver, held his breath, and finally worked up the courage to pull his shirt up, exposing his stomach. Just as quickly, he wrenched the garment down and held his jacket closed, swaying back and forth. He had a hole in his midsection just above his belly button the size of a golf ball. Black, crusted, and oozing... something.

"No..." He gasped, still holding himself tightly. He had to go find the doctor. He had to do something, didn't he? A rush of dizziness overcame him along with a whisper... *sleep*. The world went dim.

"You must sleep." The thought coalesced in his mind, not quite his own. His legs buckled, and he slumped to the floor.

"I need to help... my friends," he whispered to himself.

"You must sleep." The feeling soothed him, quieting his thoughts before everything started to spin and he fell unconscious.

*

"AI cores should be running, Ryan," Anna said, glancing worriedly at David's empty seat; it had been a while since he left.

"Thanks, Anna. Don't worry, he'll be fine. He's probably realizing just how much he needs something to eat." His stomach growled. "Hopefully he remembers to grab some for us."

Ryan looked around, not noticing any indications that the cores were running. "Aurora?"

"Captain, what can I do for you?" Aurora's silky tones sounded in his ear and over the bridge speakers.

"How are you doing?"

"Well. Currently I am analyzing the logs and attempting to ascertain why my systems went into safe mode. The experience was... disconcerting."

"Yeah, welcome to our world. Uh, we're kind of pressed for time here."

"Analyzing. Yes, of course, the matter-energy wave that is approaching the ship will cause a deadly gamma ray outburst on contact with the hull. I can see why you're concerned."

"Can you help? We can't move the ship, and personally I'd like to stay alive."

"Aurora, can the reaction engines or slip drive be repaired?" Elizabeth cut in.

"Of course, Commander Miller. Reaction engines one and three could be repaired within minutes; however, they do not contain enough thrust to outrun the matter-energy wave. Engines two and four have damaged thrust chambers and require a visual inspection to determine if they can safely be used. The quantum field manipulation drive cannot be repaired with equipment on hand. I have queried the drive's subsystems and am afraid that they are reporting errors consistent with a number of damaged external emitters."

"Can't we repair them?" Ryan said.

"No, the emitters run along the surface of the hull, and even if they could be repaired, we lack the specialized superconducting material."

The bridge went silent as Ryan, Elizabeth, and Anna struggled with the news.

"Aurora, what do we need to do to get the mains working?" Ryan said, finally breaking the silence.

"A number of physical breakers have tripped in engineering. I have sent the information to your display."

"Anna, call Johnson, get his team down to engineering and reset those breakers double-time. Aurora can assist them."

"You heard the computer... the engines won't do any good." Elizabeth said, crossing her arms.

"Well, I refuse to sit here and wait for that thing to kill us. At least we can buy some time to think." Ryan countered.

Anna immediately called down to the conference room. After a few hurried words, she tapped her display and turned.

"They're on the way, ETA two minutes."

"Okay, as soon as we get engines back, I want to get underway." He looked back at the doorway to the bridge. "Okay, we need him, where's David?"

"Lieutenant Kim is in the lavatory. Would you like me to contact him?" Aurora said.

"I can point the ship in a straight line," Elizabeth scoffed, touching her panel. "I'd prefer not to marinate in that particular stench just yet,"

"Ouch," Ryan said motioning for her to go ahead.

Thrusters around the ship fired and pointed the nose directly away from the expanding sphere that was rapidly closing.

"Power has been restored to engines two and three," Aurora announced a short time later.

"Nice and easy, keep the G's down so everyone can get strapped in."

The two centerline main engines of the *Explorer* glowed softly as the ship started to accelerate away from the wave. Onscreen, the intercept timer, which was morbidly counting down the minutes before they were killed, slowed.

"Okay, that bought us a few more minutes. Increase thrust to military and keep it there. They can take the damage out of my paycheck."

"There's got to be something else... Aurora, are there enough... uhhhh, emitters to take us partially into slip? I mean, maybe we can just get a little speed out of it?"

Elizabeth cut in. "Aurora, forget Anders's stupid question and scan our path for any asteroids or large bodies." She looked back at him. "The slip drive doesn't work that way, but if we can find a mass large enough, we might use it for cover and reduce our exposure."

"No bodies of sufficient mass exist on or around our path," Aurora responded.

"At our current speed, will the gamma ray exposure be lessened enough for us to survive or maybe survive long enough to get back to Earth and get treatment?" Anna asked hopefully.

As Aurora explained that they would only be given a few extra minutes to live, Ryan scrolled through the *Explorer*'s schematics. They were complicated, but the interface helpfully allowed him to dumb it down so he could see each space, color coded, and labeled with its function until he spotted what he was looking for: the water holding tanks. During early missions to Mars, he read that astronauts would hide behind tanks of water to absorb radiation; it was cheap and effective.

"Aurora, how much water would we need to block or at least attenuate the radiation enough to survive?"

"Nearly fourteen feet."

"What about the big tanks by the galley? Can we just point that at the source and get behind it?"

"No. Based on analysis of the structure, there is not sufficient mass to shield the crew and passengers."

"Come on, there has to be something, some system on this brand-new and supposedly advanced ship for this? We deal with radiation all the time... it's space." Ryan swiped the schematic in frustration, causing it to randomly bounce around before landing on a curiously large, empty space right next to the engine room labeled "Classified."

"I think Ryan may be onto something. If we can pump as much water as possible into these spaces. Maybe move the secondary holding tanks and engine coolant tanks and flood… Ryan, are you listening?" Elizabeth said.

"Aurora, what am I looking at here?" Ryan held up his hand to forestall Elizabeth's annoyance.

"ONR Projects have been classified to flag ranks or above."

"ONR? You mean Naval Research? Is it a weapon?"

"I am not at liberty to discuss classified projects."

He glanced up at the counter, which was still quickly ticking down.

"Aurora, I know you want to do the right thing, and rules are rules, but we're in mortal danger here. I'm sure the ISA would grant an exception in this case when we have a hangar full of civilians and diplomats on board. Plus, you saw what that wave did to the Forge." He thought for a second. "I know you didn't like being offline. We hate it too… so maybe give us a hint?"

When Aurora didn't immediately shoot down his idea, he pressed on.

"Is it a weapon?"

"No."

"Is it a new type of shield?" he asked hopefully.

"No."

"A matter transportation device like on that show?" he said, grasping at straws.

"Not exactly."

"What?" Elizabeth said, intrigued, now standing next to Ryan. Anna unbuckled and came over to stand with them as well.

"Wait, wait," Ryan said, holding up his hands. "Not exactly isn't a no. You mean to tell me the ISA knows how to beam us to another ship… or a planet?"

"I am unsure of your reference, Captain, but I cannot discuss the details of Project Daedalus."

"Come on, Aurora," he said in frustration. "This could save all of us." He hesitated, knowing that using a device to transport them might leave her behind, but pushed the thought down. "Hey, we've bent a few rules together, you needed my help to get the engines started, remember? What's one more?"

"What have you two been doing exactly?" Elizabeth said, crossing her arms.

"Yeah, what's she mean by that?" Anna said, standing next to her, her stance nearly identical, making Ryan do a double take.

"That's not important right now." He blew it off, deciding to take a different tack. "Aurora, we'll be dead in a few minutes anyway, so what's the harm in telling us? Do you want me to make Elizabeth leave the room? She's the only one that would snitch."

"Hey!"

"Project Daedalus was conceived by Dr. Henry Thorp of the Office of Naval Research Special Projects Division. He observed that slip drive malfunctions at high output powers did not immediately destroy the ships in question. He surmised that at specific powers and field configurations, the stability of quantum drives could be increased, protecting the ship and allowing travel up to fifty percent the speed of light."

Ryan whistled. "Are you saying we have one of these improved slip drives on board?"

"No. It was found that large masses regularly lost at least partial atomic cohesion above speeds and powers equating to roughly thirty-five percent the speed of light and therefore could not reliably function using current technologies."

"So if it's not an improved slip drive, what is it?"

"A new form of transportation."

"So we *can* beam ourselves." Ryan's face lit up.

"No. During a later experiment, Dr. Thorp found that by inverting high power quantum fields momentarily, he could effectively change the world line of an object, taking it outside normal spacetime."

Elizabeth put her hand on Ryan's shoulder, interrupting his next question.

"Aurora, are you saying that he found a way to manipulate time?"

"The doctor and ONR believed they had the ability to slow time relative to the ship."

"Well, that doesn't do us much good, does it?" Ryan said. "How does slowing time... or speeding up time on the ship help?"

"The device installed on this ship does not slow time."

"You just said it did." He held out both hands in exasperation.

"No. I said the doctor believed it did. I have analyzed all relevant data, and he was mistaken. The device entangles the ship and everything in it to the quantum field. In doing so, his measurements seemed to indicate a difference in the passage of time. Instead, he simply introduced uncertainty into his measurements."

"Quantum uncertainty?" Anna said, shifting her weight between her feet in nervousness as the clock ticked down below the five-minute mark.

"Once the ship is fully entangled, it exists outside the timeline in superposition. Once a bias is introduced, the waveform collapses and the ship is reintegrated into normal spacetime."

"I am so lost," Ryan said, garnering nods from Anna and Elizabeth both. "Aurora, can you put that into terms I can understand?"

"Not likely." Elizabeth couldn't help but zing Ryan, who crossed his eyes and made a "meh" noise at her in response.

"When the device is activated, the ship no longer exists in this universe. By precisely measuring its position, we can reappear in a place of our choosing."

"Holy shit... Hyperspace," Ryan said, grinning.

"That isn't at all what she said, Ryan," Elizabeth scoffed and rolled her eyes.

"It is... it's like in the movies where the ship goes into hyperspace and: Poof. Poof." He made little explosions with his fingers in one spot, then another some distance away.

"Uh, not so sure, Ryan," Anna said, glancing at Elizabeth, who looked like she was going to smack him.

He wasn't sure, but for a moment, he felt like they were ganging up on him, which felt really, really unfair.

"Whatever, we have less than five minutes... does it work?" Ryan said.

"Onboard diagnostics show the Daedalus project equipment is undamaged."

"Hot damn... Power it up and let's get out of here."

"As there are no operational tests of the new equipment, I estimate our chances of success at less than twenty percent."

"But we won't die, right?"

"Immediate fatality is not the most probable result. The most likely outcome would be a randomized exit vector somewhere in the solar system biased toward our calculated point of reappearance by approximately thirty-one percent."

Ryan thought about it for a second, looking first at Anna, then at Elizabeth.

"I'm game," Anna said, picking at her clothing. "Anything to end the torture of being in this dress and hot-ass pressure suit for one more minute."

"I suppose we've little choice. But if this gets us killed, I swear I'll find you in the afterlife and make you regret it," Elizabeth added in all seriousness.

He didn't want to make the decision for the rest of the people on board, but time was growing perilously short, and wasn't that what captains were supposed to do?

"Our chances of surviving that energy wave are zero... So, let's do it," he said, cinching up the straps on his acceleration harness.

Both Anna and Elizabeth went to their stations and strapped in. At that moment, June walked through the doorway at the back of the bridge.

"Permission to take my post, Captain?" Her eyes were red and her hair slightly disheveled. She had swapped her old clothing for a blue coverall, and a look of grim determination set her expression.

"Absolutely, Lieutenant, glad to have you back with us."

She walked over and sat, following suit and pulling her harness taut.

"Call all hands to acceleration stations," Ryan said. "We're about to get out of here."

"What do I have to do?" Elizabeth asked Aurora, unsure how to interact with the device.

"I will make the necessary calculations, Commander. Where would you like to reposition the ship, Captain?" Aurora said.

He pondered the choice for a few seconds before deciding. "Mars. Not too close, but close enough to get a message to the *Britannia*, wherever she is at the moment."

"Extending booms and calculating reposition."

A loud clanking sound nearly made Ryan jump out of his chair. He looked around wildly, thinking everything had already gone wrong before he realized it was probably normal.

"Look," Elizabeth said, pointing at the main viewscreen.

The unidentified bulbous shapes that were tucked into the midline of the ship scissored out on the end of hefty-looking arms. What must have been huge power cables were attached in bundles along the arms, almost looking like an afterthought to the design. Each one of them looked to be as large as a passageway. They were attached to the hull with massive connectors and ended in equally large connectors under the pods.

Each clanked as they locked into position, sending a shudder through the hull.

"Calculations complete. Power buffers are charging. I have enabled the initiator on your panel, Captain." Aurora said.

Ryan looked down at his panel and noticed the large, mysterious red button on the right arm of his chair was lit from behind. It pulsed ominously behind its clear plexiglass guard. The symbol printed onto the button started to make some sort of sense to him now. It looked like several wavey lines stacked on top of each other over a circle. He thought it was maybe some engineer's idea of riding under the waves like a submarine. Go under in one area and pop up in another… he could be wrong, but he went with that. The slow pulsing became faster till it went solid red.

"Well, here goes nothing." He flipped up the guard, then paused. "Will we feel anything?"

"As Project Daedalus is untested, I cannot say, but if the unit malfunctions, I don't believe you will experience any pain, as atomic disassociation travels at nearly the speed of light," Aurora said.

"Thanks, Aurora. Remind me to talk to you later about your bedside manner."

"Um. What are we doing?" June looked to Ryan, concern crossing her face.

"Going to Mars." He cringed and pressed the button.

After five seconds, he looked at Elizabeth.

Ten seconds.

"What happ—"

A wave of vertigo washed over him while simultaneously all light in the room ceased. He reached out to grasp the arms of his chair and found not only was the chair not there, but he also didn't seem to have any hands. Panic started to set in as he realized he couldn't breathe. Ryan grunted in desperation as one might do if they found themselves stuck, upside down in a dark hole deep underwater, but regardless of how hard he tried, he could hear no sound, breathe no air, and even his heartbeat seemed to have left him.

The twinkling of a light caught his attention. Somewhere far off in the distance, impossibly far away, or so close he couldn't focus on it. Ryan calmed as he realized he could perceive light once again. The warmth of it flowed over him or through him, he wasn't sure. The light was joined by another, then another, before the heavens opened and there were thousands, millions, billions of lights all around him. The vastness of the star field was unlike anything he'd ever experienced. Were they stars? He wondered. Were they motes of dust so close to his face that he couldn't quite see them, lit from some unknown source he couldn't fathom?

He felt a great connection to the lights, as if they were him and he was looking down like some sort of specter floating above his body. He tried to reach out, and this time he felt a pull. It was like reaching out only to realize you are spinning and the farther you stretch, the harder your arm is pulled to the side.

One light started to shine brighter than the others. Pulling, pulling so desperately at Ryan's being that he felt like he needed to be there, with that light.

That one light outshone the entire universe. He was being drawn in as if sucked down a drain, a whirlpool so intense there was no way to stop it, torn towards it until: darkness.

Something tugged at his consciousness. Curiosity overcame him as it pulsed. As if it had always been there, always pulsing, it was something familiar enough to be remembered. No, it wasn't pulsing; it was beeping.

Ryan's eyes fluttered open, but he could see absolutely nothing. Something was beeping slowly in the background. A rising panic started to take hold of him as he reached up and rubbed his eyes. Flashes of light met the pressure of his fingers.

Power must be out. He slowly relaxed before something like a half-remembered dream tugged at the edges of his mind. Floating, stars, bright lights…

"Anna? Elizabeth?" he croaked.

A shudder and moaning noise answered—the ship.

He became aware of a light coming from somewhere. It was bluish and muted.

"Ryan," a whisper called from his right. The light brightened as something moved in the same direction as the whisper.

"Elizabeth? I… I can't see anything. Do you see that light?"

She must have moved something as the light now shone bright. A blinking bit of text on her otherwise dark panel accompanied the beeping noise.

"Everything is offline." Her voice, at first weak, became stronger as she cleared her throat. "Restarting."

He unhooked his harness and immediately felt a strange wooziness as he almost fell out of his seat. Grabbing his chair, he stayed low to maintain his balance. He almost felt like he was spinning. Making his way in the darkness, he made it to Anna's station and felt the warmth of her back, her steady breath a welcome feeling under his hand.

Lights started to flicker around the bridge as emergency lamps came to life, throwing a shadowy illumination around. Elizabeth unhooked her harness as well, and from her expression her stomach wasn't happy. She took a few steps toward June before settling down to the floor taking deep breaths.

Nothing seemed damaged or out of place. Besides the power being out and the trippy dreams, there was no indication anything had happened.

"Sensors?" Ryan said.

"Nothing. I don't know if anything is operating. We're on battery backup." She gulped.

"Yeah, my PDD too," he added before finally remembering. "The wave! How long before it hits us?"

"Less than five minutes… I believe."

"Okay." He mentally tried to calculate how long it would have taken him to wake up and the time he'd spent speaking to Elizabeth. "So maybe another couple minutes at most?"

She didn't answer, but he realized that she didn't have to. Ryan sat next to her on the floor, and they both waited in dim silence.

Ryan exhaled slowly, the sound almost lost beneath the hum of emergency circulation fans. "Well," he muttered, forcing a crooked smile, "at least it's quiet. I always figured my last moments would involve a lot more screaming."

Elizabeth let out a soft huff, somewhere between a scoff and a laugh. "You're remarkably calm about possibly dying."

"I've had practice," he said, shrugging as if it were a joke, though he didn't smile.

Elizabeth looked over at him, her face unreadable in the dim glow of the emergency lighting. After a pause, she said, "You did… surprisingly well, considering the circumstances."

Ryan blinked. "High praise."

"Don't get used to it," she said quickly.

He nodded slowly, then turned to face her more fully. "You know, if this is the end… you made a hell of an XO," he said, extending his hand toward her.

Elizabeth glanced at it, hesitating. Then, with a quiet breath, she reached out and shook it—firm and professional at first, but it lingered just a beat longer than necessary.

She met his eyes. "And you're not the worst captain I've served under."

"I'm the only captain you've served under." He grinned, this time genuine, with maybe a hint of sadness.

She didn't respond, but a small smile tugged at the corner of her mouth.

They both quickly pulled back their hands.

"That has to be at least five minutes," Elizabeth said changing the subject. She stood, a bit unsteady, getting her rebellious stomach under control.

"Maybe it worked?" Ryan said joining her feeling somewhat relieved. "Keep trying to get systems online. If we're anywhere near Mars, the buoys should pick us up and a patrol ship should be along. We're safe as long as they don't think we're aliens and shoot us."

"Wonderful. Do keep those thoughts to yourself, Anders."

Ryan grinned. Still feeling woozy he checked June's breathing, then slowly walked over to Anna's station and put her head gently back onto the headrest.

Elizabeth sat back at her station, looking at the readouts scrolling on her panel. "A few more minutes, the reactors are in startup. Computers should be online shortly after."

"Okay, stay here, I'm going to make sure everyone in the hangar is okay and connect with Johnson."

Anna groaned and started to come to.

"Fine," Elizabeth said, brushing her hair back with a sigh. "I'll babysit. But bring back some food and water while you're at it."

"You got it. Beer and a hot dog coming right up."

"God, you're such a grub." She shook her head, watching him as he reached the sealed bridge door and waved half-heartedly at the dead control panel before kneeling to open the manual release.

"Ryan," she said uncertainly.

He paused, looking back at her.

"I know, I'll try not to get in any trouble," he winked.

Elizabeth rolled her eyes. "Ugh, shut up and go do something useful."

He smiled then walked away, feeling the smallest bit of optimism.

"Huh, there might be a person under there after all…" he mumbled before wondering if David was still in the bathroom.

He walked cautiously toward an emergency locker outside the bridge, using his hands to steady himself on the cool metal of the passageway bulkhead. Set into the wall, a plexiglass lid was lit softly from within by an emergency light strip. He opened the magnetic latch and grabbed a flashlight from the assorted contents. Pulling the activation ring, it filled the passage with an intensely bright cone of light.

He squinted till his eyes became accustomed and carefully made his way aft.

"The pseudo gravity must be screwed up," he thought, feeling like he was walking up a hill.

CHAPTER 23

David lay wedged between the stainless-steel toilet and the bulkhead of the bathroom near the bridge. As the pain of his contorted position finally overrode the shock-induced unconsciousness, he slowly came to and realized that his neck and back were absolutely killing him. His thoughts were incoherent, and his mouth was foul, as if he'd eaten a spoonful of spoiled yogurt before passing out.

"How long have I been asleep?" he groaned.

His head was lying on his chest at an odd angle with one of his arms twisted behind him painfully. Now if he could just remember where he was.

For a moment he thought that he must have been out drinking with Ryan and Anna. This wouldn't be the first time he'd woken up after sleeping by the toilet in his small quarters. His roommates normally would bang around to get his attention before finally asking him to get out so they could shower for duty.

He cracked open one eye and then another, finding that indeed he was in a bathroom, but it wasn't one he recognized. The lights were low and coming from the far side of the room. His clothes were a mess, and something smelled awful. His shirt seemed crusted over, which he assumed was due to him vomiting… or did Ryan throw up on him again?

"Was I going somewhere? I remember needing to do something." He struggled to sit, mentally retracing his steps.

He remembered getting dressed to go to the launch party for the *Cosmic Explorer*, speaking to Anna, Ryan showing up, and then Elizabeth.

"The attack," he said aloud, causing his throat to spasm and a coughing fit to follow.

He could only manage a foggy recollection of the attack and of the journey up to the *Explorer*. He remembered someone, an unfamiliar woman with blue hair, then… Slaunder. His memory was so hazy he wasn't sure what happened. He must have gone to the bathroom and passed out after reaching the ship. He looked down and saw a rumpled and stained pressure suit laying on the floor in a pile.

The door to the bathroom clanked open. Metal hinges squeaked slightly, but it was enough to make him cringe.

"David, you in there, buddy?" Ryan's voice called out.

He sighed in relief. Explaining his actions to a stranger was the last thing he wanted to do right now.

"Uh, yeah, sorry, Ryan, I must have passed out. Lemme just get cleaned up."

"You sure you're okay?" Ryan said with way more concern than David thought necessary.

"I didn't shit myself if that's what you're asking," he shot back.

"Well… you sound a lot better." After a short pause, he added, "I'm headed down to the hangar to check on our guests… you wanna join me in a bit?"

"Yeah, sure, I'll meet you down there," David said, listening to Ryan close the hatch, muttering something.

"Guests?" David mused before vaguely recalling the civilians that followed them to the ship. Ryan didn't seem too concerned, so maybe the attack was over?

*

"Guess he just needed to use the can and pass out …" Ryan muttered, closing the hatch to the bathroom and thankfully cutting off the stench coming from within.

He continued down the passage, slowing for a few steps as he thought about David. He'd sounded like his old self again, so maybe it was just some blowback from his narrow escape or something. He made a mental note to check on him if he didn't show, but for now Ryan knew the civvies were probably freaking out, and that seemed more pressing. At least the emergency lighting had come back on, so he shoved the flashlight into his jacket pocket.

The walk to the hangar still felt strange. The pseudo gravity was still wonky, but if anyone could figure it out, it was Elizabeth and Anna.

He cringed. "Well, maybe if they don't pull each other's hair out first."

Finally arriving at what he thought was the correct hatch, he pushed open the door as the automatic door controls were still dark. He walked into the hangar vestibule: a long wide room that doubled as both an observation post and a cargo passthrough. Thick armored windows were set into the wall, showing the hangar deck in its entirety. From here, crewmembers could watch as shuttles arrived or departed the ship, stage cargo or personnel, or transition into the airlock to access the bay. The only other feature was a ladder going up to the next deck where the hangar control officers and crew would be posted to control and maintain order in the bay.

Both doors of the control room airlock were locked wide open, as the bay wasn't being used for anything other than cargo storage during the outfitting of the ship. Ryan wasn't even sure if the hangar doors were actually functional yet.

The low sound of talking met him as he walked into the hangar itself. The echoey walls of the large chamber did little to dampen the noise, allowing the murmur to mix into a hodgepodge of sound. Along the back of the deck, civilians were milling about, and one person was gesturing wildly amongst a group of ten to fifteen others. Small handheld lights made puddles of warmth here and there amongst the crates, signifying gatherings of people. The overhead emergency lights only served to cast harsh shadows on everything, giving the space a cavernous feel.

Ryan smoothed his jacket, putting on his best "captain" persona and walking over like he owned the place.

"Captain!" the voice of the Martian ambassador rang out loudly, making him cringe internally as every eye in the place turned towards him.

"You see, I told you we were safe and sound in the good captain's care," the ambassador said to the small group he was with.

The robed man broke away with his assistant following closely on his heels. As he intercepted Ryan, the others looked on with concern in their faces.

Lowering his voice, he spoke quickly. "Captain, I must insist that I be taken away from here. I am fatigued and afraid all the wild gyrations have made me quite ill. I may have actually fainted earlier."

"We all did, sir," his assistant added.

"I apologize for the rough ride, but the enemy ship didn't give us much choice. Luckily, we should be near Mars now, and once the power is restored, I'm sure they would like to hear directly from you."

"Oh, how splendid, Captain, just splendid."

Ryan decided to change subjects before the man decided he wanted to come to the bridge. "How are the passengers doing, Ambassador?"

"They were scared, of course, but after some calming words, I was able to organize them into small groups and keep them safe." He sniffed, pulling out an embroidered handkerchief and dabbing his nose. "Plus, the, ah… commoners mustn't be allowed to congregate into large groups."

"Ambassador," his assistant stepped in. "I'll work with the captain to see to your accommodations if you'd like to sit. You look positively exhausted."

"Yes, Emily, that would be fine. I doubt such a vessel would have much in the way of civilized quarters, but do your best." The ambassador patted her on the hand, then made his way to one of the acceleration chairs set into the walls of the hangar and collapsed into it in rather dramatic fashion.

The young woman waited until he was out of earshot. "Captain, could you give me an update?"

"I told the ambassador—"

"Of course. I heard what you told him, but we were only in slip space for a few minutes before we dropped out. I assumed a drive failure, but…" She hesitated. "…but unless I was unconscious for longer than I realized, we couldn't be that close to Mars?"

"Oh no, it wasn't, well, it was…" Ryan caught himself before potentially divulging state secrets to a rival government. "I'm sorry, it was Mrs....?"

"Ms. Drake."

Ryan gave her his best smile. "I'm sorry, Ms. Drake, I'm not at liberty to discuss what happened at this time. I'm sure the ISA will fill in the ambassador's office once the after-action reports are filed. Paperwork, you know."

"How very diplomatic of you, Captain," Ms. Drake said, giving him a once-over. "I'm sure you're familiar with the ISA treaties concerning Mars as Captain of this ship, but I'd like to remind you that I was assigned by the ISA council on foreign affairs as the ambassador's liaison and am not a citizen of the Martian emirates." She made a show of glancing around. "As such, Captain, I'd appreciate it if you would fill me in on what's going on out there."

"I'm sorry, Ms. Drake, until I can verify your identity, I can't say much beyond what I told him. We should be in the vicinity of Mars, and as long as it wasn't attacked like we were, we should hear something soon. If we're lucky, they should have already picked us up on their sensors and sent help." He realized that if she were telling him the truth, he should probably throw her a bone. Also, it didn't hurt that she was cute.

"Okay, just between us." He thought quickly, deciding some truth was acceptable. "The *Columbia* took out the last alien ship, but she didn't survive." He paused, emotion suddenly swelling before he could regain control and tamp it down.

He cleared his throat. "So, on that front we're safe, but we had to escape the explosion by entering slip, and now we're here... unusually quickly." He patted himself on the back at the implication that it was a slip drive issue that got them here so fast. If this woman was a Martian operative or something along those lines, a little disinformation would hopefully not land him in hot water.

"As soon as power comes back up, I'll be contacting the *Britannia* to set up a rendezvous. I'm betting they'll take charge of the *Explorer* and everyone here."

"I see," she said, pondering the information. "When we're in range of the *Britannia*, I'd appreciate a personal heads-up."

"You got it." Ryan flashed his best smile at her.

She pondered for a moment, seemingly slipping into a completely different persona. "Not bad getting the ship away... for a Lieutenant J.G. right out of the Academy."

"What? How did...?"

"Oh, and Omandi is going to shit a brick if he doesn't get some quarters, so you might want to work on that posthaste. I don't think he's ever been this long without room service."

She turned on her heel and walked back to the ambassador's side, once again assuming the role of assistant.

Standing there stunned, he realized that someone else was walking toward him.

"Sir." Johnson saluted. "Just the man I wanted to see."

"Oh, ah, hey, Johnson, good work getting the mains back online." Ryan still felt flabbergasted that the demure Emily might be some kind of ISA spy? Agent?

"No problem, sir. I was just in medical getting a sitrep from Specialist Lata and the doc. He wants to talk to you, by the way, says it's urgent."

Ryan didn't need to ask. Johnson's face told him that the team's leader, Sergeant Martinez, wasn't doing great.

"I'll head there next." He nodded grimly. "What's the situation down here?"

"Most of the civvies are okay. Some of them got banged up, but overall, nothing serious. There are some ISA here too, we've put 'em to work but kept them with everyone else since we couldn't verify identities. Oh, and the Martian chief wants to meet with you too."

"Just once I'd like some downtime," Ryan mumbled.

"I'm surprised the Martians aren't down here standing guard over their ambassador," Ryan said.

"He's as safe as we can make him on the ship. My guys rotate down here to keep an eye on things, but I don't think the chief and the ambassador get along, sir. Something about political classes being... well, I don't know the word he used, but I think it might have meant 'elitist' or something. Maybe 'coward'? I thought he was gonna spit on the ground when he said it."

"Between you and me, Johnson, either is probably right on the money." They traded knowing glances. "Okay, I'll head to medical. You tell the chief I'll meet with him after."

"You got it, sir. Oh, and if it isn't a secret… what happened and where are we?"

"Show me the way to medical and I'll tell you," Ryan said, motioning him to lead the way.

*

David stood in front of the four stainless-steel sinks lining one wall of the bathroom opposite a small bank of lockers. Over each sink was a polycarbonate sheet that did a decent, if not perfect, job of approximating a mirror. The emergency lighting gave him a haunted, gaunt look with long shadows carving deep grooves into his face. His stomach was growling like mad, and his insides felt all twisted. It took him almost ten minutes to finally get the strength together to leave the stall.

He stank like an open sewer filled with rotting meat.

He peeled off his crusty jacket and sniffed, nearly giving himself the dry heaves. Tossing it to the floor, he noticed the front of his uniform shirt was unbuttoned, ripped and crusty as well. His t-shirt was also darkly stained and stiff. A momentary panic nearly overcame him as he thought that the stain might be dried blood. He raised his t-shirt and sighed in relief. His stomach was uninjured.

Silently chiding himself for his overreaction, he decided he needed a change of clothes.

"Where am I going to get a uniform?" He saw the reflection of the lockers behind him. Turning, he walked over and opened the first, finding only empty shelves. He made his way down, clicking open each till he got to the last one, which contained several pairs of blue maintenance coveralls hanging inside.

He pulled one out that seemed to be about his size and stripped down to his underwear, then decided to pull those off as well. He had stains down his legs and even into his shoes. Lucky for him, they cleaned pretty easily in the sink along with his socks. He then gave himself the best sink bath he could manage.

Sometime later, he zipped up his new coveralls and felt a million times better. He dropped his ruined uniform into the trash chute and walked out feeling like a new man. His stomach growled again, this time with an accompanying wave of hunger he could scarcely imagine.

*

Ryan carefully slid the door aside, trying not to make too much noise. The medical bay wasn't too far away from the bridge, its door looking like every other except for the small red cross on a placard about eye height set into the larger double door.

It was only one deck up from the chow hall, where Johnson headed after their talk. He played it safe and kept the noise down in case someone was resting.

"Can I help you?" a low voice sounded from the small office near the door.

"Doc?" Ryan walked in and saw an older gentleman who didn't much look like a doctor. He was stout, some would say overweight, but he had thick arms and a torso that looked like he knew hard labor. He was wearing a white, stained button-up shirt that just fit him with a jacket hanging on the back of his chair.

"Oh, Captain." The man stood, tiredly holding out his hand.

"Giuseppe Ravani, you can call me Jack," he said, with the tone of someone who'd used that line a hundred times before.

"Thanks for lending a hand, Mr. Ravani, I was told you wanted to speak to me?"

"Yeah, it's about the sergeant." He looked Ryan up and down in a very familiar way. "No offense... but how long you been out of the Academy, kid?"

Ryan didn't flinch away from the question, instead sizing up the man with a more critical eye.

"How long you been out of jail?" Ryan said, seeing the reaction he needed to know he was right.

"I don't know what you're talking about."

"Take it easy, I can spot someone who might not be a hundred percent on the up-and-up. I was there myself and I could care less as long as we don't have a problem," Ryan said, giving him a serious look.

Jack scrunched up his face before relaxing. "No offense, okay?" He gave Ryan a closer look. "So, you're not one of those rich kid officers. Who are you?"

"The captain for now. Listen, Johnson said you needed to see me. You need to see me or not?" Ryan's speech and even his mannerisms shifted closer to how he spoke to people in the camps where he grew up. He'd fought hard to bury that side of himself, but men like this had a way of dragging it back out.

"That injured soldier we got back here." He pushed himself up and walked past Ryan, leading him to a small private room close by. Ryan noticed his movements were artificially slow, with the man making a show of his aches and pains. Walking through the door, they were met by a series of electronic beeps, the monitor on the wall displaying the sergeant's vitals.

Ryan inspected the setup surrounding the young woman. He expected for her to be buried under a mountain of equipment and sensors, but she was simply sleeping with some sort of oxygen mask setup and several remote monitoring devices. One on her chest and one attached to the bandage that was securely wrapped around her head. He wasn't sure if that was due to the advanced equipment or the lack thereof.

"She's not gonna make it," Ravani said, pointing to the display. "She's got a serious bleed somewhere in her brain. I stabilized it the best I could, but she needs a real hospital and a real doctor. Half this shit isn't working even when the power does stay on."

"Damn it. How long she got?" Ryan said, still trying to figure out who this guy was.

"Half a day, a day tops. We got her on some emergency meds that stopped the bleed and reduced the swelling, but eventually she'll eat it."

The man's matter-of-fact tone was getting on Ryan's nerves, and he wasn't sure why.

"Do what you can, we should be able to get her to better facilities soon." He turned before stopping in the doorway. "Oh, Jack... have some respect. Her guys got you off that station in one piece."

"Yes, sir," Ravani said, snidely flipping him a salute as Ryan walked out.

*

Ryan was in a bad mood by the time he got back to the hangar. His emotions were bubbling even before Ravani's attitude and disagreeable demeanor had gotten under his skin.

"That is a look I've seen before," a familiar voice said.

"David. Damn, buddy, you look a million times better."

"I always look pretty good, Ryan. Except after Anna's birthday party."

Ryan eyed his friend up and down. He really did seem like the old David, almost better in some ways. His skin looked clearer despite the pitiful attempt he'd made washing the muck and dirt off, and inexplicably his hair looked fuller and thicker. He didn't have that gaunt look anymore. He looked healthy and full of life.

"I see you found some new clothes, and you stink a lot less now." Ryan smiled.

"Yeah, I have no idea what I rolled in. I found these in a locker, but I was going to ask." He looked sheepishly at Ryan, scratching his head. "What happened? I'm having a little trouble remembering how I got into that bathroom after we got here."

"After we dropped out of slip, you left the bridge... you said you were going to get something to eat. After that, no idea. The computer said you were in the head before we... we got here."

"Out of slip?" David scrunched up his face. "Ryan, Anna and I got to the ship with the civilians, then, then I can't quite remember."

Ryan studied his friend's confused expression. He really didn't seem to remember the events after they'd arrived. His trip to the Forge, the narrow escape. It dawned on him that maybe his friend was suffering some kind of traumatic amnesia. Maybe a form of shock?

Ryan filled him in, watching closely to make sure he wasn't going to pass out or anything. David seemed to take it in stride, only shaking his head in confusion at the mention of the alien creature, but more from the outrageousness of the situation rather than a denial that it happened.

"You okay?"

"I guess… yeah, I'm fine. If you'd told me that last week, I'd have called you a lunatic." He shrugged, then glanced toward something in the darkness. "Guess you've got captain things to do."

Ryan looked around in confusion. The darkened edges of the hangar and harsh shadows weren't conducive to seeing anything.

Before he could ask David what he meant, a large shadow seemed to coalesce out of the darkness. Ryan never heard the person's approach, but as the figure walked into the dim wash of the overhead emergency light, he recognized the imposing bulk of Private Nguyen. He was wearing a holstered pistol and was still decked out in his black tactical gear, but now instead of his primary weapon, he was carrying a handful of wrapped energy bars.

"Hey, Lieutenant…" Nguyen spoke to David before becoming more formal and nodding at Ryan. "Captain."

"Damn, you're like a friggin' black cat in the dark, Nguyen. Nearly gave me a heart attack," Ryan said.

"Sarge always said I could sneak up on a ghost." He grinned before remembering his manners and offering a few of the bars to them. "Civvies found a load of these in one of the crates in the hangar. Want one?"

David grabbed a handful from the private before looking sheepishly at Ryan. "Did you want any?"

"Uh, nah, you go for it, buddy. I'm gonna hit the chow hall before I head back to the bridge."

David had unwrapped several and began stuffing them in his face.

"Ugh, I hate these artificial flavors," David said, barely slowing down. "Not bad, though."

Ryan became concerned he would choke himself, but several rough swallows later and he was stuffing more into his mouth.

Nguyen unwrapped one and sniffed it. "Can't smell a thing." He looked at the wrapper. "Uhh, says Tuna-Peanut Crunch."

David seemed undeterred.

The lights brightened all around with relays audibly clicking up and down the passage while the ship hummed back to life. Gradually, the pseudo gravity fields normalized, and Ryan no longer felt like he was standing on the side of a hill. A curious high-pitched whining noise he didn't recognize was coming from all around them, but it was low enough to be ignorable. Ryan made a note to ask Elizabeth what it was.

"Glad they got that fixed, it was starting to give me a headache," Nguyen said, handing the rest of the bars to David, who greedily snatched them up. "You remind me of me... sir." His smile widened as he watched David wolf down more bars.

Ryan counted the seconds, waiting for Elizabeth's wonderful voice. As if on cue, a beep sounded in his ear. "Go ahead."

"Ryan, main power and systems are back online, but you need to get up here. We have a situation."

"On the way." He sighed. "Private, get everyone down here prepared. It sounds like we have some more trouble brewing."

"Aliens?"

"Doesn't sound like it, but just in case, make sure the civvies are prepped."

"Aye, sir."

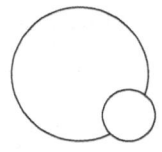

CHAPTER 24

Ryan and David had no sooner stepped foot in the hallway when another chime sounded in his ear.

"Elizabeth, we're coming," he said, waving David forward.

"Forgive the intrusion, Captain," Aurora's silky voice sounded in his earpiece.

"Oh, Aurora, glad to have you back."

"Thank you, Captain. Apparently, an unexpected side effect of Project Daedalus reset my entire quantum data plane. This is the second time I have experienced a period of forced inactivity, and again I found the experience quite unpleasant."

"Yeah, passing out sucks. At least I had some trippy dreams during this last one."

"Actually, I believe you most likely retained consciousness during the event. Biologically based brains do not rely on quantum effects like my processors do. Only certain functions like your sense of smell would be affected."

"Oh, so that's why Nguyen couldn't smell those bars." Ryan touched David's shoulder. "Let me see that."

David passed him one of the newly unwrapped bars and Ryan gave it a good sniff.

"Nothing... is it temporary?" He read the label and grimaced. *Beef and Banana.* Who thought that was a good idea?

"Yes." Aurora replied.

"How are you still... working, then?"

"The conventional processors on board act as a bootloader in the event of a failure of my matrix. If all power is lost, these simple devices act in much the same way as your organic ones."

"Good, I'd hate to lose you," he mused. "Oh, sorry, what did you need?"

"I am experiencing an anomaly with my internal sensors. I cannot detect Lieutenant Kim; however, I see that he is with you on the security feed. My other sensors do read a fifteen percent increase in O2 consumption in your space above baseline and some other abnormal readings."

"Okay, that is strange. Let's maybe file that under 'oddities' and deal with it later. Hopefully the Mars techs will have an answer soon."

"Commander Miller is requesting your presence on the bridge."

"Of course she is."

*

On the bridge, Elizabeth struggled to find any working exterior sensor. Anna and June were both attempting to assist, but something was interfering with the scientific as well as the tactical arrays.

"Anything from the cameras?" Elizabeth said in frustration.

"For the fourth time, no. I've even tried to open the missile bay doors to use their sensors before I realized that they haven't loaded any god damned missiles," Anna snapped back.

"I'm hearing so much noise on the coms channels, I'd swear we were orbiting too close to the sun," June added.

"Our receiver might be out of commission, try our transmitter, standard hail on all channels." Elizabeth ignored Anna's outburst.

"Okay, so is everything down or just malfunctioning... and where the hell is Ryan?" Anna threw up her hands.

"*Captain* Anders was in the hangar and found this guy," Ryan said, walking onto the bridge.

"David!" Anna said, rushing over and wrapping her arms around him forcefully, squeezing for all she was worth.

"Three minutes, Anders. That's how long I've been waiting." Elizabeth said over her shoulder.

"Ignoring the fact that it takes that long to get back here, I would have known if it was an emergency… we've had so many of those around here lately, I feel like I'm getting a sixth sense about that stuff."

"A sixth sense, is it?" Elizabeth said. "Does your sixth sense tell you how to get our cameras working, or the sensors?"

Ryan rubbed his chin absentmindedly. "Aurora? What do you make of this?"

"I'm not sure, Ryan, I'm… having trouble," the AI replied with an odd tone that made Ryan cock his head and look around to see if anyone else had noticed. Nobody responded, which made him think it had answered directly to him.

"Aurora?"

"Yes, Captain, how can I help you?"

"What's happening with you?"

"I am currently running a broad-spectrum scan of the interference to assist Lieutenant Rodriguez, a full diagnostic of the basic ship subsystems for Commander Miller—"

"Okay, thanks, but that isn't what I'm asking. You're acting strange."

"Of course Ryan, stand by while I run a diagnostic."

"That's what I'm talking about." He paused, waiting, but no answer came. "Aurora?" Then realized Elizabeth was watching him. "We may have to figure this out on our own. I think I broke our AI," Ryan said.

"Honestly, Anders, you behave like an unruly schoolboy with a box of matches. And don't even think about flashing that ridiculous smile at me," Elizabeth said, putting her hand up toward Ryan as if to physically stop him from looking at her.

"Elizabeth, look at these power levels," Anna said.

Elizabeth was tapping her console before Anna had finished speaking. "Pseudo gravity field is drawing twice the usual power. Can you check the numbers and tell me which way they are biased?"

"Biased to port, 330 degrees negative 40." Anna said.

"Are you getting any temperature readings from the hull?"

Anna looked confused. "I'm getting readings, but totally normal... about 2.7K."

"What's going on, Elizabeth? What does that have to do with anything?" Ryan leaned over her shoulder, looking at her console, but couldn't make hide nor hair of her complex setup and gobs of equations scattered across several windows.

She chewed her fingernail. "I'm right, I know I am."

"Right about what?" Ryan said, putting his face between her and her console, fully expecting to be slapped.

Instead, she pushed his head out of the way and pointed to the pseudo gravity diagnostics tab. "That's showing me something is exerting a strong gravitational pull on the ship." She then gestured toward the temperature data Anna sent. "If it were a star, we'd see significant heating on the hull by now... no."

She tapped another tab, scanning the data, eyes narrowing. "...no pulsed magnetic fields either." She went quiet, staring at the screen, lost in thought.

Ryan waited. "So... what are we looking at?"

"The only thing that fits..." Her voice was far away.

He reached out and placed a hand on her shoulder. "Elizabeth?"

She blinked, snapping out of it. "A black hole."

Ryan stepped back bumping into his station and plopped down into the chair.

If it had been anyone but Elizabeth, Ryan would have told them to stop bullshitting and be serious. He looked to Anna first, catching the end of her emotional journey as it played out wordlessly on her face. She shrugged at him unconvincingly, but he could see that she agreed with Elizabeth.

June seemed to take the news in stride, nodding but otherwise keeping to her duties, continuing to scan in the hopes she could pick up any kind of signal.

He looked to David who just seemed fascinated. "David, buddy, how about we get out of here?"

"You got it," David said, sliding into his station chair. The ship swung around its axis soon after, powered by the large thrusters.

"June, tell everyone to buckle in."

The background whine Ryan noticed earlier changed pitch as the ship maneuvered before coming back to full power again. For a second, another wave of vertigo washed over him, and judging by the reactions of the others, they felt it as well.

David calculated his escape trajectory and slowly increased the power.

"We're still down to two engines," David reminded them as the low rumble reached the bridge.

Vibrations started to ripple through the superstructure of the ship. The groaning they had heard intermittently till now became louder and more pronounced. They could all feel the gravitational pull of the massive black hole on their bodies despite the best efforts of the pseudo gravity generators.

"Okay, ramping up to full thrust. Recalculating trajectory," David said, his hand casually on the console next to him, keeping himself upright. Ryan, however, was struggling and noticed everyone but David seemed to be having difficulty with the changing gravity.

"Ryan, the fusion drives of the ship don't have enough thrust to escape." Aurora spoke directly to Ryan through his PDD.

Ryan was taken aback. The AI seemed more casual than ever, almost flippant in its tone. "Uh, okay, you sure? David hasn't finished his calculations."

"I would never lead you astray. With our reduced output, we are only traveling at 900 kilometers per second, " she answered back, using the same strange tone. He looked expectantly at David, trusting his friend more than the AI.

"Dave, are we getting anywhere?" Ryan grunted.

"Hold on, yeah, the computer just finished crunching the numbers. Oh... not good."

"Not good isn't an answer, Lieutenant," Elizabeth said, nearly gasping with effort as more gravity spilled past the counteracting field.

"We're losing ground... Ryan." He made a face at Elizabeth. "Maybe if we had all the engines, but this is what we've got."

Aurora added an unhelpful "Told you so" into his ear.

"You and I are going to have to have a talk later," he said under his breath as another metallic groan ran through the ship, causing everyone to look around.

"I look forward to it," Aurora purred.

"Mr. Anders, Johnson is reporting that a cargo container broke loose in the hangar. Minimal damage, but they are holding on for dear life down there," June said, using the intercom to pipe her voice directly into everyone's PDDs, as she was barely able to speak.

"Shit!" Ryan yelled, his emotions bubbling over again. "Can't we catch one break? ... Okay, slow us down, David." Ryan tried to catch his breath and calm himself. As they started to slow and the pressure of their acceleration lessened, Elizabeth was the first to fill the relative silence.

"Infall time is... not good," she said mimicking David, who in turn swiveled around with his mouth open, ready to shoot a barb in her direction.

"Infall what? Forget it, what's the bad news, Elizabeth?" Ryan cut off the argument, starting to feel like the universe definitely wanted him dead.

"Time to the point of no return." She let out an uncharacteristic sigh. "From these mass readings and our current velocity. I calculate twenty-one hours to the event horizon. Even at full thrust, we don't have enough velocity to escape."

Ryan looked around the bridge in defeat. He ran his hands through his hair and slammed them down on the armrests of his chair. "Anyone want to take over? Elizabeth? No?"

"Captain," June said.

Ryan had his head in both hands, answering back a muffled "Yeah?"

"I'm getting a signal."

"What did you say?" His head popped up.

It was Aurora who answered instead. "Captain, we are receiving a high-power narrowband burst at 10.221 exahertz, encoding shows ISA standard encryption, but the contents of that signal are odd."

"Is it another ship? How could it be here? What does it say, June?" Ryan asked, trusting the young lieutenant over the glitchy AI.

"I'm just seeing a standard hail, but millions of them all sequentially arranged." She touched several other controls. "Analyzing the encryption, I think it's ours—I mean our encryption signature, from the *Explorer*. It might just be our own signal bouncing back to us."

"Negative, Lieutenant Armstrong, while the message and encryption may be ours, the sequence of the data suggests otherwise," Aurora added.

"What sequence?" June said absently, her fingers now flying across her panel. "Oh, I see... the spacing of the messages," she said excitedly. "Each of the repeated messages are in groups, the groups are all prime numbers!"

"What are you telling me? I'm lost," Ryan said.

"This isn't earth-shattering news to me," Elizabeth said, tapping her own controls and bringing up the sequence. The computer analyzed the transmission, removing the original message strings, substituting the base ten prime number sequence. She ran her finger along the sequence, counting to herself.

"...521...523...441?"

"June, transmit the following on the same channel we received." Elizabeth tapped a sequence and forwarded it to June's station.

"Hold on, what exactly are you sending?" Ryan said, frowning.

June hesitated, her eyes flicking to Ryan for confirmation.

Ryan sighed, his frustration bleeding into sarcasm. "Right, because I probably wouldn't understand it anyway, right, Elizabeth?"

"I'm just transmitting a single number back: 541; there was an error in the sequence, and they went from 523 to 441, which isn't prime. See?" She forwarded the sequence to Ryan.

Ryan studied it for a second. "No, it isn't," he paused scratching his chin. "But it *is* the hundredth prime..."

This stopped Elizabeth short. She looked back at her console and tapped another button, arranging the data into a grid of hundreds. There at the bottom of each row, was a sequence of incorrect primes.

She looked over her shoulder, trying not to be too obvious, but Ryan was looking right at her. She looked forward again, ignoring him and his dumb smile. "Aurora, can you isolate the sequence and analyze those numbers?"

"The captain was correct, the sequence has a two-group series encoded. I believe it is a frequency and a number." Aurora sounded almost smug to Ryan.

"What the hell is wrong with that thing?" he thought.

"June, transmit using that frequency and number," Ryan said, trying to keep his tone neutral so Elizabeth wouldn't try to push him down the stairs when he wasn't looking. "What's the number, by the way?"

June tapped her screen. "It's Pi." She looked at Ryan expectantly. "Um... how many digits do you want me to send?"

"Oh." He paused. "Ideas?" He looked around the bridge.

"Maybe send back the same length message," Anna chimed in, after watching the back and forth with amusement and a little curiosity.

"Sounds good. June, send it back with as many digits will fit in the same message length."

"Transmitting Pi using the frequency offset they provided." She queued the message into the transmit buffer and hit send.

"Okay, now what," Ryan said just as the lights started to flicker.

"Ryan..." Aurora's voice sounded strangely in his ear before cutting out completely.

"Quantum field generator is going offline!" Elizabeth said. "Diagnostics aren't responding."

"Tactical control is down." Anna looked up at Ryan.

The ship shuddered once again before going completely silent. Everyone on the bridge looked at each other in alarm.

"Do I want to know?" Ryan said.

"Are you feeling lighter or is that just me?" David said to nobody in particular.

"Checking the pseudo gravity systems. They're offline, we've had a complete field collapse." Elizabeth looked around, puzzled. "Why do we still have gravity?"

The bridge screen, which to this point was a flickering static-filled mess, restarted. The boot sequence cleared quickly and a crystal-clear picture filled the previously messy display. What showed there stopped everyone in their tracks.

The surreal scene almost short-circuited Ryan's mind. It was a structure, no doubt. One so large that it filled the display almost to the edges. It hovered in space between the *Cosmic Explorer* and the blackness of the singularity beyond. Around the perimeter of that perfectly black hole in space, a shimmering swirl of light played along the edges. The intense gravity of the hole caused the light of the stars behind to be bent around in the most bizarre patterns. It reminded him of the mythical Medusa, her snake-like hair wriggling, undulating, never still.

Nobody said a thing.

It wasn't until Ryan realized that the image on the screen was now beyond the edges that his brain started working again. "Are we getting closer to… that?"

David finally spoke. "I don't know. Main propulsion isn't responding, and I can't get a fix on our position. The reactors are in standby, but from my panel, we're no longer accelerating toward the black hole."

"Elizabeth? Anna? What are you guys seeing?" Ryan said, wrenching his gaze from the main viewscreen.

Miller was trying to regain her composure. She looked at her panel as if she'd just remembered where she was. "Yes." She tapped her controls clearing her throat. "Well, primary systems seem to be in standby, but I'm seeing the same thing. We're definitely moving, but radiation levels have dropped, and gravitational effects are… well, they are—nearly normal. Point eight five g."

Anna sounded more concerned. "Ryan, tactical systems are online, but without primary power, we don't have much. Well, not that we had any ordnance onboard."

"Are we not going to talk about that?" June interjected, pointing at the bridge screen, which now showed quite a bit more detail as the ship drew closer.

What they thought was a rough spheroid crystalline structure was resolving into a much more complicated and multifaceted surface. It had a deep color pattern with reds and purples near the inner structure moving out on trunks that slowly evolved into patterns of emerald greens and shimmering blues.

Ryan couldn't quite figure out if it was a trick of the camera or if it was glowing from within. There wasn't a light source nearby, only the stars behind and around the ship.

"Whoa, where are we going... is that you, David?" Ryan said as the bow of the ship moved downward, pointing at a roughly circular dark spot. Around it, the spiny structures seemed to be opening like the petals of a flower until what looked like a portal appeared.

"I don't even have attitude control," he said, holding up his hands.

The *Explorer* quickly approached the dark portal, seemingly accelerating, but not even the slightest movement could be felt by her crew.

As they passed the portal, it dawned on Ryan why the structure looked so familiar. "Those spines, look." He pointed as they passed through the outer portal. "Those remind you of something?"

Anna took in a sharp breath. "The enemy ships."

"Johnson, come in." Ryan tapped his com panel.

"Sir, glad to hear from you. Are we okay? Things have been getting strange down here."

"You're not going to believe this, but we may be getting company soon." He waited for Johnson to ask questions, but all he received was a simple: "Yes, sir, we'll be ready."

"Lieutenant Rodriguez will send you more info when we get it, bridge out."

*

When the com connection dropped, Warrant Officer Johnson spent several seconds pondering the captain's words. Nguyen was standing nearby and stepped up to him. He'd always been the perceptive one on the team and this was no different, which is why he'd given him a promotion to Corporal and made him second in command.

"I know that look." the big man said, chewing on yet another granola bar.

"Get the team together in the ready room, full kit, prepare to be boarded." He looked at his PDD. "Grab Lata from the infirmary and any of the ISA folks and civvies who look like they can fight."

He walked off, checking to see if the lieutenant had sent him anything.

"Hey, Alex, grab the Martians too. They'll probably get a kick out of this."

Nguyen gave a huge smile. "I guarantee it."

*

Ten minutes later, he walked into the makeshift ready room. The lively banter died down as soon as he entered. His team, of course, was positioned around the central table. Cooper, who was the team's hand-to-hand specialist, was arm wrestling Chico, the team's pilot. While Samantha Cooper was by no means a pushover, she was outclassed by Chico by almost twenty pounds. Chico was trying to play it off, but he was struggling despite putting a good face on it. He kept glancing over at Inna, the second in command of the Martians, who looked on in amusement.

"Watch out there, Chico," Specialist Lata, their medic, prodded. "She's gonna win this time." She looked a bit tired, but she seemed as ready as the rest of them.

Close behind the excitement was the Martian chief and his second. They both looked relaxed and ready, making occasional comments to each other and watching the contest, their swords still strapped to their hips.

Besides that core of fighters, there were four others. Two ISA members who were in brand-new coveralls with the *Cosmic Explorer*'s patch on the sleeve, and a couple of roughnecks who were probably from the Forge rigs. Both were wearing light blue long-sleeved shirts and heavy denim coats, their rough hands and faces looked like they'd seen too much heat.

"Listen up," he said, killing the last of the conversation and granting Chico a reprieve.

"I know there are rumors going around about what's going on, but I can tell you right now, they are all wrong." He waited a beat. "The *Explorer*'s systems have been disabled, and we believe the ship has been captured by unknown... forces." He let that sink in for a minute. Nobody seemed to be ready to ask questions or freak out, so he continued. "We're currently being dragged into a vessel of unknown origin, but the captain believes that it shares the same structure as the ships we fought near the Forge."

That got the room going. The ISA members and the roughnecks both spoke over each other. Chico, of course, made a joke about being short and wanting out of the fight.

"Listen!" he said, raising his voice. "We have very little idea what is happening, but if they do want to take this ship, they're going to have a fight on their hands—Alex, what did you find in the ship's armory?"

"Not much, the lockers are all empty, but we found one container in the cargo bay with powerpacks, some tac gear, and body armor."

"Okay, divvy the body armor and tac gear out to whoever needs it. After the briefing, link up with Lieutenant Kim. He's going to rig the reactors to blow if things get bad."

That got everyone's attention.

"We aren't going to let it get to that, but we have strict orders from command to not let the ship be taken by hostile forces. Is that clear?"

"Yes, sir." his team all said in unison.

"Roch!" Both the chief and his second banged their armored fists against their battered chest plates.

He looked at the others, who hesitantly nodded their acceptance.

"Good. Now our primary objective is to secure the main boarding hatch. The cargo hatch at the rear of the ship has a manual locking mechanism, and once the door controls are disconnected, that shouldn't be an issue. The main boarding hatch, however, cannot be completely disconnected from the computers by design." This elicited scoffs from his team.

"I know, I know. Whoever built this tub didn't think that far ahead. Since the enemy seems to have a fair bit of control over our systems, we have to assume this will be their primary entry point." He tapped his PDD, sending diagrams to each member.

"We will break into three squads. First squad will be Nguyen, Chief Huatare, and Inna. Second squad will be myself, Sam, and Chico. We will position ourselves here, and here." He annotated the diagrams. "Third squad will be Specialist Lata, and…?" He pointed at the two ISA guys in coveralls.

"Private Jackson, Forge Ops," one said before he pointed at the other.

"PFC King, uh… flight crew," he stammered.

"Thank you, gentleman. Okay, what about you two?" He pointed to the two Forge workers.

"I'm Brian, that's Eric," the man said gruffly.

"Have any of you fired a weapon recently?" he asked, knowing Nguyen probably screened them before picking this lot. When they all affirmed, he looked to his team.

"Okay, pistols and ammo to third squad."

There was some grumbling, but all of them knew the small caliber weapons were useless against the squids, so they slid them across the table to the conscripts.

"Now that we have that sorted. We don't have many rounds for the mark fours, so watch your ammo usage. Corporal Nguyen has the most effective weapon, so he'll start the party."

Nguyen smiled, patting the large weapon, which was propped up on the side of the table.

Chief Huatare laughed loudly while hefting his sword. "Effective weapon!" he called out in his strange accent, eliciting a round of laughter from the rest of the assembled group.

"The Chief is right. From what I saw, our submachine guns just slow those things down. Be ready to switch to… well, switch to swords as your secondary."

"The captain will lock the ship down and monitor from the bridge. Nobody's a hero—we fall back until we hit an airtight hatch. Once through, we set up ambush. I spoke to Lieutenant Kim, and he is working on some improvised explosives, which we will pre-position along the fallback routes marked on your PDDs." He looked around, making sure to make eye contact with each person.

"Third squad, you'll act as medics, reinforcements, and door closers. If either combat squad has to fall back, you be ready to close the hatches and weld them shut." There was a palpable relief from third squad, except for Lata, who was all business.

"Okay, Charlie team link up with Specialist Lata, she'll go over what you have to do. Everyone else, check your kit and meet me at the boarding hatch."

He wheeled around and walked out the door as the room behind him erupted in activity.

*

When Warrant Officer Johnson made it to the main boarding hatch, Captain Anders was already there waiting.

"Sir? Shouldn't you be on the bridge?"

"Anna is going to run the doors from there. I'm basically useless at this point. Don't worry, I'll stay out of your way," he said, seeing the skeptical look on the soldier's face. "Who knows, if it's not who we think it is, you might need someone down here to do the talking." He grinned at the now very skeptical warrant officer.

"Well, if you wouldn't mind staying back till we know what's going on."

"Hundred percent, you won't even know I'm here," he said before a strange thrumming sound caught their attention.

"Ryan, I think we're here," Elizabeth said through his PDD. "We've stopped forward movement, and from what I can tell, something is approaching the side of the ship. Anna is standing by on the doors."

"Thanks, Commander, lock down the ship," he said before turning to Johnson. "I think we're here."

Johnson whistled and spun his hand above his head. "Game time, people. Come on, sir." He moved backwards toward the hatch leading to the main passageway.

Up and down the long primary passage, large, recessed doors slammed down every fifty feet with a thud. First squad was stationed in the small security office directly off the entrance. It had a thick armored window, behind which Nguyen posted himself. The Martian chief and his second pulled their blades and waited near the open hatch to the room, ready to meet whoever or whatever came through the outer door.

Second squad formed around Johnson, everyone now wearing soft body armor and helmets. They racked the actions on their submachine guns, chambering a round and flipping off the safeties.

Johnson pulled his own sidearm and handed it to Ryan. "Just in case."

Third squad was just beyond the first airtight door toward the bridge. They were all armed with pistols and small welding packs except Specialist Lata, who'd recruited several other civilians and had set up a battlefield triage one deck above.

"Ryan, the outer hatch is opening!" Anna said though his PDD, making him wince.

"I hear it. Just get ready on the doors if we have to fall back."

"I'm watching," she said. "Ryan, if these reading are correct, the atmospheric composition on the other side of the hatch is, well, normal. Pressure is slightly higher, and there's increased O2 and decreased nitrogen, but everything is in the green."

"Roger."

"Anders," Elizabeth cut in. "Lieutenant Kim says he's in engineering and just needs you to tell him when to…" She paused.

"Let's hope it doesn't come to that."

"Yes well, don't try to be heroic." Elizabeth said before dropping off the connection.

The outer door thudded against its stops. The inner hatch showed two green lights and one red—meaning both the interior and exterior were pressurized and the inner door was locked.

Nguyen racked his assault shotgun.

Muzzles protruded out of the hatch near Ryan, pointing toward the inner pressure door as each of the second squad members readied themselves to fight.

Ryan closed his eyes, blowing out a steady breath before opening them again, ready for whatever might come.

The red light on the inner hatch turned green, and everyone held their breath.

It swung open with mechanical precision, coming to a stop with a click as the hold open lock engaged. A soft bluish light flooded into the passageway along with a peculiar smell, something akin to salt water.

Ten seconds went by, then a minute. Ryan was tensed so long his neck started to hurt.

"Anna, do you see anything?" he said as quietly as he could, drawing a look from Johnson.

"Let me try to reconfigure the hatch camera. Okay, stand by, I'm moving it."

He could hear the whine of a small motor somewhere in front of him.

"Ryan, I see… it looks like a room." She sounded confused. "Yeah, there isn't anything in… wait. Something is moving, it looks like." She stopped.

"Anna?" Ryan moved forward a hair, gripping the pistol tightly, trying to see over Johnson's shoulder, but the light was dim on the other side of the hatch.

"It's a person! At least I think it is. Ryan, there's a… girl standing against the far wall of that room. She's just standing there." Her voice was tight.

Ryan stood frozen, trying to imagine any scenario where a girl would be out here… next to a black hole, on an alien ship, in deep space. None of it made sense.

He moved a little farther out from behind Johnson.

"Sir, don't silhouette yourself," he warned.

Ryan thought for a moment before lowering his pistol and holding it out to Johnson. "Hold your fire."

Both of the other members of second squad glanced at him. He just put his hands out and made a little waving motion, asking them to part the way. They glanced at Johnson, who shook his head in confusion before withdrawing his weapon from the doorway. Both Samantha and Chico followed suit.

"I don't know what you think you're doing, sir," Chico whispered, "but I'll tell the story of how big your balls are if you don't make it back." Chico took two fingers and held them under the brim of his helmet in a modified salute.

Ryan smirked, feeling only somewhat less terrified as he stepped through the hatch and into the passage leading to the outer door, Johnson close behind.

Ryan waved off the Martians, who looked ready to jump into the breach with him. They nodded back, each placing fists against their chest plates in silent salute.

"I got you, sir," Johnson said, gripping his submachine gun tight across his chest.

Ryan nodded and walked forward, crossing the threshold of the inner door into the small vestibule, just behind the outer door.

Taking one last deep breath, he stepped forward onto a soft surface. The experience of his feet slightly sinking into the material caught him off guard, and he looked down instinctively before whipping his gaze up, straining to see in the soft blue light of the room beyond.

His eyes were having problems adjusting. Everything seemed to be a similar hue with no real source of light. Then he picked out a shape. His heart jumped into his throat and his pulse pounded. After several calming breaths, he squinted, trying to make it out.

It *was* a person.

He looked over his shoulder at Johnson, who already had his weapon trained on her, or it.

"It's okay, Johnson." Ryan motioned for him to lower the barrel of his weapon then turned and held up both hands in front of him, palms out in a show of peace.

"Hello?" he said hesitantly. "I'm Ryan Anders, captain of the *Cosmic Explorer*."

Now that his eyes adjusted, he could see it was a woman, maybe five foot six or so. She had what looked to be shoulder-length black or brown hair, and she was thin, her arms hanging down by her sides. He didn't recognize her clothing; it was odd, looked foreign, with strips of some type of material criss-crossing her body. No shoes he could see, and she had her head angled slightly away from them, not making eye contact. She stood very still.

He glanced at Johnson again, who gave him a slight shake of the head.

"Did you send the signal?" He asked making sure not to make any sudden movements.

A crackling in his ear nearly made him jump out of his skin. "Anders, what on Earth are you doing out there?" Elizabeth's concern was palpable.

"Standby," he said firmly touching his PDD, muting the channel.

"Miss?" He took a step forward. "Can you hear me?" He took another step. She shivered slightly, bringing him to a stop.

He said the first thing that came to mind. "We come in peace." He smiled big, which she must have noticed as she shivered again and closed her eyes tightly as if she were waiting for him to pounce.

"Shit." Ryan muttered under his breath. He still had no idea what he was supposed to do, but he was the captain now. Straightening, he gave the order. "Johnson, stand down." His eyes flicked to the gun in his hand, then back to the darkness behind him. "Fall back to the hatch."

Johnson looked hesitant but finally gave a nod and took a few steps backwards, disappearing into the dark vestibule. Ryan had no doubt his weapon was at the ready.

Ryan switched gears and put his hands down. Deciding to go for broke, he sat down slowly, crossed his legs, and waited.

For ten more minutes, he waited. Trying not to move, being as still as the woman.

The darkened room, the soft blue light, the quiet. It tugged on the memory of something long past—that perfect day, the last happy evening with his mom, her smile, the way she hummed that song. Without even thinking about it, he started humming as she had. "Twinkle, Twinkle, Little Star."

The woman moved. He kept humming softly.

She turned and looked at him. He kept on humming.

Finally, she moved closer, her steps so light they made almost no sound, and settled in front of him. Her eyes were unusually large, far bigger than any human's, with amber pupils that caught the light. Her hair wasn't fine like his but broad and flat, the strands scalloped at the edges as though carved into shape. Her clothing shimmered with a slick, almost living sheen, as if it were perpetually damp. Wide, glistening bands crossed her chest in a careful lattice, overlapping like woven strands that shifted with her slightest movement, an alien weave both strange and graceful. Her feet were bare, but her toes lacked definition. They looked as though soft clay had been pressed into the suggestion of feet, convincing at first glance but strange when studied more closely.

Ryan stopped humming and turned up the corners of his mouth in a closed smile, making sure not to bare his teeth. "Hello," he said softly, slowly putting his hand to his chest. "Ryan."

She waved her hand slowly in front of her chest before placing it as he had. "Aela'ris," she said in a melodic near-whisper. He could see teeth in her mouth when she spoke, but they were smaller, maybe thinner and blunted, and he didn't see any canines at the corners. They almost looked like a doll's teeth.

"It is a pleasure to meet you, Aea-lar-is?" He struggled to make the same sounds.

Just then, a door he hadn't seen behind the woman started to slide aside, and light poured into the space as it opened wider, causing him to squint. It was a strangely familiar reddish orange hue, like seeing a sunset. In fact, that's exactly what it looked like—sunlight.

Aela'ris stood, both hands crossed on her chest. She backed slowly toward the opening and looked away as she did before.

"Sir?" Johnson's warned.

"Stand down. Keep the others ready to defend the ship, but under no circumstances are you to try to rescue me if this turns bad." He turned, hesitated, then turned back. "Hey, if I get eaten, close the door." He flashed a smile at the dark-skinned man then moved to follow the woman leaving the gobsmacked warrant officer behind.

As he walked closer, the light became brighter. It was very much like a low sunset and felt like real sunlight. Even the way it cast shadows—straight lines, not like an overhead or even spotlight.

The woman Aela'ris passed through the door, which was arched along the top in a way that wasn't like a machine-made door with perfect angles. He slowed as he reached the threshold, his eyes attempting to become accustomed to the brightness, and then he gasped.

Through the archway, he saw the last thing he would have ever guessed: a pinkish blue sky... and a city.

THANKS
AND A SNEAK PEEK.

My sincere thanks for choosing *Fleet of the Forgotten*. I hope you enjoyed reading it as much as I did writing it!

If you did enjoy this book, please consider leaving a review online. Reviews are extremely useful to prospective buyers and to authors, alike.

Please visit the website (thorntonbooks.com) and sign up for my newsletter. It's the best way to keep in touch.

Finally, by way of a more tangible 'thank you', here's a sneak peek at the next book in the *Exiles War* series...

Dan Thornton
September 2025

CHAPTER 1

From afar, it could have been mistaken for a fragment of an ancient celestial body. A vast, hollowed shell of rock and crystal drifting silently through the void. Its surface was a maze of jagged spires, and age had worn deep scars into its skin. The ship bore no engines, no ports, no windows just a shell that held a fragile world.

Nearly forgotten, in a disused section of the biosphere, a lush wetland surrounded the warm waters of a small brackish lake. Near the shore, shrubs and reeds gave way to sedges and grasses of all types. Tucked into one of these thickly grassed areas was a small clearing of moss; spongy and burbling. A perfect place to get away from the noisy bustle of the city that dominated the center of the ship.

Aela'ris lay hidden on the comfortable mossy bed. Her delicate hands cupped, supporting her head, she sighed heavily in contemplation. Overhead, past the blades of long grass, the sky glowed a deep purplish red signifying the dawning of their home star of Veyshara. The disk of dust and rock around the ancient flame caught the light and cast it back, spilling a pale glow that left her wide, sensitive eyes barely aware of the dawn shadows.

She had grown up in the city ship of *Nym'elari* like all the other Currents her age. Training for a future where the ship reached its final destination - a real world. Water and rock and salt, with a warming star that her people could call home. Not this simulation of one.

This little hidden corner of the fen was where she came to think. Unlike the older generations, she and many of her peers were beginning to see solitude differently. Being alone wasn't something to be feared or avoided, but a place where one's mind could roam freely. For the elders, staying together was the apex of being - what it truly meant to be Krynnid. To be alone was to be shunned, cut off from the very thing that gave you worth.

"Ancestors, what should I do?" She let her thoughts drift into the void, hoping for a sign, some spark of inspiration to guide her. The night before, her father had all but commanded her to abandon the School of Science and serve as his assistant instead. Among the Krynnid, such a post was one of the highest honors, something her peers would envy. Yet to Aela'ris, it felt like betrayal.

Unbidden, her mind wandered to the final verse of her soul-song, gifted to her by her mother so long ago.

Shora-thyn vela'sharan veynira —"Guide me through the shadowed current, until dawn's first light".

It was sacred to her, something that no other living being other than her birth mother had ever heard, as was tradition. A song she might one day pass to her own Newlings if she ever felt like she wanted to take that fork in the stream.

Aela'ris calmed her mind letting the thought of raising a child push away the thoughts of disappointing her father once again.

She tittered at the absurdity of her raising a little one.

"Which soul would be granted to her?" She wondered, recalling the countless great men and women recorded in the archives of her people.

Since being cut off from the birthing waters of their home system no Krynnid woman had conceived naturally for five generations, instead their colony had been forced to rely on cloning. It was mostly effective at keeping their population stable, but the technology was failing and not a single successful Newling had been birthed in over four years.

Her father had pestered her now and again about bringing a child into the family group, as if the failing process might correct itself through sheer will alone. Each time, she brushed the thought aside. How could she guide a Newling when she still needed guiding herself?

Her friends longed to raise the next generation, but Aela'ris had never shared that dream. She was too contrary, too headstrong. The group of women who had raised her chastised endlessly as she grew from Newling to a young Spring and now to a Current. They kept insisting she should follow in her birth mother Val'yra's footsteps and bring a powerful elder into the world.

She hummed a discordant note, trying to swallow the anger rising in her chest. She didn't feel powerful... she felt trapped. Everyone called her the embodiment of Thal'yssae, the legendary founder of the very School of Science she now attended. But to Aela'ris, that legacy was a curse. Thal'yssae had saved the city ship from destruction, yes, but she had also failed to free their people from the black hole that still held them prisoner. And what of her, a clone born generations later? Did they expect her to somehow succeed where countless others had failed? Or was she destined, like Thal'yssae, to fall short?

Her anger flared at the memory of her father's lectures, always about legacy and the accomplishments of a woman dead for generations. He never spoke of the other side, of how she had failed so utterly in the end: dabbling in forbidden science all the while deceiving everyone around her. Promising redemption but instead found dead at the controls of a forbidden device that could have destroyed the city.

She pushed herself up from the sedge, stretching her back and letting her legs dangle into the warm waters. "I am *not* Thal'yssae. I am Aela'ris." She said to the grass casually running her hands through the thin green whisps that curled from their tops.

Could she tell her father that the cool, never changing certainty of science was the only thing that gave her even the smallest bit of happiness? Should she just admit that she wasn't like the older generations who longed to live in harmony, lost in a sea of anonymity? That she just wanted to be herself and not what he and society expected her to be?

By the time she had become a Current and gathered with the other young adults, she had learned to hide herself, putting on a mask of togetherness with the others and keeping her irregular views silent.

Aela'ris had found some measure of comradery in the halls of science, but even there her strong individuality had become apparent to the elders who looked too closely so she kept everyone at a comfortable distance.

Her thoughts drifted back to her first days at the school, where she had learned of the universe's vastness, of stars burning in endless rivers of light, and of the distant world their people were meant to claim. That world teemed with life, species spun out of the cosmos in forms both strange and beautiful. The thought of stepping onto its soil after such a long journey was exhilarating, the one dream that kept her heart fixed on the future.

It was in this study of the cosmos that she had accidentally connected with several other like-minded souls who, like her, felt that there was something else. Something beyond the cloth and rigid societal structures that bound them all together so tightly. Something beyond just the collective society of the Krynnid.

They were young, like her. Brash in their own way, but guarded as they had to be in a society that valued the group over the individual. They introduced her to an ancient word: Tharyn. It represented a single flame in the darkness, burning alone, like a star in the vast emptiness of space. It was the very ability to act without consensus, to express total individuality that had frightened her at first, and eventually freed her mind.

The soul-song bubbled in her thoughts again.

Something about the last verse brushed across her inner being, calling out, pushing her to hum the sacred song once again, the pigments of her skin started shimmering a pale pink as she gained a measure of peace.

After years, the group of Tharyn had grown. There were many more than she would have suspected but all about her age. She had made contact with others beyond the School of Science. In the end encompassing all seven of the Krynnid schools, scattered like embers.

They had communicated, hesitantly at first, trading messages in secret, afraid to be found out by their peers, mates, or families. Aela'ris had slowly fallen into a position of leadership within the group - organizing meetings, distributing writings. The irony was never lost on her that it was in gathering together that gave them comfort, and even hope.

When her father rose to Speaker of the Currents, the highest position among the Krynnid, the group realized she might be privy to information directly from the council of Elders. But it wasn't until she let slip that she was the clone of Thal'yssae that they made their choice. In an instant she was named their leader, and the decision stung. Like her father, they looked at her and saw only borrowed blood. In the end she grudgingly agreed. After all, they were more her people than the rest of the Krynnid aboard the city ship, and they understood her in ways no one else could, especially not her father.

Suddenly her thoughts clear. Her soul-song sounding loudly in her mind. She could no longer take the shadowed way of deception and whatever happened would be the way forward.

"I must tell him the truth," she said aloud, pulling her legs from the water, then rising to her knees. "Whatever might happen." She raised her head, peeking above the tall grasses. The first light of their simulated home star warmed her face, filling her with a quiet sense of peace. She drew a deep breath and dipped her fingers into the lake, tracing gentle lines from her forehead down the sides of her eyes, ending near the corners of her mouth.

She silently thanked her ancestors and stood sure-footed on the sedge. With a light leap, she landed on solid ground and followed the narrow path back toward the city, passing old equipment long forgotten and slowly being claimed by moss and creeping vines.

A part of her ached at the decision. Her father had said he wanted her close, that he longed to reconnect after so many years of distance. The words had surprised her, warmed her even, but they tangled her mind with confusion. He had always dismissed her, always regarded the School of Science with veiled disdain, and yet now he expected her loyalty as his assistant.

She had seen what such closeness demanded. Her brother, once her refuge from their father's chill, had been bright-eyed and fearless, laughing loudest when she faltered and standing guard when she felt sad. But those days were gone. Their father had placed him at the head of the School of Protection, and the role had carved away his joy. His eyes were now guarded, his words clipped, his presence colder than the people he commanded. Watching him change, Aela'ris knew she could not follow in his path. To join her father now would be to lose herself as he had lost himself.

"I must trust in the truth." She said repeating a mantra that had been instilled in her by every teacher, every Elder, every Guide within the collective for as long as she could remember.

Her pace slowed, a feeling playing on the edges of her thought. It felt like she was missing something, some crucial bit of information.

"Perhaps I should speak to mother first," she said padding down the nearly invisible path toward the main walkway which itself was showing signs of age with its formerly marbled surface, pitted and cracked.

While her other mothers had raised her as was customary, she and Val'yra seemed to share something deeper, an unspoken connection that felt like slipping into a warm pool. There was a trust there that she couldn't quantify. She wasn't outwardly different than the birth mothers of her friends, but when she questioned them about it, none spoke of any closeness beyond what they felt for the mothers who had shared in raising them. Of course, everyone had a favorite, something that only her generation seemed to acknowledge, but warmth? Connection? No.

She hoisted herself up onto the raised walkway where the rays of the simulated star warmed her face and the path underfoot. She closed her eyes and inhaled once again letting the uncertainty flow out of her before continuing.

As she drew closer to the city, the light strengthened and the air warmed. Small clusters of older Krynnid eyed her with suspicion. Walking alone was unusual for their generation, who preferred tight-knit groups and shared spaces. Her own cohort was different. They were rebellious, independent, often seeking room to breathe and choosing paths outside the family norm. She didn't doubt that the older Krynnid would frown, perhaps even scold her, for straying from their ways.

She forced a contrite look and coaxed her skin to ripple with the soft blush of embarrassment. The pigments slowly shifted to her will, something else the older Krynnid, and many from her own generation could not control. But in her, they sometimes obeyed.

It was rumored that those in the School of Protection were taught to suppress their outward displays of emotion, to *still the waters* as it was called, but it wasn't something people discussed in polite company.

Crossing a long, arched stone walkway, she finally saw her home. It was one of the largest buildings in the leadership cove of the city, and the single largest home, befitting the Speaker of the Currents.

She suppressed her emotions as best she could, taking a moment before entering through the shimmering fabric of the portal.

"There you are." Her mother's tone was soft. There was a familiar strength to the richness of it and not a hint of anger at catching her daughter who hadn't spent last night at home.

Aela'ris put her hands across her chest, bowing her head. "Mother. Are you at peace?"

"Please child, save the formal greeting for those who don't know you."

Aela'ris looked up to see a slight smile from the woman, a glint of mischief in her eye. It tugged the heavy weight of the morning from Aela'ris's shoulders.

"Now tell me where you were and don't you say with Thal'ara." Her mother's shoulders bent forward in mock exasperation.

"I was…" she paused trying to think of what to say. Her skin mirrored the turmoil inside her, muted greys and pale blues spiraling across its surface like ink drifting through water.

Her mother gave her a knowing look. "Out with it now."

"I was in the fen near the edge of the dome. I needed some time to think… alone." She cringed looking at the floor.

Her mother touched her shoulder and guided her to the sitting area where they both sunk into the firm but soft green surface. "Is it the Dance of Acceptance?"

Aela'ris shook her head. The ceremonial dance was the capstone of her education and the moment she would be recognized as an adult. More than that, it marked her formal joining of the School of Science, the great collective she had studied under but not yet belonged to. All her friends would be there, and though she was excited, her father's disapproval dulled the joy.

"Father doesn't understand. He wants me to work for him at the council as his assistant, but I don't want that. I don't want to be some great leader; all I want to do is…"

Val'yra leaned over and placed an arm around her. Almost immediately, Aela'ris' skin rippled in bands of cyan and gold that moved in gentle waves across her head and chest, like the fading light of sunset across the sky. Soon, her mother's skin mirrored the pattern. They remained like that for several minutes until her mother gave her a comforting squeeze and then released her.

"You know how traditional your father is, I can speak to him again and…" She was interrupted by a soft chime from the other room. "Forgive me," she stood gracefully. "I've been waiting for a message about the food for your celebration."

Aela'ris watched her leave the room. Her mother had insisted on throwing a celebration after the dance and of course it hadn't gone to plan. Fully half of the guests were now only there because they wanted to curry favor with her father.

Val'yra walked back into the room looking concerned but her patterns were calm so it must have been minor. Aela'ris could tell her mother was contemplating something.

"You should go and speak to your father right now." She said giving her a curt nod.

"But I thought you would speak to him."

"Aela'ris," she said sternly. "You are nearly as old as a guide. Before long you will have to mentor someone as I have mentored you. Part of that is standing up for yourself." She reached out and helped Aela'ris to her feet, looking somewhat saddened. "Go now, before he leaves for the council chamber."

Val'yra shooed her toward her father's office down a small hallway near the back of their home.

"How am I supposed to tell him," She mumbled. "I don't even know what

I want." She walked the short distance and stood outside his door. She could hear him speaking to someone through the thin door so she decided to wait and gather her thoughts.

From within, it was clear he was speaking to someone else from the council, the formality of his tone leaving no doubt. His words were firm and commanding, pressing them to act.

Then, suddenly, his voice dropped, soft and almost secretive. This was something no Krynnid in a position of power should ever do, least of all the Speaker of the Currents. Among her people, hidden words and half-truths were the marks of the criminal or the unwell. Yet here was her father, veiling his voice as though he had something to hide.

"I will not request a meeting with the council, Sea'tah."

Aela'ris perked up at the name. Sea'tah was head of her very own School of Science.

She knew she shouldn't be listening, yet she had a duty to report anything important to the other Tharyn like herself. Since her brother had been promoted to head of the School of Protection, the group had received troubling reports, including crackdowns on independent thinking and even the detention of some Krynnid found alone, supposedly for questioning.

"The city isn't our concern right now." Her father spoke quickly. "The ship is the only thing..." Sea'tah must have spoken over her father. She could almost feel his impatience until he started speaking again.

"Listen to me," he said urgently. "Your job is to find out where that ship came from and how we can best use it to our advantage. The people are restless and it is only a matter of time before they discover that the city is doomed."

Aela'ris froze, her pulse hammering in her ears. Had her father truly ordered the head of the School of Science to conceal the truth? Her skin rippled with confusion and dread before she forced it still. What did he mean that the city was doomed, and what was this ship he spoke of?

"It is your job to find out how they could suddenly appear. If this is a technology the council can use to escape, then we must do whatever is necessary." He paused, considering what Sea'tah must have said, then added with finality, "Yes, by force if necessary."

Aela'ris stumbled back from the door, fighting to breathe. The corridor seemed to tilt beneath her feet as she turned and hurried away. Her mother stood in the hall, a swatch of iridescent fabric draped across her arms, but Aela'ris couldn't bring herself to meet her gaze. She rushed past, the patterns of her skin a raging storm.

"Where are you going?" her mother called after her, worry creasing her features.

Aela'ris didn't slow. The words barely reached her through the pounding in her head. If she stopped, if she even looked at her mother, she would crumble. She bolted through the entryway and into the open air, running from the house, from the questions, from a truth she wasn't ready to face.

ACKNOWLEDGEMENTS

This book wouldn't be what it is today without the support of the incredible people in my life. To the most important people of all, my family. To my daughter, thank you for keeping me young and for all the joy you bring into my life. And to my wife, thank you for always supporting my every endeavor, no matter how silly or strange. This book is for you.

I also want to give a huge thank you to my amazing editor, Sara. I still remember the day I nervously asked her if my writing was even worth publishing. Her response, which was something along the lines of, "It's not half bad," helped me realize this book had a shot.

To my cover designer, Mark, thank you for your wonderful work. I especially appreciate your great sense of humor and your gentle hand in guiding me to the right cover design decisions. A true professional, I couldn't have done this without you. When *Caliban's Hamster* releases, I'm sure it will be a worldwide phenomenon.

Finally, to anyone else who cheered me on: from friends and family to the early readers and fellow writers, your encouragement and belief keep me going. This book is a testament to the fact that no creative journey is ever a solo flight, and I am grateful for everyone that helped me along the way.

ABOUT THE AUTHOR

Based in Denver, Colorado, Dan Thornton is a science fiction author and a veteran of the U.S. Navy. His love for writing began with fantasy and the works of Tolkien, but his journey truly started when he discovered Larry Niven's *Ringworld*. He served aboard the USS America during the Gulf War, spending his days on the flight deck wrangling F-14 Tomcats. That real-world chaos and camaraderie became the inspiration behind his stories and is why he leans so heavily into military science fiction.

Dan's debut novel, *Fleet of the Forgotten*, has been years in the making, with parts of it taking root while he was still in the service. When he's not writing, he can be found building replica props, attending his local Comic-Con, or enjoying his favorite video games. A true fan of all things sci-fi, he counts among his favorites books by classic masters such as Isaac Asimov, Arthur C. Clarke, and Philip K. Dick, as well as modern titans like M.R. Forbes, John Scalzi, and Andy Weir. He also loves diving into modern sci-fi films like *Edge of Tomorrow, Blade Runner 2049*, and *Dune*.

Dan believes that no creative journey is a solo flight, and he is deeply grateful to the entire indie writing community for helping to keep him motivated.

EXILESWAR.COM